Other Fomite Titles by John Michael Flynn

Off to the Next Wherever

Vintage Vinyl Playlist

Answer Only

John Michael Flynn

Fomite

Burlington, VT

t

ISBN-13: 978-1-959984-64-1
Library of Congress Control Number: 2024943477

Fomite
58 Peru Street
Burlington, VT 05401
www.fomitepress.com

11/01/2024

ONE

When I dropped to the pavement in Queens, none of my blood splattered onlookers. Twilight had settled in by the time an ambulance arrived and yellow police tape cordoned off the scene. Rubbernecking strangers sounded moans of disgust. Nobody stole the half-dozen roses that had fallen from my hands. At last I was free from the lost world. Its nightmares were over.

Now that I'm a phantom, I can admit it. Agnes Bailey Kotas didn't steal my heart. I yearned to give it to her, willingly so, fearing but not expecting her refusal.

When I began to move through the floating world, I heard someone whisper my name, "Ennis…Ennis Railsback."

It was my mother, Doris, seeking her only son, a child of the Lone Star Conspiracy. My Dad, Carter, was with her. We were family again back in Gail, Texas, population 250, the seat of Borden County, named after the inventor of condensed milk.

❦

I was dressed sharply that evening, some might even say I made an attractive stiff. It was a Tuesday. I had a bottle of Syrah in one hand, wrapped in a brown bag that shattered on the pavement when I fell. As a stat under the headings *Homicides*, or *Gun Violence*, no one interrogated at the scene knew or had seen who'd shot me. No artist painted a mural of my face to perhaps incite riots or gain political influence. I wasn't even buried. No funeral either. Professionals zipped up the bag and drove my corpse to the morgue where I joined a pile of many other such bags.

❧

We swing our lanterns and find our way. If fortunate, certain stars align as objectives are achieved. Perhaps a few get maimed in the process. As I began to swing mine in a new reality, I never told myself I had a good run in the lost world or that I didn't regret anything. On the contrary, I thought back about how for most of my life I'd felt like a misfit, but I'd done what I wanted to.

A lonely kid without siblings, having lost my father when I was ten, I found solace in reading with pleasure from *David Copperfield* while my peers rubbed Tung oil into their saddles or baseball mitts, imitating the leg kick of pitcher Nolan Ryan and the "make my day" stoicism of actor Clint Eastwood. I can say with modesty that I followed in the footsteps but failed to live up to the accomplishments of my impish hero, Billy Wilder, becoming not only a maverick film director but an indie producer and founding partner with my friend Avi Lovitz of Rain-Or-Rust Pictures, LLC.

For ten years starting in 1999, Avi and I gathered investors together to put up money to make small films that we assured them would get national and sometimes international distribution. And they did. Some of these films prompted inspired performances. Others challenged the status quo and sometimes earned praise from elitist critics. A few were duds, and many failed to turn a profit.

Having shuffled off my mortal coil, though not face down like William Holden in a swimming pool off Sunset Boulevard, I had enough saved to live without working for about seven more years. This would have taken me to retirement at the age of 62. Money I'd socked away through shrewd investments, per a will I'd had drawn prior to my demise, would have gone to my spouse. If I had one. This spouse would have never needed to work a day in her life.

I died a bachelor. Unlike Gloria Swanson, I never had any years arguing that I was still big and that the pictures had gotten small. I went out in a flash. All my holdings now go to charities seeking cures for the prostate cancer that took my father early, and the ALS that destroyed my mother. Maybe that's splendid. I hope so.

Throughout my time in the lost world, I felt sorry for myself. I can say this now without feeling shame. I marveled at hacks and charlatans who enacted cruelties on the innocent and under-prepared. They exploited each day as if it were an opportunity to land a knockout sucker punch and conscience be damned.

When the bullet pierced my heart, I was still a man eager to prove his worth to an imaginary audience of skeptics. I was unmarried too, as I've told you, though I was in love and increasingly less befuddled in my search to understand its meaning.

That's the tragedy in all this, I suppose. If one chooses to view any human's sudden physical eclipse in such a way. I don't. Much like Erich von Stroheim, I maintain my own consistently stern fortitude, seeing death as release and the start of a new journey.

—⁓—

Many of Rain-Or-Rust's bleak yet comic and slightly perverse films were influenced by my abiding interest in the enigmatic John Waters. This oddball made his reputation by creating cultish rather twisted joints such as *Pink Flamingos, Hairspray,* and *Lust In The Dust.* Each of these three featured a star by the name of Divine. In one, *Cecil B. Demented*, Waters spoofed Teamsters and their role in the making of movies.

Enter Agnes Bailey Kotas. Given her erudition and arcane interests, it came as a surprise that she didn't know much about Waters and hadn't seen *Cecil B. Demented*, so I invited her over one evening to watch it with me. This was when Agnes worked for Rain-Or-Rust as a location scout. She had a husband then: Derek. She loved movies and thought the Waters flick fun but banal. She wasn't incorrect in that assessment, but I argued that banality was part of that quirky schlock-meister's charm. We don't need to be so serious all the time.

Agnes Bailey Kotas. Allow me to blow a mournful sigh.

———⁂———

I didn't battle but rather assessed phlegmatically my inclinations toward Agnes. I remember we watched more Waters movies on two other occasions. Her man Derek, unfortunately, was with us for the second viewing.

"But I ain't dealing with no Teamsters crap," were Derek's first choice words after the film ended.

Derek had nothing to worry about. I dealt with Teamsters directly. No one else in our company except Avi was allowed that role. Avi, though, preferred to be hands-off. He rarely came downtown to the office. Many who worked for him didn't know who he was.

By and large, I found the Teamsters I met to be a genial reticent lot. Some reminded me of ranchers, welders and drivers I'd known from my childhood. My father had been a truck driver, long-haul, criss-crossing the country, gone for weeks at a time. A rugged type, he could have been a Teamster himself. I sometimes think that was really all I knew about him.

Waters lampooned the process of making all payments to Teamsters in cash only. Like everyone else I'd dealt with in the movie business, these men didn't suffer twinges of conscience regarding how they operated by certain questionable codes. Most were rough-hewn and not wealthy enough to live in the borough of Manhattan. In this way, they were like New York cops and firefighters, most of whom reside outside of the grid they serve. Due to their builds and craggy facial features, some landed small roles in serial dramas such as *Oz*, which was in its final season and holding auditions in the same building where Rain-Or-Rust rented office space.

The only glimpses of emotion I witnessed from a Teamsters rep came when I failed to make a cash payment on time. Lucky for me, this didn't happen often. These were sometimes surreally intimidating encounters. Otherwise, as a goon squad, those gents tended to show up, take care of business and leave on time.

Derek once remarked, "Those meat-heads, they get a reputation for being tough. Maybe they are, but I ain't buying it. The trick is you don't show it unless you have to. That's what being tough is."

Derek knew this topic inside and out, though he was by all accounts a moron. Still, I sort of liked him. I understood why Agnes went for him. He carried that bad-boy whiff of danger and invincibility that's stirring to be around. He worked for *real* criminals with limo drivers and off-shore bank accounts to go with their getaways in the Caribbean. More than once he'd told me a bit boastfully, "Those players got one religion. The almighty dollar."

Speak for yourself, Derek.

Agnes didn't always approve of Derek's "business ventures," though for the most part she looked away. I think she stayed married to him because she liked the almighty dollar too.

Agnes also didn't approve of my abiding curiosity in Derek, so I talked to him in private, especially when it came to his dealing narcotics. You see, I was developing a dystopian TV series idea in which I hoped to blend the intensity of *The Sopranos* with the specificity of the many Manhattan-based CSI-procedurals that Dick Wolf had produced.

I wanted this series grounded in a fresh believable day-to-day look at gangsters and the law. Regarding underworld practices, the language used, the expectations, I gained insights from Derek that only a criminal could provide. They helped me incorporate verisimilitude into my story lines, that edgy sense of intelligence and humor that marked so much of David Chase's work, for example.

Derek didn't have to understand or accept any of this. He wasn't equipped to. I think he liked boasting in private to his gangster buddies of his exploits in showbiz. He could be rather coarse and cruel, but he was far from unimaginative. Agnes, though, had him by the short hairs. He'd clam up whenever she was present, wouldn't dare boast about anything.

I never pressed him. He spoke to me candidly and downright decorously whenever I sat him down alone.

At first, he'd play the shy rube. Then he'd relax and share. "Don't even know their names. I don't wanna know. Nah, Mr. Railsback I'm sorry. Maybe this TV series thing of yours ain't such a good idea."

It was always Mr. Railsback. Never Ennis. His awkward expressing of dutiful respect made me uncomfortable, especially since I savored erotic fantasies regarding his wife.

Then he'd loosen up.

"See, it's like this," he'd say. "My guy usually has a wing man and he's seated in the front seat with a nine mil., or maybe a Glock resting on his lap. I sit next to my guy in the back and all I do is sweat bullets while my guy and his assistant take turns counting the Benjamins. They do it slowly like, keeping me on simmer while I'm wishing I can split with my cut before some diehard gets the nut-job idea to dispatch me. Guys get dispatched all the time. Part of the business."

There was always a driver involved. Not all of them were assassins. Most could be, but they preferred to show poise. Some even appeared skittish. These types remained, by Derek's reasoning, the most dangerous.

"Never say a word to them drivers or the quiet types, the little guys," he'd say. "Cuz you never can tell what they're tossing over in their heads. The smaller the guy, the bigger the anger, that's what I say."

Derek didn't know how many "Benjamins" filled the envelopes he was paid to carry. He didn't open these envelopes. Wouldn't dare. His job was to sit in a car and stew and fidget like he was in school detention.

What I'm describing is Derek's role in the movement of cash. Even in this era of cryptocurrency and electronic fund transfers, an astounding number of banknotes move between hands as part of an economy that allegedly doesn't exist.

I'd be lying if I said Avi and I hadn't benefited from this invisible torrent. Capitalism, it should be noted, is a greasy enterprise of winners and losers. In many instances, the losers are those who play by the rules. The winners are those who make them. If anyone knew this, it was Derek. It guided the decisions he made as a player in the narcotics game.

He "moved the poison," exploiting a limited degree of freedom to raise his asking price depending on his customer. I viewed him as a middle man, and he agreed with that assessment. He bought from and sold to those who couldn't be trusted in his subset of lost-world travelers.

When Derek showed up to make either a sale or a purchase, he was always armed, his hand gun concealed. It wasn't a big weapon or expensive. He needed to fire it only now and then, though he often needed to get rid of it, which is why he preferred a used .38 or even a .22 caliber, its serial numbers filed off. They were easy to ditch and cheap to replace. It's only in movies, of course, that a thug or hero brandishes a silver .45 with a pearl handle in one hand, returning fire while riding a motorcycle at high speed.

Transactions didn't always occur in cars. They "went down" usually in Brooklyn or the Bronx, on side streets out of view of security cameras. He'd pay one back-up sidekick who'd stay hidden. This sidekick might be armed. He might run off, as well, succumbing to fear. Sidekicks were hard to find and could never be relied on. They were often dispatched for alleged acts of insubordination.

The men Derek referred to as The Scientists knew he was in the habit of upping his asking price while transacting sales. They didn't care. Apparently, Derek's customers didn't either. Or else they didn't know any better.

Before the Covid pandemic, many of them were high-paid errand boys for Wall Street cokeheads, low-level street hoods, successful performers, fashionistas, trust-fund kiddies with unlimited bank accounts or unionized techies who worked for me at Rain-Or-Rust or for other production companies and ad agencies throughout the region. Along with the creative types, these many techies he sold to, whether IT gurus, grips, best boys, sound men or electricians, were part of a cadre of esteemed professionals.

Many I knew labored in the city but didn't live there. As part of a team, they worked on a movie or TV set to earn union wages before going to the next set, sometimes in another city, too busy to search local drugstores for cheaper prices for their recreational highs. Those like me who hired these techies considered them members of a tight-knit extended family.

Working while coked-up on set at five a.m., as some were wont to do, was frowned on. Still, it happened all the time. I looked the other way. I didn't like such drug use, none of us clean and sober types did, but we told ourselves that what others did to harm themselves was none of our business as long as it didn't hamper their work. Or else our profit margins. Most of the time, it didn't.

Agnes, often the only female on set except for maybe the script supervisor and a make-up artist, didn't like this either. She scowled at me and threw her hands in the air whenever I asked why she didn't just divorce Derek. She had to know by my signals that I was interested in more than a professional relationship.

"I can't do it," she'd say. "Call it love or whatever, but I just can't."

It wasn't as if Derek lived like Heisenberg in *Breaking Bad* either. He was low-key, and he liked to stay home. He played his role as one minor link in what I suspected was a long filthy chain.

Derek never cut the heroin or cocaine he peddled, though he knew and had seen how the diluting process worked. He schooled me.

As I understood it, heroin was always "stepped on," no question about it. For black tar heroin from Mexico, a "cheese" was made either from Tylenol PM, acetaminophen, or the antihistamine known as diphenhydramine. Brown sugar was also used, believe it or not.

For creating whiter variants, quinine was the most commonly used agent. What was also used, ironically, was the agent that President Trump had supported for treatment of SARS-CoV 2, the Covid-19 virus. This was the drug hydroxychloroquine sulfate, used for treatment of malaria as well as rheumatoid arthritis and lupus.

Having once approved hydroxychloroquine for Covid treatment, the FDA backed off and withdrew its approval. Nobody really knew why, or whether this was the miracle drug for the pandemic. It might have been. I think it didn't get used because Trump supported it and established political elites who never liked him had their own plans in mind for profiting off a new vaccine.

Who knows? In most sectors, the default setting on Trump was to reject anything he put forth. Orange man bad, and all that. Nonetheless, his favored Covid remedy was quite effective when it came to heroin dilution.

—◦◦◦—

When the pandemic and the ensuing lockdowns hit, the supplies of cocaine and heroin began to dry up. Enter Fentanyl and another irony. This drug was rumored to be produced in Wuhan, China, perhaps not far from the lab where gain-of-function research allegedly created the leak that began the pandemic.

As lockdowns sent more people spiraling into isolation and depression, the coke and heroin market dried up and the sale of synthetics such as Fentanyl, OxyContin and Benzodiazepine began to explode. I mean it boomed. Demand was so high that Derek couldn't sell it quickly enough.

There were times when Derek, like myself, thought the citizenry of the entire world was desperately and obsessively getting high on anything available. If not alcohol, food, then on aspirin, baby powder, caffeine and lactose. Or Fentanyl, the most notoriously dangerous and powerful of these chemical agents. Lastly, for the elites, there was Phenacetin, banned in the States, though dealers knew how to get their hands on it.

I had to agree with Derek's smarmy assessment: "If all this shit that's come to light during Covid ain't better living through chemistry, I don't know what is."

Think about it. Baking soda, for one. It was useful for diluting cocaine because it didn't smell or cause nosebleeds.

Procaine, which was commonly used by dentists, as well as lidocaine and benzocaine were also used because they weren't hard to find and a pinky finger's amount to the tongue provided an immediate numbing effect. A tester could be fooled with ease.

Many felt lonely, isolated and hopeless under pandemic house arrest. Drugs were suddenly everywhere in the same way Speakeasies and bathtub gin became ubiquitous during Prohibition.

To make freebase cocaine, ammonia and ether were used. For crack, the coke was dissolved in water and mixed with ammonia or baking soda, but crack was yesterday's high *du jour* and who needed such a poor-man's choice when the supply of Fentanyl appeared to be limitless.

"Before the pandemic I never once," Derek told me, "sold anybody real pure blow. It just don't happen. When the pandemic hit, forget about it. Nobody was selling Skag or China White or Horse or blow like back in the day. Not to nobody nowhere in the world. It was all Oxy and Fentanyl. The legal shit. And it was everywhere, I mean all over the place."

Lost world, indeed.

Yet as Agnes had warned, the more money Derek brought in, the more he moved in a constant state of anxiety. Twitching, paranoid, glancing over his shoulder and expecting retribution whenever he was startled by a sudden noise.

He told me, "They think they got me by the short and curlies, like they're gonna ice me. When? I dunno. I ain't toast yet. Far from it. But I gotta walk with eyes in the back of my head."

Oddly enough, Derek didn't look like a bone-crusher. He reminded me of a character named Rave played so unctuously by the great Lawrence Harvey in one my favorite Brit noirs, *The Good Die Young*. Rave lives without conscience, not so much desperate as he is cunning and determined, maliciously so, starved to obtain money by any means possible.

There's no shouting from Rave, no posturing, yet no moral barometer within. There's no weeping or regret in his heart. Nor does Rave see himself as a victim of the war in Germany where he killed men and received medals for it. Rave wants cravenly and he'll get what he wants, no matter who must die to make it happen.

However, when our LLC was making two films a year and garnering positive reviews from the likes of Roger Ebert, Derek spent less time doing dangerous things. When Avi and I reduced our operation, we couldn't keep paying Derek, Agnes or the other creatives we'd come to appreciate. Those with experience found other production companies. Some left the business. A few made a logical move to LA.

Not Agnes. She couldn't. You see, she was due to give birth to their first child.

Not Derek either, who appeared flummoxed by the reality he was going to become a father. Derek shifted his dealing of opioids into a higher gear and started making more money than he'd ever dreamed possible.

Remember this. Derek had *never* been like a son to me. He was a crime encyclopedia that I kept close at hand. I used him selfishly; I had my own designs on making my mark from behind the scenes in the same way a hero of mine, David Chase, made his with *The Rockford*

Files, *Kojak*, and *The Sopranos*. I never met Mr. Chase, but I followed his career. One must have a mentor, a hero, a model. Without him knowing it, he tutored me each step of the way.

—◦◦◦—

I had my hunger for Agnes too, pregnant or not. She was that rare New York resident who found it sweet and charming that I hailed from Texas. She liked that I was older, as well. She thought of me as distinguished. I'd managed to convince her to view me as a guiding hand for Derek, perhaps possibly steering him away from his Fentanyl-dealing lifestyle.

Even after I fired her, Agnes kept me in her life, insisting on it.

Then she miscarried and everything changed yet again.

After I learned she would never bear children, I found myself doing what I could to make her happy. She spiraled into depression. She encouraged my continued influencing of Derek, keeping him busy, away from the dealing, but I failed at that, unfortunately.

I didn't have any street cred, nor did I want any or even know what that phrase really meant. I was the proverbial outsider, not a yahoo in snakeskin boots as played by Jon Voight in *Midnight Cowboy*, just one solitary Texan from a vast sometimes desolate landscape where residents drove for two hours to visit their nearest neighbors.

Long before I left Texas and took many a lesson from others in business, I came to understand that in order to get ahead, I had to realize I'd never fully have my own way. I'd have to form teams. Get input and funding from other investors. Lead by delegating, and lead by knowing when to step in and express the final word. One may be driven to succeed, but one must also be willing to compromise. This was some of the wisdom I tried to share with Derek.

I found it impossible to know whether Derek was listening or not. I think most of the time he wasn't. Not to me, and not to Agnes.

⸺﹏⸺

By the way, in brief, what led to the ruin of Rain-Or-Rust was that Avi started pre-production on a project funded by an investor who turned out to have mob ties. This investor was nabbed by the IRS, and all assets committed to our project, whether directly from him or not, were frozen.

There was an exhausting and militant audit of our books. Fourteen million dollars – not a penny of it could be touched. It happens. I had an idea, I suppose, but not really. Talk about feeling like a twerp from the boonies. I'd phone Avi and we'd talk for hours seeking comfort from each other, telling ourselves to hang in there, reduce expenses, try not to panic.

Four years passed before that mess got cleaned up. Avi and I kept piling up debt. We fired our staff and relinquished our office space. It wasn't until 2009 when everything changed.

Working out of our separate apartments, Avi uptown and me down in Chelsea, we funded the dark comedy, *Kill Me If I'm Wrong*.

The movie was pure rubbish, I know, but it held the interest of the Weinstein brothers, (long before Harvey's misdeeds came to light). It was mostly Bob who backed us, and he picked it up for distribution and made himself a few million. It sold a lot of popcorn as big tent summer fare and allowed us to dissolve our LLC with our dignity intact.

Avi and I then went separate ways. We remain polite though increasingly aloof former business partners. We recouped profits enough to get out of debt, pay our lawyers and finalize the audit and bankruptcy proceedings. Unlike David Chase, who remained my hero, I was no longer a hotshot. A lot of my so-called friends disappeared.

Not Agnes, most importantly. She and I grew closer.

⸻ ∾ ⸻

Agnes, dear Agnes. Known as Shooter to her closest friends.

I never called her that. Not once. I thought it horribly vulgar, especially in America.

Agnes was the type who forever weighed the pros and cons in any situation, as if conversing endlessly with herself. One such situation was her off-and-on sexual affair and so-called friendship with Holly Greene.

Would she run to Holly because she was bored? Was she tired of what remained of her and Derek as a couple? It appeared the slow ruination between Agnes and Derek had begun with the miscarriage. An event she said that, in retrospect, felt to her like it had never happened.

Yet it was there. One more failure. What she could have been. What they might have had. The map of her life felt like a lattice of lines linked between one failure after another.

Derek didn't help. He could be blunt, crude, a misguided heat-seeking missile, no matter how much he understood consequences. He'd slept with Holly many times.

So had Agnes. After the miscarriage, the three of them made a pact. They called it their "triangle game." They agreed to live by its rather loose rules.

Holly was all for it. She had no scruples. Neither did Derek. Agnes often said this explained why Derek and Holly were so fond of each other.

Agnes didn't run from them. She was willing to offer support. She couldn't resist the triangle game, I suppose. Yet she remained my friend, too, but she didn't run to me. I wanted her to, I tried to lure her, but she'd drawn a border that she wouldn't let herself cross.

Each time Derek visited Holly and returned, he'd start telling Agnes everything that he felt. He'd really open up. Holly brought this out of him in a way that Agnes couldn't.

According to Holly, Derek also shared his darkest secrets and she kept her promise to keep them to herself. Agnes did the same with Holly, told her everything.

These three shared secrets. They made promises. It seemed to be working, with Holly acting as a lynchpin and sounding board, and the three of them supporting one another to form a whole. Why should any whole be limited to two, anyway?

Holly was a narcissist, so it pleased her to entertain two lovers at the same time, both of whom she knew how to control. Derek could barely pronounce the word narcissism, but he got the gist.

True enough, Holly couldn't always be trusted, but neither could Derek, who didn't see Holly's narcissism as a fault or a weakness. He viewed it as confidence. He thought Agnes should view it the same way. Fat chance that was going to happen.

Agnes didn't need approval the way Holly did. Ever since learning she wasn't destined to have children, she'd begun to consider whether she could live alone, happily so, without either of them. She was the least dominant of the trio, but she wasn't their tool or plaything. Those two should remember this.

She believed Derek told Holly everything because Holly didn't absorb what Derek shared without inserting herself into his confessions. Maybe Derek clung too much to Holly because a man couldn't confide in his wife without feeling guilty about his transgressions.

Who could he confide in? His mother? Perhaps, but Derek believed he deserved to enjoy another woman's intimacy and trust, especially if she were as attractive as Holly. In a word, he was selfish. This was how he played it, even though he could and should have, indeed, confided more honestly in his wife.

Agnes, willing to listen, was allowing herself to be used. She'd complain that Derek had stopped talking to her. She wasn't sure she could trust him. She'd open up to me and I'd warn and advise of her getting hurt, but she didn't listen. She pretended to. I think she just needed to vent, and I was convenient and not judgmental.

Perhaps Agnes should have been, but she wasn't one to judge. Loyal to a fault, she saw herself as more than just Derek's lover. Okay, maybe she was a tad jealous of Holly. She said sometimes it felt like a three-legged race to nowhere, all of its permutations so confusing, but the triangle game was theirs, nobody else's. It made them unique. Didn't that matter?

———⌇∿∿⌇———

A dream from his childhood in Queens came back to Derek. Eyes watering with the white fumes of Borax detergent and ammonia that filled a tiny kitchen, he kneaded his little fists against a pair of trousers inside a shallow pail of soapy steaming water that scalded his knuckles. He kept pushing, wanting to help Ma, to make it easier for her, squinting in pain. He saw shock and dismay on Ma's face as she leaned over to help.

This dream forever haunting him. During those laundry sessions together, did Ma wonder how such a creature like him had sprung from her womb?

Agnes described Derek as "imperious" and "masochistic." Derek thought them funny words, but he liked them. If asked, how would his Ma describe her only son? He didn't know. He wasn't sure he really cared all that much.

Derek felt safe in this dream. A boy again in that cubbyhole kitchen. He liked those ammonia fumes and the headaches they brought on. He liked helping Ma. Made him feel useful, but it was just a dream. He was no longer that little boy, even though he could remember it all in brilliant detail, just like he remembered each visit to Ma during her days in the hospital after her first TIA.

One association, one color or object didn't take much to put Derek back there.

He loved that Shooter talked to him about his issues of dreaming and lack of control. She was a better listener than Holly, who for some reason he talked to a lot more.

Holly was the one for a romp and lots of sex. Shooter was more thoughtful and grounded. He loved Shooter's creative streak too. But he feared it. Maybe that explained why he didn't like opening up to her too much. Holly just smiled and brushed off what he told her. Shooter absorbed and pondered his ideas and spent a lot of time spying on other people and brooding about them afterwards. She liked to tell him that she imagined the lives of people behind the windows and walls in their neighborhood.

Derek couldn't stay on that "brainy-stuff" channel. He had to make a plan before some punk-ass decided to kill him. Shooter should be aware of the danger he was in, it was her right, but he wouldn't tell her. She had a clue, though.

What to do? He'd make a list of final tasks to accomplish. Start hustling that list. He hated to admit it, but his days, of late, felt like desperate ones. The clock was ticking. Might be a few more months. Might not. Either way, he heard that clock growing louder.

All he needed was to look around. Pandemic time. The list of dead was growing so fast that his checking out wouldn't even be noticed.

He'd hate for that to happen, since the only thing to live for was making an impact.

He figured Holly would be okay, since she was loaded. Harder to say with Shooter, but she was a survivor. Give her a camera and she was happy.

It was Ma he worried about. Derek didn't want to leave her a childless widow. He had to plan. Really make something that would stick.

TWO

Thinking nothing at all, Agnes studied them one at a time. She called them the "anger-faces." She saw their noses pressed against the smutty walls of their imprisoned minds. Then, as if freed at once, each anger face was flung like an oily fried egg against the pavement. They forced her to accept that life was in one's head.

This acceptance led to moments when Agnes started percolating again. She burned her eyes into the dirty faces around her, all so full of murderous intent.

She was walking downtown in Manhattan. All the theatres empty. So many storefronts like hollowed-out eyes. Or else boarded up. Not what they used to be. Nothing was.

Starting around 1916, from the Chrysler to the Empire State building to the Twin Towers, Haudenosaunee ironworkers from the Six Nations of the Iroquois, the majority of them Mohawks, helped rivet the infrastructure beams of the city's signature skyscrapers. Agnes imagined these workers 25 stories above the ground without safety nets. It was easy to do each time she admired one of the city's more famous buildings, or she recalled the Lewis Hines photos of these workers. There was one she was particularly fond of that showed the working men seated on I-beams hundreds of feet in the air, eating their bag lunches.

These skyscrapers never failed to astonish when she considered how much risk went into their construction. For what? What did it all mean? Who were they trying to impress?

The truth was that she, like so many others, remained a dilettante, perhaps still curious, which was a plus, but merely one more lost daughter of a dying empire.

Maybe that's why she shot so many pictures. They connected her to the only abstraction she claimed as her own, namely a past that no longer existed. A past that didn't feed the present.

The only illusion to be trusted was this schism she felt between her two halves. She didn't own a thing until it was gone. She, too, embodied illusion. The past was all in her head. It was a photograph easily burned or deleted, and so was she.

She couldn't own another man either, especially the likes of Derek. Why was he, a Fentanyl dealer, still the love of her life? Had he ever really been?

Holly would say no. Holly would be right. "All mine" was what she once told her.

Wrong, wrong, wrong. And she hated Holly because she knew that about her. How wrong, indeed, she was. How lost. She'd said that about Derek back when she was sure of things. When there were audiences and big plans for her future, before any of them just disappeared. Before the pandemic. Before the miscarriage. Before the bottom dropped out.

"But I'm *not* sure, I'm never sure," she'd told Holly. "Is that what love is, just getting used to not being sure?"

Holly had said she didn't know. A lie, of course, since she did. Holly knew everything. Holly played in life's orchards, plucking whatever fruit she craved from its eclectic trees. Holly preened in front of her mirrors while Providence remained the center of her universe and

Queens remained the center of Derek's. Both of them playing it like they were so tough, so seasoned. Well, they were. Certainly tougher than she'd ever be.

Agnes thought she should just move away, maybe go back to Los Angeles where she'd lived only for a year and had never gotten used to the freeways and traffic. She could probably work there in union gigs on film or TV productions.

Was that what she wanted? Not really. Not that LA was really booming either. It wasn't. Everything, the whole wide world was shut down. What a concept to wrap her head around. She couldn't. To think of the future was to kick a corpse and expect it to move.

Nor did she want this place either, not like she used to. Dried up, dead inside, festering with maggots and thieves and as dead as she was. A mirror of her soul.

She could leave Derek. Or could she? Something about his indifference, his answer to life held her captive. There was strength and resilience in it and she wanted some.

—⁓—

Agnes hadn't gone weak in the knees the first time they'd made contact. Not love at first sight. More like the promise of a longer summer ahead, or a blissful sleep. He probably hadn't killed anyone, hard to say, but he'd witnessed murders and ran with dangerous criminals. He sold toxins that destroyed people's lives. Yet he kept her comfortable. He bought her whatever she asked for and he allowed her to go to Holly as part of their "triangle game" arrangement.

Yet there was something off about Derek. To scratch beneath the surface was to learn he was cold there, lacking compassion, selfish. He liked to play at showing empathy. An act. He and Holly, the two of them, self-obsessed birds of a feather. Not enough storm-tossed seas concealed inside of them. Yet such storm light, such wrath and fearlessness.

At night, Derek's eyes shined like precious stones underwater. Agnes dreamed of touching them and how they'd glow like tourmaline when light hit them a certain way. It was all in her imagination, of course, but maybe she wanted to believe that his eyes were more special than they really were. Maybe she just wanted to be in love. Eternally so. Was this really so inane a desire?

When she and Derek met, he told her he didn't shake hands. Too many germs. *I don't kiss on both cheeks neither.* Agnes laughed at the memory.

He loved to call her Shooter. As if it made her tougher, brought her down to his level. Most tough guys from Queens didn't want to hear about where a girl had been raised unless she was from the city like them. Only then, they might ask a few things about that girl's neighborhood or family.

Shooter ain't no New York girl, she's country.

Everything outside of the five boroughs was the sticks. Nobody was tougher or as skilled at what they did. Or so Derek and all his crews and posses thought. Of course, Agnes knew better. They were the provincial ones, not her, and they needed an audience and their boasts to prove their worth. They needed the world. Not her. Never her. All she needed was her camera.

※

Agnes had been couch-surfing between Manhattan and Providence for many years. Having finally saved enough from excelling at two dead-end jobs and selling her photos online, she got herself into a dank basement-level hole in a Brooklyn brownstone. When I hired her as a location scout, she looked like what she was: a struggling boho artist in her mid-thirties with a diploma she didn't think worthless who was rapidly passing her prime and hungry to find security and approbation.

I felt disappointed when she showed me her wedding ring. I had wanted to kiss those pearly lips, that tiny little chin. She was a small yet sturdy creature, inclined to a little plumpness, one that I could cuddle with easily, taking her under my long arms. I feared, however, due to our age difference I reminded her of her father.

She introduced me to Derek at one of my parties. He was the only one there not drinking. Even I was a little drunk that night. Agnes was sucking down wine. She was a big drinker, she said, which partly explained some of the softness in her figure. I rather liked that softness about her. She had her camera with her too, wanted to take my picture, to capture the redness in my face, the shine in my eyes, what she called my "dharma-inflected chin-line." She'd been reading Kerouac's *The Subterraneans* at the time and believed romance in my life was long overdue.

So why not with me, Agnes?

We talked in one corner, just the two of us, for a long time. She told me Derek peddled hard drugs, the worst kinds. No future in that. I already knew this, but I didn't tell her.

Perhaps Derek, she feared, knew too much. Perhaps they'd kill him. What she didn't fear was how much I already knew. It was all breathless and urgent with her. Remember, this was before the miscarriage.

She was telling me this, she said, because she'd felt at once that she could trust me even if I was her employer. She'd weathered some horrible bosses in the past, but she just knew at first glance that I'd be different. She even used the word simpatico to describe us. I thought it fitting. I found it a breeze to talk to her.

She complained that Derek was childish in so many matters. He didn't know much about photography and even less about movies, but on the plus side he was curious and "so intuitive," telling stories, showing a memory for details.

After that party, we deepened our acquaintanceship and developed a rapport to the point that I took the risk of asking if Agnes would bring some of her photographs to my office. Our company wanted to use her as more than just a location scout. She could also be a photographer and an assistant DP, to start with.

I thought she had a terrific eye. After gaining experience working with seasoned DPs, she'd make herself a valuable asset to any production company. Many would have fallen all over the opportunities that we were offering, so I figured she'd be overwhelmed by the perfume of working for us in a larger capacity.

"Come on," I said. "Be a bigger part of our family."

Curt and showing a lot of gumption, perhaps too much of it, she said she would expand her role. Money wasn't the issue. She'd do it, but we would have to hire Derek. Those were her terms and she stated them unequivocally.

I wasn't offended. That's the trick, by the way, of making it in New York or anywhere else. No brass balls, no bravado, then no brass ring.

Avi was against it, but after two weeks of thinking it over, as I phoned him daily to explain why I wanted to keep Derek around, he consented. We referred to Derek as "the kid" and paid him to complete tasks any intern from film school would perform gladly for no pay at all.

For a while, two of my staff members tried to teach Derek how to write coverage on the scripts that poured into our office. He had no talent for it, but day after day he'd show up on time to run the most tedious sorts of errands for our small family of employees at Rain-Or-Rust.

In private sessions with me, Derek would share his gangster stories. I began to develop a burgeoning file of possible ideas that could become part of my TV series. It was more than coincidence. It felt meant to be.

Agnes impressed everyone who had the pleasure of working with her. I'll never forget the first time she kissed me on the cheek in my office. This was followed by a long soft unforgettable caress.

I found myself enjoying a refreshed outlook toward life, and a growing sense that new trajectories were possible and much was about to change. These intuitions turned out to be accurate, but didn't manifest in the way I'd expected them to. They didn't come close.

There was a night when Agnes and I were sharing an Italian dinner together on Prince Street in the Village. I saw by the way she was glowing that she'd begun to realize that I was stuck on her. I didn't think we should resist the way we enjoyed such an alluring chemistry. I started letting my mind wander into more arcane realms, thinking of Schopenhauer, who at the time I was trying to read more of and understand better. I was hooked on the man's work, laboring to grasp his theories about how love is defined by the physical sexual urge, the desire to match to another who is different in order to procreate a more perfect variant on the species.

As I saw it, love as understood by Schopenhauer wasn't anything abstract or cerebral. It was purposeful lust tied to a carnal urge and a need to reproduce the species.

I didn't bring this up in conversation, of course, though I dabbled with the idea of risking it just to see how Agnes would respond. I feared I'd come across as pretentious, a simpleton, and maybe I was both.

Anyone who read Schopenhauer or worked in the movie business weaving together narratives of comic-book level morality was sordid, incomplete and pretentious. I recalled how Avi and I would talk over cocktails about how these narratives we were so intent on funding were essentially criminal interpretations of lies designed to exploit a market, especially when they became part of the fabric of what some young minds accepted as reality. Ridiculous, really, and tragic.

It made me want to vomit whenever I'd hear one of the young hopefuls in our office pass a remark such as, "We get a black man in the cast, an Eddie Murphy, and we're guaranteed fourteen percent market share."

One had to be pretentious to summon the nerve to be part of such an enterprise. Wasn't the pandemic proving that life could and would continue without any new entertainment being generated? There were enough old forms around to be rediscovered.

I didn't discus what I happened to be reading at any particular time. It could be said I threw occasional parties, but I wasn't much fun at them. In many ways, I liked the pandemic because I didn't need to throw parties. Nor did I need an audience. I lowered myself into the hold of my ship, as it were, using my home as a monastery. I read my books, kept to a strict diet, meditating, doing Yoga, and listening to music for hours on end. I found it rather easy to shut the world out and forget it had ever existed.

When spending time with Agnes, I did as I tended to in most social situations I found intimidating. I played the victim. I told Agnes that I believed I was getting too old to fight off or be afraid of any sparks I might be feeling when with another woman. I meant, specifically, her.

Agnes appeared to get this and looked astonished to hear my confession. Not that I, as a bachelor, really knew how to proceed in any long-term relationship.

What bedazzled me was that every time I saw Agnes I felt those sparks, an impulsive need for intimacy that I'd been vulnerable to since the first time we'd met. I was also wrestling with the fear that I was running out of time, that I'd never meet anyone like her again.

She said she knew how I felt, but she wouldn't act on it. Too bad we hadn't met before she married Derek. Those were her exact words. God, how they stung.

She went on to tell me that while on a date with Derek, sitting by his side, that she began to accept that he was, indeed, and always would be a criminal, but not in *her* mind, not really. She knew she was lying to herself, but she accepted the lie because she wanted to be with him. He was her provider. She needed one to practice her photography, which she referred to as her "art" and her "strength" and her "salvation."

Where had she stolen those lines from? I didn't know. I certainly didn't trust them. She said it was true love she felt with Derek, even if it was also a bending of the truth to fit her obsession with becoming famous as a photographer. This was an impulsiveness she'd known since her first days of living in Manhattan.

The more I talked with Agnes and learned how her mind worked, the more I remembered why I'd stayed a bachelor so long. Did this make me a misogynist or a pragmatist in a city full of delusional cloud chasers? I thought it a fair question.

—∞—

In a life of extremes, meeting Derek, realizing she loved him, made Agnes feel enthralled and energized. She felt this way when younger and riding the Acela train to the city to visit high school friends who already lived in Yonkers, Bed-Sty, White Plains and uptown Manhattan.

Agnes had them as community, a group of peers. She'd made the mistake of assuming that they'd always be there. They weren't. Each of those friends had moved on.

She wanted to use a movie comparison, so she said, sounding a tone of lament, "You know, like in *Boogie Nights*. There's aging and ejaculation and moving on. Every movie ends, just like every seduction."

I listened as the minutes, days and months went by, each one becoming more painful than the last. This I deemed part of a masochistic sense of loyalty to her. I believed it came out of a need that she'd like me in return. I didn't want to admit it, but I was tired of being a bachelor. Perhaps Agnes would learn to love me the way she loved Derek. Perhaps she just needed to get to know me better.

She told me about the moment that came when she embraced the notion of getting serious with Derek. A full commitment. She'd been coming to trust her own skepticism. The city was no longer a religion. Having changed for her, it would continue to change whether she liked it or not. Derek understood this too, and he appeared fine with it. This was what she'd spoken to him about the most. He listened carefully, as if amused, and made no comments to judge or insult her. He wasn't on edge, didn't play the peacock, remaining sanguine, introspective, and willing to confess how lonely he was.

Sanguine? Had she really used such a word? She had. Then what did that make me? How would I be described? What did I look like? Had this relationship of ours become a question of my being obsessed with what I couldn't have? The thought appalled me, and so did all these questions, but they existed and I couldn't avoid them.

As her conversations with Derek evolved over time and the two of them got to know each other better, Agnes felt comfortable enough to order dessert whenever they went out for dinner. Derek told her about his step-father, Buzzy, who'd died a while back, and how that had left him feeling marooned and in need of what he called "healing action."

Then he'd added, speaking to Agnes as if she'd earned his respect, as if she was one of the guys, "Yeah, *Shooter* Agnes. I feel lucky to meet someone with a name like that. Says a lot."

I listened to Agnes. I mooned. Buzzy? Shooter? What kind of names were these?

A jackass, that's what I was. I wanted what I couldn't have, which only served to make me want it more.

Agnes understood that Derek talked like a street tough, but she also saw it wasn't an act. Derek was genuine and shrewd; he knew he should conceal his inner life and share it judiciously under proper conditions. Throughout their early nights, she and Derek talked for hours, month after month of courtship, taking their walks and their conversations to Madison, Central, or Washington Square Park. Or way uptown to The Cloisters. To the museums. To Battery Park and Staten Island, where his mother hailed from.

Derek, she said, was game for anything. So was she. It was romantic, a long montage with music playing. Nights at concerts, in barrooms, at sporting events, in cafes, at movies and plays or else taking walks and then making love until falling asleep at sunrise.

Best of all, he didn't drink much, didn't smoke or use drugs. He just peddled them.

She thought she already drank and ate too much, so being with him curbed those tendencies. She started to lose a little weight. Her own father, a wealthy self-labelled "stock and bonds guru" had drunk himself to death. Her mother, who she got along with when the woman was sober, resided alone in her widow's manse in waspish Barrington, Rhode Island. She spent most of her days not far from the sea, specifically on Rumstick Point. She'd lunch on her patio in pleasant weather, doing her best to match her late husband one martini at a time until her afternoons became evenings and she could barely stand.

Agnes then shared a story of how one evening when after leaving Derek the last thing she said to him was, "Pray, that's all I can tell you. Not much else more than we can do."

Was she really such a believer? Did she trust and follow her own words of advice? She wasn't sure, but she'd liked seeing Derek hadn't resisted or rebuffed her. Not that she was all that Catholic. Just a little, and when convenient. Like most Catholics, she supposed.

These emotions she felt. Were they love? I had no answer. Why? Because at every interval whenever we met, I was asking those same questions myself.

They must be, said Agnes. They sent her mining into depths she hadn't realized she held inside. Lucky for her that Derek, it turned out, liked that she was Catholic. He said his Ma would approve. No, he didn't go to church all the time. Not a big deal. That was for other people. He went for Ma's sake and always attended for Christmas and Easter.

"We can keep doing this," he'd said. "See how it goes. Maybe make it regular."

Did he mean getting married? She'd like that. She'd never thought it possible. She'd hoped for it, of course, and she wanted to have a baby, though it was all happening so fast. That was when Derek started calling her Agnes, not just Shooter – and that was when she knew. A woman always does.

—⁓—

I called her Agnes. I understood the Shooter nickname's derivation, but I didn't like it. Nor did I like she seemed not to "know" I loved her the same way, if not more than Derek did. It made no sense, but then I reminded myself that one of the glorious delights of womankind is that they're seldom willingly as predictable as men. It's as if they're supposed to view situations according to their own sometimes diabolical and byzantine perspectives. Men, if they can even find the track, stay glued to it. Women tend to make and revise the track as they carry on.

They got married, renting an over-priced pigeonhole in Queens not far from where Derek's Ma lived. Derek kept encouraging Agnes to pursue her photography, so she ventured out night after night in search of material to shoot. She took hundreds of pictures with film, using Derek's drug money profits to process and print them.

She told me, and I'll never forget it, that this acceptance from Derek, his funding of her passions as a shutterbug, was when she became Agnes, once and for all: mature and phlegmatic, determined, growing in confidence, still shooting film and proud of it.

You heard that right. Film. She shot digital too, telling me once that she wasn't "a Luddite." Yes, she used that word. Film, however, was what she loved. Partly, it was due to color saturation and how it could be seen in the movies, for example, of Jack Cardiff.

Sure, I told her. I knew a thing or two about Mr. Cardiff. God, I loved her for simply knowing who that man was, let alone his contribution to cinema history.

Agnes mourned that Kodak and Konica were words more often associated with museums, what used to be. She could no longer buy Kodachrome 64, or Ektachrome slide film, or Fuji 1600 and a host of other products that were once part of her daily life. She shot her images, got the negatives processed, and printed them herself at home. Derek, her angel, paid for all she needed to practice her expensive hobby. He did this by contributing to and accelerating the so-called opioid crisis.

In a nutshell, that was their story.

THREE

Working as members of a corporate tribe, our first film was a tender drama with a twist in the vein of Tennessee Williams that was shot on a farm upstate not far from Oneonta. I thought it brilliant but not edgy enough. One critic compared our young director, a Fordham graduate originally from Indiana, to my fellow Texan, the auteur Terrence Malick.

High praise, indeed. Reactions came from critics on both coasts, and even in Europe and the UK, all positive, but the film wasn't a box-office draw. Its two largest audiences were at a festival in Toronto, and one in Deauville, France. It went straight to DVD. Remember them?

We happened and were eclipsed in one long breath. To hear Derek say it: "Wasteland for pissants, I'm telling ya." To see Derek *live* it: "Not *mañana*, you douchebag. I mean now."

Maybe Derek thrived in a way that he felt destined to, as he should have. Maybe this Covid variant was a modern plague. Derek couldn't say. Nor could I. At one point in Derek's life he'd decided he needed to make perfect every method of lying that he knew. Did he think his days were numbered? He did. This wouldn't stop him. He was one who seized and never waited.

Sure, Derek had scars. We all did, but the pandemic wasn't about them. It was about something different. To Derek, the pandemic was the dying time, the great eraser when a smart survivor put his mask on and learned how to shut up. Didn't matter any longer who you knew and what you'd done or what your politics were. Unless, of course, you owned a yacht and could moor it off the coast of Baja and just linger there until the virus disappeared.

Derek had words he planned to have engraved on his headstone. Even though he didn't smoke, they were inspired by some of the noirs he'd watched with me. They went like this: *I'm dying here, so light me a cigarette, will ya?*

He wouldn't put them in his will. I told him he should. He said, "Nah, Mr. Railsback, they're just a joke, really, when you look at them. Know why? Because everything is."

Derek didn't care about meaning. Swerving and dodging up Eighth Ave in a sharkskin suit that fit tightly over his pronounced contours, he moved as if he planned to cover within minutes all the blocks from Twentieth up to Seventy-Second. Sometimes he went even farther uptown, it just depended on his errands. He had a reputation and it was working for him, mostly in his favor. He didn't lie, cheat or steal. These were rare qualities among the slime he did business with.

How quickly he got a job done depended sometimes on the weather and his mood and whether he needed to visit his Ma. It also depended on how often he allowed his lungs to suck in more oxygen by pausing in front of sausage vendor carts, soaking up the stinks and steams from gutters, drains and ventilation ducts.

Wasteland. Ghosts everywhere. If anyone asked Derek on the street at any moment whether he loved the city, he'd have told that person he hated it and that Gotham stunk like a sulfur fart. That it was dying, the whole world was, but The Scientists, well, those cocksuckers were waist-high in the Benjamins and they planned to stay there.

These Scientists were the operators he feared and worked for. I was never convinced he respected them. They were thugs, too, captains of a ship that when it sank, he sank with it. Covid was what he called "the real equalizer" and it was teaching everybody just how puny they were.

⁓

Pumping up the magenta to reduce the green takes some knowledge, true, but color balancing on a computer wasn't the same for Agnes as wearing gloves and using a loupe to read a slide or a negative in her hands. What she relished was going through the process of seeing a photo develop step by step in a miasma of agonizing mystery to eventually get a result she might not like. What she mourned was that it had all become immediate. Gone was the ejaculatory moment that gathered momentum before exploding at one's fingertips. She liked to quote Derek who'd once told me, "Any douchebag with a phone can call himself a photographer, but Agnes she's an artist. There's a difference."

"He's right," Agnes had said. "I *am* an artist. *I* take the pictures. Not the equipment!"

Derek liked to agree with Agnes's assessment that she wasn't like the others, them, those "touch holes out there," as he put it, that he had no use for. He bragged that she had a gift. A seeing eye. A sensitivity to the moment. Agnes swooned when he said such things.

Yet I said such things to her all the time, but coming from me it wasn't the same. Why? She expected it from me. I was playing my role. This was where she loved me. In the role.

Pre-pandemic, Agnes would often go back to Rhode Island when there was no work or her mother needed support and companionship. In return, her mother would send money Agnes's way. Agnes needed her mother as much as her mother needed her. She slept on silk sheets in staid mostly privileged Barrington, in one of the many large bed-rooms there. She took meditative walks along the shores of hidden inlets and coves native residents knew about or had access to.

Over two decades ago, both of her older brothers had left to start their own families. One was in Utah, the other in Los Angeles. Her mother had no desire to visit either of those places. To her, LaLa Land was clotted with traffic jams and cloying Latino illegals carrying con-cealed weapons. Utah was a desert playground for Mormons where the beer didn't have a high enough alcohol count.

Agnes didn't disagree entirely, though unlike her mother she hoped to visit both brothers, if only to see her nieces and nephews. But nothing could be scheduled now. All plans were figments. Life was about getting on while being put on hold.

She still had a few friends in Providence, two of them mothers, one divorced, but she never saw them. The majority of the artsy aspirants she knew from student days had moved if not to warmer climes then to growing cities such as Denver and Boise where, allegedly, all the high-tech jobs were. It appeared, she said, that she never got the memo regarding which states to relocate to if one wanted a lucrative job in the 21st Century.

"All high tech," she said. "Everywhere you look. Tech, tech, tech."

She tended to flog herself over never fully realizing that to be an artist was to be considered a useless miscreant. That if one wants money, a career, then one should work for concerns that sought more efficient ways for humans to mend or tutor or else kill each other. One choice that I suggested would be to become a medical professional who cared for a growing population of citizens who might not have adequate insurance coverage to pay for any treatment which might keep them alive. She showed no interest, citing it as too mainstream.

Her diffidence meant she lived with a constant and troubling sense of feeling like a failure. When had she lost her once deep-seated confidence and proud anti-establishment attitude? When younger, she could have reinvented herself with ease. Instead, she'd thumbed her nose at girlfriends residing in massive homes in leafy suburban communities with gates and guard shacks and names such as Heritage Meadows. She never liked the suburban plaza-in-an-SUV lifestyle. You couldn't pay her to slurp coffee at Starbucks.

As if anybody cared now what on earth she thought about anything. Naturally, I'd cared. I'd wanted to help, but I had to work so hard to get her to see this.

Oh, she told me, when she was younger enough time had passed and she'd learned, all right. As she'd gotten older, her sneering attitudes toward authority and bourgeois standards had become harder to maintain. Financial burdens came into play. Having roommates or else couch-surfing became less tenable. Few noticed when she started smartening up, but by then it was too late. There was no interest from her peers. They had their own problems.

Meanwhile her body began sagging into premature suggestions of matronly dumpiness. But she didn't go to the gym or watch her diet carefully. She began to believe that if she wanted to wed and raise a child, she should jump on the first opportunity that came along. Time was running out. She didn't want to die alone. Especially since money was what people noticed. What they respected. Not art. This had been a difficult lesson for her to learn. She supposed some artists never did. She wasn't even sure she'd learned it.

When Derek came along, it all fell into place. Derek had money and a sense of humor. He lived under an alluring spell of risk and danger. He loved her photos and told her to keep taking them. Millions of them. She wouldn't have to break it off with Holly either. There was love there with her, too, Agnes was sure of it.

I wanted to tell her that Derek didn't love her. Not the way I did. Yet I didn't tell her this. Why? Because, I think, that with love I could never be sure. I hadn't lost confidence; I'd never had any. This was my Achilles heel. Not hers.

❧

Despite what she said about it, Agnes wasn't the type who lost confidence. Perhaps that's another trait that appealed to me so much. While living in Providence, a city which Agnes had learned by heart while saving for her move to New York, she had studied and photographed its grittier neighborhoods. Many of them had gotten more run down. Just as she had. Yet those dirty low-down 'hoods were places she revered and never tired of telling me about. I assumed she told me because Derek, as a native New Yorker, wasn't interested.

Agnes stomped around on foot in her sand-colored boots and camo cargo pants wherever any city neighborhood was different from block to block. She wandered up Chalkstone Avenue in Providence where she found three-deckers and doughnut parlors. Many of the Hmong people that lived there after arriving in boatloads following the Vietnam War had assimilated and moved out. Though this demographic was changing, she still saw some of them along Chalkstone with chickens pecking the hardpan in their little front yards behind makeshift picket fences.

A lot of the nearby three-deckers all over neighboring Smith Hill had become expensive rental properties. Smith Hill was where Holly still lived. Holly had the top floor with three bedrooms and a balcony porch of a three-decker to herself. Holly's Daddy owned the building. He owned a few buildings in the city and some office space too.

Holly never had to worry about money. Agnes envied this about her. She also kicked herself for not following Holly's lead and buying some property when it was still relatively cheap. In her defense, Agnes never had a Daddy who could pay for everything. He might have been able to help, but he was busy playing golf and getting sotted on Wallbangers at the Wampanoag Country Club.

If Agnes had been smart, she'd have pioneered and bought a place in one of the less expensive Providence neighborhoods. Unfortunately, she hadn't and it was too late. Providence had been discovered.

Not only had Holly always enjoyed having more money than Agnes, she was younger, too, by five years. Daddy's little girl, a princess, that was Holly.

Agnes used to adore her, but something had changed. She couldn't identify it. She just knew that she saw Holly differently. It was as if her adoration had with time become infused with more envy than idolatry. She found it frightening to think that she and Holly had considered marriage and living as an enlightened gay couple. Thank God, Holly had decided she needed time to play around and figure herself out sexually and that maybe Agnes should do the same.

Holly was still happy to jump from Agnes to other men and women. Agnes had fancied herself doing this too, but she'd known from the start that she wouldn't. She simply preferred men, though little of lasting consequence had happened with any man until she'd met Derek.

She loved Derek, she did, didn't she? This love question, it was tricky, and on occasion she needed her time away from it as if with any other routine.

So did Derek. They both used Holly, and Holly enjoyed using them. All seemed to be working out for the time being.

I never once believed Agnes when she told me this. I saw her triangle game as a disaster waiting to happen, but I lacked the fortitude to tell her. To warn her away from it.

⁓

What Agnes lived for was to find her images and capture them in peace. To labor all day in a darkroom, and flop on a mattress exhausted at night. She still didn't know where her creative impulses came from and why they'd endured for so long, but she didn't care to examine them. For a long time they'd irritated her, their luster fading as time went on. She'd begun to see her friends grow increasingly prosperous while her attempts at becoming the next Diane Arbus kept adding to a frustrating sense of being flawed and untalented.

What she liked about Providence, the city where many of her firsts happened, was that some neighborhoods still retained the ethnic characteristics that made them appealing to her when younger. They were well-hidden gems, she supposed. When people in Manhattan heard she was from Rhode Island, they shrugged indifferently. Many of them pictured dopey scenes from the cartoon, *Family Guy.* As for me, I knew it was a state, technically speaking, but there were counties and ranches in Texas that were bigger and, frankly, more interesting.

I learned not to tell that to those proud swamp Yankees in southern New England. I also learned their provincialism was odious to the point that the mere mention of Texas made their hair stand on end. It was as if we Texans were all bowlegged in ten-gallon hats, shouting "Yee-hah!" every time we saw the cock of a stud horse, an ICBM missile, an Apollo rocket, the American flag, a pick-up truck, a Dallas *Cowboys* cheerleader, and a long-neck bottle of beer.

And a gun, of course.

As a Texan, I took solemn pride in knowing this stereotype reflected their disgusting elitism and ignorance, not my own. And never the truth. What a relief it was to learn that Agnes could talk to me about such topics. As she saw it, New York elitism and provincialism weren't much different from the New England varieties. I agreed with her, having found that the people I'd met throughout the Northeast acted as if they'd created the diversity thing and that they owned the rulebook on how to run the country. What they preached was tolerance and openness, but what they practiced was something else entirely. Why was it, for instance, that everyone from outside of that region, and along the I-95 corridor in general, all the way south to DC, believed this not to be true?

I often discussed this with Agnes, encouraging her to get out of the straightjacket she'd allowed herself to grow up in. To her credit, there were many times when she did so and listened to my points of view. She argued that in many smaller cities of the Northeast, even in tiny Providence there was a diversity that couldn't be found anywhere else. Though I knew she was only partly correct, I didn't fight with her. I listened as she boasted about the many Puerto Ricans, Dominicans, Salvadorans, and Brazilians who weren't hiding in enclaves there. How they struggled in solidarity with Laotians, Nigerians and Vietnamese. She made them sound as if they weren't humans but rather glass figurines out of Tennessee Williams' menagerie.

Clearly, Agnes had never been to Houston or Dallas or El Paso. To Agnes, all that diversity, no matter one's country of origin, translated into subjects she hungered to photograph. "These people in these cities," she said, "are trying their best. Nobody really shows them how. Nobody shares their struggle with the world."

I wasn't sure she was right. Nor was I sure that New Bedford when compared to Fort Worth, or New Britain when compared to El Paso, could be called cities. Big towns was a better label, but that was my opinion and it wasn't heard as Agnes rambled on telling me about Broad Street in Providence, which I'd never seen. She argued that this particular street was still home to many newcomers, with its neo-Christian churches in shopping plazas full of Haitians who'd rejected Catholicism, its Guatemalan laundromats, its Liberian restaurants, its Cape Verdean night clubs, and all the little bodegas where one could purchase Panamanian and Dominican food. It seemed to her when she was spending a lot of time there that Liberians were having the toughest go of it, their numbers so high, their wages so low.

I didn't know, and I said as much. I also listened, and tried to keep an open mind as she boasted that Providence was a sanctuary city – a pairing of two words that I could never reconcile. Similar, say, to "engineered demise." I also didn't tell her that there were some, many in fact, that didn't like the idea of this free-flowing input of humanity one bit, especially those who owned property and had labored long and hard to do so, many of them who she'd disparage as "rednecks" from my native part of the globe. She was so open that she didn't want anything to do with such people.

With a sigh, and some indigestion, I took all her opining in stride. She thought their argument (and mine), inane. My belief concurred with the alleged redneck one which stipulated that creating sanctuaries meant more low-wage labor got imported while more low-wage companies kept moving their factories out of the country. No, I didn't think it was an inane perspective at all. I thought what government wanted was more serfs to their feudal estate, more future voters on their side of the red-blue color divide, and more dependency on government in order to survive. Though I wasn't anybody's version of a right-winger, I understood the mind-set of many Texans and red-state residents, not all of whom were socially conservative and pro forever wars. I'm talking about people the likes of Agnes had never really met or talked to.

These oversimplifications and politics that we'd argue could be frustrating. I'd ask her if a government should allow desperate people into its country and not provide them with a means to find a place to live. Shouldn't that government provide a path toward independence? Not dependence. And not a way to get by that didn't make poorer all the hard-working people who were playing by the rules and already over-taxed and over-paying for basic amenities.

Actions by such a government struck me as wholly irresponsible. When I took my time and explained my views in this way, Agnes never had an answer for them. She teemed with Yankee stubbornness, or maybe it was a Catholic thing, and refused to concede I might have a few valid points.

It's cliché, I know, but I told her she'd feel right at home in Austin, but not anywhere else in Texas. Not that she cared. Not that she was even remotely interested in visiting.

⁓⁓⁓

The East Providence neighborhood that Agnes had lived in was pop-ulated in large part by Cape Verdeans at that time. Her friends the Cabral boys were still around, she said. So was Willie Gomez. She had fun with them. One friend took her sailing on Narragansett Bay. She'd row in a canoe early mornings on the Seekonk River with slick Ricky Amado, but he died. She'd slept with him a bunch of times. Slick Ricky got knifed in the throat during a bar fight in the town of Brockton.

What he was doing there Agnes never knew. Probably chasing drugs, money or women, which all those boys of his ilk tended to do.

In her old neighborhood, where it could be dangerous, people liked to say they were friendly and they got along. Maybe they were, but I doubted it. This was like saying that people are shy. They aren't. They're mostly not interested and afraid to embarrass themselves. They use these behavioral definitions as acceptable cover and excuses to avoid face to face contact and interaction. These were the people who loved Covid. It allowed them to hide out in the open.

Remember, Agnes was the perpetual art girl, the astute observer. She knew how to find people like those boys in East Providence to protect her. She tended to see people not as who they were, but who she believed them to be.

She said if you were from her neighborhood, your race or religion might matter, but not always. They looked out for each other. They boasted of this. Neighborhood loyalties often cancelled racial or ethnic divides.

Agnes had come to understand that she needed to be shrewd and on the defensive as she exploited her knack for making new friends. She'd learned through practice and many disappointments how to get strangers to allow her to photograph them. This was an undervalued part of her mastery of the art form. She had brilliant examples too. Some incredible faces.

Unlike me, she was keen to talk politics. I humored her and listened.

In the world according to Agnes there weren't enough minority cops. She'd told this to one of the old Providence mayors back when he was going house to house running for office for the first time. Seeing faces like their own, in her view, would help new immigrants at least feel like they were getting representation.

If I'm not mistaken, that mayoral candidate was cunning enough to get himself elected, served at least one term and now represents the Ocean State in Washington, DC. The hiring of minority cops never happened. Just the opposite occurred. Cops were ostracized, their numbers reduced, and we were all told that because of this crime wasn't on the rise. I think as new mayor that young man may have had lots of trees planted in some rich neighborhoods. And of course he despised Trump and bad-mouthed him every chance he got.

Even if Agnes agreed with me on political issues, and sometimes (rarely) she did, she remained a true-blue liberal. This in spite of knowing that prices had to be paid by those residing in a sanctuary city, especially when its cops were mostly white and ex-military, underpaid, undervalued and retiring in droves.

I argued with her that a mayor should be concerned with more than identity politics and planting trees. A mayor should make certain that services got provided to tax payers, immigrant or not. In a place like New England, it seemed to me this meant clearing snow off the streets. Getting city school buses home before dark. The old guard, the ward-boss mayors and governors I'd read about who'd served cities all over the country, none of whom were angels, though many were beloved, had understood this. Whether blue or red, they might have been pugnacious and vile, but their constituents came first, not just party donors, and they were effective.

According to Agnes, all those mayors were beasts. All they ever wanted was for desperate newcomers to become so blended-in that it would seem like they were consumed by assimilation. Yet the constituents of those mayors, I argued, represented the rainbow in all its colors. The rainbow itself was an image of assimilation, not diversity. She disagreed. Immigrants or not, no matter race or ethnicity, she believed people should be allowed to feel what they wanted to feel or be, whether accepted, represented, a bit special. Not to be assimilated.

Well, you really know you love someone if you can respectfully disagree and still manage to spend the evening together in peace.

"They want to fit in," she told me. "But to do so they need to claw and scratch and to never surrender. Assimilation is a form of evil."

Whatever. I found it difficult not to choke on and marvel at her idealism, telling her that clawing and scratching was what she had to do, as well, especially as an art photographer. As a woman too, unfortunately. I believe she liked hearing this from me.

"Clawing and scratching is our natural state," I said.

"You listen, don't you?" she said. "Derek. He never listens."

Was I, finally, getting through?

FOUR

Do you revere those plonks, fizzles, crackles, tonal peaks and sliding elisions that spark, spit and bubble off our tongues? I do. Language like that, all those sonic collisions that remind me of film music by George Antheil, are what got me excited about getting into the movie business. Couple this with witty rapid-fire dialogue. Repartee, as it were, going back to the first time I watched *The Philadelphia Story*. Those exchanges between Jimmy Stewart, Cary Grant and Katherine Hepburn, really any dialogue exchange in a George Cukor film, or a comedy with the likes of Rosalind Russell or Thelma Ritter in it, or William Powell in *My Man Godfrey*. These films transported me to a place that helped me say "I'm home, I belong here." It had only been an accident I'd started out in rural Texas. The mission of my life would be to get out of there to New York City, in black and white, on celluloid, where I belonged.

How to pull this off? Well, it wasn't easy, but when you're poor as a kid, and we were, you don't dream. You wise up early and get on your pony and you ride. You hustle with purpose and cunning. I learned quickly to like the way my mother would look at me in awe each time I came home having figured out a way to put some money in my pocket.

This drive developed and got me through school and, while there, led me to revere all things English, and Texas, and Manhattan. I led what I thought of as a double life –to cop a title from a Ronald Colman classic for which he won an Oscar. I was a business student at UT Austin, but I was able to visit London as part of a student exchange program. I fancied myself the next David Niven or Roger Moore. I even looked like Mr. Moore.

I stayed on the straight and narrow, but in the closet laboring while others were out going to football games and getting drunk. I read constantly: Tom Stoppard, Lanford Wilson, Horton Foote, Emily Dickinson, Oscar Wilde, and Samuel Becket. Taciturn, I was a wallflower prone to entombing my emotions, lugging them around until they exploded in fits of purgative agony.

What a triumph I felt when I first read or viewed the works of playwrights and poets who spoke for the jumble of emotions I was grappling with. As a meek loner who looked more suave and sophisticated than he really was, I grew up without an appetite for sports in a state where football is nearly a religion. I played the innocent and survived. This meant I never suffered an excess of friends. I found a social outlet in theatrical productions, whether comical or absurd. These were sanctuaries. For the longest time, I thought I was gay and just as painfully closeted as William Inge had been because I was so awkward around both boys and girls. The only male friend I had at university, Mason Slidell, an Austin native, was flamboyant, a reader of Sylvia Plath and William Carlos Williams, and sometimes militantly defensive about being gay. He was determined to flee Texas forever once he graduated.

Mason died in the 80s while living on Castro Street in San Francisco. I don't know the details, though I can hazard a guess. I miss him.

After we parted ways, neither of us made an effort to stay in touch. I can't say why. Laziness, I guess, and a sense of entitlement, as if we believed we'd always be there for each other. I miss the innocence we shared as undergrads. Our eagerness to realize hidden ambitions. I visited him once in San Francisco after graduation, but we got so high and drunk during my visit that I don't remember much of it.

It seems to me I'm still a lonely lad who silently destroys in my dreams whomever and whatever I perceive as a threat. It seems I'm perpetually in a situation of some kind, but that's a definition of living, I suppose, isn't it?

As a boy, what I disliked coming to learn was that I could hear what the others, the knuckleheads, the jocks, the popular ones, said about me behind my back. Like I cared! But I did care, and I listened attentively both to haters and jealous insecure boys, and to power-mongers prone to violence. All of that mattered when I was a pipsqueak. If anything, it mattered too much and led to more isolation.

I taught myself how to deflect and avoid the philistines and to gravitate toward the other castigated ones, the thinkers and my fellow freak-show outsiders. Those who read books and went to the theatre. The mousier ones, as I thought of them, including myself.

As I matured, I learned the value of stamina and my diffidence. I moved inward steadily toward the rock where, like Peter the Apostle, I would build the church of my Self. I knew this would take time, but I also knew I could do it. Just as I knew I could find myself abusing narcotics and alcohol and getting into scrapes with the long arm of Texas law, as some of my well-to-do university classmates wound up doing. My isolation made it easy for me to avoid all of that.

Those years at UT Austin were a time of experimentation and rebellion on all fronts. My time in London, though brief, gave me perspective on just how mewling an infant the American experiment really was. Though my behavior could be deemed radical, it wasn't noticed or considered out of the ordinary for Austin. That city, which I still love, has always been the counterpoint, the opposing force to whatever synchronicity might be developing in other parts of the state. In fact, many of my classmates there were not from sagebrush Texas but from wealth. I learned the best way of coping with their pretensions was to dig further inside of myself. To learn more and work harder. To create, on one hand, escape routes and fantasies, while on the other hand developing practical schemes for getting richer.

When I wasn't reading, or working in a bank, I auditioned for plays. I had no talent and never got cast, so I volunteered my time to help build sets or work as an usher or take tickets at the box office. Anything to be involved outside of the sometimes turgid manipulations that defined management, marketing, accounting and other principles of a business degree.

I often journeyed alone to Dallas, and Houston to see concerts, plays and movies. I enjoyed what titillations Austin had to offer, especially the music. In particular Nancy Griffith, daughter of Seguin, seat of Guadalupe County, who I had such a crush on. She broke my heart when she moved to Nashville, but I understood why she did it. She had to. Just as I had to, when ready, pull up stakes for Manhattan.

What's the point of living if we don't self-actualize? I wasn't determined to fit in or to become an artist. A dilettante? Perhaps. But that came second to what I really craved, which was the security that money could bring. I started young working in Austin as a bank teller. I had a clean smile, a warm manner, a firm handshake. I worked in banks during my entire time as a student. I began investing while reading everything I could find by Milton Friedman, Warren Buffet and other such guru moguls. By the time I graduated, I'd been promoted to loan officer. I liked money; I liked even more what it might do for me if I invested it wisely.

I stayed in Austin, kept working at the same bank. I kept investing. I befriended young professionals who understood finance and brokerage firms. They knew nothing of my interest in theatre, literature, music and film. Percentages of each paycheck I earned, no matter how small, went into savings, some stocks, and some investments accounts. I had started this habit in my late teens, and by the time I earned my MBA, I had myself the foundation of a decent portfolio. Leaving Austin for Manhattan as soon as I could, I asked myself if I had a secret recipe for success. No, I didn't. Nobody does. I simply knew I'd succeed.

In my case, my start was as a trader on Wall Street. It was the 80s, the absolute best time for a Teflon-coated aspirant like me to be there. I wasn't the Wolf Of Wall Street, nor was I like Oliver Stone's character Gordon Gecko in that greed defined me, but it most assuredly drove me, just as it drove those I worked with throughout that decade. They were, many of them, a spoiled, entitled and crass lot, thinking the boom times would never end. I was unpopular in that I took a longer view. I didn't show off. I worked late and I worked weekends. I lived as if still a struggling a student, managing to save and invest throughout that decade and well into the nineties, watching not all but much of my risk-taking and patience pay significant dividends.

Tech. Microsoft. Intel. Amazon. Exxon. Starbucks. Cisco. The dot-com boom and bust. Slow growth. Pharma stocks. Short sells. Low risk and high. Even Netflix penny stocks. All stocks, you see, are affordable at one time or another. Patience helped. So did listening and keeping my mouth shut. So did persistence. It wasn't magic. I knew what I wanted and nothing distracted me. There was land development. International shipping. The rise of the container. The rise of the Internet. Transportation. Mining. There were times to buy, times to sell, and always time to listen to those who knew better. I kept working and investing. The more that funds came in, the more I diversified and listened and waited. None of the investors I admired had been impatient.

How scrupulously I managed my money. As I started to see profits grow on some investments, I sent a little money home to my mother. I tried to do this each month. I ate frugally. I seldom drank or splashed the cash on big nights out. I owned few clothes, but cared well for those I did have, and I looked sharp in them too. I didn't need a car or a gym membership, but I had ways of staying fit, and I suppose my life was boring, all about work, but it suited me. I lived not on the island, but pioneered in Hoboken before that became trendy. It was dirt cheap there, though sometimes perilous.

I kept to a rigid routine each day, rising early, making time for morning calisthenics, some reading, some extra work to augment the demands of my job, and then some reading for pleasure each night. I lived alone in a rented rather squalid room, preparing for the next step, seizing opportunities when they came my way. As I overheard one colleague say about me in the office, I didn't make friends easily, but I didn't make enemies and I got the job done. Experiencing disappointment never set me back. It stung, of course, but it helped by showing me just how much pain I was capable of enduring.

This process, this stubborn resilience in me, had started with the death of my father when I wasn't yet a teenager. I was in the fourth grade. My mother and I never found a replacement. At home, I became the father figure: stoic, independent, impecunious.

There was a little money, apparently, in my mother's family, not much and that small sum came to me later when my mother died. I was in my early thirties at the time. Put me over the top, so to speak, enabling me to invest even more, mostly into oil, tech, pharma and natural gas. Three things were going for me. I'd never needed to borrow money to go to university. I was patient and careful with every cent. I worked so much that I never had time for women or to lavishly waste what I earned.

I tried to write a play about my father, cribbing as much as I could from fellow Texans Sam Shepard, and Larry McMurtry. I imagined my father as a man who fled to Mexico with a *senorita* he'd impregnated when she was all of sixteen. It was a terrible play, a feeble attempt to discover the man who'd left me too soon.

It was my dear mother who raised me, exhausting herself as a widow, working full-time while looking after my interests. Her death should have been more of a shock because her illness came on like a zephyr, wasting her away within a year, but I'd left Texas by then and had no intentions of moving back. She understood this and never pressed me to return.

During her last year alive, I saw her three times. At Easter, on July 4th which was unbearably hot, and at Christmas when I'd already sold, at her request, the double-wide she'd raised me in. By that time, she was too weak to stand while living as a patient in a rehab center in Wichita Falls.

The vanishing of a constant parental figure in a young person's life leaves such gaping vacancies within. The vacancy I felt, and its echoes, needed with time to be shared with someone I cared about. There had been women, and a couple of men, don't get me wrong, but I wasn't interested in commitment. I also knew I preferred women, and that I was too selfish. The women I dated came to learn that too.

As I got older and grew more comfortable with Agnes, I decided that I was ready for commitment. I started to convince myself that I could earn her trust and adoration and tell her anything. Though I never felt any of this with Derek, of course, the three of us became our own family. As I understood it, Derek had lost his third father when he was too young to really know what was going on. That was followed by the death of two school friends and a step-brother who was older, and a sibling from one of his Ma's other marriages. Four marriages in total.

When Agnes lost her father, she began smoking. She was still in high school. She smoked three packs a day and she smoked as much marijuana as she could purchase. When she hit thirty, she quit smoking. Cold turkey.

I had quit around the same age. It made a difference in my stamina and in my bank account. Though at first I got a little heavier, as did Agnes, I lost the extra weight and kept it off. The problem became my improved sense of smell.

Agnes and I had this experience in common. We came to enjoy talking about it, in spite of it being such a mundane topic. For me, the more mundane, the better. I felt safer with banalities as long as there was a sense of connection.

For example, Agnes knew only too well the putrefaction emanating from the city's armpits and rotten tonsils. Though we were both used to these stenches, especially in summer, we still got overwhelmed at times. Her photos and no movie I'd ever seen, let alone produced, could capture how on hot July days it felt like we were being punched in the face by a bursting diaper full of fumes that were still ripening.

Derek went through a similar process, having also quit a cigarette habit. He didn't get winded quickly anymore. A plus for one who needed to act on his feet, though he endured constant achiness due to broken ribs never healing properly and a wound from being stabbed in the side. He'd also been shot in the leg twice, but that meant nothing to him. He liked to dismiss it by saying, "Everybody's got sob stories and wounds."

True enough, and as time passed and Derek, Agnes and myself grew closer, we veered and chugged while running our errands. We dodged one body on the street after another, broken, speed-addicted or else muddling along.

Derek was twelve years old when he started claiming his "shit-hole of an island" as his own. He loved it. He despised it. Agnes felt the same way. So did I. We learned how to deflect the city's less attractive energies without losing nerve. Keeping our vulnerable selves hidden and protected, sticking to our designs, we played cabin boy or girl to all the passengers and captains on the SS Gotham City. We flew at warp-speed into arrival modes and eclipses.

Agnes once said, summing it up for me, "Everyone has a right to die, and they have a right to find love and define both of these on their own terms, in their own time. It doesn't matter how."

I couldn't have said it better.

—◦◦◦—

There were characters, so many "dudes" Derek knew before they were shot or bludgeoned to death. They were real street-toughened "dirt," some of whom didn't get killed but were arrested and he never saw them again. Some who had vendettas against him. Others who did time at Ryker's Island and when they got sprung they couldn't make the adjustment and committed suicide. Some lasted a week on the streets and went back to prison. One ended up in Sing-Sing. He was still there. As Derek said, "Maybe he learned his lesson, but I doubt it and now it's too late. The deal is, I just ain't ending up that way."

There was from Derek no dearth of tawdry, disturbingly sexual and sometimes hair-raising stories of violence, regret, hatred and penury. I felt as a producer that these were characters I wanted to hear about in the same way I enjoyed a Quentin Tarantino movie. I didn't want to meet them. They weren't real to me. I saw them as character studies. I continued to develop story lines and to learn from David Simon and his brilliant, *Homicide*, and *The Wire*.

I can't say why, but human criminal filth on this planet appeals to me. We're all coping with recoveries and illness, trying to stay within lines demarcated by moral rectitude and lawfulness. The criminals among us either don't recognize these demarcations, or else they reject authority in all forms, including their own.

Or else there's a vacancy within that their acts of reckless abandon and lawlessness can fill. I learned much from Derek about this rejection. After he and Agnes and I watched James Cagney in *White Heat*, I summoned the courage to ask him about how disproportionately loyal Cagney's character was to his mother.

I asked him if all criminals were so loyal.

"No, Mr. Railsback. No way. How could he be such a cretin and still want to care for his own mother, for crying out loud. It's his Ma we're talking about here. He was just trying to impress her. It's just what you do. Your Ma comes first and to hell with everybody else."

His Ma. Her name was Ginger. Top of the world, Ma. Top of the world.

⁓

I met Ginger for the first time shortly after we'd viewed *White Heat* together. I found her easy to talk to. For a while, I quietly harbored schemes to get her into one of our films, something that never happened.

I found her a cross between the razor wire of an Elaine Stritch, the matronly intelligence of a Bea Arthur, and the saccharin but shrewd delicacy of a Betty White or an older Debbie Reynolds. She was the type who opened up in consort with the amount of booze going down her gullet. Each time I visited her, I downed more than a few gin and tonics, as well, regretting each one when I went to my gym the next morning to sweat them out of my system.

Ginger wasn't interested in taking life slowly. I always feared appearing naïve in front of her. I mean, did she really want to hear me talk about Texas?

She didn't. I don't think she cared one bit that I was a movie producer, but she looked tickled pink whenever Agnes would mention some of the A-list actors we'd hired for certain projects.

As a delightful source of inspiration, another real character, the more Ginger drank, the more she'd fly into rants about what she'd seen during her salad days in Manhattan. She'd seen gay co-workers drop by the dozens due to AIDS, especially the men she'd worked with uptown. A lot of them had worked as secretaries or executives while trying to be actors. Some had taken temp work. All of them were sexually active anywhere they could be, including the stalls at the public library and bath houses in the Village that are now long gone.

"I guess there were orgies, I can't say," she once remarked. "But I don't doubt it. That's what they tell me. That's what I heard. Men are men anyways. They're pigs."

I heard about her exploits at Studio 54, and at CBGB. Ginger talked and talked as if she was the only one in the room. She went to many dark places back in her youth, bouncing between cliques and social sets and inappropriately daring sexual escapades. She told us of how she lived two lives. Secretary by day, and part cobra, cougar and rattlesnake by night, complete with red leather pants. Worn tightly, of course.

She laughed when I asked her if she had dated men who wore mullets. Of course, she had. For a while she'd dyed her own hair acetylene blue. Confessing this, she cackled with a modest show of glee.

Here was a woman who'd say anything about herself, or me or Agnes or Derek, no matter how hurtful or prideful. She struck me as unapologetically judgmental and sincere, and harsher on herself, I thought, than anyone else. This, too, I found appealing.

True, her son was no angel. Yet he survived. He made a living. A decent one. According to Ginger, if Derek gave her trouble, brought about her sudden ruin, it was his fault. Not hers.

This didn't matter in the end. She'd still let him in the door. She was his son first, warts and all. She gave him a pass to run amok in a straight-laced world where neither one of them had ever fit in.

It was often while talking with Ginger that I remembered I should be grateful I'd brought Derek into my fold. What's life without a little daring and unseemliness? Derek appeared to need an older man to look up to. I guess I needed to believe that I could be such a man.

Ginger read this need in me. In spite of her health issues, there was still enough sultriness in her to show that she'd once been attractive. I don't know what fascinated me more. Her owlish glances, her narrow waist, her pointed chin or her gray-green eyes forever glassy with alcohol. For me, it was revelatory to understand while in her company just how far apart we were, and yet how much the same.

She once said to me, in private, that if she were about fifteen years younger and much healthier she'd take me on the floor after the kids had gone to bed.

"I'm sure we'd have a whale of a time too. You'd be Bogie and I'd be the most trashy Bacall you can imagine."

This had me in stitches. Though it disgusted me too. She wasn't Cagney's withering long-suffering Ma. Not at all. Nope. Just the opposite. I found her a marvel, no question about it.

As I saw it, nothing Derek had done was unusual on the streets of any large city. What was unusual was for someone like me to get so close to him, to be allowed insights into his masquerades. He saw it all as a game and he'd lost fellow players – not really friends, mostly customers and neighborhood companions – losses that were a result of bad decisions more than anything else.

He said, "My gig ain't never been about me. I've never been busted. Never snitched on nobody. I can stay clean. That's what these other knuckleheads don't get."

His ethic, he told me, came from his Ma's fourth husband, Buzzy, who took him under his wing when he was fifteen. Derek worked construction jobs, lugging bags of cement, running a jackhammer. Always working. He got strong that way. Yet he still went to the gym with Buzzy, even though he really didn't need to. There were ballgames too.

"Buzzy and me, we were *Mets* fans. Some bar stools for Buzzy, but not the way Ma liked them. For Ma, those Irish taps could be a second home. Not Buzzy. He liked to circulate."

Buzzy showed him how to play. No alcohol. No theft. No bragging about how he dodged bullets to make a score. No showing off with bling. The secret was to keep it under wraps, to live up to your word with those who mattered most. To keep it hush around those who didn't.

"The best thing Buzzy told me was to stay away from the life when I wasn't on the clock. And that's what I did. Still doing it now. We tried to keep it a secret from Ma, but she knew. She always knew. I took my lessons. Cash and carry. No sudden large deposits into personal accounts. That sort of thing."

When Buzzy married Ginger, he got out of the game, which Derek cherished him for. Buzzy was devoted to Ginger, who was smart enough to use inheritance money when her father died to buy an apartment on the fringes of Astoria when they were considerably cheaper. This was before Derek's street "got clean and respectable and the old-timers from the Europe countries started dying off or else leaving for Florida and got replaced by young professionals."

This slow gentrification began to spread. Derek never thought he'd see it. "But that's just how it goes. Change or die."

I'd never hear him utter the words "trust me" or "I promise." There had never been a time when he wasn't looking over his shoulder. Racial issues?

"Screw that racist talk. Everybody's racist. Especially them that can't stop talking about it. What spins my gears is survival. I started out early figuring out problems on my own. I took my lumps. I got over 'em. It's the best way."

Buzzy was consistent as his "ace mentor." He was "old-school" and used to walk "like he owned the streets," his slacks pleated, in pointed leather shoes. One minute Buzzy moved like a hyena and the next he was crabby, coughing and telling Derek that he had no idea what was wrong with his health. He thought he was getting sick. Ginger belittled him as a hypochondriac.

"It's a word I like, Mr. Railsback. I even think there should be a band named it. Come to think of it, there probably is. The Hypochondriacs. I like that."

Buzzy turned out to be right about being ill. More and more tired, then really exhausted, and this went on for about three months until he, Derek and Ginger were at Jones Beach. Buzzy was swimming and when he waded out of the water, his fingernails were bright blue. This got Ginger worried, so she started talking to a doctor and he explained the blue nails were due to a lack of circulation, not uncommon in a man his age.

What really scared Ginger was Buzzy's first loss of appetite. About a month went by and he refused to eat. Ginger forced him to get some blood tests done. They showed no Lyme disease, which her doctor had feared, but there was an elevated white blood cell count.

The doctor hadn't minced words. The blood test results were bad news. The doctor recommended an oncologist.

"I say that right? It's a hard word to say," said Derek.

Another blood test was done, the results conclusive. Buzzy's white blood cell count was too high. One word: leukemia.

"I gotta tell ya, Mr. Railsback, it's a word I'll hate to my dying day. I knew hardly nothing about Buzzy's past and his family. Whatever Ma knew, she didn't share with me."

With time, Ginger and Derek became experts. Derek liked learning new things, though he disliked school, any institutional experience, and watching Buzzy die.

They looked into donors. Ginger, a pious Catholic, pro-life, researched every possibility, but if the ethnic make-up between mother and father was different, it was nearly impossible to find a donor. Ginger knew little about Buzzy's past, and even less about the ethnic make-up of his parents. To worsen matters, Buzzy wasn't willing to share that information.

"My guess is that Buzzy, like me, was mongrel. I mean, my father was supposedly Puerto-Rican, that's what Ma said, but I don't think she knows. My last name, Kotas, is Greek, after my grandfather. That guy was a hard-ass, even though his wife, my grandmother, was like a saint. She was Irish and Polish Catholic and raised Ma on Staten Island."

Ginger needed 36 categories to match with a donor. Most people only match to five or six of them. For a while Buzzy was brave. He wore a wig and different hats. No flowers allowed in his room. No raw foods, salads or bread flour. Only peeled fruit. No movie theatres. No subway trains. Only cabs.

As weeks passed, he grew thinner and weaker and didn't want to be treated differently. Two weeks out of chemo he was exhausted, and every ten minutes he was splashing water on his face in the bathroom. He took deep breaths all the time and it seemed he'd keel over if he held one in for too long.

"He had more courage in one pinky finger than I got in my whole body."

Buzzy had asked Derek why this was happening to him. Derek had thought this a weak question, but what could he say? Buzzy wasn't supposed to be weak. Derek told Buzzy the truth: Sometimes there aren't any answers.

"What a rotten thing to say to someone you care about," he told me.

Having learned Buzzy's story from Derek, I began to see the young man more clearly. I had swung my lantern and found two surprises. One was a better understanding of how I'd handled and endured the death of my own parents. The other, more stirring, was a dimensionality to the stamina, and a depth to the compassion and endurance I'd been too ignorant and vain to appreciate from Derek and Ginger.

They weren't characters. I couldn't degrade them by writing them into the plot line of anything put on film. I began seeing them in a new light, as if for the first time, with a vivid measure of due respect.

FIVE

Agnes drifted into City Opera Thrift Shop. This was a place to air herself out for a while, her mask on while she browsed amidst racks of vintage blouses, blazers and sweaters. She looked over the odd desk lamp, knick-knacks, record albums, bric-a-brac, books, plates, bowls, saucers, tea cups, coffee mugs and jars of buttons. She opened one jar and took a few out, finding delight in all their colors, textures, shapes and sizes. They were made of wood, faux amber, bone, faux pearl, Bakelite, brittle plastic, and cheap metals. A few were covered in cloth. Some were on cards in pairs or quartets, back before ready-to-wear days when clothing wasn't made to be chucked out but to endure and make a statement.

These wonderful buttons! They appealed to her in different ways. Like candies. Like circles within circles. She could shoot a series of them, each one featured under elegant lighting the way photographer Larry Stein had shot Malcolm Forbes' collection of Fabergé eggs. No button too small, no whimsy brought to light too insignificant to leave unchecked. Oh, such small and yet inspiring discoveries, the pleasure of the smells of a rummage amidst old books and vinyl and vintage fabric. Larry's Fabergé eggs as she remembered them. Her days meeting Larry and other pro shooters in the Fashion District. The many techniques and approaches she learned from them that submerged her into a melancholy over the disappearance of days gone by. Days when she was more hopeful about how her pictures would not only be discovered, but would add to what she believed John Berger meant when he wrote about the "language of images." When she believed her images would help redefine herself as she added not only to the canon of photography, but to a visual narrative that would one day define the past.

Those quixotic days, those noble beliefs, those hopes had vanished. To think of them now, to view how she'd concerned herself with such lofty ambitions, was to see how ridiculously pretentious she'd been. She would think instead about the usefulness of buttons. They proved how the least significant of objects from the past had been made to endure and to outlive their owners. Back when waste culture wasn't yet the author of so many prevailing norms.

To buy something, anything, was what she needed. To hold the past in her hand to prove her connection to it. *Not all can exist in an infinite present.* To support the shop and its mission and to simply feel linkage, and a little better about her ever-evolving acceptance of mortality.

Though she browsed for about hour, Agnes found nothing that she could justify spending money on to help her feel better. As it was, she had more than enough kitsch in her apartment. Derek often complained about her figurines, ash trays and vintage tourist souvenirs, deriding them as trash and clutter. To a degree, he was right, but they had all made excellent subjects for photographs. Besides, they brought her comfort. They made a house a home.

Yet Derek did have a point. Sometimes, no matter how she felt about her objects, her various collections, things were just a burden. She had plenty of things. Too many of them. Maybe next time, she thought, deciding instead to make a ten dollar donation, the clerk accepting it with a smile and a thank you. This allowed Agnes to exit feeling less melancholy and a bit more prepared for Manhattan's sunless canyons with their echoes and shouts.

As she walked, however, Agnes felt an amorphous feeling of uncertainty. It was adding to her melancholy. The problem as she saw it was that she was still in a browsing mood. She blamed it on recalling perfume traces while looking over a purse in the shop. It was the kind of accessory her late grandmother might have owned. Agnes had almost chosen to buy it along with a 20s-era cloche with a velvety maroon texture.

She should have bought them. What was wrong with her? Why was she always talking herself out of the little pleasures that sustained her?

No doubt on another occasion, prior to the pandemic when all felt more open whenever she thought about the future, she would have made those purchases. Now, looking ahead, she saw no welcoming horizons or blossoming ideas. This meant she must hold back, restrain herself. High castle doors that could withstand battering rams were used to keep marauders at bay during medieval times. She saw darkness. She felt grief. That cloche and the purse wouldn't be there during her next visit. So be it. Let someone younger perhaps more hopeful pick them up for a song.

This browsing, this hunger, God, this wanting to capture the transitory and hold it still within a frame, it was pathological, an endless need for new definitions of reality. As if framing objects and landmarks brought them to life. A silly and vain indulgence, she knew this, but necessary at times.

There were no rules for her or for the pandemic. Each person needed to find their own way to keep sane.

Mask still on, accustomed to it, she took a quick snapshot of the storefront. Such shops tended to suddenly disappear or move to a new address. She then puffed her way along to another of her quaint shopping getaways, the Housing Works Thrift Shop, where she was happily surprised to see that it was open again after being closed for so long.

There, she engaged in more of the same browsing. She'd been hoping for quite a while to find a vintage *Rolleiflex*, or a *Brownie*, even a Kodak *Instamatic* from the late 60s. She could buy one online, but that wasn't any fun or form of adventure.

It wouldn't matter if these cameras functioned. She just liked having cameras around the apartment. She'd pick them up and fondle them the way others might fondle worry beads or an old book.

She found no items in the shop related to photography and left without speaking to the clerk or making a purchase. All so lonely, so dreary, like she was a dying vulture poisoned after pecking at toxic carrion.

Nonetheless, her camera's eye wasn't yet dead. Nor were its promises.

A sturdy all-manual-controlled Minolta SLR, it featured a basic 50 mm bayonet lens with a polarizer stacked over a UV filter. She liked shooting manually, using different filters, because it challenged her.

Due to her camera's lack of electronics it would function in any kind of weather. A suitable tool for a journalist on the go. Manual shooting also meant she controlled the speed and the F-stop. She, not the camera, snapped the pictures, and she should never forget this.

While walking aimlessly block by block, stunned to see how quiet the streets were, Agnes made it all the way to Second Avenue. Though disappointed to see that the Clover Delicatessen was closed perhaps permanently, she decided to shoot a series of it, with an emphasis on the lush pinks and greens in its neon sign. She liked how they reflected off the deli's chrome trim façade, spreading to wash its black Bakelite panels.

She already had some shots of this classic deli neon, but she'd taken them at daytime and none exuded the after-dark moodiness she was after. She found the neon so vibrant, certainly worthy of one personal archive, her favorite one, which she labelled Night Shots Of Doomed Landmarks.

If The Clover was going to shut down for good, and this was what she'd heard rumored, she'd at least have it for herself. She'd keep it for posterity, from all sorts of angles.

It was in this archive of Doomed Landmarks that Agnes stored what she considered her best nocturnal images of businesses, signs, and buildings that were going to vanish. Such landmarks vanished daily, rapidly so, in such a metropolis.

One day, perhaps, her archive might be valued as a historical record. Future photographers could examine her work in the same way that she had viewed and learned from the paintings of John Sloan, Robert Henri, and George Bellows. Their renderings of Gotham were, in her opinion, a necessity when it came to understanding what a city or a person could be over the course of, say, eighty years.

With this thought, inspired by a sensation that she was providing a service to humanity, Agnes shot 48 images of The Clover. She didn't linger before heading west uptown toward Penn Station.

———∾∾∾———

What did she want from these signets of the past doomed to be erased? A legacy? What a horrible word. What a stupid idea. Her own past, she supposed, couldn't be traversed as if a map opened in front on a desk in front of an explorer with a compass.

This pursuit of hers was touched with madness, wasn't it? When she was younger, it had felt like a slyer, diffident choice, a way to flow against conventional means of making a name for one's self. She'd lived to sustain the idea that art shouldn't be nor had it ever been deemed conventional. Now, she wasn't so sure. She didn't feel so cool or hip. She felt, shuddering with the thought, like she was engaged in a bit of necrophilia.

She kept asking herself why she continued. She was hoping, as she did with all her shots, that each one would be a journey. She wanted to drift back into time, add a few more coastlines to the new continents developing inside of her, while at the same time observing other continents erode.

By looking out, she was looking in. She was the walking archive. Her body and its five senses, along with her lens, created a membrane. Osmosis created her, image by image. Each photo developed her inner geography, capturing what she believed her eyes had witnessed.

The mystery of sight. Of comprehension and evaluation in the moment. All so intriguing. She lived to understand, to experience shooting again and again, lost in the steam of railroad history at one of her favorite bars, Tracks Raw Bar and Grill at Penn Station, where she now loitered debating whether or not to go in.

She'd arrived. She knew the streets so well that she hadn't even seen them, keeping her head down, her legs pumping, her mask on, the outer margins of her flesh on alert at all times, quick to respond to shouts or sudden movement. She was infatuated with movement, with light, just as her favorite classical composer, the Czech Antonin Dvorak, or the New York fashion photographer O. Winston Link, were fascinated with trains.

She'd go inward by going outward to a place where she could ruminate on objects in motion and the tracks they followed or else left behind. Not just people or animals but engineering marvels such as boats, delivery trucks, argon gas trapped in glass tubes, subway trains, familiar sights in the terra firma at her fingertips when it came to a yen to feel safer and warmer inside of her own skin.

Pausing, catching her breath, she saw that the rumors were true. Tracks had closed permanently at the end of the summer as part of the restoration of Penn Station. It wouldn't be gone for good, however, as it was moving to a new location across the street from Madison Square Garden.

Though this news pleased Agnes, she still suspected that Tracks wouldn't be the same haven she'd experienced in the past. It had been an island within an island, a respite from the urban lunacy that tended, due to its location, to attract travelers willing to strike up serendipitous conversations. It was the best part of the old Penn Station which, in her opinion, really did need a significant upheaval and was, at last, getting one.

She suspected other regulars felt the same way and that some would frequent the new version of Tracks, if it was going to be called by that name. Of course, due to the pandemic nobody knew when this would happen.

Even without a name change, the Tracks bar wouldn't be the same. It was one more little death for all the opinionated travelers, mercenaries, pervs, sales reps, drunks, office workers, train enthusiasts, sports fans, lost souls and lottery ticket holders to mourn over. Her archive, she supposed, was for them, and for their grandchildren.

Absolutely, it was worth her time to take some new shots. Worth the effort, the risks she was taking as a woman alone at night.

She was always vulnerable, flashing gear easily fenced or pawned for pocket change. She was always engrossed in her work and tended to forget where she was. This added tension and fear that she believed came through in her photographs. There was no other way other than to be out there, on the street, building an archive. All the great shooters had done this. They'd taken untold risks to create something as ubiquitous and pedestrian as an image.

Fertile, wasn't she, likening her images to her children, just as she likened them all, the many drinkers she'd met in bars such as Tracks, to members of her extended family. They'd each have to find another oasis where they could waste free time in alcoholic bouts with loneliness. She saw them as Kerouac inspired angels of desolation.

She'd told this to Holly once, but in spite of her Ivy League education Holly hadn't grasped what she'd been referring to. Nonetheless, Holly was smarter than she presented herself to be. She read a lot, but only to amuse herself. Janet Evanovich, and Sue Grafton rather than Margaret Atwood, or Jane Austen. Without guile or pretense, she took pride in being lazy.

Agnes didn't care one bit. Friends or not, people were consistent in that they usually disappointed her.

—⁓—

As Agnes shot what she could of the old Tracks, in limited light, she remembered again it was the action, the taking of her photos, the steadiness in her stance, her hands, her breathing, that kept her going. The ordeal was a physical, emotional and visual exercise. She was amassing an ever larger personal archive, creating continents and nations within, jaunting about to watering holes that she enjoyed as one of her own pleasures, a private one.

She took no comfort in thinking that Holly, and certainly Derek, at times, didn't always enjoy or appreciate her photos. Nor did they approve of the spirited shows of eccentricity she was prone to when sharing them. She must share with *someone*. She'd just explode if she kept all this geography in. This was where I came in. She could show me anything and I'd show her, in return, respect for the intention in her work, whether I liked it or not.

She loved to frequent the city's bars, hunt down bungholes, warts, diamonds and idiosyncratic flourishes. The city wasn't about one image. It was about the bleeding together of the blemishes and happenings, the ghosts, the failures, the plain old scars and signs of rot and revelry. Drunk strangers wouldn't always listen or usually laugh out of politeness at a clever joke or play on words, but they didn't mind seeing a photograph. She could take one out to show it from the little album she always carried with her.

Or else, depending on the person, she could open her phone and show them off from various files, proving what she'd done and was capable of doing. Strangers wouldn't always marvel at her shots, but most of the time they were intrigued if not impressed. Agnes was crafty that way. She knew when to stop showing them, having whetted their appetites and leaving them to wanting to see more.

Just a few frames. A nibble. Then let them be changed as they imagined the others, if not their own shots, that were capable of being had.

She needed to sigh. To blow it out. The game-playing with her little album, especially before the pandemic, was all part of the old world, the old Agnes, the pre-pandemic, pre-miscarriage one.

She couldn't remember the last time she'd sat in public and spoken to a stranger, let alone shared some of her pictures. It really was over, wasn't it? God, she hoped not.

A touch of the circus sideshow. Neither Holly nor Derek had that in them, but Agnes did. She knew this and wasn't ashamed of it. She thought of herself as part magpie, part all-seeing eyeball, and part barometer. She had questions, all sorts of them, and to find answers she needed time away from Derek.

She needed a woman's hands to touch her body now. Holly's in particular. Holly could be annoying, but she was warm and oversexed and had kept the door open by agreeing to the triangle game. Anytime Agnes wanted, just call and they'd find themselves in a cuddle or else getting audacious.

Not out of love. Out of hunger.

Holly had agreed to the triangle game because she knew herself well enough to manage her responses to Agnes's mood swings. Agnes also needed the manageable size of Providence in all its provincialism. She should remember that she'd once loved Providence even if now every American city struck her as a tad provincial after having made herself at home in Queens.

Like Derek, Holly didn't always get Agnes's sense of humor, but she'd allow Agnes to wade back into her past, probing forms of misery, cynicism and angst without any aim or goals in mind in order to reshape some of herself in the present. Derek of late had become too obsessed with both his mother and his perilous maneuverings in the drug trade. Agnes believed if she stayed away from him a while, he might start to miss her. Perhaps he'd realize how lucky he was to have her in his life.

He'd never appeared upset enough over the miscarriage. He'd been tight-lipped, taking it on the chin, choosing to move on. That was his strength, of course, but it suggested an indifference that Agnes found difficult to accept. There was no complicated geography and fusing of continents inside of Derek. He was one big chunk of terrain, mostly an emotional desert made of shale. He maintained it in his own arid way.

Emptiness, a low-hanging cloud within her sternum had begun expanding to drain Agnes of energy. Such a constant aching emptiness. A baby would have changed everything. What had she done wrong? What was she not hearing and seeing? What was this horrible loss trying to teach her? It had to mean something. Fate just couldn't rob her of the opportunity to be a mother.

She wanted to fill herself up on fast food, shovel it down until her ribs ached. Taking a brief look around, she was unable to spot any place where she could part with her money and punish her body. Better to keep walking, then, and fight off the urge to drown her intestines in consoling grease.

She decided to head uptown to The Roosevelt Hotel for no other reason than she liked the name of it. Both of the Roosevelts, for different reasons, were presidents she admired. She knew a few things about presidents, having started young and inspired by her father to become a student of some of the history of the country she'd been born in. She didn't regret her penchant for reading biographies of not only presidents, but the real heroes, their wives. As she walked, she thought it a shame that the summer rioters, the BLMers and the Antifa mobs had gone as far as to knock over the statue of Teddy in front of the Natural History Museum. To what end? To prove that they could be violent and destructive? Lots of emotions from those camps, but no *answers*. Never an answer. If only an answer. Any idiot could complain, just as any idiot could shoot a photo with a cellphone.

She'd been disappointed, heartbroken to learn about their acts of aggression. Why Teddy? He was the man who created what eventually became the Teamsters and the New York subway system. Were those racist developments? She was sure that such juvenile narrow-minded acts triggered questions in many about the real vision and motives, if they existed, of all those proud anarchists, most of them bored college-age millennials with too much free time on their hands.

Sure, Teddy was no saint. Who was? She'd hated to agree with Derek when he'd said that once the first statue went down, then all the others would go down too. That it wasn't logical or productive or all that smart. "They got nothing better to do," was how Derek had put it. "That's why it's so easy to sell 'em Fentanyl."

Initially, she'd disagreed, in part, with Derek, and sided with the rioters. Now, she saw it differently. What had all their violence brought? Nothing. No answers. Step up to the microphone, Loudmouth, answers only. The rest of us got enough questions to choke an army of horses. They struck her as wholly miserable, self-serving, hopeless and without a vision.

She couldn't say this to anyone. That was the worst part of it. Was that freedom? She didn't think so. Her mask was on. Her lips covered. Everyone was learning how to clam up.

She'd discussed this on the phone with Holly who'd agreed with her.

"On the spot," Holly had said, "you'll be called a racist and a cop lover and possibly a Nazi. They'll cancel you. Do those people really think knocking down statues because of annoying chapters from history, is a way to solve present-day problems?"

A reasonable question. Holly, for a change, was showing insight.

Agnes viewed it as a show of entitled anger and disenfranchisement.

Entitled because in many other countries such summer-long looting and rioting would not be financed or condoned, but rather all involved would likely be locked up or executed.

She thought what all the shouting would do in the long run was embolden those to take action against anyone who might disagree with them. So, this was the whole point of democracy. She didn't think so. Holly had agreed with her. Violence led to more violence, whether in a war or a riot that lacked any focus.

Why were humans so *destructive*? Was their first primordial impulse to create or destroy? Which of those overheated rioters pondered such a questions? Few, she suspected, and it was a shame.

From what she'd read, for all the good Theodore Roosevelt had once done in New York, and for the country as a whole by establishing the national park system, he'd done much harm exploiting people in places such as Panama and Cuba. Still, she couldn't name one male politician, no matter his Party affiliation, with a blemish-free record and no blood on his hands. Not a single one.

Were female or black politicians likely to be any different? Holly had answered that one for her, saying, "No, I doubt it. But I still think it's about time we had a woman president."

Where would those rioters have been without the New York subway? Where would American eco-warriors go to find balm for their souls if there were no National Park system? Teddy Roosevelt was a *progressive* for his era, not a backward-looking conservative. In many ways, he'd been ahead of his time, a true conservationist. Didn't those strident spoon-fed anarchists care to know any history outside of what they deemed convenient to use in order to support their narrative?

No, they didn't. No nuance in their thinking. No vision.

Yet they expected nuance from everyone else. None of the tenor in all their uproar was about informed reasoning. Orange man bad, yes, she got the Trump Derangement Syndrome, especially from her mother, who went shrill despising the man, comparing him to Satan and yet during Trump's time in office found herself living better and more comfortably as she cashed in stock dividends.

It wasn't as if Agnes was a Trump fan or loyalist, not in the least. She'd voted Hilary all the way. It was time for a woman, long overdue, maybe Tulsi Gabbard one day who both she and Holly really liked, but to rebel for the sake of feeling better, just to tear things down in a knee-jerk fashion, was to surrender to an infantile impulse. It wasn't a rational choice. It didn't provide answers. How could her mother, who spent weeks pondering over which color and design to select for wallpaper to revamp rooms she seldom even entered, be so devoid of any enlightened vision or deliberate reasoning when it came to politics?

Long ago, her mother had chosen her color, her Party affiliation, and she wouldn't deviate. She refused to, preferring to remain insufferably ill-informed and opinionated, soaking in the televised babble those awful celebrity hens spat out each morning on programs such as *The View*, with no concern over what was just or needed to create a path toward a better future. Her poor, poor mother. So very comfortable, and so drunk all the time. Every day, in fact.

Agnes believed she was probably more liberal than her mother. She was certainly more willing to hear or examine as many sides of an issue as possible before making any decision on it. Sadly, her mother was like many others of her ilk in that she couldn't be bothered to take the extra step, to view the other side, to examine some of the history around any issue *du jour*. It was too much work. It would demand she clear her head.

Prone to hysteria, her mother took whatever bait that came her way. The woman was bored, empty inside, hooked on the fear narrative and the thrills it offered her. The woman wanted, it seemed, to feel like everything was falling apart. Wanted suffrage as if she were like one of the barflies in the play I had encouraged her to read, *The Iceman Cometh*, by O'Neill.

In that play when Harry Hope, as if the second coming of Jesus, comes to the bar to rescue the drunkards from their anguish, they all sign on. They give it a try. Eventually, they slide back one at a time into their despair, taking so much comfort in complaining about it.

No answers anywhere, thought Agnes. Nothing but angst and fury. Dirt could be found on all men and women alike, everywhere in the world. Of what value was trashing city streets and tearing down statues?

Agnes had discussed this with me, with Holly, but few else. She had admitted to Holly she felt terrified about what was happening and found it disturbing and at the same time strangely exhilarating to ponder the whole post-George-Floyd ordeal. The man wasn't a hero or even a decent citizen, but the way he'd died, the tragedy of his death merited no excuses.

Even Derek had agreed with her. He hated all cops and, unlike Holly, he'd had his share of run-ins with them.

Those two awful words: social justice. Agnes thought them part of a fantasy narrative, a utopian pipe dream, a narcotic that helped one's mind get distorted while one's ideas became erased and edited as soon as the questions of race, genders and religions came into play.

What better method, she thought, than race to divide and conquer all the munchkins in Oz. All it took was one phone raised to create a video – an image – not a reality but a framed distortion of the truth that within minutes could be disseminated and manipulated in order to fuel rage across the land. If only one of her photos could do that.

How awful she had felt watching the coverage of those riots, viewing such a disturbing show of undisciplined anger and confusion made worse by language manipulated by political operatives on all sides of the issue. It was a seizing of the American mind, a corporate move if ever there was one. Nothing working class or grassroots about it, in her opinion.

Didn't anyone see what to her was so obvious? She couldn't say. Everyone had vanished from her life. They were stuck at home, gripped by fear with a mask on dreading that they'd die as a victim, one more zombie in the Covid apocalypse.

———✦✦✦———

As time had passed and Agnes had been able to step back from the way she'd normally viewed and studied prevailing political narratives, she'd phoned Holly often to talk about it. She was changing. She didn't understand it. In the past, she would have sided with the younger more rebellious types. Not this time, and it was leading her to question who she was. She just didn't know any longer.

Holly was receptive to her questions and to the reality that Agnes was seeing her political views begin to change. Agnes still considered herself a liberal, still liked to think of herself as open-minded, but what she'd begun to understand was that the government and the country that her late father had believed in, the one she'd been raised in, no longer existed. When and how had that happened? And so quickly, at that.

Holly listened and remained receptive to everything Agnes had to say. Agnes thought of her as a blessing, a real friend, a bit of salvation. The new government appeared to show no interest in people, or in stopping Covid, but rather in profiting by a fear narrative. The pandemic was about learning how to silence one's self as operatives pushed a Hold button and kept working puppets dangling on their strings. They were all on pause, baited with a tiny check akin to a welfare payment. Rejecting any reasonable form of discussion that might lead to new methods and significant change.

So, first she'd not only lost her child, her hope for the future, which had been difficult enough, but now it was worsened by having to live under house arrest, masked and gloved and unable to go out. How had she reached such a dismal juncture? She'd watched life pass her by on a screen, feeling a need to follow screens more and more often, to live according to narratives, to seek them out – one more voice, another opinion, perhaps a fresh one, not a man or a woman since that wasn't allowed anymore. That was how. By expecting others to answer questions for her, and not to answer them herself.

She and Holly spoke often, losing track of time, not even caring about time or what day it was, arguing over all the pressing issues such as how a person had to be gender fluid these days, screaming down the he-she-it racist-homophobic-fascistic rabbit hole as if overnight it had been automatically accepted as the only way to think about gender. It had felt to Agnes as if all the freaks, the one-percent of her high school graduating class who never participated in anything had seized power. They were so angry and vindictive and closed off to debate that they would take whatever steps possible to infuriate and stifle their locked-down minions and detractors in the mainstream.

Apologize just because she was born with fair skin. Apologize just because she viewed herself as a woman. A mammal. A biological creature who through her womb created children and through her breasts gave milk, not through her mind or imagination. A womb that had failed. A mind that struggled to accept that failure. God, the feeling of being trapped under glass. Nothing was in any sense honest. A corporatized scheme to profit by what Holly had called "cognitive dissonance."

Not even the epidemiologists, especially the honest ones, could agree on anything. Those who dissented from the narrative had been shut down. Divide and conquer. Those had been Holly's words too.

Derek had put it succinctly, "If those fuckers really wanted to end this pandemic, you know, world-wide, all the masks and those anti-germ ointments and wet wipes would be free of charge everywhere. Richer countries would have handed them out to the poorer ones with bigger populations. Doled them out to their own people too. But that's not what they want, is it?"

Divide and conquer. The words kept ringing in her head.

Derek's voice returned: "They're keeping the zombies under wraps. Forcing them to take a vaccine that maybe works, maybe doesn't. Make it a law. That ain't freedom. That ain't even choice. They say it don't matter that it ain't been tested enough. They're gonna make the people so scared they'll do anything to comply."

Not even the air could be trusted. Fear it all. Find a cave. Hide there. Watch it all get revised and feel hopeless to do anything about it.

She'd go to The Roosevelt another time. If the pandemic had given her anything, it was too much time to think. The hour had come to catch a subway, find her way home and into bed. Derek might be there waiting. He might not. She really didn't care. She'd had enough of his and all the other voices ringing and banging and buzzing between her ears.

⸺ᴗᴗᴗ⸺

Agnes had changed her mind. She'd go to The Roosevelt, after all. If it was open, she'd visit the Madison Lounge which was inside and accessible without an elevator up a small flight of stairs from the lobby waiting area. There, she'd have herself a cocktail, maybe many cocktails while she got smashed and slowed her breathing and let her mind fall into reveries of a 30s era movie version of life in soft focus, ever so luminous.

The light she imagined was filtered, smoky, black and white. Into each frame stepped one of those lean handsome leading men of the time in sharp lapels with cufflinks and tie. Those men who spoke kindly and with respect to a woman in heels and gown that glittered each time she sashayed in any direction.

She must accept the miscarriage, but it would be easier to do it while getting loaded on martinis. The pandemic, death in all its certainty would help her find a way to be reborn into a new etiquette and ways to practice her life.

She must write herself some new guidelines. Maybe she could adopt. Wasn't the same, though, was it? These new guidelines would include how to breathe despite what remained of the Delta and the Omicron variants. What remained of her sanity. Time was so weird now, so shapeless, and she must follow rules of her own devising as if they were a creed or an adage she'd learned while doing a Sunday crossword created by Patrick Berry, a favorite Sunday *Times* crossword maker, second only to Elizabeth C. Gorski.

A crossword fiend, Agnes knew this hobby was one reason she might survive any holocaust or desertion in the remote wilderness of Alaska. The crossword adage she had in mind was a quotation from Mark Twain: *Pity is for the living, envy is for the dead.*

She wouldn't choose envy. Though she'd keep her options open while seeking to breathe more often through her nose.

The Madison was closed. Dammit. So much for that idea.

The masked doorman wouldn't even let her into The Roosevelt's lobby. Agnes was polite to him as she toddled off.

Her camera, her urge for vision, the shutter, stayed in its bag. It would have to stay there a while. Which day was it again? She still didn't know. It didn't matter at all.

She wouldn't shoot. She'd walk with her mask on and marvel at how deserted the streets appeared to be. Not completely, of course, but she felt none of the electric charge that once filled her on such jaunts.

There was something banal and hopeless about it all and she wondered if it was her or the city itself. A little of both. As she walked, getting needed exercise, she began to feel better. She trekked all the way uptown to La Dinastia Latin-Chinese on West 72nd Street. Then, meandering along, she found herself in Central Park, glad the sun was shining as she allowed herself time to unravel.

She was alone and could, at long last, take off her stupid mask to inhale the chlorophyll elixirs of trees and grass. After about an hour, she decided to head back downtown and maybe sit in a barroom, if she could find one that was open.

She walked and walked and thought of crossword puzzles and Bill Clinton and the comic Jon Stewart. These were two men she learned were crossword mavens when I turned her on to the movie, *Wordplay*, viewing it together in my apartment. They were also two men who had let her down. Clinton proving himself a jaded dishonest womanizing heel, and Jon Stewart just a tool of the blue party who had chosen to infect his comedy with blue politics and turn *The Daily Show* into a platform for the Democrats. In her opinion, a comic shouldn't have political ties. No artist should in any genre. They should be obsessed by the human condition in all its shapes and colors. They should slay the political machines, not support them. How much money had they snared Stewart with, and the other one, Colbert, turning them into mouthpieces lacking a single original idea? Sad, she thought, but it proved how rare an artist really was, and that money was all either one of those two cads had ever cared about.

Speaking of crosswords, I recall that it was during this time when the pandemic was really making her miserable, that in an attempt to cheer her up I had told Agnes about a 60s film, *Soldier In The Rain* with Tuesday Weld, and Steve McQueen. It also features New York's own Jackie Gleason, who plays a Master Sargent with an abiding yen for crossword puzzles to ease his loneliness. This was the element of the film that spurred on Agnes to want to see it, so after searching online and finding it, I insisted on another movie night.

I must have sounded like a geezer telling Agnes that not too many years back such a movie was really difficult to find. I'd never seen a copy of it on DVD, and only one on VHS at a well-stocked Kim's Video rental store in Chelsea. I'd had my own copy once which I'd taped off Turner Classic Movies. Hearing myself drone on like this, I realized I was only widening the age gap between us. Because she worked in the movie business, she knew who Steve McQueen was, and she worked up the nerve to tell me she couldn't name any movies he'd been in. She said the same about the other two stars.

"Not *Bullitt*, best car chase ever filmed, or *The Hustler*? Gleason plays Minnesota Fats in some of the smokiest, grimiest and most tense pool-room scenes you'd ever want to see."

"Nope. Not into pool or car chases. Not really my thing."

Did she *want* to see them? She so fond of Jack Cardiff. I didn't ask. I ascribed her indifference to them being movies for guys. Maybe Derek had seen them. Perhaps I should have insisted he come. To think of the appeal of those movies, their levels of excellence, however, and to think of Agnes's youth, the distance that would sometimes loom between us, really upset me. Perhaps I should have known better. I couldn't be sure.

All this had bothered me only briefly, because after watching *Soldier In The Rain* again, I felt that it was as fine and quirky a film as I'd remembered it to be. That the story and performances had held up. I was also thrilled to see Agnes had enjoyed it. Astonishing now to think, pre-streaming, how difficult it was to find such old films. Just as astonishing, and heartbreaking, was my realization that there would always exist a divide between Agnes and me, one that might be more than a little difficult to cross.

—◦∾◦—

Back, then, to Agnes alone as she walked and walked, not really seeing, not looking either, until she had wandered all the way to Walter's Bar with its lavender canopy above the door and its name scripted in white across the canopy's front edge. This was a dive for darts and pool and a juke box. A real Manhattan dump of a bar, though it had become more of a hipster's destination rather than the seedier gin mill for misanthropes it was when she'd first discovered it. Her interest in such dives and the fact she'd never seen *The Hustler* was one of those discrepancies within her, one of many, that I never could reconcile.

Agnes liked to believe that if she drank in such a watering hole that she'd see a city no one had ever photographed. That the experience would deepen her photos in various ways. What those ways were she could never tell me. She also believed that no one would bother to trouble her in such places. This was just folly, but I never said so. Let her learn for herself. She was smart enough to understand that one never knows, especially a woman alone, when it comes to bars of any kind.

She decided she wouldn't drink there. The pandemic had altered the mechanism of yearning when it came to existing in public with others. She'd gotten comfortable feeding off her isolation. She'd amuse herself just by admiring the bar from the outside and thinking of how much she enjoyed shooting storefronts and neon signs in close-up, at various speeds, with different kinds of film, from different angles, hoping she'd capture a hidden gem in the light, or the chiaroscuro vibration of one color as it faded off glass tubes to become another.

Such a *cold* aloof woman she'd become, hadn't she? Such desire she felt for any sense of emergence from Covid and her miscarriage, as if she'd been snared into them. Was this a trap she was falling into, or was she simply paranoid? Was Covid even real? Was it killing off a generation? Was it killing her too? She couldn't say and this frustrated her to no end.

The miscarriage, though, was real, but it hadn't killed her. She could say that much, though there were times when she remembered the experience that it still didn't feel at all real. It felt like a diabolical ploy that had forced her into preferring celibacy or leaving Derek, perhaps, in order to possibly wed Holly. They could do that now. Wed legally. Some progress had been made in the culture wars and hurray for that.

No, she was wrong. Covid was real. It was reducing all her expectations of what life could be, whether crystalline bright or gloomy. It wasn't defining what she craved, but what she had to get accustomed to. Too many had died. Too many exploiters like Anthony Fauci and Andrew Cuomo had manipulated and killed too many people and profited from it. What she needed was an antidote, so to speak, to Covid's echoes and prevailing winds.

With vague desires in mind, she took her camera from her bag.

She moved with it as if armed with a weapon. Stepping from side to side, she took advantage of having the pavement to herself. She knew this wouldn't last long. She worked quickly, keeping the F-stop open wide, the speed slow, hoping not for concrete images but for darts and squiggles of color.

These squiggles would speak for her tapped-out soul. They'd represent the arteries and veins in the others who were walking about, moving as if wounded, homeless, or else senile and elderly and dying in nursing home beds. Nothing was clear to anyone. Each moment, each breath was a tinted trace, a vapor blending prismatic hues that fired through darkness.

Where was she now? Was she losing her mind? She must, at least for a while each day, *know* something, so she stopped shooting. She stood dazed on the sidewalk and felt herself drifting in place, the sidewalk tilting up, the city walls pulsing around her. As her breath shortened, she shook her head, squinting, trying to free the clogs in what she thought of as the pipes running through her head. She needed to move about, to free herself of this sudden feverish spell of inertia.

It was her own fault. She'd snooped about too much, sometimes almost marching because she was so intent on capturing images she thought she saw in front of, behind or inside of her. All an illusion, proven by what she remembered having read in an interview with one of her heroes, Henri Cartier Bresson. The Frenchman had stated modestly that his best photographs were accidents. Unplanned. Pure luck. To get them, however, he'd needed to shoot constantly and without fear.

So Agnes kept moving uncertain of what she hoped to find. Let the accidents happen, she thought.

It was overcast, which helped even the contrasts between light and shadows. She didn't want it to rain. Not yet. Not until she could sit somewhere, find a park bench, a café, anywhere, to get herself back on track.

Sleep, that's what she needed. Rest. Quiet. A consoling sense that she'd found her accidents.

The idea of spending time with Holly loomed brighter and more alluring as Agnes forced herself along, stumbling. There was no place she could walk into without showing her proof of vaccination and going through the rigmarole, so she kept pushing herself to move. Was this it, was this all her life would be from now on?

She tried to block out the city and the noise, eventually finding a bench. Without seeing any of it, just lowering herself down, she sat feeling achy and swollen. She dropped her head between her knees, taking one slow breath at a time, sliding her mask off, allowing herself to recover.

⁓

Agnes viewed the bland, concrete slab edifice that was the Fashion Institute of Technology. Just another day of wandering Manhattan Island and seeking ways to imprison for future generations what a moment's voltage had once offered.

It wasn't worth shooting, not considering the mood she was in. She couldn't say why, but the building had caused her, in a way she didn't understand, to feel drained.

She'd just spent three days home in bed doing very little. She should have more energy, but she didn't. She needed to sit for a moment. There was no place to sit. There was no place to pee either and she began searching, gritting her teeth until, at last, she found a McDonalds that was open. Astounding. A message, she supposed, not to give up hope. She was able to get inside, all masked up, and order a cup of coffee. She found herself less disgusted by the ladies room than she thought she'd be. With diligence, accustomed to it now, she scrubbed her hands and then used disinfectant gel on them. She thought the proliferation of these anti-bacterial gels, whether effective or not, a positive side-effect of the pandemic. She'd never again take for granted how many germs and potentially harmful organisms that doorknobs, counters, her phone, camera and purse carried on them. Let alone revolving office entryway doors, public toilets, and the turn-stiles of subway train stations.

The weak coffee comforted as she sat alone. She looked forward to a feeling of relief once she got home and could stop wearing her mask. Did they even work? She didn't think so, but she didn't want to obsess over the pandemic. Plenty of other loud voices were already doing too much of that. Her mind, instead, wandered as if a small plane flying over various landscapes of fashion, as it was wont to do because she loved everything about it. She felt inspired by the thought she'd love to visit the museum at FIT, but it still wasn't open.

She remembered an allegation she'd read on a blog that skirts for women tended to get longer during difficult economic times. From what she'd seen while visiting favorite sites online, as well as on some of the female pedestrians courageous enough to walk in the city, this appeared to be true.

Mommy jeans, as well, appeared to be making a comeback. She liked wearing jeans, but not the Mommy style, never did. She was all in with the campaign against them waged by Stacy and Clinton, the stars of *What Not To Wear*, a show that for ten years she'd watched religiously.

Just thinking about that old favorite show, she began to feel less vacant. She felt empowered. She could accept that nothing would ever be the same. It was merely one more reality. She could handle it. Everyone could. Humans had endured much worse.

Perhaps the best years of her life, a time when feeling beautiful, though not always looking that way but caring about how she presented herself, had passed and would not come again. Perhaps not. There was an outside chance she could experience a renaissance of sorts. It was possible, but any hope she felt was met again by the frigid reality of the pandemic's restrictions. They brought a finality to her ruminations, slamming doors she once considered possible to breeze through.

Other than photography, which was becoming increasingly expensive, what was left that would keep her excited? What would steer her from these bouts of vertigo and nausea, this nagging hunger to drink and smoke too much, overeat and oversleep. She'd been shrinking between the walls of a tomb. She'd been plunging each day into quicksand in order to protect herself from the despair, ever so bleak, that she saw no matter in which direction she looked.

Holly, yes, and Derek. The three of them were like the bohemians she'd read about who lived at Charleston House in 19th Century rural England. Like those bohemians, they painted in squares, talked in circles and loved in triangles.

Love, love, love. There was no hope of it. She'd never birth or raise a child. Derek didn't want to adopt. She and Derek and Holly and Ginger. And me, as well. That was it. Her family. And her Mom, too, couldn't forget her.

Derek had, at least, talked to her about adoption. Then he'd stopped without offering any explanation. He'd made his point of view clear, sharing it, and he no longer wanted to approach the matter. What was worse, they barely talked now about anything. Derek had even gone so far as to ask her not to bring up the past, saying it was gone and nothing they said could change it. He believed the pandemic had changed everything. "There's no future now," he'd said to her one night during a ranting show of fatalism. "There's no time for dreaming and wanting things. You just got to accept the lousy cards. We all do."

Nor was there gainful honest work to be had. He'd keep playing the mule, running cash, and selling Fentanyl or whatever forms of dope the customers out there wanted. No doubt, they wanted anything they could get their hands on. The government was now sending out checks. The whole city was on welfare and getting high. The whole country was, as she saw it. The only stable constants, it appeared, were the number of tattoo parlors, sports betting rooms, cellphone dealerships replacing storefronts that were once cozy little delis, bakeries, Mom and Pop shops, boutiques or cafes.

It was now possible for Agnes to sit home alone all day, baked out of her gourd, watching in horror as her hips spread wider apart, no matter how much she exercised. She was a toad on a stool. A mushroom. A fungus. She could sell herself to graphic design firms as a freelancer who could doctor and format other people's photos from home, but did she really want to spend even more time in front of the computer considering how little it now paid?

No, she didn't. She'd take her chances trying to sell her own photos. She'd fight the urge to die as if an inert slug on a leaf of lettuce. She wouldn't bury herself alive. She'd keep venturing out; she'd break the rules, wouldn't quit, and never surrender to what she viewed as a conspiracy to force the world to conform to a dystopian nightmare.

Another paranoid thought: who were the people Derek called "the bloodsuckers"? What did they want? To kill her and all other freethinkers slowly, to shut them all down. She was no different than any other creative spirit, and there'd be no relief from misery until this pandemic, or whatever it really was, passed away once and for all.

Normal, she supposed, to feel anger, fear and paranoia, a loss of power and sense of self. She'd take Derek's advice: "Go on, Shooter, don't give up. What you do is take pictures," he said. "You take 'em. You can sell 'em. You got nothing to lose by trying. Look at me. I'm not staying home. I'm out there every night risking my neck, and I'm earning more than ever."

He was right about that. There was cash money hidden all over the apartment. Under cushions, in the medicine cabinet, rolled inside old tins in the kitchen cupboards. Such a gift, perhaps, to be as stubborn, feckless and rock-headed as Derek. She really did love him, after all.

—◦◦◦—

At 23ʳᵈ Street, west of Broadway and in Chelsea, my neighborhood, she began to shoot the Bright Food Shop, with three words running vertically down its marquee: *Steaks Chops Seafood*. It was closed. Maybe for good. Probably. This saddened her, so she set about shooting it, her standard 48 images, though they wouldn't go into the Night Shots archive, they'd go into her Daylight Doomed Landmarks file.

Steaks, chops, seafood. She remembered those three words were the title of a script by Robin Feldman, a gay man she'd met before getting married. Robin was the only man she'd ever known who was raised in Los Angeles.

Robin had ventured east to try his luck in Manhattan. She'd had a crush on him and she missed him and wondered if she'd ever see him again. She had followed his Facebook page for a while, before shutting down her social media life, learning he was back in LA.

Agnes could, she supposed, text him, but that wasn't the same thing. Not even close to the long conversations they'd enjoyed while walking the Village before stopping to have a coffee in a diner.

Robin had told her he wrote his script in six months. She remembered that it wasn't all that bad either. She'd convinced Robin to talk to me to see maybe if I could help gather the funds to produce it. That never happened. I did try, though.

I think Agnes was partly right. It wasn't a bad script, but not a great one either, mostly a pedestrian love story that made it different because it involved two gay men. Boy meets boy. Nothing wrong with that, of course, and it can be done well. It has been, but it's a ton of work to get investor funding, and it's most likely not going to recoup expenses. Not that most movies do. The dirty secret is one big smash makes up for all the losses any company pumps out year after year. I also thought the script lacked zest and comic turns and the bizarre twists and tenderness that audiences often like in such a story.

I never learned what Robin chose to do. Agnes never did either. She missed him, poor Agnes, as she drooped and moved along like a barge on a slow river, burdened at once with memories of all the creative types she'd met and befriended in the city, none of them able, apparently, to produce work that would find an audience, whether it was music, film or theatre. Those she knew who were writers had left the city and were holed-up in other cities and towns, some still clinging to their delusions.

Friends who, like her, had shot photos, had also left the city. Did she really have friends any longer? Facebook names. Memes. But friends? Not to her. Not anymore. She had Holly. She had me. She found comfort in holding on to what she knew, meaning Derek, for better or worse. He was a modicum of stability, a source of financing. She needed only to stay in his good graces.

Among all the budding artists she once knew in the city, was she the only one who'd stayed? It sometimes felt this way. Just as it felt she'd never get beyond the pandemic's restrictions and her pathological needs for acceptance and encouragement.

The others had fled in droves. She'd stayed. She'd even been paid for some of her photos and featured in magazines and on websites. She could say she still had a career as a photographer. This should have made her feel satisfied in a small way. Instead, it helped her see how many creatives out there were still at it, most of them failures. The pandemic had reduced what she or any of them had accomplished, none of it all that unique or necessary.

If she desired a wider audience, it had never been a question of the style and quality of her work. Or the profundity of her artistic vision. The deterrent was her ability to market her photos, knowing the right people, being part of various circles within circles within circles.

Mastery, its pursuit, remained an unavoidable first curse. She had the stomach for it.

Marketing remained a second curse. For this, she had no stomach. Agnes knew this too. She accepted it. She just wanted to make her pictures and archive them.

She told herself she had to stay positive, upbeat, looking toward the light. She had new negatives to print and new potentially doomed landmarks to shoot. She was still doing it in Manhattan. Was this *all*? It was. Yet why did she still feel such bleak dejection? She should be used to darkness by now, comfortable with accepting less as she made her adjustments.

She wasn't. She'd never get used to it. While on her deathbed, nobody would accuse her of not trying. Nonetheless, when she walked, sometimes mannishly so, swinging her arms no matter in which direction or to which purpose, she continued to pummel the air with her fists. She seldom hesitated to avoid or stomp on any forces who attempted to impede her.

She'd go slowly or quickly, open or closed, it didn't matter. She'd been doing this for most of her adult life and it had helped her feel better. She had to forget about her miscarriage, the rising tide of unemployment, social distancing, hygiene, ventilation, sheltering in place, getting vaccinated once and then getting a booster, and those whose parents had died due to executive orders, state government mandates forcing elderly, already sick people to stay indoors sealed into airless rooms, completely unhealthy situations where they'd died alone without dignity, without their families able to visit them.

Compliance. What a horrible word. As if anybody in any government really knew what was best for people.

She had to stay angry. She had to be shallow, stubborn, resistant. She also had to remember Derek's advice to walk fast and make her eyes "scream." Derek had said, "Your eyes should shout get outta my way and look out I'm coming."

Having perfected such a walk, attitude and stance, Agnes had found that sometimes it worked, even though she wasn't anybody's definition of a tough broad from Queens. She'd met some of those broads, including Ginger. She couldn't, she *wouldn't* be that way. Though she'd grown more of a spine, grown wiser too and some of her girlish perkiness had faded, she still had to accept she was well-mannered, an intellectual. In spite of her parents and their alcoholism, and how it had killed her father and caused all kinds of rifts between her and her mother, she'd been raised in what by all accounts could be deemed a prosperous almost genteel family situation.

She was still speedy for her age, too, something of a lady guerilla soldier dodging hazards. She could read the messages in various looks and sneers. Light made a face. Subtleties spoke volumes. Evasions were necessary; they helped her stay in motion. They also helped her feel more empathy toward the faces she shot. This empathy improved her photos. The myriad reflections she captured, always by accident, that made her work transcendent, she believed, was due to her being open to them as possibilities.

Not all the image-stories were about intersecting lines and the spray of light from window glass. There were human sorrows to be found in the rubble. Joy in the echoes. Ghosts in every chamber. She sought to uncover examples of woe that were defining the pandemic. Examples of diffidence and survival when facing the open-air prison that the city had become. Freedom in the lock-down. Flight, shows of mercy, shows of gratitude. Her images were about battling the promoted narratives which all those who were forced to stay at home had to absorb day after day while fretting over how they were going to pay their bills. No wonder they took their welfare money and got high.

Maybe she was getting tougher, but she'd never been callow. She never would be. No artist could survive or practice without a broken heart. By now, she should be used to her lapses into self-pity and self-doubt. Her life had value because it meant her work was getting done. So many others out there couldn't do what came naturally and obsessively to her. She must not forget this was the secret ingredient: to fight back against the tide by producing unselfish, high-quality work that sought a reflection of the immortal.

———〜〜〜———

At Todaro Brothers at 555 Second Avenue, Agnes thought about buying fresh oranges and apples, but she learned something new that really appalled her. After 102 years in business, these one-time Italian immigrant fruit vendors were going to close their business.

Such a wonderful shop. Oh God, she thought. She wanted to cry. She couldn't believe it. Covid again and its so-called management was slaughtering all in its path.

She had to get out of there. She'd come back, another time, and shoot it. Not now. It was too much for her right now.

Agnes thundered along on foot, dodging the fat, the slow, the speedy, the homeless, the drug-addicted, the filth that was always prevalent on the sidewalk. Where was she? Eighth Avenue. Okay, but how far uptown? Again, she stopped and looked around. Had she really walked so far, so fast? She had.

She was standing across from the Tick Tock Diner and could see half a block in both directions from Madison Square Garden. At the corner of West Thirty-Third and Eighth there stood a small block of low dilapidated buildings one of which was four stories high and had etched in cursive across its face BRIGHAMS, and next to it was GOLD'S, a pawn shop. The three gold balls were still hanging from a bracket over its door and she wondered if it, too, was a doomed landmark and she thought of a novel I'd told her about, one that I'd read back in college, *The Pawnbroker*. She couldn't remember the author's name, but she remembered watching the movie that starred Rod Steiger, viewing it with me during one of our movie nights.

She'd loved that early Sidney Lumet drama, the intensity in Steiger's performance, the high contrast black and white cinematography. The movie, she'd said, had made her think with more compassion of Jewry and what Manhattan, in general, had meant for post-war generations of refugees from Europe. A movie that she didn't think would be as powerful if filmed in color. When she'd shared that one point, I'd known she was finally allowing herself to trust her instincts, so many of which were incisive and accurate.

She'd loved the tradition we'd started of movie nights. First, they'd been once a week. Then twice. Then three times. They allowed us to talk in detail, indulge ourselves, get carried away examining how the city would change, and so would her images, especially as she changed and her compassion for others deepened. Her eye, her sense of mastery would develop, in time. This, too, she had to remember. One day maybe works from her archive would be viewed by a large audience to show what liars we are, especially about ourselves. She believed this was the value in the works of a director such as Lumet when at his best. Lower art, more commercial films didn't have to carry a message. They could hold a mirror up to the audience and allow them to see who they were or maybe were not. The telling of truth, the examining of social issues, in her opinion, should not be preachy but open and allowing for interpretations.

No, she wasn't taking pictures for her own pleasure. She was trying to contribute. Let the audience see themselves and then decide if they liked, wanted or needed what they saw. Nobody escaped outside of themselves when viewing a movie or a photograph. They did just the opposite. They went inside, whether consciously or not.

She needed more film. Did she need to keep shooting? She did. She had to!

Knowing it was open, she walked to the colossus, her go-to, B and H Photo. Its period of closure, nearly a year in duration, had ended in March. Though she marveled at the size and the efficiency of the B and H operation, curious about the lives of the many Orthodox Jews who worked there, she felt a little uncomfortable with the stranglehold they had on the market. Similar feelings overwhelmed her when she thought about Amazon, as well, which had turned into such a gluttonous behemoth, reminding her, as Derek often had said, the gambit of capitalism was designed for a few massive winners versus hordes of struggling losers.

After leaving B and H, moving on, she paused in front of where Calumet Photo used to be. Everything changed. It was inevitable. She shouldn't mourn. Calumet had been gone for a while now, but she'd never photographed it for her archive. A small regret.

Allowing herself a self-pitying sigh, she moved on again to visit what used to be Adorama on West Eighteenth Street. This had become a business called Printique. Adorama was another landmark she'd neglected to photograph, never learning until too late.

Why was she doing this to herself? It was masochistic.

A few doors down stood the Academy Records store. When Agnes saw that it was open, she couldn't resist the urge, though she knew she shouldn't.

The shop felt so empty. Judging by the amount of vinyl in the bins, walk-in business had slowed to a crawl and inventory levels of cut-outs were high. Who even bought CDs any longer? She did and since the shop was open, in business, and she had cash in her pocket and a place to linger and get lost in for a while, she indulged herself. She found it a pleasing distraction to rifle through second-hand CDs, scooping up three of them for ten dollars.

One dream gone stale was that one of her photos might be used for an album or CD cover. It was unlikely, but she still harbored it. The problem was that she didn't know young musicians the way she'd known them when she, too, was younger and starting out. The ones she'd known, thoroughly disillusioned, had left the city.

To be out and about, to be looking at forms of music and not seeing it on a screen but holding an album, smelling the vinyl, reading the liner notes, being possessed for a moment by the thing was such a comfort. A relief. Things still existed! Not all music had become reduced to its digital articulation on sites such as Spotify. Call her a troglodyte in such matters, she didn't mind. This was an utter delight.

Out the door and back on the street, discs in hand, she loitered a moment in front of Skyline Books across the street. It was closed. It might not open again. She added it to her list of future sites to photograph. Small used bookstores, especially, found their way with ease to extinction.

She had a soft spot for this one because it was here that she had once found a signed copy of a James T. Farrell novel that she bought for an old girlfriend from college days, Ellen Sheehan. Ellen had studied Irish-American literature, had even spent a year as a student in Dublin. Agnes couldn't remember the last time she and misanthropic Ellen had talked. She didn't know where Ellen lived or what she was doing. Probably teaching somewhere. Agnes had always liked Ellen and should try to find out, simply out of kindness and curiosity, but she knew she wouldn't. She was too lazy, too willing to accept that her once piquant friendship with Ellen had faded into one more sepia image from her past. Toned in sepia, she supposed, because it suggested a warmth she felt whenever she thought of Ellen espousing on how degrading patriarchal Irish men could be. She liked to call them "peacocks," admitting she stole the label from a Sean O'Casey play.

One less friend, sadly, and one with a barbed wit and an encyclopedic knowledge of Celtic myth and urban American literature. She hoped Ellen was fine. Married and in a tenure position and with the two children she'd always wanted. Agnes assumed she was. She had to assume because she knew she could ask Derek to go on Facebook and look her up, but she wouldn't do it. To what end? Just to arrange a Zoom meeting and say hello look at me I'm older now and a little heavier and still shooting photos on film that cost a lot of money and aren't really making me famous. What would Ellen say? Look at me. House, kids, car, job, bills. Health issues. Diet issues. Marital issues and disappointments.

Then again, it sometimes sickened her to think about her past. How naïve she and the likes of Ellen had once been. Ellen might agree with her. Why even bother to go back there?

So, walking then. On with it. Pumping her legs forward and back. It helped her forget.

She headed to Willoughby's at Thirty-First Street in the Garment District, close to Fifth Avenue and one of the city's oldest photo shops. Her feet were starting to throb, but she could endure such discomfort because she knew where it came from. She'd walked countless times up and down this island grid, often seeing more of it in a day than many saw in a month.

The walking was her choice. A way to cope. Just like Whitman, another famous walker in the city and a poet she'd told me was one of her favorites along with Anne Sexton and Mary Oliver. The woman read poetry. Imagine my surprise when I learned that. Imagine hers when she learned that I did too.

Agnes slid her mask down from her nose whenever she could, but she kept it on. Kept her head down too, her camera hidden. If a day came when she'd leave the city, walking the gridlines was what she'd miss most. It struck her as funny and soothing how she could leave massive B and H on foot, and had done so many times, to shoot locations such as the Cheyenne Diner nearby. She'd known many nights in all four seasons of shooting this diner, one of her favorites. She had a gorgeous 8 x 10 of it in a winter setting, surfaces frosted with snow.

This particular image I'm referring to was one she captured at night. When I saw it, I liked it so much that I bought from her an 11 x 14 made just for me. I had it framed and matted by a professional before I hung it on my bedroom wall.

She could also hoof it one block around the central post office building, which she'd shot many times for both of her doomed landmark archives. She understood that it would soon be converted as part of the new Penn Station. When that happened was anyone's guess, but it would eventually. The plans had been announced, the funding was in place.

She could look east, as well, to see the Empire State Building. Just for kicks, she could snap all the touristy images of that building her heart desired. Tourist shots. She loved them. They were the real chronicle of so many people's lives. She had to laugh about this. How often had she seen people younger than herself who couldn't even walk down the street, at last visiting this city, living their dreams, without stopping fifty times to photograph themselves while doing it. Selfie addiction. Pictures of one's life, the record of it, had become more important than the experience itself. Would all future statues of venerated leaders feature them standing with a phone raised in front of their noses? As if to say it's true, it happened, only because of the selfie.

No selfie? Then it never happened. Of course she'd shot her share of them when younger, but now she rejected them. She didn't despise them. They were for others who loved rather than needed to take pictures. Who kept Instagram and Tik Tok and Facebook accounts. Derek did all that for her. Too much of a time suck considering she spent hours in the dark room each day.

The numbers of these selfie-shooting visitors had dwindled considerably. No eager mobs of tourists were around. Nobody was. People were present on the street, but individuals mostly, the occasional pair, but they were hunkered down, zipping about, masked and fully distant and anti-social, per the mandates. As she saw it, they were really else-where. Mostly, inside of their heads. This would be the re-set, as she viewed it, post-pandemic. Humans would need to re-learn their sense of connectedness and shared humanity. Many wouldn't. Many more wouldn't even bother. They'd find it easier to stay under lock-down protocols, sealed off, scheming ways to keep the checks coming in, to stay on the dole, to stay high, forever in front of their computers, alone, at home, on their phone working the hustles from the caverns within their minds, still in their pajamas all day.

The walking, sometimes, was enough. She didn't have to shoot or record anything. The images she was after would come to her later. They'd be discovered, revealing themselves, one frame on the strip of negatives after another. She felt those negatives drying inside of her lungs. These she thought of as her voices, as her memory pictures. They weren't pictures of what she found out in the city. They were what she threw into the air each time she breathed and clicked the shutter.

In the taking of each picture, an act of larceny to a degree, Agnes had found her own built-in denial of expectations. This she'd learned to trust. With film, too, there was no immediacy. A period of wait-ing was part of the process. There was more of a mystery behind each shot, a hope that the lighting, composition, all of it was right in that it wasn't what she'd expected. It was better. It discovered her. Defined her. There was also the ratio to contend with, quite a large one, between so few adequate photos compared to so many duds. Forget about good photos. They were like rare butterflies in a rain forest.

Derek had been right when he complained that any idiot could stick a phone in the air and press a button. This was another reason why Agnes kept going with film. She controlled the vision apparatus. She staked her claim. It forged her. She stood removed from the horde. Her film, as she chose it, followed the speeds and aperture openings that she dictated. Then it dished up something entirely different. What followed, the developing and printing, were a nurturing process. More choices. More failures, mostly, but she lived to breathe and gasp and emote through the agony of every single one of them.

Photographs were her armor, a form of protection. After all, how easy it would be for the propaganda mongers, perpetually lying, to keep her in fear. Not when she had her photos. Each was a child, yes, but also a shield. Like a cop's badge. Developed in silver nitrate. One could be garrulous, another could be spontaneously cheerful. People, it seemed, weren't that way any longer. Yet in some ways they were larger than she'd ever imagined them to be.

Thinking in this way, Agnes sometimes felt akin to Will Smith in *I Am Legend*, except that she lacked a canine and guns to scare away mutants that might eat her. She wasn't fleeing mutants; she was pursuing a way to imprison the moments that creased and defined and scarred their faces. She was capturing holes in their stories, those secret places they themselves didn't realize they inhabited.

The questions her subjects shared, seen always in their faces or their reactions to other faces, the battles they fought, the answers the provided were often the same: Why am I still here? How did this happen?

Like her, most people wanted to feel better. She believed they would. They just needed time to heal. That was all. More time and a return to interaction.

SIX

Babies died. Happened all the time. This was how Derek put it to his Ma. He saw the miscarriage as a tragedy. He never used that word with anyone, though one night in bed he did ask Agnes: "Without death what edge does a guy have?"

Agnes had answered with a line from Ginger's friend and caregiver, Sister Nancy: "I think we all need those precious deeper meanings when we're lucky enough to find them."

Beautiful benevolent Sister Nancy. The only nun Agnes had ever gotten to know. She was as earnest and compassionate as she was prone to striking an occasionally poetic note.

Why would such a woman even talk to Derek? Because of her heart, her sense of forgiveness. Because of Ginger. It wasn't immediately evident on the surface, but when it mattered, Ginger believed in and acted upon any appreciation of Godliness by doing charitable work for others. Sister Nancy saw this impulse in Ginger and respected it as true.

Not for a minute had Ginger scrimped when it came to sacrificing and doing what was right for her son who, knowing this and fearing it, lived in awe of her. He'd been loved. Maybe, thought Agnes, if Derek's customers had felt such maternal love they wouldn't need to lose themselves in hard drugs so often. They'd put Derek out of business.

A pedestrian thought. Silliness. Agnes pushed it aside bored by her own sense of morality. The miscarriage hadn't been Derek's fault. Nothing had been. He'd done his part, spreading his seed. She wasn't to blame either, of course, but she still thought of herself as guilty, incomplete, a failure. These thoughts kept coming up during sessions with her psychiatrist.

Derek told her often, "Don't take it so it hard, you did nothing wrong, it happens."

For about a month she'd mothballed all her photo equipment. No pictures at all. When she finally got back to it again, she started shooting what she called "toxic incubation cells." Nobody got the gist of what she was doing. Not that it mattered. It was her thing.

She liked the sound of those three words. Meaning wasn't important. Ironically, the images she was creating at that time brought praise from a few cliquish trendsetters online who followed photography. She sold a couple of images to a magazine and a web site. Maybe it was because her pics were in black and white, tended toward the abstract, and weren't afraid to ask questions. Agnes couldn't say. What surprised her most was that they didn't offend as many people as she'd hoped they would.

Derek called them "sick."

She told him: "Sick is what sells. You, for one, ought to know. As if you should criticize. Look at what you sell. It destroys their lives."

"But they don't have to buy it."

"And people don't have to buy my photos either."

"Look, if you want, I'll shut it down. I'll get out. You don't like the money, I'll try to live on what I've saved until this Covid bullshit ends. It ain't about nothing else but the money. You know that, Shooter. You ever see me using? Never. So don't be getting so high and mighty just because you sold a couple of pictures."

Screw Derek. He didn't get it. Not a nuanced bone in his body and he couldn't be relied on to discuss such topics. Not that she'd expected him to. She wasn't kidding anybody. Derek was her bank. The sex, anything romantic between them, it had ended after the miscarriage. Put a fork in it. As a couple of lovers, they were done.

This was why Agnes wasn't surprised when Derek suggested she should avoid trying to hang toxic incubation cell pictures in a gallery. He didn't really want her to succeed, did he? She didn't listen to him. Thanks to Holly, she found a gallery in Providence that even during the pandemic was willing to feature a dozen of her images. She could show and sell her work. She could maybe even find a new bank.

The cruelest images and most difficult to view were the blurry ones influenced by X-rays of her own womb. They showed her fetus, her baby when the girl (she hoped, she believed it was a girl) was still in it. Her future daughter dying but still alive. Talk about heartbreak. Yet those images sold the best and for the highest prices.

More than demented. Fucked up. Maybe that's what art had to be. It showed Derek, for one, he knew nothing about the arts. No surprise there. No pain either. What hurt was her coming to understand that he also knew nothing about the woman he'd married.

Was it really starting to end between them? Some people would do anything for attention. Right, Derek. Go to hell, Derek. *She* was one of those people. She'd had enough of his nonsense.

Huffing and puffing. Pausing. Waiting. Shooting. Studying. Shooting again. Enough time had passed so that she'd gotten her mean city face back. She kept it glaring from behind her mask and, to defend herself, sometimes kept her middle finger raised in both of her eyes. This allowed her to cleave the fumes and the wretchedness, some of it dangerous, whenever she moved down a street. To sneer at strangers was to invite confrontation, but to wear a mask atop her mask, to air herself out was a way to rid her mind of knots and congestion.

She'd had a list of baby names. All girls. She'd had tentative dates for a shower and planned on inviting Ginger for a weekend trip to Barrington to meet her mother. How badly she'd wanted those two women to enjoy getting acquainted.

Now, she didn't care, but while pregnant nothing mattered more than making sure all went according to plan. That all felt magical in spite of the physical pains which she never complained about. She could have, but she wanted Derek to feel comfortable around her. She doted on him. He appeared to be fine. They had many gentle nights of sweet intimacy. He kept telling her she was angelic, "all rosy like." They'd raise their daughter and be a family. If all went well, they'd raise two.

The shock of it had blind-sided her. The adage proved true that death came in threes: her baby, her job at Rain-Or-Rust, and then all hope thanks to the pandemic. Who she thought she'd been, who she and Derek had hoped to become, what they'd expected, what they were becoming wasn't anything she recognized any longer. It had all changed. It was changing yet again. Just as it was teaching her, yet again, how to really see.

———∽∽∽———

Permit me as one adrift in the floating world to examine all this from Derek's perspective. Though I wanted to, I struggled to do this until I was unshackled from the lost world. Now that I can, it assists me in comprehending that it's fruitless to try to make sense of anything that happens. What I examine and gain insight from are my own and others' responses. Not the events themselves.

After Buzzy's death, better things were supposed to happen. Not worse ones. Not his Ma having another TIA. Would Shooter ever get over the miscarriage? He couldn't be certain. Women tended to hold on. He didn't. Let it all go as soon as possible. Ma had been right. Give Shooter time to heal, that's what she'd said. All he needed was to be there, doing his thing in the background, making sure she could lean on him for help.

None of it had panned out. Ma believed Shooter was strong and time was all she'd need. "She'll come around" is what she'd kept saying.

Derek hoped Ma was right. That Shooter's mother was right too. A couple of lushes both of them. He'd been following their suggestions, but it still hurt when he thought of that moment when the news came. Another punch to the gut like the one he'd felt when Buzzy died.

There'd be no little kid. No son. Bummed him out. No new branch on the family tree for Ginger, no Christmas meals and presents, no birthdays, baseball games and first rides on the subway. No board games on the living room floor, no walks to a park or ferry rides or playing catch. No exciting stories of the *Mets* the way Buzzy had shared them. No hope for him and Shooter to ever conceive. That was the crummiest part of it. The finality. Sure, they could adopt, but he didn't want that. It just wasn't the same.

So why bother staying together? They should separate. He'd give her cash enough to keep her photo habit going, settle it all calm-like and then find someone else. Not just because he wanted to be Dad, but because he wasn't sure he even loved her anymore.

All sour grapes, a real downer now, moping about, dazed. He didn't need the aggravation. Guys were breathing down his neck all the time. One wrong move, one slip and he was meat. The whole family dream, it was over, just like that. Wasn't meant to be.

His once sparkly angel, his Shooter, had gone inward. She'd changed beyond recognition. She was spooky quiet now, ate a lot of prescription meds her doctor thought would help her sleep. They did. She slept all day, liked it, had gotten used to it and started to pack on the pounds. He didn't go for heavy women.

Sometimes, he couldn't hack looking at her. Instead of lecturing or fighting her, he stayed away. He had his crew, his work. The dealing life. Had to stay sharp.

He went to Holly to get laid. Holly was a wire. She got him, took him in, was there for him one-hundred percent holding to her end of their triangle game. He didn't care if it broke the rules of his Catholic upbringing. Wasn't like selling Fentanyl was going to land him in heaven.

His Ma and Sister Nancy, if only they knew, they'd be mortified. That was why they'd never know. The money was adding up, and the edge he felt, knowing so many relied on him, it was, like always, keeping him sane.

Holly knew she could help him. Who cared about rules when you made a living by breaking the rules? Holly got the gist of that. They kept their time together a secret from Agnes, even though it was within bounds and by the rules. It was working for him. What he needed. It was still working.

Now, he was back in Queens. Holly was in Providence doing her thing. Like it never happened between them. Shooter wasn't any closer to being her old self, but she'd made some adjustments, had maybe found what she needed to recover momentum and keep going. So had he. So had Holly.

If he didn't really know who Shooter was anymore, maybe he never had. The egg that once symbolized their happy life had been heaved against a wall, smashed there, dripping its bloodied yoke. He still loved her in a way, he supposed, but what the hell was love? What did that word even mean? This was part of the problem. Plus, he was busy, and he was always looking over his shoulder. Couldn't be sure about nothing. If he put his head into the clouds thinking about love, some animal was going to blow it clean off.

None of the knowledge he used to rely on could be trusted. Had to admit there'd been a special anticipation, a bond they'd shared during the pregnancy. It had gone to hell. Everything was going that way, but he'd never made more money in his life. The pandemic had rewritten all the rules. Wasteland for pissants and vipers, that's all the city was now. One frothing face at a time like a bee freed from a jar, nipping at his skin as it swelled and burned. He was in the moment all the time blending with the smoke in the city's lungs. Enough already with painful ordeals. He wouldn't slow down, he'd burn like a comet. *I ain't ready to join you yet Buzzy.*

In five years, he'd be forty. What did that mean? Just a number. One day older, maybe wiser, even though he knew he wouldn't live to be old. Might not live past this very day. He saw death everywhere he turned. Just how it was. All he knew was misery. He could trust and rely on it. Everything else was a lie. When night came down, he told himself he had one less day. Some nights he welcomed death. This could be his last, his *lucky* night.

He'd been counting backwards from the end for a while. It hadn't started with the miscarriage. It started when Ma had her first of what the doctors called TIA's. Transient Ischemic Attacks. They were strokes at the bush-league level. Didn't last long and usually the victim recovered, just as Ma did, but she had to keep watching what she ate, get herself some exercise. When Buzzy died, she plunged into booze, bad food and depression. She put on a brave face each day and went to work, but once home she drank and smoked and ate too much pizza and ice cream. Many a night she'd find a bar stool and drink to the point that a cabbie had to drive her home. Once there she'd order more lousy food, have it delivered and then pass out while eating in front of the television.

This took its toll. If only he'd said more, forced her to slow down and get healthy, tried to pick her up somehow. But he was lost in his own head, dodging bullets, selling heroin before the pandemic hit and the supply chain dynamic shifted to Oxy. And then later Fentanyl. Shifted all the time, so that was nothing new. What made him crazy stupid was that during the same time Ma was recovering there was a regular customer, Hassan from the Bronx, who blamed him over a user, just a kid, who'd OD'd on Mexican cheese he'd sold him. He knew Hassan watered the cheese down with anything he could find and then sold it to poorer users way uptown. Yet he got blamed for the kid's death since Hassan was banging the kid's sister.

The Scientists, though Derek asked them, had offered no protection. Hassan stopped buying, spread some nasty rumors that nobody accepted, and then wound up doing time for another infraction, a robbery.

Now, Hassan was out. He was still dealing, still with that same girl who wanted revenge for her little brother's death.

Derek felt badly about that kid dying. About the kid using in the first place, being so desperate, but people lived and died by their own choices. He hadn't forced the kid to buy. Nor had he been the one who'd cut the heroin. There was no point in feeling guilty about it. Hassan had his name, though not his address. Not yet anyway, but the reality stood that Derek could get capped at any time just so Hassan could keep his girlfriend happy. What kind of person was this girlfriend anyway, letting her kid brother buy H from her boyfriend? Such people were scum. Yet he was in business with them, scumbags all over the place getting rich or going broke on their choices.

What did that make him?

SEVEN

Holly was all hers to lavish with kisses. It would be different and much better *in the moment* if she could rid her mind of Derek completely, but Agnes couldn't and she knew why. She still wanted a man in her life. If not Derek, then perhaps me. There is a line in T.S. Eliot's poem, The Wasteland, that states: *The dead tree gives no shelter.* Agnes would keep such a dead tree alive in any way possible. She might be wrong to trust another man, or to stay loyal to Derek, but she believed herself prepared to reject the triangle game as the self-indulgent irresponsible lark that it had been. She was seeing better now. She didn't need a tripod to stand on. She didn't need a man either. She wanted one. There was a difference. New solutions, perspectives, angles and degrees of nuance were necessary to produce her life as a new image. Plenty of dead trees littered her landscape. She needn't become one herself, obeying those such as Derek who didn't really love her any longer and wanted to control her.

This wasn't paranoia. Holly wanted to control her too. They'd been watching lots of movies, snuggling on Holly's sofa, but it never felt quite as fulfilling as she'd hoped it to be. Scenes from their cuddle sessions had started to creep into her dreams. Agnes kept returning to one dream that she was in a French *noir* lying flat on a sidewalk in Marseilles in grainy black and white, asking a fellow gangster, a woman dressed like her, like a man in a 40s-era suit, for one last cigarette. No filter, of course. A Galois. She loved that name. There was a look of melancholy in her eyes as she whispered, "*Je compris. J'ai fini.*"

In French the words sounded better, especially as she heard the hiss while she dragged on that Galois and *FIN* in big white letters appeared on the screen.

Where all this came from she had no idea. It wasn't important that she didn't smoke and had never found the habit appealing. Though it scared her to a degree, she still revered the dream. She thought it spoke for an understanding of finality that the miscarriage had brought her.

Derek just didn't get it. His life, the drug dealing, it would come to a bad end. Anyone could see that. Sex with Holly wouldn't lead anywhere either, though Holly had been right to say she should give herself credit for staying away from Derek a while to focus on what mattered.

What did matter, especially now that everything felt different?

"It is *all* off a cliff, isn't it?" Agnes had asked.

Holly, nodding, had replied, "You've outgrown him. It was bound to happen. He's not any good for you. It's time now to find out who you are. The real Agnes. Not who you were or wanted or thought others expected you to become."

She was, indeed, *Shooter* Agnes. Or Agnes the Shooter. Or was she just plain Agnes? Or Shooter? How frustrating this was to realize at her age she was still so many types of women. Being with Holly had brought her back to remembering this.

The pictures she took, they completed her somehow. They made her one woman. Maybe she should change her name. The Ukrainian, Usher Fellig, had done it, calling himself Weegee. Emmanuel Radnitzky had done it too. Man Ray. She'd call herself Woman Ray, perhaps, and move to Paris to create a Neo Surrealism movement. Agnes giggled with the thought.

She could admit it. She was struggling at different level now. The initial period of depression, coupled with the side effects of the medications she'd been taking, had passed. They'd brought up her weight. Not any longer. She'd started to trim down. This was always a sign she was moving in a positive direction.

Holly understood this and forced Agnes to exercise, taking her as a guest to her gym. The sex with Holly was vigorous, as well. Her sexual appetite had returned and her sleep had improved. For too long, she'd been limp and doltish with Derek in bed.

It was about time she made her peace. Came to a decision. Perhaps moved on.

—∿—

Holly was tonguing her ear, whispering, "No young beauty in the prime of her fertile years should have to suffer a miscarriage and then learn she'll never be able to conceive. No woman, do you hear me? Ever."

She had to learn to love being *Shooter* Agnes again, didn't she? It felt like the most natural path, the easiest to take. Nobody had ever said it would be easy. Nor had anyone told her that life would feel so crushingly banal, so draining, so empty.

Holly was nibbling now the nape of Agnes's neck. Agnes, giving way, felt herself floating as she sounded little gasps of delight. She thought some are born blind, some are dreamers, some are behind the eight ball. Some are born all three. What was she? Over-sensitive, for one, too intelligent, misunderstood, seldom part of a group in any situation. Always the outsider looking in, recording the event for posterity.

Why Derek? His body? They had nothing in common. Yet the man wouldn't go away. Derek didn't criticize, so maybe that was why. Or maybe because he was the only one who'd asked. She had panicked, doubting her appeal to men, fearing she'd be alone until death. She'd thought no one else would ask her. *Don't want to become an old maid now, do you?* Her mother's voice, she could admit that now, she'd wanted to show her mother that there was a man out there who found her attractive. God, how stupid she'd been. She'd fallen for Derek in such a short time, loving the breezy way he just got along with people, the confidence he showed, the nerve, that acerbic New York skepticism, riding the waves, making his own decisions, living by his own rules and never concerning himself with what others thought.

That Derek was behind her now. Like a slow flame, thought Agnes, they'd endured until they'd burned out. It happened to most couples. They weren't any different.

It was her turn now to take Holly. She shifted her position in the bed and held Holly's face in two hands, assertively so, though with a gentle touch. She began kissing Holly on the lips. One moist kiss at a time.

There was goodness in her heart, she knew this. In Derek's? She couldn't say. What had Derek ever seen in her? He must have likened choosing her to picking the runt out of a litter. He must have pitied her, believing he could control her. The man consorted with and worked for scum and he sanctioned or participated in horrible acts to help them get richer. He'd selected her, Agnes The Nerd, the kid from some hick place in New England who won a school spelling bee once upon a time. Agnes the clumsy, the hobbled, the artsy type.

It was the pity in Derek that disgusted her now. Ironically, if she was honest with herself, it's what had appealed to her, too, at the start. Money appealed too. She had to be honest. There hadn't been as much innocence behind her intentions as she liked to tell others there'd been. She'd been his slut for his money and she'd hoped to start a family and now that she understood this wasn't going to happen she didn't like her situation and she had no one else but herself to blame for it.

Agnes stopped kissing Holly, but she kept Holly's face cradled in her hands and said, "Derek doesn't even know what empathy means. He pitied me. I just thought it was empathy."

Holly, who'd been staring at Agnes, showing fervent devotion, lowered her eyelids. "The man sells drugs. He was your bad boy. All that danger maybe it was an aphrodisiac. Your way of getting back at your parents."

After a moment of thought, a nod from Agnes, and a little grin of appreciation, Agnes heard Derek's voice echoing: *Seriously, how many guys like me you even know?*

"You don't mind talking about him? Especially now?" asked Holly.

Agnes shook her head no. "I think it's over."

"Agnes, tell me something, why do marriages exist?"

"Too hard alone, I guess."

"There you go. So don't be so hard on yourself."

Of course, thought Agnes. She hadn't expected such wisdom from Holly. "Where'd that come from?" she asked.

"Beats me," said Holly with a shrug. She sat up and faced Agnes, leaning back on her hands. "It's a choice, right? Marriage and a family. Even if I'm not sold on it. But I have my choices and my priorities when it comes to Derek. You should know that by now."

"I do." Or maybe I think I do. All the time maybe, thought Agnes. "Holly, you ever think beauty in the world is in danger?"

"It is," said Holly. "We all are. Nothing lasts forever."

She liked how coolly Holly had expressed this. As if she really knew. "All this anxiety I feel," said Agnes, wanting to confess now, to talk for a long time. "Sometimes, it's too much. It's off the charts."

Holly, nodding and grinning, took her by the shoulders. She said "Just let go" as she forced herself on top of Agnes while kissing her neck and collarbone.

As Agnes thrilled to a tingling sensation, she breathed in Holly's scent. She absorbed Holly's kisses one at a time and remembered that by exploiting the triangle game with Holly she had given herself permission to escape herself, to find needed bliss outside of norms and rules and her usual pangs of self-doubt. How sweetly, she thought, they folded themselves into each other. How they perspired and grew redder as if a pair of rose blossoms that glistened with dew.

EIGHT

Though Buzzy had been gone a while, Derek knew Ginger was still grieving over him. She was always sad about everything and he couldn't be angry with her, but she really had to find the strength to move on.

It was tough. The pandemic was putting everyone into a funk. He listened best he could when she had too much to drink and started reliving each anniversary, from the day she'd gotten hitched to Buzzy, back to the day he proposed, back to the times they had together when they'd first met. So many better more pleasant times. All gone now. The poor woman. Thank God she had Sister Nancy. How else account for her showing some signs of progress. Ma had slowed her drinking, though there was still too much of it, and she still refused to eat right.

Ma hadn't stopped working either, which he found amazing. Though maybe work took her mind off the past and Buzzy. She'd returned to the office two weeks after his funeral. She'd always worked hard, like it was the only thing she could do well. Hard as steel from the inside out. Tireless.

That's what happened, he supposed. People were like trees. They swelled and developed ugly deformities and if they didn't get chopped down or struck by lightning, they rotted from the inside out while they kept leaning in the direction of their bad habits. Most people were their own worst enemies. Buzzy used to say that all the time.

During his last visit to Ma, she'd told Derek about a girlfriend she'd known for decades, also a secretary, who'd died of Covid. There was no funeral. Only the woman's husband and daughter, masks on, mourned at a Catholic cemetery where a priest said a few prayers. The funeral home made a video and posted it online.

Derek watched this video with Ginger, out of respect, but it made him feel so damn depressed that he'd needed to be alone a while, lying down in the dark of his room. He hated seeing his Ma bawling her eyes out, knowing her girlfriend deserved better. Yet so many had died and were still dying that way, a lot of them younger than Ma's girlfriend and with larger families. Covid was wiping out a whole forest of hardened trees, and it made thinking about Agnes and the miscarriage really difficult. Which was why he didn't think about them at all.

Ma knew better to bring up the subject. More than anything in the world, Ma had wanted to be a grandmother. Wasn't gonna happen. One more reason for her to get shit-faced and feel sorry for herself. Sure, he got the gist of that, he did, a baby meant continuation. Big-time. It explained how Ma got up each morning and could still log on to her computer and, even when working from home, do data entry and type boring letters and emails and suck up online to pompous suits with MBAs.

Ma could do anything. She could wear the mask even though she was feeling the same lousy depression he was. Even though her clothes didn't fit like they used to, and her figure no longer turned heads. Ma didn't care. She just kept going. She took her mind off by keeping busy.

She kept smoking too, stinking up her apartment. Bad enough there was already a reek in the walls that stunk of pee from her cat's litter box.

Sister Nancy bailed Ma out, came by to clean and to check on her. Sister Nancy deserved sainthood. If any of the stress of the pandemic fazed her, she didn't show it. She'd told Derek that the TIAs were like volcanic eruptions inside Ma's body shouting to stop before one final huge eruption ended it all. So, Ma had to stop. Not because she wanted but because she had to.

She'd tried, but she hadn't succeeded. What could he do? That was how it went with people. They wised up or else they took solace in habits that ended up killing them.

Derek tried not to dwell on this too much. What he feared, he knew, was Ma's death. Then he'd really be alone. There'd be nobody. Then what?

Screw it. Time would tell.

He kept running his errands, cashing in, keeping his nose clean. He stayed on high alert for one of Hassan's bullets, shifting gears, schooling himself the way he had when Buzzy got sick. What did Sister Nancy call him? A caregiver. No, that wasn't him. He stole from life. He didn't give it back. In that old-school song Buzzy liked when the line goes *I'm your pusherman*, it was him, nobody else, Curtis Mayfield was singing about. A crummy feeling. What could he say to his conscience? What did it matter that he was there for his Ma if she was gonna die anyway? Shit, it wasn't like he'd been good to anyone, or faithful to his wife. When he wasn't banging Holly on the side, he was tearing into some fresh who put out in exchange for grams. He got more than enough pussy, and he had cred, but all that was overrated, especially when what he wanted was more of it. More of the big empty charade.

Not like he could tell any of this to Sister Nancy. Not even to Agnes. Sister Nancy didn't visit as often as she had in the past. For quite a time she'd showed up every day. Her visits were usually twice a week now. The woman was such a help, such a blessing. He couldn't have done squat without her during those days after Ma's TIAs, and this was another lesson the pandemic was teaching him. No such thing as a lone wolf. It was a myth. Wolves ran in packs. The strong guided the weak, propped each other up.

Like rats, people were stuck with each other. So many rats in Ma's basement. So many rings in Ma's trunk. So many forgotten old songs in her heart. Ma the tree that sucked vodka tonics through her roots like they were water. Crazy now to think that for a while she'd been in a rehab center and couldn't get around without one of those aluminum walkers with rubber-tipped legs. During that time, when Ma had to live at a window and didn't dare to brave the outdoors, she'd needed prescription shades like she was a character wearing a Star Trek costume.

Derek wanted to think that the more he coped with the idea of Ma's death – and it was coming, he knew it – the easier it would be. Derek knew better. Death couldn't be ignored. This was what he figured defined love. Knowing that life ended but not thinking about it, not fearing it, just getting out there into the street each day and putting out energy to help Agnes, Holly, Ma, Sister Nancy, helping everyone he met to find some comfort. He was lousy at it, for sure, a total wreck, but at least he knew it. No flies on him, no delusions of grandeur either.

NINE

Accepting advice and payments from her father, Holly Greene got into real estate at the age of nineteen long before Providence had what its late mayor, Vincent Buddy Cianci, had once touted as a renaissance. She'd bought for $40,000 dollars a three-decker unit that once housed a trio of working-class families on Smith Hill, not too far from the State House.

Again with her father's assistance, she renovated the entire property. She rented out the first and second floors, moving into the renovated top floor. As her only foray into real estate, it had been a success. After two decades of paying a relatively small mortgage, she now owned the property outright, knowing that in the current market it was valued at ten times her purchasing price.

Though she owned a car, a Toyota *Prius*, Holly could live in Providence without one. She enjoyed walking to her preferred cafes and restaurants in the Downcity neighborhood, along South Main Street, and in the warren of streets of the city's East Side. She could also catch an Amtrak train, or a Greyhound bus, with ease, to any major city on the Eastern seaboard.

Despite feeling twinges of pride as a minor success in real estate, Holly nurtured an enduring affection for this city she was raised in. She mourned, at times, the vanishing of the city as it once was, though granted, while growing up, Providence had been poorer and in some neighborhoods much dirtier and more dangerous. She'd heard stories, too, from her parents and grandparents on both sides about a Providence that didn't feature WaterFire events on the city's river, or gay lovers walking hand in hand downtown inside the huge mall that had been built there back when Cianci, indicted as a mobbed-up felon, had seen his long reign as mayor come to an end.

On the nights when there were concerts at the Civic Center, the Ocean State Theatre, or Providence *Bruins* hockey games, or a WaterFire event, she'd marvel at how the city had changed. She could now take pride in feeling safer while observing the families that would drive in from the suburbs, parking at the downtown mall. They, too, felt a sense of security, a pride in the charm that the city in its renewed state now had to offer. For older long-time residents, especially the Italians, it explained some of the fondness they shared when recalling the former mayor, despite his crude malfeasant practices while in office.

On WaterFire nights, Holly would sit among these older residents and newcomers alike on the banks of the river. She'd watch gondoliers light the flames that reflected off the river's surface, sending smoke into the air that breezed along to the accompaniment of cerebral music by the likes of Enya, and Vangelis. It was a stroke of genius, really, such a simple choice to situate fires one after another in the middle of the river canal. These controlled bonfires lit up the night, coaxing residents out of their shells so they could gather and think and socialize a while.

She'd see fathers rising taller in front of sons, sometimes menacing them with silence. She'd watch mothers collapsing during stolen moments alone behind horizons of exhaustion. Seated on their blankets, or in the lightweight chairs they brought with them, residents and visitors alike snacked on potato chips or carrot sticks, the lines in their faces enhanced by the firelight.

Watching them, Holly would think of how the firelight proved a certain depletion in the human spirit. She'd study the faces of so many strangers, actual tourists to the city and view them as they endured the burden of recalling failed ambitions and forms of happiness now etched into their memories. She saw often in the people from the suburbs, as she saw in her friends, as well, the framed family pictures, creased, out of focus, fading, taken perhaps by ancestors in an older country far away.

Such a puzzling and compelling array of thoughts she'd experience when observing people, almost as if she wasn't one of them. This was similar to the many cerebral flights of fancy that accompanied her ruminations when studying the images that Agnes would often share with her.

As Agnes liked to say: "Every image reveals a little bit of who we are within, but, of course, mostly who we're not and would like to be."

Shooter Agnes was a genius. The world didn't know it yet, but it would, one day. Holly fully believed this. Not that she was an artist herself, but she had what her mother called an artistic temperament. The closest she'd gotten to art was playing small roles in school theatre productions. She soaked life in and tended to spend a lot of time alone. She didn't mind solitude. She preferred it. As a steady companion, she had her cat, Prince, named after the late musician. A cinder-colored shorthair, Prince, like her, didn't eat enough and so was mostly bones and liked to sleep all day.

Agnes, too, was one to feel emotions strongly. She clung to them and brooded. Not Holly. She set them free and Agnes liked to call her "a divine" and a "princess," and Holly never knew what to make of such labels.

Agnes could be sarcastic, too, outspoken, using over-the-top language that she had to apologize for later. She was a sweetheart under the skin and she'd come back to her. They were on again, so to speak, living the triangle game with no concern for rules. Perfect for her. Even better for Derek. Not so much for Agnes, though she was still in. For how long, though, was tricky to say.

This particular period of intimacy with Agnes wouldn't last. None of them did. Fine. No expectations. She'd seize their time together and make the best of it. This meant feasting on salacious impulses in the face of limitations due to the pandemic. It meant burning like the fire on the water. Burning up the night. Throwing off sparks.

⸎

Dawn had come. Holly, awake, lay in bed naked allowing Agnes a full view of her body in the rising light. She looked up and saw Agnes in her camo pants with her denim jacket on. Agnes had straps running over both her shoulders that held cases that protected her various cameras. She was moving around the bed, firing one click at a time on her camera's shutter, wanting Holly un-posed, still naked, vulnerable. While shooting her pictures she talked about her cameras as if they were her children. One was a Minolta, the other a Nikon, what she called an FM2, and the third was her Nikon F1. Agnes had two lenses and some slow film for color saturation, some faster film for action shots. She had a digital Canon point-and-shoot for quick back-up images.

Holly had heard all this more than once, and didn't mind hearing it again. Agnes needed support and a willing and appreciative pupil and model. The day before they'd visited a hair salon and the stylist where one of Holly's gay male friends had been cute about snipping Agnes's mane really short. Agnes had then dyed her hair bright purple so that she looked like a New Wave rocker from the 80s.

"I like the hair, seeing it now," she said.

"Don't talk," said Agnes from behind her camera. The shutter went click. She spun the camera swiftly. Another click. "Just be still. I'm almost done."

Click. Click. Click. More pictures. Holly remained silent. She thought the purple hair suited the way Agnes thought of herself as a commando photographer, but a little different, not to be dismissed as conventional. Holly found it all a rather adorable flirtation with excess.

Ever so fey and lissome, Holly started to pose, just a little, allowing Agnes to feast her eyes on her body. She was prone to enjoying such flirtations. Greene, incidentally, was not her family name. She'd been born Consuela Giordano to parents who were both the children of Italian immigrants. Nobody's fool, a name change early helped her fit in at an elite Catholic school before she earned a degree from Brown university, all of it paid for by her father who never divulged where his money came from.

Agnes would be borrowing Holly's car, having taken a shower and choosing to skip breakfast, Holly assumed, because she wanted to get out early into the dank yet vivid morning air and light.

Holly craved none of that. "Are we done now?" she asked. She was admittedly lazy. She'd never had to work hard for anything and didn't see this as a flaw in her character. As she viewed it, some people were born to stay in bed until noon simply because they could, so why shouldn't she be one of them?

Her mother was the same way. Let the men bring them money, perfumes, flowers and chocolates, and ask no questions about the sources. Women, after all, were born for shopping sprees. This was how she preferred to live. The rent she collected from her tenants was more than enough to cover daily and rather tedious expenses. Daddy still sent her allowance, as well, some of which she invested, the rest she used for traveling or shoes or wardrobe upgrades.

Lazy she was, true enough, but she wasn't stupid. She was shrewd with her money. One day, when her looks began to fade, she'd sell her apartment building and pay in cash for a villa somewhere in southern Europe. She flew to Italy, Spain and Portugal throughout the year, having developed connections there with brokers, bankers and lovers both male and female, single and married.

"I'm done, that's it," said Agnes. "You go back to sleep."

"I most certainly will." Holly pulled sheet and blanket over her body. "You have fun," she said. "And be careful with my car."

Before leaving, Agnes kissed her lightly on top of the head.

⸺◦◦◦⸺

Each day, Holly took her sweet time with her morning Pilates routine before putting on make-up and clothes. She prepared coffee, nothing else, and then read for a while. She read at least one sometimes two novels week, favoring mysteries of all sorts, and women writers from across the world, particularly feminist ones.

It was late afternoon. As her habit, she started thinking about her first meal of the day. Agnes would most likely be back soon with the car. They could go for an early dinner together in the city. Al Forno would be suitable, but they'd have to wait until it opened at 4:30 and settle on take-out from the reduced pandemic menu.

They could get a grilled pizza and bring it back to her place and enjoy it. This would be splendid in all its simplicity. They'd buy a bottle of Asti too and drink together as twilight came on. Then they'd start all over again in bed, some quiet music playing as they ravished each other with honeyed kisses.

Oh, she thought, the dreamy whispers, the deep sleep, the flashing days between sultry and sullen episodes in this long lingering fantastic of life of hers…she could remember years ago, back before it became yet another pizza establishment aligned with Federal Hill, how she went with Agnes to watch her in action. Agnes had been trying to capture some magic from what was then left of the Castle Hill Cinema marquee on Chalkstone Avenue, closed long ago, now gone, once a centerpiece in a neighborhood not far from where she lived.

She remembered falling in love while Agnes was bent over or else crouched down while snapping her pictures, complaining she hadn't stopped for a cup of black coffee at Dunkin Donuts. Holly had laughed at Agnes's pretenses of being working class, so rough and tumble, drinking coffee out of paper cups when she could have imbibed espresso with her at any number of fine eateries in the city.

This was Agnes's charm. She was dead set on pretending to be who she wasn't. She'd become a person rather different from who she'd been raised as, defying her mother's rather elitist expectations. They talked about this at times. Agnes didn't feel she'd let herself down, but that she was following through on her passionate obsession to become a great photographer. Her mother, however, viewed the photography as a phase, not a career choice, and still expected Agnes to grow up, marry a lawyer or a broker and get on with the business of living. She derided Agnes as selfish, bohemian, ungrateful. From what Holly had seen of Agnes's mother, the apple didn't fall far from the tree.

Whenever they talked, Holly found that she told Agnes nothing that she hadn't already known about herself and her situation. It was the rapport, she supposed, being there for Agnes, listening to her, that mattered. There were so many holes in that poor girl.

They'd talked and talked about what the city was when they were younger. Holly knew the city well. Agnes knew it from her student days. They both remembered how the Castle Cinema had been a place where kids for decades had flocked to in order not to just watch movies but to play with other kids and get out of their crowded apartments on Smith Hill or Federal Hill, screaming and running all day long up and down the aisles in that cinema. Kids like her own father when he was a boy, one of many in a big Catholic family, spending each Saturday afternoon with the other kids, meeting girls, having a life of their own outside of the poverty of their always crowded and noisy urban apartments. At night, couples without a television in their homes stepped out to watch a movie starring the likes of Lana Turner, Joan Fontaine or Bette Davis after dining in one of the local restaurants on Federal Hill. Some drove. Most of them walked. Women wore leather gloves. Heels. Crinoline dresses. Men wore hats. Cuff links. They dressed with a desire to show elegance and class beyond their station. When Holly's mother and her girlfriend Sylvia, both natives to the city just like Daddy, watched movies there, they bought two tickets that cost them two wrinkled one-dollar bills.

In one incarnation, as Holly knew well, the new owner of the Castle had installed car seats on wheels with little tables between them. He'd paid wait staff to serve customers alcohol and snacks during the film, but even that hadn't sufficed to boost ticket sales. All the cinemas had moved into homes. Everything had changed.

That morning seemed buried now in the past, and Holly had been fascinated with Agnes. She still was. She'd been in awe of her. Agnes had appeared fearless on the street, brazenly setting up her tripod and camera on the sidewalk. She'd photographed the theatre's marquee with its neon letters *CASTLE* running horizontally atop both sides and angling out over the sidewalk. The vanilla-colored tiles framing each side of the wide lobby entryway had created a glazed ceramic border with an etched-in and fanciful grapevine motif, all of it catching a hard, ascending white light. The hour had been somewhere between five and six a.m. Few pedestrians at that hour, and only an occasional car passed by disturbing briefly the otherwise placid morning silence of the neighborhood.

That had been Holly's first and most memorable glimpse of the other Agnes. The real artist. Agnes had shown such poise. Holly remembered Agnes saying how pleased she was there weren't shadows yet. Shadows? Holly hadn't even thought about such things, but from Agnes's point of view it made sense. The two of them had marveled at the roseate quality that had begun to alter the light.

It was Agnes who'd brought Holly a new understanding of light and how it affected mood and resonance. Light was powerfully simple. It was everything. Agnes herself was light. So was Jesus or Buddha or Allah or any other divine force one might care to worship.

Agnes had shot the Castle Cinema from different angles, at various speeds, isolating architectural flourishes. She'd used her telephoto lens, explaining that she also used what she called a polarizing filter that altered the light. She used an ultraviolet one too, stacking her filters, she said, threading them to the end of her lenses to reduce glare and create certain effects. Masterful, really, a whole new way of not taking for granted what the eyes feasted on each day.

Pitiful vacant me, thought Holly. She'd perish adoring an artist with purple hair who, like her, was obsessed with light. One could, she supposed, laughing at herself, do a lot worse.

She found it easy to admit that the two of them were in synch. Her time with Agnes kept her wanting to remain in a perpetually adolescent state of anticipation. She didn't feel that way with men. Not with Derek, as sweet as he was in bed, or any of her others. With her men it was about letting them adore her, feeding their fantasies that she was the only force that brought contentment in their universe. *Worship me, spoil me you with your sword and your musky scent and I'll save you from yourself.* Oh yes, men. She couldn't, unfortunately, live without them.

The glory of her time with Agnes was, however, of a more satisfying nature. She never felt she had to bring anything. She could be young Holly and in awe, perhaps naïve, and didn't need to know enough about any particular subject to impress her. To live with Agnes was to live for the surprises and disappointments that came as unpredictably as the images that would appear magically in the solutions that Agnes developed her negatives in. With digital tools, as Holly understood them, there was less of this magic and chemical alchemy. Again, it was about light, but there were few risks and even fewer surprises. This was why Agnes lamented their popularity. Convenience, Agnes had said, but to a fault. Just last night Agnes had carped on and on about there being too many pictures now, too many selfies, too many hacks and amateurs and photo-shopping charlatans that didn't bleed for their art.

Holly, amused by this outpouring of frustration and emotion, had agreed with Agnes. The ease of technology led people to take far too many steps away from each other. Human movement, as it struck her, was one that drifted now away from an essentially human core. It inched closer to defining the illusion rather than the real thing as what it meant to be fully alive. It suggested via screens that people were actually in each other's company. In truth, so much of living had become an exchange of images creating one paradigm and narrative after another, none of which adequately captured the human experience as she saw it. She wondered if others saw things this way too. It was hard to say, especially for one such as herself who spent so much time alone.

Technology, and she'd said this to Agnes, made it too easy to hurt each other. Too easy to arrange into reality what were once deemed collages of perceptions of the real. Not the real thing itself. All a bit like Dadaism blended with science fiction. A profound thought? Holly didn't think so, but she was grateful to think philosophically along any lines and this was all thanks to Agnes, She Goddess Of The Camera And Lens, igniter of bonfires in her imagination that sent Holly's blood into a boil.

TEN

While eating pizza and drinking wine Holly admitted she found it tedious the way Agnes expended so much energy fretting over issues she couldn't control. She reduced Agnes, saying she was cute in all her diligence and idealism, but that she wrapped herself in delusions of what she hoped she and the world could become rather than what they were. The comment had stung and Agnes didn't hold back, insisting Holly apologize.

"Never," said Holly. "You know I'm right."

"I can't believe you'd say that to my face."

"But how I do love the still innocent girl in you, Agnes, though I worry one day you'll wake up – and that day will come, believe me – and you'll realize you have no money, no fame, nothing but a bunch of photographs to show you silly you've been. And the worst thing will be that nobody cares."

"Where is this coming from? You sound like my mother."

"So master your art," said Holly. "Prove us wrong."

Agnes, clenching her teeth, countered with, "Eventually, someone will notice. They'll come for me. You watch. Even if it happens after I'm gone."

"Look, I know you're a genius," said Holly, undeterred. "But a dose of reality. If it goes like you say, you won't enjoy it."

"I enjoy it now. With you. You spoil me. So does Derek. I don't have it so bad."

"I thought you two were finished."

"I'm going to leave him once I figure out the money."

"He's your bank account. I get that."

"Oh, stop it, will you," shouted Agnes, popping out of her chair and glaring at Holly. "Just stop it."

"I'm sorry," said Holly. "It's the wine and all."

Holly then asked Agnes where she'd gone to shoot her pictures this time. Relieved to change the subject, Agnes told her she'd visited where the Castle Cinema marquee used to be. She described how people had milled past her on the sidewalk while she'd stood there looking thoughtful and dejected, her camera in one hand, a strap and its case over one shoulder. The pedestrians had stared as if wondering why anyone would be on such a street with a camera.

Agnes knew Holly had seen the many enlargements of her photos from past excursions to this mostly forgotten local landmark. It was their place, after all. Where they'd fallen in love. There'd been a time when fearing real estate developers were going to level it, Agnes had assembled a memory album of the theatre to go along with all her other archives.

Holly spoke in a diplomatic tone. "You know, Agnes, I think it's like you don't trust that one constant in life is change. It's like you need to hold on to the past, to keep it in a safe place for posterity because you can't handle that day by day it's going to be different."

Agnes, listening, had nothing to add. The best of her archives might make a glorious coffee table book. What was wrong with that? Someone had to chronicle the past, and Holly had never been convinced the city or the owner of the building would level the cinema, and this point of view had become, for a while, a point of contention between them. In the end, Holly had turned out to be right. It was no longer a cinema, but the building was still there and it housed a pizza franchise. So that meant chronicling what it had been was certainly worth a photographer's time.

"So what was your impression after being a way for a time?" asked Holly.

"I didn't shoot it. I couldn't. It's a pizza restaurant. Besides, I want to remember it as our special place. You do know that, don't you?"

Holly brushed aside her long black hair, keeping it off her eyes. "I do. I do."

Agnes thought of what she'd seen, the shell of the theatre building and how, though decayed, it had remained as if to remind her that decay ruled all. It hadn't been restored or returned it to its former glory. For those who didn't know better, it was just another building.

She said, "I think it looks like it should be something else."

Holly, wilting, leaned back in her chair. She'd been too hard on Agnes, had really levelled her with the criticism. It was the wine, it did that sometimes, freed all her inhibitions. They were in the kitchen, plenty of light, warmth, a simplicity to the embellishments there. She blamed herself for not allowing Agnes to enjoy it.

"I remember," said Holly, "when I first learned the marquee had been taken down. I went there and it was true. I couldn't believe it. Honestly. The building's face stripped of all its unique little designs and doodads. No marquee at all. Just vanished! I'm still sad about it."

"So am I," said Agnes. "I wish I hadn't gone back there. I couldn't sleep, and I'm not like you, I can't stay in bed all day. Besides, I wanted some fresh images to update my blog."

This blog, which Agnes had started years ago when still living in Providence, archived images of theatres and other landmarks, no matter the city, which she and others agreed were doomed. It was the only project she maintained online, an archive that had grown in popularity and included photos of many decaying, doomed and neglected gems. Agnes and other urban archeologists, as she thought of them, whether architects, amateur historians or photo buffs, used it as a forum to celebrate what was slated to be or already vanquished.

Why had she even been concerned with the Castle Cinema and its marquee? It was dead. It should be buried, incinerated. Her interest, though not easy to admit, stemmed from a desire to journey back to her early days with Holly. To who they'd been. Not who they'd become.

"If only I could look to the future a little more," she said. "Or at least to the positive changes in the city's landscape."

"Lots of them here," said Holly, gawking into space, flinging strands of her long hair out of her eyes, seated at the table in a loose linen top with big wooden buttons. Such a cute top, too, thought Agnes, but she thought Holly looked so unhappy. Dreaming perhaps, just as she had been, of where their life together, the cinema in it, used to be. Struggling or else unwilling to accept it was no longer there.

"We've got to stop living in the past," said Agnes.

"No, we don't." Holly didn't raise her eyes. She stared instead at the glass of white wine in her hand, swirling it around. "I like the past. It's in front of me. I can see it coming."

To a degree, Agnes understood. The Castle Cinema had represented a safe oasis for children in the neighborhood. For a young girl like Holly who was no longer young. Cinemas and movies were places associated with fantasy and escape. More than ever, in light of the pandemic, escape was alluring. Even Holly's father had, over the years, admitted he felt sad the cinema had started to look dingy, the black paint of its metal front beginning to peel, its chaser lights always dark, no longer blinking, the O and S missing in its posted letters: F R ALE.

The cinema was like the fish and chips joints and grocers' shops that used to hum in that neighborhood. One more site that spoke of what could never be recaptured. Natural, thought Agnes, for anyone to mourn, so she could forgive Holly for probing and brooding so restlessly.

Agnes wanted to shout at Holly that if her Daddy could get over the cinema's disappearance, then so could she. Shouting wasn't her style. Nor would it move Holly one bit. She tried a softer approach. "Please don't wallow." She said this in a gently fashion. "Holly, let's go somewhere else, where things are newer. We need that."

In the past, Agnes would have never been able to speak with such conviction to Holly. Their time together, apart and together again had allowed her more ease, clarity and confidence. She didn't have to make Holly feel comfortable. It was best to be honest and direct.

"What do you expect?" Holly sounded a pleading note. "I loved that cinema."

"I did too, but finding another subject. It's what photographers do."

Holly dropped her head a moment. She brooded, both of them seated in silence, and then raised her head and eyed Agnes. "You're right, I guess, but it all happens so fast. Look at us. We're like old or something now."

"We're not old. We're *older*." Agnes had to laugh at this. Poor Holly, she could afford to wallow in such emotions. "We get used to it. That's all."

Nodding glumly, Holly asked, "Am I a freak? Be honest."

"You're not. You're just more pure of heart than others. More than you're willing to admit. It's one reason why I love you. But if only you could learn to trust yourself."

"There's no normalcy anymore. Not anywhere," said Holly.

"Maybe," said Agnes. "Or maybe you're too limited in your thinking. You need to embrace the word 'strange' for what it is – one more definition of what doesn't need to be defined."

Agnes felt she'd hit a grace note. She'd gotten inside of Holly and led her to a place where she needed to be. She could keep going now and pull from memory any number of mental pictures that on one hand could be deemed strange and, on the other hand, if one accepted life in all its forms, weren't strange at all. These might help Holly see the sometimes overheated stubbornness in her that refused to accept the unfolding of one's days as little more than an endlessly absurd play. Sometimes tragic, sometimes not. Always an adventure at best.

Of all the girlfriends whose company Agnes had enjoyed, from Flora in DC, to Caroline in San Francisco, Holly was the one most prone to drowning under such waves of despair. Holly had taken the mantle years ago, deciding to never be a negative influence, seeing herself as both friend and spiritual advisor. Though she'd never say it, Holly knew it was her own fault she wasn't daring enough to break out of certain behavioral patterns. She was too comfortable. This was common, fear-based, alive in many people, and one more reason why Holly sometimes punished herself with self-loathing.

Agnes labored to get the words out, speaking deliberately. "It's like I've gotten nowhere in my life. In any careerist sense. I don't even have a job anymore. I just run around taking pictures. But it doesn't matter. Not at all."

"I don't have a job either. I've never had one."

"But you don't need one. You're different," said Agnes.

"So are you."

"Don't compare us, Holly. And don't make excuses."

Holly paused, stopping herself. She sighed. "Look Agnes, it's not as if a career were the only important measurement of success. All I want is what I already have. Money and my own place. I don't have a problem if there's no career, or any sense of urgency."

"So you still think you have a lot to live for?"

"Of course I do," said Holly. "We both do."

"I suppose you're right."

"Okay, then, so let's go shopping. Let's be typical, for a change," said Holly. "Despair is overrated."

❧

They walked. Holly had wanted the mall, but Agnes had argued she needed to move outdoors, away from people whether in masks or not. She also felt more comfortable speaking about her feelings while covering familiar streets, so they chose to climb the hill up past the grounds of Rhode Island School Of Design, and Brown University.

As they walked Thayer Street toward Wickenden, Agnes told Holly how much she had needed all this time away from Derek. Time to find her center and a clearer sense of self. With the pandemic, she felt she'd lost her identity. Without a job or a place to be or a schedule, she'd begun to see how limits and structure kept her mind and body from feeling as if it were turning into mush. "I don't like this sense that I'm decaying into sloth."

"Some of us," said Holly. "Need to stay busy."

Agnes agreed and explained how she felt better when she was alone moving about Manhattan on foot, taking photos, editing an image or two online, selling one now and then. Was that enough? Was that a job? Not in her book. It was more than that. It defined her. A job, the money part of it, was merely one small piece of the larger puzzle.

"But it really upsets Derek," she said.

"That you take pictures or that you think that way?" asked Holly.

"He gets testy each time I tell him I'm happy with what I'm doing, and that I suggest he try something different to make a living. Maybe consider moving to one of the other boroughs. Changing his life completely."

"Dangerous territory, that's not Derek," said Holly. "And what does he say, usually?"

"I suggested Brooklyn, which I like, especially Prospect Park, even though we can't afford it. But he said Brooklyn is an over-priced mosh pit full of hipsters and thugs."

"And Queens is the center of the universe. Yeah, I get it. Kind of a stupid thing to say," said Holly.

"But Derek isn't stupid."

"But he is," said Holly. "He is."

"I don't know what I ever saw in him."

"Same that I saw. He's a man, he goes along with our game. He brings me drugs. He brings you money. Not so bad, I suppose. But what I don't get is why the soft spot for Brooklyn."

"It was where I started my New York life alone. I don't take such a harsh view. I stay open-minded. You know, I really do try to understand Derek. I really do."

Agnes stopped talking. She wanted to cry. She couldn't even look at Holly as the two of them kept walking along. Just thinking about Derek, about what he could be, what might have been – it was all too much.

By the time they reached Wickenden, the smell of the ocean, the sound of freeway traffic, glimpses of the tip of Narragansett Bay that fringed the city helped Agnes pull herself together. When had salty air not revived her? It always did. Quietly, calmly, she continued to walk, pleased that she hadn't broken down in front of Holly.

"So what's next?" asked Holly. "Do you want to stay married or not?"

Agnes thought the question appropriate and fair. Holly had a knack for asking them at the right time. She told her that to think of Derek meant to think of Queens. No other place. It was all he knew. To think of marriage meant to think of tolerance, compromise and flexibility. Regarding Derek on these issues, Agnes wasn't so sure she had an answer.

"I think you should be grateful for our triangle. At least he agrees to that."

"I am."

"Lighten up, Agnes. Don't worry about definitions so much."

Definitions, yes. Her yearning to keep all in focus. To maintain perspective. Concerns a photographer had to keep in mind. It occurred to Agnes that Holly understood her better than anyone she knew. Holly had become more than a lover. She'd become a refuge. They were both, indeed, older, but that was good, wasn't it? Older meant more mature, wiser, proceeding gainfully through life. Had she really expected her life would never change? Foolishly so, yes, she had.

Holly said, "This is how the triangle game works. It's supposed to make you happy. That's why the church won't allow it. Happy people don't throw themselves at father figures like the Pope."

"Marriage is serious, though, and what we're doing," said Agnes. "it's a dangerous game, don't you think?"

Holly, shrugging, told Agnes not to worry, that she needed more time to heal, to absorb other points of view. She didn't condemn. Nor did she condone. Holly knew how to stay in the middle and help make Agnes feel protected. Agnes had always wanted to feel this way with her mother, but she never had. She felt judged by her mother, a failure.

Not with Holly, who believed in her, made love to her, lifted her up. Holly had listened when Agnes had confessed how much she missed her father. That her mother, at times, behaved as if she didn't miss the man at all. Yet she'd seen how lonely her mother was. Why else would the woman drink so much? Her mother put up a front, presenting herself as supremely comfortable, which she was thanks to her late husband.

"It's good medicine to air yourself out," said Holly. "Nothing's as big as it seems once you free it from your imagination."

It was a useful thought, and when they returned to Holly's apartment, since the weather allowed it, Agnes asked if they could sit on Holly's third-floor balcony in Adirondack chairs. They did so and looked east across the city at College Hill where, above the Providence River, lush tree cover was dotted with the gables and mansard windows of Victorian-era manses and university buildings. The lowering sun left twilight golds and lavenders that gleamed softly across those rooftops, glinting in places, melting and flashing against the windows that spied back at them from between the trees.

It was a view Agnes had forgotten about, and she found it soothing. A gift. She fought urges to photograph it. Not this time, no, she'd just sit an enjoy it. She had in the past savored a lot of quiet time on this very balcony thinking about the choices she'd made, reveling in memories of her father when the man had been sober and congenial. When her mother had been less candid in her criticism, more supportive, not pickled all the time.

Agnes marveled over how the sun gelled in margarine and brandy bursts that bled off windowpanes and spread meek fire across trees and shadows. She drifted back to the pudgy and inquisitive little Agnes she'd once been, thrilled by New England as a place of colonial-era ghosts and Native tribes headed by leaders with names like Metacomet. It was there on that balcony, at a party, that she and Holly had first been introduced. They were both older than seventeen yet still learning "the truth about beauty queens," a line that came to Agnes from an old Janis Ian song.

Always in her mind that song. Her mother's song. *God why can't I just have happiness with my mother?* Agnes wondered sadly if anyone remembered it. She and her mother would listen to it from a vinyl copy on her father's turntable. Her mother had been right when she'd said that she could feel her age when she thought about pop culture references. How the feeling became an ache whenever she tried to share such references with anyone younger.

"We have such short memories now," her mother had said. "I can't remember anything anymore. I need Google to do it for me."

Agnes wouldn't let decay continue to happen. She wouldn't erase her memory. She remembered everything. Just as she remembered in fine air-brushed detail meeting Holly for the first time who on that day was garbed all in white cotton, her summer dress cut low across her breasts, showing a little cleavage, hugging her long lean lines. Tanned, Holly's black hair had flowed down her finely hewn shoulders. After private high school, where she'd been a model student, she'd graduated with a BA in Liberal Arts from Brown. She'd looked every bit a daughter of privilege, poise and breeding. From the moment they'd met, Holly had astonished her, made her feel underdeveloped and insignificant.

Agnes remembered how during the party she'd had such fantasies, such flights of lust while watching Holly from a distance. They'd been introduced by a mutual friend and the two of them had just started babbling about the sunset. Holly had made a reference to how H.P. Lovecraft once "resided" in one of those "stately edifices" of the city's east side that could be seen from the balcony. Holly didn't use typical words. She had a language, a polished style of her own. She could it turn on or off at will.

Enthralled, an admirer of Lovecraft's stories and a recent graduate from Providence College, Agnes had been eager to tell Holly that she knew this bit of trivia. When she did so, appearing to amuse Holly, it had the effect of loosening them up. They'd spoken about how the past could be so close yet embedded deeply within at the same time. Holly's comments had made Agnes's eyes and heart bloom larger and that was when, Agnes supposed, she knew she'd found a potential new friend and soulmate.

With the pandemic, she'd grown comfortable retreating further into isolation. They both had. They discussed this and much to Agnes's relief, Holly confessed that she'd gotten more difficult, contentious, more stubborn, harder to read.

"I've just stopped talking," she said. "It's like I can't accept that every-one's life is on hold. Like it's trauma or shock. During the worst time of lockdown it was like there was no point in even discussing tomorrow."

Agnes had little to add. She knew precisely the feelings Holly was alluding to.

"I don't have any friends any more," said Holly. "Except you, of course."

Agnes had always burned through friendships. The pandemic had helped make that easier. Time kept slipping away. Friends she'd held to, or thought still cared about her, had moved, had married, had lost interest in a woman who appeared to be content to do nothing with her life other than to take pictures. It had been different with Holly, who preferred her isolation and let everyone know it. Months might pass and they wouldn't communicate. Holly would never say she missed Agnes after long absences. They'd pick up where they left off as if it had only been a few days.

"We go back, don't we," said Agnes.

"We do," said Holly. "I miss it sometimes."

During Holly's first summer as a new grad, after a trip to Cozumel, she'd worked as a box office manager at a summer stock theatre in Dennis, on Cape Cod. Agnes had gone to see plays there, contacting Holly in advance, asking if she could visit backstage after the show. Yes, of course, she could. "Of course, of course, anytime, please come see me," she'd said.

They'd kept in touch. Holly had welcomed Agnes with open arms. During her first visit, Agnes had ended up staying the night, sleeping with Holly, overwhelmed by the sudden intimacy they shared in all of its intensity. That summer developed into episodes of play-going, beach-combing, swimming, partying and sex.

Agnes still viewed that summer as a turning point in her life. She came out. Men were okay, but so were women. She was different. She'd never be like the others. She shot photo after photo of the actors performing on stage. Holly liked them and secured Agnes a position as the theatre's new on-site publicity photographer, essentially creating the position.

Agnes rented one room, sharing an apartment with a costume designer, a precocious black queen named Tye who kept her in stitches. She photographed the actors before shows, in costume and posed, and then had the photos printed and enlarged before posting the best ones either in front of the theatre or inside the lobby.

She hadn't known at the time and learned only years later, much to her disappointment, that the money for her position had come from Holly's father who'd gifted the theatre a contribution large enough to allow Agnes to rent her room and stay all summer. Holly had also taken measures to ensure this funding source remained confidential. One of the reasons for her success, and her job security in a less than stable profession, was the reputation she'd developed as one who could procure funding.

When Agnes had learned of this, she'd felt betrayed. She'd wanted to get ahead on her own merit. Not on the charity of Holly's rich father. The issue had turned into a point of contention between them, leading to a drunken argument and invectives which had so infuriated Agnes that it was two years before they began speaking to each other again.

What had mended their friendship was Agnes making the effort to explain to Holly that all she expected of her was that she be honest. Holly, who hadn't been nearly as injured by their falling out, had invited her over to stay a while. She'd talked about how secrets were her specialty. She'd insisted Agnes be less demanding of others, and more grateful to be given any opportunities to practice her art.

What Agnes had learned from Holly, who had forgiven her, was how to lower her standards. How to be more fatalistic and detached in her outlook. She'd never forget Holly telling her, "Make me come to you. I like the hunt. If it's too easy, I get bored fast."

After their reunion, rather than viewing herself as occupying a vaunted position, Agnes began to comprehend her role in Holly's life. She was merely one more suitor in a mix between men and women. Holly's whimsical romantic arrangements were calculated and maintained through her evolved sense of guile. When Holly drove her hooks into Derek, she was the one who introduced him to Agnes.

"We're in this together," Holly had said. "Just play along to get along. Derek might be loyal to you, and he'll provide what you need, but I probably won't."

"And what if I don't play along?" had been Agnes's question. "What if I don't agree with what he does to get his money?"

With a shrug, nonchalant, looking a bit annoyed, Holly had said. "First, don't look a gift horse in the mouth. Second, it hurts too much to fight all time. And third, if you do fight it, you'll lose one of us. Maybe both of us."

"Is that how you love me? By contract?"

Again, a nonchalant shrug. "I'm afraid so. You see, Agnes, Derek and I couldn't be more different. On the surface. But we think alike. Now, if we had a kid together, that would all change. No more triangle."

"And if you don't? Have a kid, I mean, then it would stay the same?"

One nod from Holly. *Why had she stayed with him?* Because, as she'd told Agnes, she loved them both. "That's *my* problem," she'd said. "Not yours."

Agnes struggled to admit it, but when she looked back she saw herself as the wounded soul she'd been that both Derek and Holly had needed to rescue and raise up. She'd been their child, the one they'd pitied, supported and had worked so hard for. This was the truth and it disgusted her.

What Agnes envied about Holly was that she no longer had big plans. She'd ceased all discussions about starting her own business. There'd been times when she'd dallied with maybe creating a new line of make-up, or perhaps an agency of some kind to help budding artists. All that was out the window.

Though she still said she loved to travel, Holly had stopped during the pandemic. Nor did she appear to miss it. Agnes believed Holly's deflation and surrender, if it could be named that, was due to her father dying suddenly of a heart attack. He'd come home one evening to his summer place in Westerly, sat in his favorite chair and just dropped to the floor. He'd been dead by the time his wife found him.

There was money for Holly, and property, though most of it was in her mother's name and wouldn't become Holly's until her mother died. With her father's death, a spark had fizzled inside Holly. She'd lost her confidence and snarky tone of entitlement. She'd retreated and started to allow herself to age. She no longer dyed her hair to shine raven black, looking a bit like Cher. Streaks of silver shone through, and there were crow's feet visible now around her eyes. Not a rapid aging. A distinguished one. She remained stunningly elegant and graceful despite a gradual show of withering.

She probably shouldn't have married Derek, but she'd wanted a child. Derek had been kind and wanted a child, as well. Well, she should leave Derek. She had to admit it was selfish the way she was using him. Their apartment, her photographs – all due to his earnings. She was betraying herself by hanging on, and she wasn't even sure she wanted Holly any longer. Not to share her, not with Derek. It was what Holly wanted, though and, knowing her, what she'd get. Holly always got what she wanted.

It had all changed when she'd met her "long, tall Texan" as she liked to call me. She felt a frisson of lust whenever we two were alone and could speak about our feelings. Could she risk dumping Derek? Could she even ask Holly what she thought about the idea? A layer of ice had begun to cover her, thin, omnipresent, without which she couldn't appear in public without giving away the complex jumble of feelings that was eating at her.

What did I offer Agnes? One thing. A hunger to be accepted. This was my appeal. I came with so few conditions. I was there, waiting eagerly in the wings. What Agnes felt for me she found difficult to express. She respected me, but could she love me? I never brought this up in conversation, though it was a question that plagued us both.

Agnes, you see, had learned the hard way one rule to live by. Whatever she wanted wouldn't just happen. She had to cultivate it. What she wanted more than anything was not a long, tall Texan. Not Derek. Not Holly either. She wanted absolute mastery as a photographer. Approbation less so than respect from her peers. Nothing less would do.

She could hear her father as he spoke from the grave. *Becoming who you are, Sweetie, takes time. What you're trying to achieve is difficult because you're already good, but so are many others.*

Was she good? What had her father even meant by that? She'd asked this to me.

"You're a born artist," I told her. "When you're younger, it's cool. You think you're a trendsetter. But now, don't you see?"

"It's a curse?"

My smile was sardonic. "You'll never be happy, Agnes. It's just who you are."

I then took her arm and tucked it under my own.

"So don't even try?"

"No, try. There's nothing to lose. But be realistic about it."

We walked on together to a wine shop. It was one I liked to frequent mid-town that featured excellent reds. I was in a red mood that night, so I bought a Malbec from Argentina.

Agnes was in a red mood. This is what she said to Holly as they sat in those Adirondack chairs. The sun had set now over the balcony, and there was a slight chill, but nothing a sweater couldn't cure. Holly said she had a nice bottle. A Zinfandel from Sonoma. This was fine with

Agnes. Could they order a pizza too, just a cheap plain one and have it delivered? Of course they could, said Holly, calling it perfectly divine as a choice in all its simplicity.

ELEVEN

I jump around in time, shape-shifting, assembling or gathering pieces, completing jigsaw puzzles in the floating world. Contrary to this, when adrift yet earthbound in the lost world, I was seldom able to complete a single puzzle with ease. Now, I laugh because they're a cinch. I remember I got so jealous one time of Holly that I phoned her out of the blue under the pretext of talking about a position for her in a future project. I knew she had experience in the theatre and that she was a lovely and intelligent woman. I also knew, having met her on more than one occasion, that she was the type who talked about being interested in producing a film but really wasn't steely or driven enough to do it. What I really wanted was to assess her as a way to examine my competition and my chances when it came to marrying Agnes. I didn't expect that Holly would be on the level with me, but I hoped she'd shed some light on the subject.

Holly was remarkably detached and yet at the same time forthcoming when it came to discussing Agnes and their relationship. I envied this about her. She didn't wear a mask in any sense of that word. Holly *was* the mask. I couldn't trust a word she said.

I knew Agnes admired me. She'd become my friend. She had, quite possibly, more ambitious ideas about how our friendship might develop. As I spoke with Holly I began to see that Agnes was not so much a subject but rather an unsolved riddle between the two of us.

Holly pulled no punches. "I think our dear Agnes," she said, "mostly appears to be craving stability now and a sense of commitment to herself."

"What do *you* crave?" I asked.

"Sex. Good food. Shoes. Expensive clothes. And more sex." She laughed. "But not with you. So don't get any ideas."

"I'm too old, I know."

"Oh, it's not about age, Ennis. Your sights are on Agnes. I've know that for a while."

"It's a narrow window, isn't it?"

"For a woman? Yes, but that's not our fault."

"I'm not saying it is."

"Ennis," she said. "Let me put it this way. I just worry that Agnes will become one more conquest discarded among the plethora of other hopefuls who never made much of their lives even though they let men like you exploit them."

This comment I thought unfair. I wasn't Harvey Weinstein. Never had been. Though I knew the man, and many others like him. It's no secret the world is a filthy place.

"The circus of ambition, it's not pretty. I think Agnes is aware. But you, Holly, what are you going to do?"

"Nothing. Why should I? In a lot of ways, I've never been happier."

I asked if she worried that Agnes wouldn't be happy, as such. That she might want to hazard a slightly more conventional arrangement.

"It depends. Tell me about the arrangement you have," she said. "I need to know more."

"You're the one," I said, "who should be telling me about arrangements. I still find it astonishing that three seemingly normal individuals are living such an experiment."

"It's like this," said Holly. "I pursue a caprice because I prefer to forget how difficult life can be. And Agnes, she's perfected the art of turning all her attention away from herself."

"And Derek, meanwhile, he just goes along?"

"Ennis, honestly, I think if I were a man I'd find such an arrangement quite accommodating. Wouldn't you?"

"I'm too much of a prude. And I'm too busy. And one more thing. I'm still trying to understand what love is. What the word means. I don't see it, geometrically speaking, as a triangle."

"Please don't tell me it's heart-shaped, please."

I chuckled at that one. Holly really was a charmer. "I think it's about giving, isn't it?"

"I believe, Ennis, you've had enough of the movie business. That makes sense since you self-made tycoons like to compensate for any guilt you feel over your wealth by presenting the appearance of generosity toward the poor."

"Spoken like a true Marxist."

"So you think if you understood Agnes better, you might gain needed insights into what makes her tick. I'm here to tell you there's no recipe. You'll never really know. You'll just have to find out what works."

We were getting somewhere. I wasn't, for a moment, regretting any of our time together.

I leaned over the table. "Tell me, Holly, and be honest. Is my enduring and heated curiosity about Agnes a form of proof that I love her? It isn't an absurd question."

After sipping her cocktail and moistening her lips, Holly said, "I don't feel guilty about the money I have. First of all, in a lot of circles, it's not that much. And second, my father, may he rest in peace, worked extremely hard to get it. And since we're cross-examining each other, what I'd like to know is why you don't summon the nerve to move out of Manhattan. I'm sure Derek would appreciate having you out of the picture. And if Agnes really did love you, she'd probably find a way to be closer to you."

"So you're saying I fear just being who I am."

"What are you afraid of? You'd be star material back in Texas. Isn't everyone moving there? This is what I hear, anyway."

Holly was the type who respected strength shown in others, no matter how unseemly. The pause and the silence between us lasted longer than she'd expected. It made her uncomfortable. I think she'd hoped I'd get rattled by her little barbs, but I wasn't. Not at all. I respected strength in others too.

She said, "It works better, our triangle, when I'm not in the same zip code. I think of it as a kind of separation therapy. Furthermore, I like being the only spoiled princess on my street. I've gotten used to it."

"Gives you purchase and identity," I said. "But does it garner any respect, empathy or admiration?"

"As if I care," she said. "Empathy. Spare me. What an overused and misunderstood word. A big part of me needs to be despised. If I want to be emulated by other princesses, I know which rivers and tracks to cross."

"I'm not sure that Agnes does."

"Agnes is not a princess."

"She's not as capable as you are when it comes to connivance."

"You love her," she said. "Admit it."

"I've told you my state of mind concerning love."

"You'd cross the Sahara for her if she'd have you."

"Maybe as a protective figure. In a fatherly way."

"Oh, I doubt that very much my Texas friend."

"So do I. So do I. To be fair."

She laughed and laughed, devilish and smug.

I ordered us another round of cocktails. Dinner was on me, as well, and I wasn't surprised, rather liking it when she ordered the most expensive items on the menu.

TWELVE

It was a weekend night, quite cool after a rain that had passed through as if in a hurry to end. Agnes was in Providence again walking back to Holly's place after making a purchase at Academy Market. She was passing a Thai restaurant, recalling how Holly had commented on the quality of the food when Derek's words returned, broken, shared breathlessly and in a hurry when she'd last seen him. Derek had been running and he'd burst into the apartment in a sweat, panting: "Gonna kill me…Hassan…like they kill everybody…I can see it… need this time… gotta think…maybe ditch Queens…ditch the whole country.…"

That was all he'd said, which was a lot for him when it came to talking about work. He'd hurried into the shower and after drying off slipped into pajamas and fell immediately to sleep. Agnes hadn't bothered to get into bed with him, choosing instead to watch a Bruce Willis movie and pass out in her clothes on the couch. She often slept this way, finding Derek gone when she got up in the morning.

It was all wrong. Going nowhere. Nothing of value would come of it.

The lights of signs and slicks of rain on pavement and the swishing of passing cars presented themselves in cinematic detail. Agnes kept a brown bag of four chicken breasts in one hand. The plan was a return to Holly's place to enjoy dinner. Holly had agreed to cook her Chicken Kiev recipe with lots of butter. Her reason for this was that she wanted to show Agnes some gratitude. A strange word choice, thought Agnes, since she'd done nothing at all unusual for Holly who'd started speaking and behaving so formally of late.

The Thai restaurant was one of those cubbyholes where customers could bring their own liquor. Holly often said she'd always liked the place. Agnes thought it was just okay, knowing Holly had eaten there more than once with Derek, getting drunk on cheap wine and having sex with him all night afterward.

Agnes didn't wanted to think about Derek, or be reminded of him, but she couldn't help doing so in this neighborhood. Both she and Holly had dined with Derek there more than once, especially at an Italian place next to the Thai one. Derek had loved the veal marsala there and, as he'd put it, "Kind of redeems Providence for me. Just a little."

Derek thought everyone in Providence bratty, snot-nosed and ignorant. He often tried to explain this, with no justifications, bemoaning how difficult it was for him to like or accept anything outside of Queens. Holly liked to upbraid Derek for his provincialism, to which Derek would reply, without apology, "I'm like Popeye. I am what I am."

Agnes felt a warm glow that surprised her. She smiled as she remembered nights when the three of them together had enjoyed dinners out. Those had been more hopeful and innocent periods. She'd eaten veal scaloppini during their last visit together, as a trio, to a place called Vinnie's Kitchen, which appeared to no longer exist.

Why would she remember such an insignificant detail? How many times had she ordered veal, her favorite kind of meat, at different places? She remembered, too, there had been a Bolivian restaurant in the neighborhood. Fewer empty storefronts. The *Vitto and Veto* law office which had made Derek laugh out loud when he'd seen it.

Laws. The marriage sacrament. They meant nothing to Holly. What did they mean to Derek? And to her? She doubted that, if asked, she could answer such a question. She might recite some cant as a byproduct of her Catholic upbringing, but she wouldn't speak with conviction or knowledge.

Was it so wrong to *want* change? To *know* who she was in the present time? To *live* in a different way, to break old affiliations and find other goals and rules to follow? Want, know, live. Such a trio of words. She shouldn't be easy on Derek. She believed she had a moral code. She wanted a male husband, an honest man willing to provide support. That husband wasn't Derek. Nor was it Holly. She wasn't the same old Shooter Agnes any longer.

She couldn't stop thinking of me. I never had to say it, but she knew I'd be there for her.

The triangle game. It hissed and spat like a cobra in her face.

Their last conversation. How distant Derek had been, how frazzled. He was up to something and afraid of it. Making plans. She shouldn't be dense. She should be ready for anything. Derek had an expiration date. Granted, he had the nerve to act according to his own set of rules, but that took a person only so far. Like Holly, he was too vain to accept this.

Darkness. So much of it. Domino's Pizza, Dunkin Donuts, Dollar General. Each franchise sign dull and repetitive and fully lit as a way to deny the darkness its reign. To give drivers and neighborhood residents a destination. She disliked them all. She wanted darkness, complete, unyielding, vast.

Agnes approached a local laundromat. A yellow wash of light

emanated from the pearls of steam occluding its front window. No sign out front. Like a warm buttery spot along an otherwise chilly wet worm of a street. There was a travel agency, too, closed for the night. A package shipping service, large fliers in Spanish *tarjeta aqui* filling its window. Agnes saw that "ship" was spelled in English with a *c* to read: *pack and chip*. This made her smile and that's what she was doing when a Latino teenager in a hooded sweatshirt crossed her path and blocked her way.

At first, she didn't fear him. She tried to pass, but he wouldn't let her. Fists in the pockets of his baggy sweatshirt, he glared at her from under his raised hood. He wore a skinny mustache. His dark eyes shined.

Growing alert, conscious of her breathing, Agnes started to worry. Not that much traffic now. Her return to Holly's apartment would require walking quite a few more blocks. What was this *muchacho* planning to do? Why was he blocking her way? Agnes understood she had no idea of what she was up against, so she wouldn't dare take the boy lightly. She remembered what Derek had once told her. "Never show your fear."

Perhaps her *muchacho* was afraid of what he was capable of and unwilling to admit it. The male side of Agnes, that boy who was a part of her whole self, had been that way at his age too. Agnes had a method, though, of coping with confused aggressive impulses. It was to act out violently. Maybe now she'd benefit, get some payback for all those fights she'd never started with those ridiculous *other* girls in school, so few she'd ever liked.

Maybe, as Derek would say, she'd get a shiv stabbed into her *Anglo* butt. Or else this boy would make her sweat and then he'd kick her teeth in. Or else he'd just run. He was just a boy, after all.

Agnes saw in him that he wanted her to be afraid, to get prickly, lose her cool, fire off a racist expletive. Anything to provide motive. Then again, no, maybe not. He was just a child. Angry, puzzled, unwilling to admit he was afraid.

Within the silent moment there was an expansion, one Agnes believed she and the boy were witnessing together. It was as if they'd begun realizing at the same time that the moment was rife with potential violence, a confrontation, yes, truly, this was a *thing* now.

It would become a larger moment, day by day, into the future, supporting a comprehension that she had strength enough to kill another human in self-defense if need be. She wasn't sure she liked knowing this about herself, that her anger, from a deep reservoir within, could be tapped at will and put to use. Was this valuable knowledge? She couldn't say.

She began to resent that the boy no doubt hated her dyed purple hair and her pale blue eyes. She had to remember that in such a neighborhood it was seen by some as a crime to have fair skin and too many presumed advantages. Could she pull her phone out in time to call Holly or the police? Why did Holly insist on living in such a neighborhood? Did she experience such encounters? Probably not. Holly knew how to avoid these kinds of interactions. If she did see them, she ignored them or pretended they didn't happen. Holly was an expert in defining her life as whatever fib she felt convinced it was.

Maybe some misguided force in this boy hated women. There was a time Agnes might have lashed out to damage him, but not now. She was no stupid girl, she was a woman, had lived some, could handle this. She felt no need to be offended by the daggers in the boy's eyes.

If he pulled out a weapon, she'd be ready. She'd run. If he demanded her money and her camera and her chicken breasts (God, how silly), he could have them. It had to be the camera, she thought, that had brought on this macho posturing. She should have hidden it better.

With her eyes lowered, Agnes didn't pity the boy's wolfish assertiveness. In such a neighborhood it was common to use the threat of violence to rob from the landscape in compensation for whatever squalor one had been brave enough to endure or escape from. If this boy wanted to embrace his identity as a thug, that was his choice and he'd need to live with its consequences. If he thought her a gringo *putana* then fine, let him. He could die in prison as a thug. Like she cared what he thought of her. His animus was driven by semen wanting to burst free, ridding his glands briefly of a machismo-inspired attitude toward fear, along with hatred and resentment of the Other, the Oppressor, the Anglo *Puta* with a camera.

Dear God I ask you please tell me, are you a dim-wit? Look at the two of us, God. Is this the best you can create in mankind?

Perhaps her *muchacho* believed his version of street-thug culture was taking over the world. Maybe his belief was accurate. Maybe God really was a dim-wit. What Agnes knew, and what the boy didn't, not yet anyway, was that he couldn't rob her of anything. He might overpower, injure or rape her, but he wouldn't win. He'd only strengthen her disdain for the human race. In knowing this, Agnes derived resolve. She heard herself breathing. She could handle this boy. She wouldn't show fear.

About sixty seconds passed, heavily so, the two of them locked into a face-off. Agnes had to stay sanguine, become a sort of murderer, though she didn't want to. She had no choice. Did this boy feel the same way? Could she communicate with him? The answer was no and it lay in understanding Thanatos. A concept. Another cerebral idealistic notion. The dictation of full expression of one's true self, which meant if Agnes was honest with herself, she should murder the boy first and ask questions later.

Thanatos. She'd been reading about this. Little had she imagined that it would help her in such a moment. Thanatos, to move away from Freud was better understood in words from Derek who'd once tutored her, saying, "If you can't run, then ambush the motherfucker before he ambushes you."

Run as fast as possible and don't look back. Why? Because she couldn't murder anybody other than herself. Nor could she find any words. It was because she didn't want to. This made her a thug, too, didn't it?

How on earth did I get myself into this situation? What would Derek do? He'd run. For one, he wouldn't stop walking. He'd just keep going. Derek was big enough to bowl the boy over, taking him by surprise. He'd move so quickly that the boy would struggle to keep pace.

What should I do? The stare-down continued. Agnes began to feel drained as a stabbing ache increased its pounding in her ribs. Face flushed, a warmth spread with the heightened speed of her pulse, but she remained stone-faced, prepared to run, to fight, to die.

Beat it, you idiot! Why are you standing still?

She stood because she believed in her stoicism. In an almighty nothingness, and it would work on this boy. She'd win this battle by her own strategy, by applying her own rules.

Agnes couldn't say she knew when it was almost over, but she sensed it. She studied the boy in his baggy hooded sweatshirt and sweatpants with stripes running down their sides. A kind of typical thug uniform, his face in shadow under his pointed hood. Once upon a time a designer on Madison Ave or in a Hollywood ad agency had shown this gangster-in-training look to a boardroom of investors.

Such ads would for decades teach criminals and adolescent males how to dress.

It struck her as absurd and tragic that there was nothing original or inspired about his presence; he was just one more boy for her to pity and endure while trying to keep any shows of defensiveness out of her eyes or posture. As this boy got older, he'd get more and more tattoos. He might harm more and more women. As if any of that meant anything, though of course it did. It meant everything.

Her stoicism, held so steadily, appeared to make the boy uneasy. This was not what he'd expected. He was dangerous because of his misreading of these expectations. Agnes believed she understood him now. The boy was weak; he smelled like one unproven, a follower, though the weakest in any pack were the ones to fear the most.

"Hey, how you doing?" Agnes had said this in her best roughest street accent, bluntly so, as if she owned the street and the boy. As if she were channeling Derek, a master at whipping up lingo. "What's up?"

She made bold eye contact, searing into his dark pupils where she sought and found the corrupted, contemptible and confused gearworks of his soul. She held her stare, let it sear in.

She heard words percolate through her: *Let the kid be, let him flow in the rivers of purgatory.*

She would be perceived the racist in this, the killer and victim at the same time. Honkey that she was, raised in Barrington of all places. His discomfort and anger were *her* fault. That's just how messed up the system was.

Naturally, she found such a presumption ridiculous and impossible to accept, but she lived with it, as all women did, no matter their race, each in peril from one day to the next. Anyone could fling labels or aspersions or identities, but to live side by side with the malcontented and ignorant meant one had to labor to empathize and understand. Nothing she learned in school would serve to help. Here, the only teacher of value was experience.

Hate, she thought, feeling a twinge of sadness, is what these boys have been sold. Advertised as the power to make them exemplary. Be the hate, personify and redefine it. Drive the wedge that drives us all apart. It was a profitable hatred in some quarters but not worth her paying attention to, even though it was sold around the clock and so easy to find. Nobody got rich selling the fashion statement that most people simply wanted to get along.

Society, culture, identity – these were just vague associations. A drag. All she'd wanted was to buy chicken breasts and maybe snap a few pictures.

Finally, she saw the boy slump, back down and move on. She'd done nothing and in that she'd done something right and it had worked. Maybe because she'd said nothing of consequence. She didn't know, she never would, but she might trust herself more in future situations, knowing that she could find the patience and inner resources again.

Agnes felt her whole body sag, weary now, heavy, sick of so many scenarios still playing out in her head. *Girl, you don't fight it, you rule the temple within.* She shuddered and then she tucked her chicken breasts tighter under her arm and she ran, hurrying back to Holly's place.

So much of anything, all of it bad, could have happened. She got it, she always thought she'd gotten it, but not really. She'd never tasted it so intimately and in dinky Providence, not Queens. Ironic, wasn't it, but now she could abide by a certain knowledge about herself. Its taste on her tongue, its smell from her pores, tensions stating she must live by her own codes. When necessary, she'd make them up as she went along.

How naïve she'd been. When she arrived to Holly's front door and began to unlock it, she saw this clearly and felt another shudder, a kind of aftershock that reminded her that so many horrible things could have happened. But they hadn't. She'd take this as more than a lesson. It was a gift. She wouldn't even discuss it with Holly. She'd keep it to herself, and she'd see when she looked in the mirror that she was tougher, a little more tested.

From now on, behind her eyes, there would be more than a camera. There'd be mace and possibly a gun. She could get one. If it meant her safety, legal or not, Derek would approve of it. There'd be a force, too, and she wouldn't know its name. She'd know how it felt and where to find it. She'd trust it to be there when called on.

⁂

In spite of her disdain for men who drank to excess, Agnes, seizing the light, began to photograph a dive bar. She chose it as a subject because she could see that gentrification, franchise sprawl and demographic shifts had already conspired to erase the neighborhood as she remembered it.

Such a dive stood little chance of surviving. She had talked about this to Holly who, slightly amused and at times condescending, confessed to no interest in such places whatsoever.

Agnes had even told her that one day she might just wander in. Holly could be flighty and impractical, but she knew Agnes cold. Such a flirtation with danger would never happen. Agnes smiled with the memory of their conversation.

Holly had said, "You can say what you want, but I think you take photos because you need to prove to yourself that love isn't real. It's an impossible delusion."

Agnes had argued that love existed in everything, and where it didn't, it should be created. Photos could be a form of love. Memories, too. Together, they reminded her of another old song, one by Jim Croce that her mother liked.

She shouldn't exhaust herself with such thoughts. Better to remember her purpose for coming to this neighborhood.

As she recalled the boy she'd had her stand-off with, she tried to look street-level mean, not to be messed with as she took her pictures of the bar. Strange and unnerving how in Manhattan she'd seldom felt a need to do this, but here she felt she must.

Tiring quickly of the bar, she walked on to Grasso's Auto Sales, which intrigued. Not the exterior, but as an inner-city car dealership that still featured an indoor showroom. Closed for the time being, she leaned gently toward plate glass and peered in to marvel at a silver Jaguar inside under a low ceiling. She felt a touch of daring from the glitzy allure of that Jag, her car of choice to drive off a cliff with Holly like Thelma and Louise in that movie, both of them buckled in and screaming toward infinity.

She shot the Jag just two times with her digital camera, knowing that through glass her images would lack adequate clarity. Maybe she'd clean them up in Photoshop.

She then moved on to Chalkstone Supermarket and remembered that this block used to look quite different and that it had once been called Academy Market and it was in business across the street from the Castle Cinema. Oh, the Castle again. Talk about love. Talk about vanished. Talk about misery. Holly had really admired her then, following her around enchanted by the way she worked. What happened to *that* Holly? What had happened to enchantment?

The street had not only changed, but what remained still felt temporary, on the brink of extermination. Agnes wondered if any of these new businesses were family-owned. Most likely, some wouldn't survive in the wake of the pandemic. Everything felt so doomed.

The memory of a night came back to her from years ago when she and Holly were walking this avenue arm in arm, openly displaying their affection for each other. This was when such a display was still a tiny bit risky for gay lovers in such a neighborhood.

This was a fond memory from their earlier and some of their best times together. She hadn't met Derek yet or moved to New York, but she was working and saving. Her rent was cheap, her needs simple and she was still spry enough to sleep drunk on a couch at a party and pop up the next morning to go to work without a hangover or a sore back. She was always broke then, too, or so it seemed, Holly often helping her to meet expenses.

Like the Castle Cinema, Tracks Raw Bar, The Clover Deli and others, those days had vanished. There blew new winds over the sterile plains within her now, a landscape potent with a sense of gloom. It wasn't easy to feel happy. What had happened? Saucy, quick with a joke, proud to make others laugh, she used to cherish being alive. Holly had really liked that about her, but that was back then, as if another life, when just to walk with Holly was like elevating herself.

If she had any reasonable concept of what was going on, it meant she didn't understand anything. She felt no motivation to share her doubts, suspecting, like many, that she was being lied to. This was the brave new world she'd once read about it high school. It had been used as a blueprint. She and her friends would go to their graves knowing they were cloaked in lies. Everyone would.

Holly had been right on one issue. They were all complicit. They'd let it happen. Some had raged against cops and racism, but they'd done nothing about the larger manipulations regarding vaccines and mandates and a re-writing of history. There was nothing dystopian or accidental about it. The mask, as symbol, said it all. Hide your face. Hide your questions.

Still, Agnes believed it right to understand that this was the time to clam up, cowed by the narrative as the wrath of a vengeful god. To think for herself, to reject the narrative down deep where it counted, wasn't what any government operative wanted.

She'd rejected it all silently. She'd keep rejecting until her death. What she used to hope for, and what she saw now was unlikely to come, was a time, an era, one day when it would be celebrated to act toward one's more constructive choices, to build up communities not to break them down. To improve and unify, not to isolate and desecrate through the cuts and scars of the new identity-prioritized religion.

Better perhaps that she hadn't given birth, after all. Better that she remain an empty vessel. Why bring a child into the realities of this era? Not a time of reasoned discourse and forward-thinking ideas, but a time to die inside, smoldering, silenced by snarling mobs and corporate cancel culture. Keep the mask on. Answer only with your eyes.

If she could just capture in one photograph all the suffering the pandemic represented.

The comfort and horrors of a separate reality. A different drug of choice, the cyber-version of existence, a Kabuki theatre which didn't allow for intense examinations of the complex threads of what might be seen as a real version. For centuries, pernicious actors had peddled agendas and objectives, trafficking in lies. She wanted no part of them. Wouldn't it be nice to move to Alaska, drop out, homestead, commune with seals, polar bears and migrating salmon.

She had to sound a laugh. A big one from deep in her belly. Such a life would ruin her. She'd spend all her time with a chainsaw and an axe and she'd still end up frozen to death like hapless Christopher McCandless from *Into The Wild*, both her hands clutching a camera, the meat on her bones picked clean by wolves.

Agnes put on her mask and stepped inside the Chalkstone Supermarket to pick up a few grocery items. With only one register, the wait in line was unbearably slow. She lingered behind an elderly woman who was wearing two masks, double the protection apparently, while buying a single roll of toilet paper.

The woman looked lost as she counted pennies from her change purse, her fingers trembling. She didn't have enough. When had people gotten so poor in America? Agnes got her attention and gave her some of her loose change, which shocked the old woman and the middle-aged clerk, as well. At least, thought Agnes, we will both exit this establishment on a happy note.

One should never underestimate the value of adding a little joy to another's day. If God was alive, thought Agnes, this would happen all the time. Yet it didn't. So maybe God wasn't alive. Maybe God was on holiday due to the pandemic.

The old woman left, thanking Agnes, and now it was her turn. Agnes felt a tad entitled because she'd displayed such an act of generosity. Yet just as she was about to make her purchase, there appeared a matronly brunette in a panic, not wearing a mask, pushing a baby stroller, a pair of toddlers at her feet. Neither toddler wore a mask and they pulled on their mother's arms and ranted and shouted in Spanish while the mother burst into a chat in Spanish to the clerk. Every word in Spanish, a voluptuous language, one Agnes had studied along with

French in high school and she was glad that she did, though her French was better.

Agnes understood a few words of what this poor frenzied mother was saying. She was begging for help. She spoke urgently, using idioms and slang, her voice pitched as if she was about to burst into flames if she didn't get her groceries back to her apartment to feed her starving toddlers.

The infant in the stroller started to bawl, her shrieks piercing the air. The toddlers, one a boy, the other female, faced the stroller and did their best to comfort the infant. Meanwhile their young mother showed the clerk a fistful of government-issued WIC coupons. The clerk, unsure at first, decided to abandon her cash register, leaving Agnes waiting. The clerk didn't even acknowledge Agnes as she hurried off into the short narrow aisles to help the woman navigate items from the shelves, collecting six cans of Enfamil, a stack of diapers, three boxes of cereal, small jars of baby food, packets of cookies, a loaf of bread, a jar of jam, and two boxes of muffin mix. No fruit, no vegetables, no meat.

This new Land of The Free, thought Agnes, where the poorest still arrived thinking their lives would change and improve. Maybe they did. She doubted it. Then again, maybe such mothers made out all right. Maybe their children lived better than they had. Maybe God and the Virgin Mary were still alive in their souls, helping them along the way. Agnes liked to think so. She had to. Otherwise, it was impossible to accept reality. Besides, she still wanted to believe in the American Dream, in spite of all the doubts she harbored. Holly, for one, dismissed her as inane for even thinking such a dream still existed, or that a belief in God granted freedom, and that Jesus and the Virgin Mary stood for grace and forgiveness.

How could this poor undereducated woman raise three children? Why not six? Why not twelve? The government, after all, was feeding them, paying for their diapers. No doubt that in her native country, a big family was a sign of wealth. No doubt that the woman's various priests had told her to accept male seed, to reproduce, no matter what the cost or whether the father chose to stick around once he'd performed his insemination.

To think, by comparison, she and Derek had been doing okay. All thanks to drug addiction. Pernicious Heroin, Cocaine, Meth, Fentanyl. Criminal exchanges of laundered cash. They had saved and prospered thanks to Derek's nightly illegal activities. This said everything to her about how wrong life was. *Her* life.

Before the miscarriage, Derek had even been talking about moving to the Jersey shore, slowing life down and raising their baby in a secure neighborhood with decent schools. All a lie. To think, all of that had died. They could have afforded to make it happen, and here was this raw-boned undereducated hard-working woman, uncomfortable speaking English, no money, probably no husband, maybe got through fourth grade back in her native land, a place she fled from when young and fertile, just a girl. Now, too old too soon, too burdened, no ring on her finger to prove she was married, nothing but debt, hunger and a nagging want in her children's eyes, and exhaustion in her own.

What a mess people make of their lives. Easier to profit by cheating, robbing and breaking the law. How hopeless some are, born into nothing and destined, at best, to secure a table and bread one grueling day at a time while totally in need of the government's help. A government in all nations that has perfected the art of thievery. Always far from home, disoriented, outside of anything that smacked of comfort. Children of God, each and every one of them, to be loved but not to be pitied.

Pity was what Derek had used to lure her in. Nobody was to be pitied. Nor could Agnes be angry with this woman who was likely following what priests or parents had told her, living a mission to get nearer to God by birthing more Catholics, to raise her *niñas* and *niños* on chemically-enhanced lactose out of tin cans. Not to raise them up and out of poverty, but to keep them one bite shy of absolute hunger and malnourishment.

For this woman, there was no shame in being on the dole. The State, the church, the neighborhood would save her. It wasn't a far-flung idea. It was an expectation she'd brought with her. Assimilation, well, that was for her children, if they wanted it.

What did it even mean any longer to live in a country? To be a nation or show national pride? It meant nothing. Did Agnes believe any of her overwrought thoughts as she waited there losing patience? She didn't know. Some days, frankly, she suffered through wild-haired reactionary ideas. She vacillated. Growing up as a so-called child of privilege, she'd heard all the jingoistic talk, the blather about evil, but would any politician anywhere even consider standing in line in such a little bodega? Never, not on their lives.

Narratives, these politicians approved and designed them to enflame and bifurcate and confuse. Like anyone who'd grown up in the States, Agnes had learned to live with and to resist them. She'd taken one action already. She'd helped an old woman buy toilet paper. How could she help this struggling mother? Should she? Would an act of charity be seen as condescension?

A tricky slope, she thought, between absolute strangers.

She watched the clerk and the mother pile up the groceries on the counter. Perhaps the problem was that government – whatever that was or meant – pretended not to really see this happening. Government planned it and knew it and wanted it. The whole point of getting rich and powerful, after all, was to secure insulation from discomfiting realities. The same insulation Holly enjoyed and, at times, took for granted.

Agnes couldn't endure thinking about Holly living in such a neighborhood. Nor could she continue thinking about government and immigration and the constant guilt she was supposed to feel. Why guilt? Because she was born white to a father who'd been born into money and had earned lots more of it while still alive? Yes, that was the narrative, a lie she was supposed to hate herself over.

No guilt. None at all. She decided to imagine Derek on those nights before the miscarriage when they were more physical and intimate. Derek arguing that she romanticized the experience of motherhood and didn't like accepting she would need to get used to loneliness as an essential part of becoming an adult. Agnes had showed no interest in rearing children for the longest time, but she had probably been lying to herself. This, perhaps, was why she'd had the miscarriage. Some would say God's work, but Agnes knew it was her own. She had willed herself into that miscarriage. She'd never really wanted to give birth.

Still, no guilt. It had happened. It had never been destined.

Here was this little boy. This cute little girl. They looked sad and hungry. Agnes smiled at them. The boy sneered and ignored her, still tugging on his mother's arm. The girl saw her, didn't sneer, but she didn't smile back. If anything, she looked afraid of this *gringa* stranger.

If Agnes believed in anything, it was an allegiance to helping those who suffered, not just to art but to pathologies, as well, all part of the poetry in human souls. If only she could photograph this woman, capture the frenzied desperation in an act as simple as buying groceries with food stamps. She wouldn't dare, even though she had her camera with her.

No, as much as she wanted, she just wouldn't dare.

It appeared the woman was expressing her gratitude to the clerk. Wait. Were those cigarettes the woman was buying? A carton of them. Were those lottery tickets? Could you buy lottery tickets with food stamps? Something wasn't right here. Something was way off, and if Agnes was translating the woman's Spanish correctly the two of them were relatives of some kind, helping each other out, ignoring whatever rules were applied to possible abuses regarding food stamp purchases.

After putting one big grocery bag in each of her toddler's arms, lecturing them to be careful, the woman got out of there quickly as if she knew a certain amount of larcenous behavior had been practiced. Agnes just looked the other way. She neither said nor assumed any-thing. It seemed right to her that struggling people should steal from the government, taking any chance they could to win lottery pay-outs. Ultimately, this meant stealing from hard-working tax payers, certainly not from comfortable government suits. So, it wasn't right or fair, but neither was all that cash Derek stashed in his hideaway places when he came home each night.

Perhaps the woman knew this. Perhaps she'd run out of the store boiling in shame as she pushed her stroller home. Perhaps not. Perhaps she didn't care and saw her actions as yet another form of risk that was part and parcel of maintaining a difficult life. Perhaps there was, indeed, a father in the picture, and he came home from work in a dif-ficult job, laboring long hours for little pay, wanting the comfort of a cigarette. Agnes hoped this was the case, but she'd never know.

Still, shouldn't morality prevail? Shouldn't shame be felt by that clerk and that poor woman? Maybe not. *God, if you're listening, I pray let her find what she needs to survive.*

As always when she thought about money, Agnes felt her stomach becoming an empty burning pit. Even if she wanted to know, she'd never find out if she'd make a good mother. It was one more cloying ache to endure, much like watching that mother cash in her food stamps for lottery tickets.

That woman, that mother could have been her. The accident of birth and all the fate that it entailed, nothing more, was the only difference between them.

※

It was early. For the time being, Agnes had finished taking photos, mostly of facades, windows and doorways not far from Holly's Smith Hill neighborhood. In digital. Not film. Later on, she'd sit at her laptop and run them through Photoshop, pumping up contrasts, making them less than suggestions of architectural details and more like Rorschach images. Something different and vague with more pretensions toward the post-modern, for a change.

As usual after a fevered trip down memory lane and a hyper tense photo-shoot, she was experiencing an unnerving quake of emptiness inside. She walked, head down, the dirty asphalt lit, visible, but without radiance. A profound feeling of loneliness overwhelmed her.

An urban shooter needed to trust her sense of acuity when it came to definitions, destinations and a purposeful rendering of densities in light. Her mentors and heroes knew this: Berenice Abbot. Edward Hopper. Margaret Bourke-White. Dorothea Lange. Alfred Sticglitz. Gordon Parks. Julia Margaret Cameron. Charles Sheeler. There were many others, their numbers always growing, but this group comprised the core of her A-Team and helped her define her own aesthetic. She'd know nothing about photography without what their work had taught her.

There were so many talented shooters out there. Those of the era, the moment and those out of the past. They taught her something new when she studied their images. Not enough women among them, though, which could be said for all art forms, and that was where she came in. She wanted to lengthen the list of female shooters, make her mark so that one day the establishment snobs would take notice. As much as she loved the work of Vivian Maier, and as much as she followed her example by shooting scads of photos and sticking to her aesthetic, she didn't want to be ignored all her life because she didn't know the right people or how to market herself. If Netflix hadn't made the documentary about Maier available, that obsessive and hermetic woman's 100,000 photographs would likely still be rotting in obscurity.

It made Agnes wonder how many others were out there like Maier, like her, compiling images to no fanfare at all. Which was why, frankly, she had to hold back an urge to vomit whenever she saw photos by Cindy Sherman or William Wegman. She saw the banal appeal, but they were masters of self-promotion, venerated by so many without an aesthetic or decent taste. She thought their work puerile. She also knew this didn't mean anything because nobody cared what she thought, and everybody had an opinion.

Holly liked to remark: "Don't you worry, Babe, your ship will come in."

Could happen, but she had her doubts. She needed a gallery or museum visit, but most of them were still closed and there weren't many in Providence to begin with. She was really missing her Manhattan museums too, and her regular visits to the International Center for Photography. Once again, the Internet would have to suffice. Granted, the virus was still around, a Delta variant but still as real as the body count, though statistical numbers would always be debatable and prone to manipulations. It was so easy to think of the pandemic as a conspiracy to keep everyone indoors where they could be watched through the screens that they were watching. What a disillusioning thought.

She not only missed museums but libraries and live theatre. People needed these distractions. For her, they were always more important than punching a time clock at any soul-killing job. Why? Because she liked learning and needed to feel inspired by the efforts that day by day showed her she'd absorbed intelligence and perspective from others. Allowing herself to be humbled by the brilliance and commitment of others, getting out of her shell, letting her teach herself who she was. Really, what had she learned at school? Pretense, most of it.

If she was a shooter of any value, she'd know she could, from any reasonable distance, capture the seam in a plum on a windowsill from another window across the street where her camera would be fixed on a tripod. No one could teach this. It had to be learned through diligent practice. A shooter needed patience, eyesight and control over her breathing. It was through such practice, not bombastic lectures or reading, that she would hone these skills.

She had to continue to learn, and she had to remain quiet. She might live or die by plans and dreams, but she couldn't disrespect or speak carelessly about them. Like anyone suffering the delusion of becoming an artist, she brimmed full of opinions and she could be narrow-minded, but she found liberation and humility in knowing this about herself. In her opinion, a shooter was more than an observer. She was an articulator of visions, sharing what she knew she couldn't capture. Being popular had nothing to do with it. Popularity, she believed, was about marketing. It was pompousness, mediocrity, and spin. It was appealing to the mass of people who really didn't want art that challenged them.

She'd read much during the pandemic and recently, for the third time, *On Photography*, by Susan Sontag, one of her feminist intellectual heroes. She remembered Sontag writing that "The camera doesn't rape or even possess," describing what a camera did by using words like "presume, intrude, trespass, distort" and "assassinate."

All from a distance, of course, with "some detachment."

How Agnes yearned to regain the feeling of excitement she'd experienced while reading that book for the first time. Maybe this idea of the photo as assassin explained why some Amish, with their insistence on not being photographed, made so much sense.

Crazy Horse, too, who refused to have himself photographed. There was a tribe in the Brazilian Amazon, the Kayapo, who used the phrase *Akaron kaba*, which meant "to take a picture." It also meant "to steal a soul."

Not by accident, and Agnes liked the honesty in that.

Call her twisted, but Agnes agreed with Sontag. The shooter as archivist took observation to the point of theft and murder. She didn't articulate anything new. By using filters and angles, she assassinated, captured and erased all that was natural. The image ultimately conformed to the shooter's equipment, technique and eye. Not the other way around, though Agnes wished selfishly this were so.

There lived only one certainty in a photograph: that it was a lie. So, the shooter must watch and breathe with stealth while waiting. Always waiting. Ready to kindle the lie. Once the shot was taken, all innocence was eclipsed. The lie had been made whole.

If Agnes could say anything to future shooters, it would be to make no wish for any soulfulness, healthy enthusiasm, vivid energy or promises of resurrection in their images. It was quality of light and degrees of angles and, mostly, dumb luck. It was time framed, composed,

unnatural, post-post-modern and post-audience and all the preten-
tiousness that accompanied such labels.

A shooter must destroy within herself all notions of miraculous
advances in talent or technique, or some form of suddenly redemp-
tive and cathartic style. Agnes told herself repeatedly that there was
no glory in knowing she might die by suffocating due to fumes while
inside a toilet stall shooting close-ups of the turds or the graffiti there.

She waited. She hoped for nothing. Pleasure, then, lived in her
active hungers. If not for what she couldn't have, namely a perfectly
realized ideal photo – because there was no such animal – then to
ignite that twitch of a nerve in her spine that helped restore her confidence in herself and the way she was playing the game, seeking what
couldn't be had. Any restorations of confidence were welcomed, even
if they lasted briefly.

She believed she was ready to go back to Manhattan. She wasn't
sure the city wanted her back. She was never sure of this, but she felt
glad and fortunate to have spent so much time with Holly. Now, she
needed to get back to reality. If Derek didn't want her, let him say it. Let
them split up and get on with their lives.

To be grounded again, to at least feel confident in her delusions,
was what Agnes now craved. The ugliness that defined so much of
Derek's universe would be hers again. Being there, not hating herself was like the five stages of grief that came with any death. She was
moving from one into the next but without an agenda, time limits or
expectations of victory.

She couldn't conceive. It was not a disappointment. It was a fact.
She'd been in denial about this, overcome by guilt and grief, but in all
its basic truth it was there. She was flawed; she had not acted wrongly.
She was no longer naïve about this. It just wasn't meant to be. Time now

to accept and move on, get back to herself again, on her own, without Holly's whimsically decadent displays of self-serving disinterest.

Her idea of birth, the one that thrilled, was capturing a crystalline raindrop dripping from a sunflower, or a green spiral of light worming down the edges of that sunflower's spine. To be and to do good, to heal, to inspire with her photos, to encourage the best from others – this is what she would live for.

She'd used her time well with Holly. None of their arguments and discussions had been painful, though a few had been exhausting. The arguments she had with herself were still there, hadn't gone away, and they'd remain.

If she loved another person, she did so for the same reason she shot an image, because to capture another also meant to enslave them even while finding one's own freedom. She liked her more mature comprehension of this idea. It empowered and vitalized her spirit.

Why should love be about chiffon and candy hearts? Love, like photography, could be assassination. It could be both taking and giving, and nuanced control of one's self.

THIRTEEN

Agnes moved like a small lambent wave under moonlight that never broke twice the same way on the same beach. She moved like a lozenge of sun going down over the skyline of an empire's capital, fingering rooms with a blushing scarlet. Derek on top of her supported his weight with arms like marble columns. He seethed and thrust his hips forward and the two of them fused, their bodies oars slowing to sound creaks in their locks, allowing Agnes to remember that coitus with anyone was never the same each time, though it might suggest a reek of the familiar.

She didn't know if she'd ever felt quite like this before. Maybe she had. She ravished the moment and how supple Derek's body felt. She gripped his upper arms, squeezing them. How fully there he was with her all the way and in the moment. Bliss, heavenly bliss, and when Derek released, giving out spent on top of her, there came a slight crackling sound and Agnes feared she'd injured her spine. Derek had heard it, as well, and he asked if she was okay. She said she was fine and she meant it. What they'd shared had been a proper little tussle into oblivion.

Derek rolled away, but not too far, draping one hairy leg over both of hers while laying one arm across dewy splotches of perspiration that had formed on her stomach. So muscular he was, so brutish, especially after Holly.

He rested his head against her breast. She began envisioning them as if an eye was there in the room watching and recording them. She was a turquoise pool shaped like a teardrop and he an arid twisted length of Mastodon bone taken from a Dali mural.

Sweetly fatiguing, whatever it may be, so just keep feeling it, thought Agnes. She heard a purling stream. Intense movement brought a profundity to the restful time they were poaching in. She could hear the musical components of their two bodies eliding, that crude phrase "getting it on" annoying her. She felt neither ashamed nor contrite. She had put herself where she wanted and it had felt as if she belonged there.

Finding herself willing, capable, serene, Agnes imagined herself opening a door, frozen a moment on its threshold, flooded by light. As she stepped into that light, she paused, looking back, and then made sure to wipe away her fingerprints from the door handle. This was her secret passage. No one else would know of it.

Of all her images already shot and developed, which one would she choose as the one that spoke best for and shared the experience of making love? It was too easy to imagine the smile of contentment on her face that bloomed afterwards. Yet in all its simplicity it was an appropriate image. She felt so happy to lie there, melting, tingling within. Not all images should confuse. Some should be grasped, without question, at first glance. Ah bliss, heavenly bliss.

⁓⟐⁓

Derek in white crew socks, a blue pocket T-shirt and sweatpants lay sprawled all over the sofa in their living room, the television on, its sound off, images flashing, none of which he viewed though he kept the set on just the same. He was bushed, but he didn't want darkness. It was too early to sleep. Besides, Shooter had gone out for groceries. Wanted to cook. She'd seen he'd lost weight without her around to remind him to eat. She'd lost weight too. The time with Holly had done her some good.

Derek closed his eyes and sleep came fast, submerging him into a dream that he was listening to Ma sipping juice through a straw. Ma in a hospital bed and he standing over her, ever so solemn, thinking that she should die, end all this, because he knew that she didn't want to see either one of them suffer any longer. In the dream, Shooter was the nurse and how gently she held the straw to Ma's lips. He marveled at Shooter, this nurse, but he didn't know her.

How long the dream? How long had he slept? Judging by the television and what he saw of the broadcast, it had only been a few minutes. It felt much longer. Like hours.

She was a comely and yet strict black woman whose name Derek had never learned. She'd been his mother's nurse during her time of recovery from the TIA. All the nurses and therapists who had helped Ma amazed him. He never knew what to say to them. He admired them so much, the way they gave fully of themselves without showing any doubts they might be doing battle with inside. That took real nerve.

Derek remembered how Ma would close her eyes and try to suck residual sweetness through the straw from her juice, a disguised medical concoction. Meanwhile, Derek had sipped vending machine coffee from a paper cup, careful not to burn his tongue. He'd nibbled stale cookies also bought from the vending machine. He remembered how Ma's teeth were like pearls. Her mind wasn't clear, but her teeth were lovely.

So manic and inconsistent her energy levels had been. He'd often feared she no longer knew who he was. There'd been many times when he'd started speaking to her as if rousing her from sleep. *It's me, Ma. Derek. Remember?*

She'd just gawked at him, looking bewildered, a filament of drool running down from one corner of her mouth. *Ma, I'm here for you.*

He'd reach over to wipe away the spittle, but she'd swat at his hand, scowling at him.

Not a dream. It all happened. Seemed a long time in the past. Yet it seemed liked yesterday.

Let it go. Try to get some rest.

He thought about how Ma had never really *disliked* the women he'd dated. She'd never really *liked* or been impressed by any of them either. He thought the compatibility Ma shared with Shooter was the result of Shooter treating Ma with full-on respect. Shooter never took on airs. She talked up to Ma, not down. Maybe they shouldn't have gotten married, but he'd wanted a kid and Shooter had been willing. He hadn't seen any harm in trying. Though he wasn't crazy about her from the get-go, he'd liked her. She had her own thing, too, with taking pictures. This gave him breathing room, what he needed. He liked how they just got along and chewed the fat like old pals that had known each other forever. He'd had no idea there would be a miscarriage. That kind of thing happened in soap operas, not in life. Not his life, anyway.

What were they going to do now? The sex had been okay, good, not great. Then what? Meals? Then what? More meals. He hated to admit it, but he was bored. Holly was the one who charged him up. She was cunning, erotic, willing to do anything in bed. A real flirt too and he still felt hungry whenever he thought about her. Holly wasn't like any woman he'd known. It was all highly charged sexual vibes with her, super-charged play and daring and no talking allowed. She didn't want it to be soft and comfortable. She liked an edge. She'd handcuff his arms to her bedposts and scissor her legs around his head as he gnawed on that sweet bush of hers the way a man should.

Not Shooter, none of that. He'd get on top of Shooter and he'd try to make it special, but she'd just lie there and perspire and sound her little moans. She never grunted or howled or shrieked with ferocious abandon the way Holly did. With Shooter it was all kinds of gentle and thoughtful, no sense of rugged play involved. All that was fine, too, but it grew old fast.

Holly could be boyish in her own nasty ways, with a mean streak in her, a playful pixie quality, a sparkly cuteness to go along with her sharp-tongued demands. The way she'd bite and slap and fight him off, making him earn it. All that was a plus. Holly was the vixen with a thinner more lively body, more athleticism and endless amounts of energy. Sex was never simple with Holly. She'd do anything, always a game, living in the present. He felt with Holly that she gave her all, really let herself go, and he liked trying to last as long as possible and to match it. They never went gradually and with care the way he did with Shooter.

A dangerous adventure, that's what he wanted and Holly could provide it. Not that he wasn't fond of Shooter, but it was more of a cozy visit, not a wild ride. He just didn't want that any longer. He knew what that visit felt like. It was too consistent. No surprises. No fireworks. He'd been there too many times.

Man, the things that happened to people. Including him. Shooter was still struggling with it, even after her long visit with Holly. She always would, and so that was that. Shooter liked to come across as the zany artist type but mostly she wanted to be kind of normal, if that was even possible anymore. Holly wouldn't even use the word "normal." She believed abnormal, if anything, was really normal. Maybe Shooter believed this too, but only up in her head, not in practice on the ground where it counted.

They still had their triangle game. He could go to Holly just as Shooter had. Maybe he should before Holly lost interest in their game. Nothing lasted forever.

Ma knew nothing about Holly. Never would either. Ma liked Shooter and how dedicated she was to photography. She thought Shooter talented and had said, "She can walk the walk."

High praise from Ma, who'd been crushed to learn she wouldn't be a grandmother.

After the miscarriage, he and Ma had a long talk. Ma had said he should just stick to his role as husband, breadwinner, a kind of old-fashioned taste to it all. He hadn't told his Ma he didn't want that. He wanted to take his savings and get the hell out of Queens.

He couldn't take Shooter with him, but he could go to Holly with his money and he could hide for a while. Nobody would know where to find him. Hell, he wasn't stupid. He had nothing to prove; he didn't need to feel ashamed of wanting to bolt. The sell-by date on dealers came up fast. And it was a final one. No going back.

He'd tried to play electric guitar for a while, but during the years of dating Shooter, whenever he brought up his guitar and maybe playing in a band, Shooter mostly ignored him. Holly, on the other hand, begged him to play his guitar naked while she lay on her bed, also naked, and masturbated.

Shooter didn't know about any of this. When he'd asked her why she was so against his guitar playing, nagging her to talk to him about it, she'd finally given in and told him that she had no issues with his interest in music. She loved music too, but she was the creative one between the two of them and there was no place in their marriage for two creative types.

Just let her take her pictures, then. He should be the breadwinner, the provider, even if what he did was illegal and she probably disapproved of it even though she never said so.

That dude, Hassan, was still at large. Still looking for him. Derek knew he had to be careful. If he holed up with Holly in Providence he might get his nerve back. Hassan would never find him there, never even think to look, but the longer he stayed in Queens, the more dangerous his life got. Any given day he could walk out of his apartment and get capped. It was more than possible, it felt like a slow train moving toward him, a train that would crash just outside his window. Dealers got capped. Happened all the time.

He could boast a clean record. No priors and the number of a lawyer who could help him. There didn't have to be a reason he was still alive, still dealing. Sure, he'd been recorded on a security camera but nobody knew he was. He had to be honest. Just a matter of time. It wasn't luck. He knew what he was doing. Extra careful all the time. They were using him as a tool. All part of the game. He'd liked it for a long time, lived for it, but since the Hassan incident he'd started feeling more paranoid. A shaking inside like what he'd felt when Ma was drooling in a hospital bed, barely conscious, sounding her moans of pain. That tube in her neck, that IV drip. Took time before Ma even knew when he was in the room with her. Yet she came around. It ended. He had to remember this. Things changed. They got better.

They got worse too. He had to be patient and make a plan. Take control. It's the watchers, the followers, they're the ones so jumpy all the time, not the leaders. They're the ones that get capped.

Shooter helped him, he had to admit it. She calmed him way down. She fed him, kept him at home when he didn't have to work. He got the gist. It was feeling helpless that paralyzed him most. Made more sense when Ma was sick, but Ma was better now, so why was he still feeling it? Because of Hassan. That bullet with his name on it. This is what he couldn't explain. Not to Shooter. Not to Ma. Only to himself.

Not that he had to, but he should. It was only fair because he was her husband. But he wouldn't. Never. Not his style. He'd act, swift and sure, and let the others figure out his motives later. Thing is, if he did it right, they'd never find him. Queens, as much as he loved any slut, would be in his rearview. Holly would take him in. A guy had to hide sometimes, release sadness, adjust, make new plans, let the past fly away in the wind.

Losers watch change. Winners make it happen.

FOURTEEN

Such pleasure I took in dispensing advice to one who hungered for it. There were evenings when Agnes would call and talk to me as if reporting out of necessity a breakdown of what she'd done that day. Derek was out making a deal somewhere, risking his life. Things were worse than lukewarm with Derek. They'd grown uninspired. He was seldom around. It was pretty much over between them.

"I've been taking your advice," she said. "Today, when I was out shooting, I was thinking to myself as I removed a lens cap and started groping toward one of my ideas for a picture and, looking without really seeing, I just began to shoot. But I knew was looking beyond what was there and really trying to see what would find me. But I just kept shooting. Does that make sense?"

I told her it did because it didn't. "My point is that the process doesn't have to make sense. As long as you grasp that, you're not going to lose interest in it."

"We never really know, do we?" She spoke at a breathless pace, enthused and eager to share. "Which image is going to expose the power, as well as the vulnerabilities in us. If you ask me, I think that in this way, the mysteries of the universe stay alive. I don't need to trek to Alaska or own the latest piece of new equipment or hardware to understand that by using my camera I'm involved in and altered by cathartic forms of invigorating loss and discovery."

I couldn't have agreed more and said so. I had to see her. These long conversations were fine, quite wonderful, but when could we meet face to face?

That's when she asked me what was wrong with the idea of the two of us writing a screenplay together. As a team. A witty comedy as if we were Elaine May and Mike Nichols. I was all for it, I told her, but we should wait. We had to be patient. I'd let her know when.

"Soon," I told her. "Let me first adjust to your sudden interest in me."

"Not sudden. I've always been interested. But I was married."

"You still are."

"I told you it's over."

"But Derek used to work for me. I don't think he'd approve."

"Who cares what he thinks. At this point, he'd be glad if I made the first move. Takes the pressure off him. He's bored out of his mind."

These conversations went on and on, with me playing the role of the phlegmatic procrastinator not in any hurry to make changes. I thought this best. I didn't trust what Derek was capable of. If Agnes had called to say she was divorced or would be soon, our talks and my stance would have been different, but she never called to say that. She called to explain she believed there were no endings or starts. No prizes. She complained that life was an existential monotony without a finishing line in sight, and she grieved over time lost pissing away so many years, as she put it, dumbfounded by it all.

She loved Derek, didn't she? Derek knew this, didn't he? These were my questions.

Not really. Not anymore. Whatever they'd once shared, call it hope, passion or a dream of the future, no longer ignited them. She wasn't ignorant. Nor was he, but he was dangerous. She still lived with him. She needed to talk to him, create something final. Until then, I shouldn't see her, not in any way other than a professional one. That's when I told her I assumed working on a screenplay together might fit into that category. Warming up to the idea, I told her so.

"It might work," I said. "Talk to Derek. Don't keep any secrets from him."

Yet she refrained from speaking to Derek about this. Her reason was that she didn't trust words, she never had. Pictures were what she lived by, especially in regards to love. This didn't help me at all. I asked her again if there was anything left between them. I thought it a reasonable question, but she took offense at it. She said she'd have to think about her answer in an earnest calculated way, waiting for a definition of love or when the need for their relationship became clearer to her. That was the core of it – *the need* for them to remain together.

This made little practical sense. Derek appeared to be stuck in neutral, bristling with a hunger for what he imagined he could have. Agnes appeared to be hardening within and she didn't mind it. Maybe this was what she needed and she viewed it as a maturation.

She did admit to needing time, but she was ready whenever I was to start working on a screenplay. We could meet once a week, but Derek couldn't know about it. I went against my better judgement and agreed to this.

In the meantime, Agnes said she would continue to do yoga at home, stay careful with her diet and continue taking pleasure in losing weight. She was slimming down, drinking less, choosing to read more, though still watching any films I recommended.

These changes. She liked them. I liked them. She began to talk to me in a different way. To describe what had altered in her tone of voice was to say there was less fear and more confidence. A little less desire. I found it incredibly arousing.

I trusted that she was sincere, and this was why I agreed we should begin working together. She could come to my place. We'd start hashing out a script. I'd pay her so that she could begin to move away from her reliance on Derek for money.

She'd keep it all a secret. So would I. Maybe not the wisest choice, but one we made and were linked to. Were we star-crossed? I didn't think so. It felt right that we shared certain working habits and preferences. We'd gotten to know each other better through our movie nights. We liked each other. I didn't want kids. I didn't want anything more than a companion and a chance to live with a woman and grow to understand romantic love. We also both liked a large coffee with cream and two sugars, a sofa, window light and maybe a cat on our laps. We could take notes by hand or peck away at our laptops.

This our latest excursion, part of a growing dream, was no fiction, fantasy or comic caper. It was real and it had the potential to sweep us off into a lifelong romantic voyage. Though I didn't show it, I was happy about all of this. I benefitted from Agnes's input, so of course I learned to listen better. She did too. It was as if we both had said yes to an idea and an adventure.

We worked in this way. She'd explain to me first the scenarios she'd dreamt up, her characters, and I'd mull them over as the reasonable and balancing force of resistance to help dampen the fires of her more outrageous and serendipitous imaginings. She didn't mind having a second creative hand in the process. Nor did I, though I reminded her often that the two of us shouldn't expect too much from each other. Photography, after all, was still her métier. It was related to film. She rebuffed me, at times, by saying that as a photographer she had to try something within her métier but also slightly newer in order to keep her mind fresh. Stanly Kubrick, she reminded me, one of the masters I was often prattling on about, had started out as a photographer for *Look* magazine.

I remember Agnes saying we were circus-freaks, she supposed, in most circles. She respected me because I'd lived longer, seen more, lost more, suffered fewer delusions than most of her friends. Yet I was still a circus freak. She enjoyed the company of someone who read as much as I did. This inspired me to open up to her in ways I hadn't thought possible.

I'd grow loquacious to the point that some of my comments such as those I shared regarding Schopenhauer, which I'd thought ludicrously ostentatious, forced me to withdraw. Yet those comments had impressed her. She liked when I wandered away from and even fell off the thin line I allowed myself to walk. She wasn't gullible. She saw intelligence in me, but she didn't allow herself to like or enjoy it too much. Neither of us did.

The experience did wonders for my self-esteem. She started to phone more often, easily five times a week and never when Derek was around. I saw her feeling freer to complain more. The pandemic had shown a new reality. She hadn't liked it. She'd found it nauseatingly dull, but she was making adjustments and getting on much better.

Had she really phoned me once to talk about the meaning of love? She had. She'd even asked me where did love between consenting adults come in? I was charmed. Smitten. Gob smacked. To Agnes, love demanded commitment. If the love was real, the commitment would be too. I agreed. Daily life could fracture attempts at love, creating separate forms of tension between what was real and alleged. We were both average persons, not that unusual and we struggled to maintain lines of division that would allow devotion to the abiding concerns of each other. We struggled with our inner concerns, our feelings. We agreed on many issues that she'd admitted had been contentious ones with Derek. We talked for hours, taking long walks with our masks on, neither us having much more to do and weary of the sedentary malaise that had crept in during the severe lockdown days. A malaise that had settled into our bones, it seemed, and required a protean effort to expunge.

As one who liked to say she had no use for yackety-yak and gossip, Agnes talked a blue streak. I let her. I listened. She needed a willing ear. So did I.

—⁓—

Our relationship developed and I learned, with time, that her thinking process, her ethos, and her undying insistence on independence was aligned to that of one influence from her early life, namely her late Uncle Roger. Her father's only sibling, Roger Bailey promoted the subversive yet joyful attitude that Agnes had adopted when it came to approaching each day. The proverbial *carpe diem*. The two had become friends rather than merely niece and uncle. He had taught her to examine others with a compassionate eye, to show respect and tolerance, not to forego judgement but to pause, to avoid haste, keeping in mind that most people quietly withstand more unspoken-of pain than she should care to imagine.

Agnes came to admire and sometimes idolize the man, a divorced bachelor and attorney who lived alone in a drab split-level ranch in the suburb of Somerset. He exuded the sense of having a shadowy past. When she got older, though still in high school, he drank with Agnes on occasion, meeting her in Providence on a Saturday where they'd see a matinee at the Cable Car Cinema and then dine on Italian food while drinking too much red wine.

On such occasions, Agnes worried her uncle wouldn't make it home by car. Eventually, this habit did him in. He perished in an accident late one night on his way home from one of the many watering holes he liked to frequent, his blood alcohol level well beyond the legal limit.

Agnes spoke with fondness about Uncle Roger encouraging her to understand that she wasn't the cause of how lonely and afraid she sometimes felt. Many felt this way, including her mother who, strangely enough, didn't think her brother-in-law a suitable influence.

The two laughed at this. Her mother was hardly one to criticize Roger's drinking or his outspoken campaigns against maudlin perspectives on life. The man defined *joie de vivre* for her, exemplified it, ever present and generous, especially in the wake of his brother dying.

Uncle Roger came by daily for about six months, visiting during a delicate period when her mother was struggling to cope with being a widow while Agnes mourned in longing for her father's steady hand.

"But he didn't make it all the way either," she said. "What I mean is that neither he nor my father saw me graduate from high school."

All those errands her father used to run had suddenly become her mother's responsibility. The woman wasn't up to the task. She, like her late husband, preferred draining another gin bottle over coping with difficult responsibilities.

Uncle Roger helped with legal matters. It was easy for him to accept the dictum that family is all. At first, her mother had resented the assistance, boozing it up night after night. This had puzzled and demoralized Agnes. Uncle Roger, unflappable, forcing himself to stay sober, responded to his sister-in-law's resentment by ignoring it. This had led Agnes to suspect that her mother and Uncle Roger shared painful and perhaps unsavory echoes from the past that had become grudges neither of them were willing to share or address in the open or in private.

When drunk, which was often, her mother took every opportunity to belittle Roger, claiming that "like all Bailey men" he suffered from "perverse delusions of grandeur."

Roger fought back, deriding her as "a spoiled kitten" who'd "married up and hadn't loved her husband adequately."

"What for? Since he turned out to be such a lush," her mother would fire back.

"Look who's calling the kettle black."

During such skirmishes, Agnes tended to retreat. She read copious amounts of fantasy novels. She ran off with her camera, borrowing her mother's car, driving the jammed-up shoreline roads to take pictures of what she described as "scenic miniatures" of the Atlantic coastline.

She often agreed with her uncle when he'd quip, "At least that old sot of a brother of mine left you plenty in his will."

⸻◦◦◦⸻

It was mid-afternoon. Agnes and I lingered on the small divan in what acted as the living room of my Chelsea apartment. The sun and shadows were creating an excess of contrast in the light from the room's one big window. Washing up the walls, they created softly outlined fingering shapes and pools.

According to Agnes, this wasn't the best time to be shooting, though not the worst either. It depended on what she was after or, as she liked to say, "What finds me."

As I understood it, Agnes viewed her attempts with the camera as a way to fight off a lethargy of the spirit that the pandemic lockdowns had allowed to seep into her plasma. Otherwise, if it was during normal times and she wanted to "escape," she'd take a page from Uncle Roger's book and find a sanctuary where she could run her lips over the salted edge of a Margarita glass until dotty. She would do that with me, pandemic or not. I was a companion she felt she could trust. She liked to say, "I can hang around with you and do nothing and not feel like I'm missing out."

I was flattered by this. More importantly, I was beginning to understand that love knew no limits within the imagination. I'd never felt so willing to give up everything I had in order to make another person happy.

"I need to be out, to be active," she said. "Whether I like wearing a mask or not."

I asked her about Derek. He came up often in our conversations, leading Agnes to respond that she didn't want to talk about him. Not with me. Not with anyone.

"Derek's got his own life," she said. "There are so many holes in him, so few linkages. I don't like how tied he is to his mother. He doesn't love me anymore. Maybe he never did. He needs to see a shrink, but he won't, of course, though it's okay if I do. He'll just sell more dope to some poor slob in order to pay for my visit. Our life together was a joke. It still is."

"Then end it."

I wasn't sorry about saying this. The ordeal of the pandemic, its ups and downs had taken a toll on my patience. Add to this that I'd not only begun to tell myself that I was in love, I was starting to believe it too.

There was a stoniness in Agnes, a rigid confidence that showed itself when she knew she was right. It showed at that moment and I found it intimidating. Yet I turned my face toward her and looked at

Agnes directly, searching her blue eyes. Such a sweetness of light and whimsy there. Such a stolid reticence, as well. They were all bizarrely compatible, but that was Agnes.

I reached over to take her left cheek and held it in the palm of one hand. She softened. The sweetness took over. We kissed for a long time. When we separated, I felt both relieved and energized. This was, indeed, love.

I watched Agnes draw in a big breath. As she let it out, controlling it, she began calming herself down. She then rose from the divan and picked up her camera and aimed its lens at the shadows on the wall. She fired her shutter. One click and then a second click, each at a high speed, the heavy mechanical clicks of an older camera done spontaneously yet with surety.

I told myself that I was a beneficent influence. That I could grasp love and abide by its teaching. Whatever she'd had with Derek could be relinquished though not quickly or with ease. I merely needed to be patient. This would be easy.

"It's all about seeing, isn't it?" I remarked.

"Yep," was all she said.

I felt with her that I was still on my way somewhere, that my life was far from over. In middle age, that's a rarer and not an unpleasant sensation. It was as if I'd begun to see and accept myself again, the loner, the outsider, some might say a maverick, but not me, especially not in matters of love and women. I was tawdry, a late bloomer. I understood money, but love was a whole other kettle of fish. I was willing to help Agnes if she needed it. I felt empowered when with her in a way similar to what she'd described feeling after her "healing time" with Holly, explaining the details of their triangle game.

For the time being, and only she knew for how long, Agnes was keeping to her marriage commitment. Yet clearly she'd found in me a needed refuge. I was finding sanctuary and self-discovery in her, as well. Was this part of love's overall meaning? I thought so. It had to be or why else would so many crave it?

I could be present for Agnes, ready to listen. In this way I'd be valuing and sharing and improving the best in myself. In spite of the dreary pandemic conditions, life was becoming an adventure again. This brought me no shortage of comfort.

FIFTEEN

Holly puckered her lips and sounded a kiss in front of her mirror. Still got it, still gorgeous, but *I'm alone again and how did this happen.* She was comfortable, wasn't she? Why else live? Not, in general, with this or any other form of isolation, which wasn't the same as solitude, but comfortable with isolation imposed on from without. Solitude felt more internal and organic, like an interest in one's self as a garden to be tended to slowly, with care. Isolation came in the form of walls and curfews and doors forever closed.

There was courage in her yet. She wasn't finished. She could still push with one exhalation at sand castles that tumbled with ease, but she could also admit that a component was missing. Agnes had described it as a force that drove her to punish and starve herself. This might explain why she was so thin.

That was the old Holly. Everything had been altered. The pandemic had sped up and heightened permutations that had begun long before mandates, mask couture and the labels on floors to demarcate proper social distancing limits were seen everywhere. The point of living was to have and do many things, and to be comfortable. Yet how had she gotten so irritably peevish, so bony, such a picture of char and cadaverous stress and near ruin?

It was useless. Nothing was happening and it was all because of this dreadful plague. House arrest. So very little was going on *anywhere in the world* and so few, she suspected, felt right about where they were or believed they were headed.

She shouldn't feel so badly. She wasn't alone. Everyone wanted this period of doom and confusion to end. People wanted to feel better. Was that asking too much? No, it wasn't, especially when she considered the poor who were dying in droves in faraway places such as Africa and India, images beamed by satellite into her living room.

She actually paid for her access to such footage and reports, as if it were a fetish, one online report after another, all of them so dreadful and negative, making her feel useless, hopeless, guilty of having clothes, food, a bed. This was why she never hesitated to write big checks once a month to support charity organizations and campaigns to end hunger.

Why guilt? She hadn't brought this on. How could she alleviate it? She really didn't know. It wasn't like she could trust any of the information she got.

That had to cease. Today, she'd cancel her Internet and television accounts, rid her soul of the agonizing close-ups and interviews with death, deprivation and misery. All such narratives felt so fear-driven, dystopian and calculated. What she craved most was the erasure, not the development of the fear component. There was too much fear. She'd always seen it in other people's eyes, but now it loomed in her own, especially when a mask covered the lower part of her face.

The masked brigades. Those strangers out there. She felt no connection to any of them. How long would this nightmare last? No one knew. It went from one stage, one message, one lie and one crude political manipulation to the next. True, the ultra-strict lockdowns had ended, but there were still demands on freedom, still all these mixed messages. Still talk of conspiracies and newer, stronger variants of the same virus. Spiking numbers. Side effects to vaccinations. Collusions and arguments between nations and politicians. Should she run to Florida? Many others had.

She'd been following news from around the world, finding it convenient and often the only thing she felt like doing. As if by paying attention she might change the narrative somehow.

That's how they get you. She'd end it. Pull the plug. No matter the country, the narrative was a similar one: hopelessness. As soon as there appeared to be a reduction in the number of jarring announcements of increased numbers of dead, especially in poorer countries, along came graphs and charts from foreign lands where the numbers had again begun spiking. It seemed no one solution was effective. It seemed there were no leaders of any quality anywhere in the world. There was also a flood of talk about authoritarianism from overnight experts and pundits. There were competing narratives and a politicization of the pandemic, using it as a weapon, a way to maneuver. There were vaccines developed at a dangerously rapid pace, but which ones were effective, fully tested, and which ones produced horrible side effects? She'd gotten her vaccinations. Two of them. The first one had produced only a mild night of insomnia, but after the second she'd felt horrible for about 48 hours, her head spinning, her sinuses and throat dried up and burning. Then she'd felt fine, though a bit weaker for another seven days. Agnes had endured a similar experience. They'd gone at separate times and to different places, both of them allegedly getting the same vaccine.

Still, doubts remained in her mind about the vaccine's effectiveness. She feared long-term side effects that would occur and damage her. She didn't want to hear that she'd need a third one, what they called a booster, and that this still might not make a difference in terms of protecting her. Nobody knew anything. So many in the world were still not privy to their first dose of the vaccine. Was this the world she'd grown up in? It wasn't.

This was a time for sacrifice and a spirit of cooperation, yet why did she repeatedly feel as if this was the last thing any of the politicians or journalists were willing to bring up or act on? They were complaining about Trump as if he were still president. He wasn't. They'd elected the mannequin, Biden, a man who'd been in politics back when her dead father was young. Back in the 1970's. Nobody in politics for that long could be trusted.

It seemed real journalism of any serious non-biased intent was dead. If it wasn't on Instagram, Twitter or Tik Tok then it hadn't happened, it wasn't real. If Holly didn't tweet her thoughts then she hadn't had them. All of it, especially the social media platforms, she wanted to be through with them, but she couldn't let them go. She wanted to hear what they had to say about cancel culture and Wokeism (whatever the hell that meant). She battled her impulses to shut them down, and instead of severing each and every capillary, she kept herself tuned in believing she needed to be linked to this unnerving culture of pulsing tom toms.

As she'd told Agnes, one day she got out of bed and could no longer trust anything she heard, but that didn't mean she was going to block her ears and eyes. In an instant, everything had changed. Still, she should pay attention. She must. Nothing in the public arena could ever again be trusted, but this didn't justify burying her head in the sand. Original thought was the real virus. The one they were trying to control. She couldn't block out her own thoughts.

There was such a genius to it really, the manipulators had pulled it off; from Texas to Timbuktu they'd closed down thinking minds across the globe. Would she hide? Not a chance. She demanded from herself that she never cease keeping track of developments, that she learn all that was possible, even if by doing so she might drive herself over the edge of sanity.

Agnes had scolded her. "Holly you luxuriate in distracting yourself with news of the world, as if by giving it attention the news will morph gradually into a more palatable and less frightening narrative."

Did she, really? Perhaps she did and so what, she wasn't hurting anyone.

Agnes was partly right in that the narrative frightened, but Holly didn't feel like she luxuriated in anything. She didn't expect the narrative to become palatable either. Why did Agnes medicate herself with such disdain for her? How did Agnes spend her free time, after all? Taking photographs, using her camera like a narcotic. They were both sick. The planet was sick.

Agnes had been right to be fatalistic, saying, "The world has always been a mess, but it was just harder and took more time to get the message out. What we both need to do is to shut it all out and look inward and focus on ourselves."

Suit yourself, Agnes. Spot on if that's what you want, but not her. Not Holly Greene, no, the news diet fed and satisfied. Whenever Holly stepped away from it she started to feel jittery and returned in a sweat, no matter where she was at the time, or to what program or voice or screen, allowing herself to use the narrative as a needed psychotropic med. By stepping away, she'd become indifferent and hence a contributor to the problems.

She'd keep her phone, upgrade her service to 5G, a choice she thought long overdue. Now was the time to call people, talk to them, seek out and discover arguments and differing points of view. Now was the time to fund and promote ways to solve issues she cared about, whether global hunger or climate change. How much money had she already donated to organizations on the front lines in various battles? Plenty. Yet Agnes, for one, never donated and remained doubtful many of these problems even existed, often criticizing the journalism as incomplete or a hoax, a money grab or a transfer of wealth. How could Agnes be so callous? Didn't she realize that the planet was damaged beyond repair? When it wasn't flooding, it was burning up.

When Holly had asked her this question, Agnes had remarked balefully, "Look, when was the last time you saw a dinosaur? The planet's always changing. Species come and go. They adapt. Just like we'll adapt. Nothing anyone in politics can do will make a difference."

To think that Agnes had even defended some of Trump's policies, too. That ogre of a man. That orange worm. That disgrace. True, Agnes hadn't voted for him, but she'd stated outright that she had no use for Biden either, calling him an "addled meat puppet and a yes man for corporations without a single new idea in his empty dementia-impaired head."

Such strong words from Agnes. Why had she ever thought Agnes would make an appropriate life-partner and companion? That was *never* going to happen. Just the same, Agnes was her friend. She listened, she tried to show empathy. The sex with her, at times, had been remarkable, but still poor Agnes struggled with her errant self-serving political and world views. There'd been other women, of course, but Holly had never let herself be as vulnerable with them as she'd been with Agnes.

Agnes really understood and knew how not to insult her ideas. Agnes talked to her supportively, from the heart, even when disagreeing with her on some issues. She knew how to address potentially delicate subjects without condescension. There was much to value in having her as a friend. Each leg of the triangle should be different. Now, perhaps, it was time to return back to Derek to fulfill her physical desires. Let Agnes have him for a short time. It wouldn't be long before he'd grow bored. Then he'd come to his Holly, she knew this, she felt it in her bones, and she'd be ready for him.

⁓

During their most recent all-night gab-fest on the phone, she and Agnes had spoken candidly about how Holly had finally realized that her "fame obsession," as Agnes had labelled it, had driven so many of her choices when younger. Agnes had been correct about that. Throughout her twenties, Holly had been ravenous for attention and hadn't even noticed how little time she'd spent addressing inner needs and concerns.

Agnes, ever sardonic, had also stated that Holly's current maladies were not due to the pandemic, but rather that her fame-obsession had died and Holly had become deflated and in need of a motivational force beyond having intercourse with members of both sexes. This, too, had made sense to Holly given her age and the changes that had occurred in her thinking in regards to how she might define happiness and a sense of living a satisfactory life.

What could replace her fame-obsession? Could it be self-love? Holly laughed with the thought. Agnes had so imperiously declared that Holly didn't know how to love herself. She'd reduced Holly's narcissism to a liability. A delusion of grandeur. Maybe she'd been right to do so, but Holly would never agree with her. Nor would she ever forget Agnes remarking so snidely, "You think the world needs you, Holly.

That you're so special. That you're supposed to be happy one day. It's a big fat lie that you refuse to accept."

Holly hadn't begun crying over the phone, though the comment from Agnes had stabbed her in the heart. Agnes, knowing this, hadn't bothered to apologize. She'd remained arch and self-righteous. "Don't blame yourself, Holly. Nobody likes admitting they feel lost."

Agnes had been right. Holly knew she ran from pain, found all sorts of ways to medicate herself and defined these medications as getting closer to who she *thought* she behaved as, rather than who she was and had been. She knew, too, that she refused to sacrifice anything if it might make her uncomfortable or look bad.

She had to admit she'd been living these practices for so long they'd come naturally to her and defined how she lived. They formed a quasi religion of escapism that gave her the means to navigate the ethers while convincing herself she was pure of heart and true to a higher calling.

Agnes, such a deadly honest soul, understood her. She respected Agnes for this, though she didn't really like her for it. Yet why had she thought she wouldn't feel twinges of emptiness and regret in the wake of Agnes's departure? Because she knew but didn't believe that Agnes loved her enough to be honest and forthright.

Holly had really wanted Agnes to leave, she'd known the time had come. Trying to control Agnes was tantamount to not respecting her. Holly could admit she loved and respected Agnes, and she'd even told her so, but that didn't mean she'd call or keep in touch or that they'd return to the intimacy they once shared.

The realm of entitlement Holly knew she lived in had no real use for such pure outspoken souls as Agnes. It was better suited for the vain, befuddled and perpetually dishonest likes of Derek. The man was hardly pure. Hardly intelligent. No matter. Holly didn't need that. She wanted Derek's body and she knew she could ravish it.

Just a question of waiting.

For the time being, she preferred to be alone. She would heal and prepare and meditate in silence, venturing inward in the hopes of discarding the old ways she'd used to once define her ambitions. Her question hadn't changed. It was basic: What did she want to do with her life?

Firstly, avoid the stench of false purity and virtue. Secondly, promote her own enlightened self-interests. The news of the world was an admission of cruelty and arrogance. Stupid, stupid world.

She wasn't an idiot. She knew where she'd been. Agnes had been correct to criticize her, saying she was getting too old to lack any sense of what her life's mission was going to be. Fine, whatever, she should water the gardens of gainful pursuits that would make the planet a better place to live. Indulge in ventures that hadn't defined themselves yet because she'd failed to take the time to seek them out. What would those ventures, that life work be? Just begin, Holly told herself, and don't look back, and be selfish about it.

⟞⟀⟞

This man, this solitary pair of boots on the street. Holly watched him. He, too, wore a mask. The man's skin color, likely of African descent, was a soft ebony, smooth and so sensual, his build and height muscular, though a little plump around the middle. In her estimation what anyone would define as a working man.

"I'm *my own* man," Holly's father used to say. "Not anybody else's. And none of the pricks out there can take that from me."

This black man. He worked hard for others. For his family. Holly

liked him immediately. He must have suffered more and in many different and disturbing ways than Holly could imagine. She found it easy
to sympathize with him from afar. Why did race have to be a variable,
a barrier? He was likely a kind, simple man. He looked tired and over-
worked. Why did a surface tone have to dictate an emotional reaction?
Yet it did, as it had for centuries.

The issue of stopping racism was about learning how to see better,
wasn't it? To see inside of each other, beyond the surface. Now she
was starting to sound like Agnes, but this wasn't necessarily a negative
development. Indeed, this was not only her question, it was everyone
else's too, particularly for those like this black man, one who'd lived and
had no doubt seen havoc, ruin, cruelties and restorations.

The man's hair was white along the edges, his mustache thin.
He was wearing a red and black plaid flannel shirt with a gray hood
attached. His was the time-eroded face of one who's heard and seen
too much of the same arguments. As if the wind had worn his face
smooth, with a touch of eroded mahogany in the higher points of his
cheekbones.

His posture was tilted forward ever so slightly, bent over due to
his belly, such a bulky presence, as if it were pulling him down. His
elbows were extended out as if to hold him up against the air. Almost
as if gravity was tugging him inexorably closer to a fall into the asphalt.

As Holly felt she, too, was getting pulled down. Gravity didn't see
race, nor did it discriminate.

It was clear the man had passed more than a few milestones. Yet
he still exuded a sturdy resilience. He wore sand-colored work boots
unlaced as if to show that his labors for the past, say, eight to ten hours
had been completed. Such a man, given his age, probably mid-fifties,
went home each day with tired feet. Such a man relied on a woman,

most likely, to clean and iron his work trousers, soiled each day at construction or clean-up sites where all the workers got dirty. He looked ready for a hot meal and perhaps a favorite chair.

He was waiting for his bus. One more pair of boots on the pavement. One more soul done with working for the day, lips parched, poaching in the blush of twilight that had begun to descend.

Glancing up for a moment and without planning on it, the man eyed Holly across the street. She was just standing there and gawking. Their eyes met. She thought his face solemn and yet tranquil and his eyes said to her: *It's misery, Pretty Lady. I know, Lord help me, I know.*

Holly then saw what she would relate later on. It would turn her inside out, a moment that would haunt her for years to come. The man started gasping, coughing, sucking in air. He gripped his sides as if embracing his soft middle, trying to force out expirations as if breathing would free him. Each breath that fluttered off his lips brought only more spasms and stabs of pain until one breath became more decisive than the rest, the man bolting upright as if poked in the behind by an electrical rod.

What Holly witnessed held her stunned in place, unable to move. There was what she thought a disturbing trace of slapstick in the man's physical suffering until there came a moment when it was impossible to evaluate or judge. In this moment, she saw a glowing from the man's aura that stated without equivocation: *It's done, at last.*

No, she thought. He's dying in front of my eyes. This can't be.

His body went slack, his legs failing to hold him up. Without anything or anyone to soften his landing, his skull sounded a crack when it landed in a faint yet alarming note against the pavement. He lay there and twitched in slow spasms for perhaps half a minute though it seemed to Holly to last much longer.

He then lay still, looking huge on the sidewalk, as if a small mound. A chill ran through Holly as she viewed the man. Viewed herself as useless, an observing outsider who should either take action or disappear. She was little more than a spectator and an assessor. What could she *do*? She couldn't believe what she was seeing. What she was thinking. She should run across the street to assist him. She should phone 911. It scared her being in the moment and recalling the moment at the same time as if they were separate realities. She felt an urge to rush to the man's aid, but she held it back because she felt unable to do it, frozen by what she'd seen, inexperienced, unprepared, gawking at the cars as they passed on the street, forcing her to tremble and fret while she stood there alone.

A woman appeared, also in a mask. She had approached by walking up a small hill that was topped by the bus stop bench. The woman had skin like cocoa butter, marcels of dark hair, the regal features and stance of a proud perhaps Cape Verdean or Dominican. This woman, who had no doubt planned to catch the same bus, must work as a nurse, thought Holly, because that stop served the line that ran each twenty minutes or so to the hospital nearby. Holly saw no hesitation as the woman took action, without panic, dialing her phone, probably 911 and knowing what to say, knowing a heart attack when she saw one.

Holly, one hand to her quivering lips, still standing there across the street, began to cross, but the regal woman, now crouching down next to the man, turned to her and shouted, "Don't. Please. Just don't. You'll only be in the way."

So Holly stopped. She stepped backwards to the sidewalk and remained there. She watched from across the street as the man stopped gagging on his own tongue, the sounds from his mouth no longer revolting to hear. Was it too late? Was he no longer alive?

The woman spanked his face, begging him, "Breathe, c'mon breathe."

A momentary dimming of light, a density forming in the air as if the sun, lower now in the sky, passed behind increasingly scarlet and opaque clouds. Holly couldn't just leave, so she decided to wait, but she had to assist in some way. She couldn't just watch and allow herself to feel so damn helpless, so she started again to cross, but the regal woman, still crouched over the man's body, waved again and shouted with more vehemence for Holly to stay back, stay away, she'd already called an ambulance. "I'm a nurse," shouted the woman. "You want to help, you just get going. You stay away."

Holly felt herself quaking, but she began to walk. She was different now, wasn't she? Acting against her own impulses, but doing what the nurse had asked. She knew this was right, that it was always best to heed one who knows through experience. Holly walked in long brisk strides. She didn't turn her head to look back. The scene came alive in her memory. She kept seeing that man buckle and fall.

When she heard the ambulance siren wailing behind her, Holly didn't glance over her shoulder. How quickly they'd arrived! She kept walking and felt in awe of that nurse. What luck for the man she'd arrived there, that the hospital was so close. Maybe by her decisive action that woman had saved his life. This was the thought Holly clung to as she strode along. She'd take it home to bed. That man. She hoped that even if compromised he'd eventually enjoy happy hours with his loved ones again. All stories required such an ending, didn't they?

Cars continued to race by, their drivers distracted or unaware of what was happening at that bus stop. A crowd didn't gather. Due to the hospital's proximity, the ambulance had arrived in a remarkably short time. The police arrived next. The regal nurse spoke to both officers, each of whom were white men and sympathetic. Race didn't play any part in their conversation. The aim was to get the man to the hospital as quickly as possible. Both officers thanked the woman who remained remarkably composed and genial.

How little control we have, thought Holly. Perhaps the fallen man had more work yet to do and would survive. Perhaps not. Why hold to the mortal coil, battling infirmities, if there was no purpose behind living? Perhaps the man was emboldened by thoughts of his wife, children and grandchildren that he still needed to support.

Holly didn't know. She never would. She phoned me one night just to tell me this story. She was sobbing, asking, "What's wrong with me, Ennis, why does my life feel so useless?"

SIXTEEN

Having risen early, unable to sleep, Derek went for a casual jog in the neighborhood. He hoped cops on patrol wouldn't roll by and see him. They didn't. He enjoyed a short jog that cleared his head. Having stuffed a roll of bills into the pocket of his sweatpants, he stopped on his way home at a neighborhood bakery and bought half a dozen bagels. He did this for Agnes, who liked bagels more than he did. He hoped to atone for what had been an unpleasant night.

Agnes had been tired and stoned on high-octane weed when he'd come home late to her, after midnight. When they'd gone to bed he'd forced her to have sex, though she'd lacked the energy or the desire. When she'd finally given in to his demands, he'd learned that he couldn't remain aroused. The result had been a litany of curses and a temper tantrum that ended with him storming out of the bedroom to spend the night on the couch.

They'd both had too much of each other. Too much history. Too many differences. Instead of them building on changes, he saw they were getting buried by them. He also thought it was wrong that he could say he still loved her even though he didn't. This made him a liar. Sort of. Because he did love her. Sort of. But not in the same way. Not physically. Sort of.

It was all twisted up. Confusing. There was nothing fresh or exciting between them. Maybe he should tell her this. He didn't know what to think. Why bother? She already knew it was over. She was no ignoramus, that one. She felt the same truth and insights that he did. If she did say anything about it, she'd be speaking honestly. So would he.

They needed to talk, air out their grievances and move on. He didn't know how. Too many details. She could have the apartment, but he wasn't going to pay for it. The lease would be changed to her name alone. First its time for renewal had to come up. Yeah, way too many details. In the meantime, he'd move in with Ma. He'd start bringing his belongings to her, little by little. He didn't care how long it took. The main thing was they made a decision and got on with it.

Derek figured a long breakfast. It was his way to contribute, to take action, to sort out a plan while they sat and gabbed together. Agnes liked to gab. He knew that once she chose to hit her tiny darkroom, he might not see her for the next eight hours.

What did he need to say? First, that his feelings about her weren't the same. He wouldn't tell her that he couldn't stop thinking about Holly. He'd just tell her that he saw Agnes had changed, as well. She didn't appear comfortable around him.

Second, it was as if during the ordeal of the miscarriage and their times apart she had matured in one direction, and he'd gone in another. He hadn't ever told her this. Maybe he should have, but he'd assumed she could see it, just there, a presence looming between them no matter the time of day.

That would be enough. If there were gaps she'd fill them in with her own concerns and questions.

Once home, having showered, Derek sat in the kitchen where he watched Agnes move to the coffeemaker and pour herself a cup. He'd made a fresh batch just for her, knowing how much she liked her coffee. He liked it, too, especially the way its aroma filled the air.

Agnes looked sleepy in her pink cotton robe, knotted at the waist, her hair a mess, her slippers sounding little scuffs as she dragged them across the floor. She stared at him, steaming cup in hand, looking puzzled when she spotted the bagels and cream cheese plated on the kitchen table. He offered to toast one.

She shook her head no. "Why is everyone trying to sabotage me? I'm trying to watch my weight."

"Just a bagel," he said. "What do you mean sabotage? I'm trying to be nice. Jesus. I know you didn't have any good New York ones during your time with Holly."

Chilly, looking suspicious, Agnes eyed him. "You worried I'll become the next Karen Carpenter?"

"What the hell you talking about?" He sounded peeved. "They're just bagels, like I said."

Agnes, sighing, pulled out her chair and leaned toward Derek as she spoke. "My mother used to listen to The Carpenters all the time. She used to say she liked Karen's voice but that she died way too young."

"Look Shooter, all I'm trying to do is help make you feel at home."

"Since when?"

"Since last night. It friggin' killed me. Okay? I said it."

She shrugged and picked up a photography magazine that she'd left on the table the night before. "Oh, that. We've had worse."

Watching her, blowing a sigh, Derek started to feel his left leg throb due to his jog. He wouldn't talk about the pain due to a gunshot wound there. As always, he'd live with it. All he wanted was to sit and feel peaceful-like with her, like their early days. What the hell had gone wrong and why so fast?

"I'm on a diet now," said Agnes. "The quarantine fifteen. I put on too much weight."

Derek softened, his face reflecting the anger and twinge of disappointment he felt. "Look, I don't want to argue first thing on a Sunday morning. Why can't you just accept that I'm doing this to make you feel happy? They're fresh out of the oven."

"I like the idea of the bagels, Derek, I really do. But maybe later. You have one first."

Derek felt a small collapsing within and for a moment it was as if he'd been sapped of energy. "I need to keep weight off too. You know that." He crossed his arms and leaned back in his chair. He knew he was lying. He'd lost ten pounds without Agnes around. All his shirts appeared too large for his frame. He took a bagel and started chewing on it.

"Can't we just have breakfast together, like we used to, just for an hour?" he asked. "I'll fry up some eggs and bacon, if you want."

After she rolled her magazine, tapping it lightly against the table, Agnes paused to think. She sounded a little hum as if realizing she was guilty of a transgression she'd finally understood. "You're right. Sure, we can have breakfast, but let me shower first."

They'd reached a compromise. Derek liked knowing this. They could move forward now.

Agnes, standing now, remarked, "You know, Derek, each day, your body and your mind they get weaker and more run down. Then one day, you die."

"That a fact?"

"Far as I know."

"Then that's why we got to be like Ninja warriors."

"No we don't." She lifted her mug off the table and sipped from it. "Did you get onion? Those are my favorite."

"Two of them," he said. "And sesame and cinnamon raisin. A half dozen in all."

With a solemn distracted nod, Agnes put down her mug and then looked at Derek, studying his features before she said, "Honey, I wanted to say this last night, but I couldn't, so I'll say it now. I think you should find – "

He cut her off mid-sentence. "I know. Another line of work. You say that all the time."

"I was going to say someone else."

"What?" He stared at her. He waited. "What is it? What do you want to say? I'm all ears, Shooter. Word up. I'm all ears."

"I'm saying it's wrong. We both know it. We should break up."

"Divorce?"

"Why so stunned? Don't tell me you haven't thought about it."

"I was. I mean, yeah, but it's not so easy. I mean, I do love you and all that."

"Oh please. Just stop. Nothing you say is going to change how I feel. And you don't love me. I doubt you ever did."

Whoa. What was this? The way she spoke, he knew, proved she meant every word. She wasn't faking it. If anything, there was too much sincerity in her, a challenge for him to face so early in the day. He stopped chewing on his bagel and decided to make a suggestion. "Maybe we should visit your Mom next weekend. This time of year, nice there in Rhode Island, ain't it? We can rent a car."

"It's over, Derek." She leaned closer to him. "Can you read my lips?"

He sounded a snort of contempt and looked away. Agnes began to hum. He'd always found this an annoying habit, but he'd never complained about the way it unnerved him. Still seated, looking up at her, he thought if they made a visit to her mother, both of them would be treated like royalty. Agnes deserved and needed a bit of pampering, though he worried that she might throw the switch that sent her into an extreme mode which allowed her to keep pace drink for drink, usually gin and tonics, with her mother. The two of them shared this combative streak, each determined to outshine the other.

"Why don't you do it? Don't you want to see your mother?" he asked.

She stopped humming. She shrugged. "Maybe. Hard to say."

Complicated. Yeah, he knew. During their last visit, she and her mother had started with cocktails for lunch at a seafood restaurant. After that, he'd driven them around until her mother wanted afternoon drinks at a hotel lounge. This was followed by another lounge, each of them cheesy places, one of them with a parquet dance floor, a happy hour and a buffet table. Another one had been a favorite where Agnes's mother knew the regulars and got herself bombed out of her mind. As had Shooter. He'd driven them home, both so drunk their breath stunk up the car. In crowded Rhode Island with its narrow roads there'd been too much traffic, too many cops parked behind bushes, but he'd played the good son-in-law, hadn't touched a drop. Drove them home to Barrington and watched them stagger off to their separate bedrooms.

What was he suggesting? Was he out of his mind? If they went again, he'd likely play the same role as designated driver, watching mother and daughter duke it out to see which one of them could pollute and devour herself faster.

"We'll see," said Agnes. "I was going to call my Mom today anyway."

Could be a bad idea, thought Derek, regretting immediately he'd brought it up. But maybe they really should get the hell out of Queens for a while. For a woman her age, Shirley O'Meara Bailey still had decent looks and plenty of money, so she tended to be active in a way

Derek thought that Agnes sometimes envied. She wouldn't admit it, but Agnes had a tough time keeping up with her mother and could lapse into a whiney mood whenever Shirley became the topic of conversation. The thing he'd always liked about Shirley was she left them alone. She'd told Derek once, "You make Agnes happy. If she's happy, then I'm happy."

Later, about four hours after they'd eaten breakfast, Agnes exited her darkroom while Derek was on the sofa resting his leg and playing a video game. Agnes made the big announcement she'd done enough work for one day. Derek commented that it was a short day for her. She explained it was Sunday and she should rest a bit.

She then phoned her mother and learned that they were too late for a visit. Shirley would be heading out of town mid-week to visit a friend about to enter the hospital for an operation. She'd be gone through the coming weekend, returning late on Sunday, so no invitation, no visit. Maybe another time.

They were now seated on the overstuffed sofa in their dank and cramped living room. Agnes was smoking from a bong, getting herself stoned. Derek had switched from his video game to watching the *Mets* baseball game on television. He didn't mind that Agnes liked to smoke weed, especially after being cramped inside the closet he'd helped her customize to use as a dark room.

Derek didn't know how she pulled it off, cramming herself inside that space every day. That room, their whole apartment reeked of photo chemical solutions. Now, it would smell of cannabis. He'd smoke with her on occasion, but in general preferred to maybe sip a beer or eat pretzels while watching a ballgame.

She offered him some, but he refused. "Maybe later," he said.

Her damp photos had started to curl. They hung from clips on a clothesline Agnes kept stretched between the living room's narrow walls. Taking another bong hit, she exhaled and coughed and told Derek, "You know my mother, she does her own thing."

"Shirley's her own woman. Just like you are."

Red-eyed, Agnes stared at Derek lolling on the sofa in a pair of sweats and a T-shirt. "Derek, look at me."

He sat up straighter, ran one hand through his hair. Rubbed his eyes. "I'm looking."

"Everything inside of me is dying. Go find yourself someone else. Okay?"

Jesus, he thought. Where'd all this come from? He wouldn't insult her with a dopey comeback, even though she was stoned. He could also see she was serious. The weed must give her courage. Not that he'd know. Not that he cared all that much as he watched her stand and plod off into the kitchen where, he assumed, she'd start eating everything in sight.

"Where you going? I thought we were talking."

After a long silence, she replied, "Munchies."

Just as he thought. He lay back down on the sofa. His left leg had not stopped throbbing. The pain sharper now, steady. This was how it would be from now on. Aches and pains. Ups and downs. Agnes getting stoned because it was just too hard to face reality sometimes, drowning in memories of how she'd felt before the miscarriage and everything had gone wrong.

She was right. They were done. She didn't want him any longer, he didn't want her, but he didn't want to be alone either, especially with Covid and nobody really able to convince anyone they knew how to deal with it.

Thinking of Holly helped him. She'd take him in, and he'd go to town on that body of hers. Man, it was all different now. He remembered from childhood his old neighbor Thurmond who used to call out to him from his front steps. Thurmond had lived in the apartment next to Ma's, on the first floor, with his wife Eunice. They were a sweet and crabby old couple. A retired machinist, he'd sit on those steps and yell at the pigeons to shut up. Eunice would sit next to him. They'd each sip a can of beer, chain-smoking, and Thurmond would ask, "You hear them, Eunice? Those God-damned rats with wings?"

Eunice would nod and keep smoking. As the sun set, they'd grow quieter and sometimes Derek, just a boy then, would sit with them and say nothing until it was dark. Since both of them suffered poor vision, neither felt comfortable staying out, so they'd say goodnight to Derek and groan about aches and pains as they shuffled back into their apartment.

Derek, eyes closed, could hear them both so clearly. It was an uncanny feeling, as if they were in the room. If asked, Derek might say, "I miss 'em, but it's times like now when I feel like they never left."

The life he'd known had disappeared, but now and then it came back. For years, Thurmond yelled at pigeons. Amazing. He was still yelling. Eunice was still loving him. For some couples, that was just how it went.

Fact. They died within a year of each other, with Thurmond going first. Together until the end. Inseparable. Not him. Not Agnes. He'd go to Holly. He'd be back online playing the singles market. But not in these parts. Somewhere else.

Something important inside had changed. He didn't see the value in trying to force the issue, to holding on unhappily for the sake of honoring an agreement. What Ma the Catholic would call a sacrament.

Nothing was set. What he and Agnes had been was now defined as the past. Lots of couples split and thought nothing of it and wondered why they hadn't done it sooner.

They weren't going to starve. Agnes could have her darkroom, her cameras, her visits into the city. He wasn't sure what he'd have, but it wouldn't be this. He'd do something new and different. The time had come, and one day soon this crummy pandemic would be history.

SEVENTEEN

For a moment, though he believed his head was clear, Derek hadn't known who he was.

Who he'd been. He became another person, one he didn't recognize, and he waited through a sleepless night in Ma's guest bedroom, what would be his new digs for a while, staring at the walls before deciding to get up to see if Ma was still there. He found her in her favorite chair, conked out in her robe, her glass empty on her lap, the television still on and flickering icy light up the walls.

He coaxed her upright and walked her toward her bedroom. After he lay her down and drew a blanket over her, he knew he shouldn't touch her body. He wanted to, at least, kiss her on the top of her head. It felt strange when his lips grazed her hair and she sounded a slight moan. This was the last time Derek saw her alive.

She went, as it was said among those who knew her well, in her sleep. Quietly so. Sister Nancy remarked, "The poor dear, her heart just gave out."

Derek had cried for quite a while, always alone, finding it easier to cry with no one around to judge him. His sobs allowed his body to surrender to a grief so large that it had frightened him. How he'd once held his mother's hand, learning to walk one nudging advancement at a time. How during her recovery periods she'd need a nurse or Sister Nancy to help her deal with simple tasks and, at times, there hadn't been any nurses available, so that was when he'd stepped in and learned how to act and think differently when caring for her.

He couldn't say when his first inklings had come that his life would soon be different, that Ma would only live another year or two, or maybe die within the week. Now, it was finished. He'd no longer need guidance from Sister Nancy to take care of her by himself. For the past few years nothing else had mattered.

Now it was really finished. He'd feel her, sense her, but he'd never lay eyes on her again.

He remembered how more than once he'd walked her into the bathroom and he'd sat her on the toilet and then waited, enduring the stink before he'd helped her stand. He'd helped wipe her and clean up afterward. All that agony was over now. Everything would be different. Maybe easier, but he'd miss her, he was missing her with each breath he took. A new agony now, one that ambushed him at times and he couldn't shake.

Her living room felt hot and smelly. A kind of earthy fume. Ma's body. Dead.

Memories and emotions were draining him. It was Sister Nancy who'd found her. Not him. He'd hurried out that next morning, had to be somewhere, hadn't bothered with breakfast or waking Ma up or even looking into her. He'd behaved this way knowing that Sister Nancy was going to come.

When he'd asked Sister Nancy what it was like, he knew by the tone in her voice that she wasn't lying to him. She'd said the skin of Ma's face had been swollen, clammy and cold. She looked as if she'd been dead for a while. Sister Nancy said she'd panicked at first, refused to believe it and had then tried to help Ma sit upright. Ma hadn't gasped or said anything or even opened her eyes. Sister Nancy had been the one who'd gasped, shocked to realize where she was and that Ginger Kotas was no longer alive.

Hello, 911. I'd like to report a death. Yes, please send someone. Here's the address. Derek had trusted the look in Sister Nancy's eyes. Like she'd been stunned into an awareness of a brutal reality. As a nurse, as a person, he thought Sister Nancy amazing and he'd watched in awe and learned from her.

Without question, as he recalled it, the most difficult task had been learning how to sit his mother on her toilet, where she'd sound those throaty gags, almost animal-like sounds. He'd look away and gag a few times himself until she was done. The smell, too, was awful, but he'd put up with it. Him, of all people, playing nurse.

He decided against phoning Shooter. He'd had it with her. They were through. He'd call her later, after all the paperwork and the plans were finished. Thanks to Sister Nancy this, too, was getting done. She'd hooked him up with a lawyer who'd helped him deal with the will, power of attorney, an arrangement with a funeral home and a cemetery.

He had power of attorney and all the documents, but he wouldn't have to do much. There'd be a burial ceremony with a priest. He and Sister Nancy. Nobody else. Not even Shooter. The funeral home would post a video online. E-condolences might be shared, though most of Ma's closest friends and relatives were already dead too.

As Sister Nancy had said, "She's just joining them now."

⌇⌇⌇

The hot stabbing pain seared through Derek and a welling of tears exploded, wrenching his ribcage, overwhelming his body. The loudest, sharpest tears he'd released as yet. He was alone in Ma/s house in his tracksuit, nobody around, so he just let the tears overtake him, standing there, waiting, his head lowered, his body shaking gently.

All the professionals had come, those hardened by their experience in such matters. One of the cops had led him aside, gently so, taking down his information. All routine. Together they had watched her body carried out in a bag. Then, just like that, everything Ma had ever owned had become his.

He owned the house outright. It was already paid for. He could live there comfortably and wouldn't need to worry about a mortgage. He started remembering all the times he'd helped her stand, held her up, kept one arm around her waist as he'd made sure the toilet paper made contact against the cold flesh of her butt as he wiped away smears. No matter what she ate, he'd gag on the stink, his eyes watering. He was no professional, but he'd gotten the job done while developing a respect for nurses.

How he'd scrub his hands in scolding water. Moisten a small towel to wash Ma's legs, patting her bum, trying always to be polite about it. After applying baby powder, he'd use another towel to wash Ma once more. He could never wash his own hands often enough.

Lastly, he'd slip her into a clean robe, turning away not to see her naked. He'd lower her to bed and make sure she took her pills, each of which he'd set out ahead of time.

Those were the days. Not what he wanted to remember, but memories that came nonetheless, that filled him, yanking down inside his body to pull at his throat, making it hard to breathe.

He remembered nights when he'd seen that she was awake, aware of her surroundings, and appeared pleased to know he was there. The TV on, the volume turned down low and she seated there making comments about the actors she tended to like while he took out the trash or killed a big cockroach or washed the dishes or scrubbed her ceramic kitchen sink until it shined. He wasn't just anybody. He was her only son. All her hard work had supported him all his life. He'd been loved. There was no question about it. Never had been.

Derek went to a window in the living room and looked out at her street. He couldn't see much. Her neighborhood, much like her clothes, her looks and the overall condition of her apartment had, with time, lost its luster. It was dumpier than it had been when growing up, some of the buildings nearby dirtied with graffiti, a few windows boarded up here and there. If asked, he'd say that the whole city, and by that he meant all five boroughs, was slipping into a rat-infested mode, with crime on the rise, weak leadership, a lack of vision.

For a while, during a childhood which in that moment felt like part of a golden time, when he'd needed most to feel safe, the neighborhood had been his own. He'd viewed each street as a theatre stage, the setting for his boyhood adventures. He'd been a tatty snot-nosed kid full of the usual nonsense that kids often tended to brag about. He'd seen an upswing in the neighborhood during his time in school as it became viewed as both affordable and respectable, with streets getting lined with more small shops, improvements made to multi-family housing units.

Residents migrated in and out. The number of burglaries and break-ins, especially to cars, spiked and dropped, was never consistent. It was hard to believe that kids like him once ran around block by block in packs. Equally hard to believe there'd been a surging gentrification that had seen the conversion of many multi-families into apartments and condos for young professionals who could afford an easy subway ride into mid-town Manhattan.

Now, it all looked and felt as if in decay. There were fewer kids, though just as many shit-heads and loudmouths on the streets. They didn't live there. They drifted about. Gangs were their families.

Yet in some ways it was tamer, too. Hard to pigeonhole it and he never trusted anyone who had. He'd made a run to Canarsie a few days back and he hadn't seen one cop or posse of gangbangers the whole time. You just never knew. That's how it was. Those who said they knew, hell, they were full of it.

Ma should have sold and gotten out before dying. They'd talked about this. He'd never liked it, but he'd understood her stubborn insistence on staying put. Familiarity was a comfort and she'd had this ridiculous fantasy that he and Shooter would move in after she died.

Shooter. Why the fuck had he ever married her? They'd settle out of court. No lawyers. No games. She could go after him for Ma's house, he supposed, but he knew she wouldn't. She didn't have the nerve or the stomach for it. She preferred to stay lost in her photo world, living in that darkroom of hers, unable to face the day without a camera in her hand. Besides, she was getting the apartment and he'd leave her enough money to live without working for a year. If she squandered it, that was her problem.

The thing about Shooter, and Ma too, was that they were a pair of outcasts, but it wasn't as if anyone cared. Ma had gotten vaccinated, had worn her mask every day during the pandemic, had avoided Covid completely because she'd spent most of her days alone, forgotten about, watching television, enjoying her visits from Sister Nancy, who'd also been in her mask constantly. Sister Nancy had kept Ma alive during her strokes. Photographs had kept Shooter alive. People simply did what they had to do.

What startled Derek was to think that Ma hadn't left Sister Nancy anything in her will. That, and the fact that Sister Nancy had never gotten Covid. God had looked after that woman. And after him, he supposed, but why would God do that? Why bother with *him*? He didn't deserve it. God sure was strange that way.

He had to get out. He'd put the place up for sale immediately. He could feel this Hassan character getting closer. Ruthless Hassan. That dude would find him and ice him. Derek could smell him coming. Any day now, any day.

One way to appease Shooter would be to split the profits of the sale of the house fifty-fifty. That would shut her up for good, give her more than enough to either stay or get out. She could do whatever the hell she wanted. What she wouldn't get would be any of the money he'd take when he closed out all of Ma's bank accounts. He'd give Sister Nancy a pile for being such a saint. Knowing her, she'd donate it to charity.

What Ma hadn't known was that he'd hidden bundles of cash all over her place. He'd now start putting them together, counting up the sums. Belize seemed the best place. He'd been looking it up online. Holly had told him about it a while back. He'd been keeping in touch with Holly. He'd have to let her know about Ma dying, about how it was the proverbial straw breaking the camel's back with Shooter, just wasn't happening, and it was finally agreed upon between the two of them that they'd end it.

Holly wouldn't come to him in the city, which was fine, probably safer. He'd go see her. Take the bus. Holly, he hoped, would keep it all a secret. Holly was loyal that way, though he didn't trust her, not really, nor did he trust Shooter. Woman were capable of anything.

Now this. The end of Ma. He'd seen it coming. He'd known, but he still hadn't been prepared for how much it hurt. If there was one consolation, it was that grieving over her death made it easier for him to leave Shooter.

He'd been thinking a lot about Belize and now here it was; he could follow through on that thinking. Had to admit it. Holly had come roaring back into his consciousness, his dreams, driving him crazy with desire. He couldn't. But he should. He wanted to. What if Holly said no? She wouldn't. He'd do it. He'd disappear. Hide out with her. Keep off the streets and enough time would pass so that Hassan might lose interest in him.

He had money enough, and there'd be more after the sale of Ma's place. He felt as if Holly was calling out to him. He imagined her naked in her bed with her long black hair shining as it draped over her pillow, and the almost porcelain shine in her long thin legs. Her toenails painted in different colors. That silver ankle bracelet she wore. Real silver, of course, nothing but the best for Holly.

She'd give him the lowdown on what he might need visa-wise, if anything. They spoke English down there in Belize, though he knew some street Spanish, enough to buy basics and take a taxi. It was a stellar plan. By passing on, Ma had given her blessings.

Shooter would be free too, and he, Derek Kotas, would vanish. After a few years, things would cool down, the pandemic would be forgotten, and Hassan would be dead or back in prison. Otherwise, who was he kidding? If nothing changed, he'd end up at the pearly gates asking for Ma to let him in.

EIGHTEEN

Agnes, perturbed, ill at ease in her own skin and unable to think clearly, had become obsessed with Ginger and what their dreams had been when they'd first met and how none of those dreams had materialized. Such memories, she knew, affected her moods, but they were altering her photography, as well. She saw this kinship with death in all her photos. She, not Derek, was the one upset, unable to function, sodden with grief. Derek seemed buoyant and garrulous, behaving as if Ginger's death meant a burden had been released from his shoulders.

Maybe it had. She should talk to him about this, but they weren't talking much any longer. She didn't like admitting he'd never be around again. That she was on her own. The papers had been signed. He was going to leave her with some money. Maybe he had loved something in her, after all.

She had admired the way he'd taken care of the funeral, and then the emptying and sale of Ginger's place. He'd done it promptly, without much emotion, including her in a very generous share of the profits. She had more money now than ever.

Yet Agnes had been weeping in her sleep, though that, she knew, had to eventually cease. It started when she'd learned that Derek had gone away, saying he needed to be alone. He'd refused to tell her where he was going. "Don't get in touch with me," was all he'd said.

She respected his need for privacy. It wasn't as if she had any choice. But the house was sold. He had no place, nothing to come back to. Where had he gone? Why? Agnes felt she deserved to know, but she also suspected Derek would disagree. More proof that it really was over, once and for all. A double death, in a way. Ginger and Derek.

On the other hand, she was free. She had money. She could do whatever she pleased. Never, in her life, had she been able to say that. I was now hers for the asking, and we had our screenplay project and were seeing more of each other. We'd started sleeping together and behaving like a couple, unable to stop touching each other in or out of bed.

Along with the screenplay, Agnes immersed herself deeper into her photography work. She talked for hours on end about photography and this led to what I saw in her as a serene joy. It was obvious, wasn't it, that the right turn of events had occurred. The Titanic had sunk, but everyone had survived. Ginger had been the iceberg.

She didn't need to ask if I was enjoying her company. The answer was written all over my smiling face. This shift, this moving from dream into reality, this kinship we felt. Such a word, kinship. Such a notion. Not like one of her regular dreams that tended to morph into nightmares of different stalkers tracking her down, their hands around her throat while she was gagging. She didn't usually share them, though she'd started to with me.

Once memories evolved into dreams, and she experienced this often, she looked for them in her photos. One memory involved her Uncle Roger looking bloodshot and bereft of hope after his divorce. Roger had had no children after a marriage that had lasted two years. His wife had run off with another lawyer who earned more money and owned a house in Hawaii.

She'd told me this about her Uncle Roger, a man I felt I was getting to know. While listening, I'd become droll, mournful and silent. Afterwards, still silent, I took her out for brunch at a café where we could behave as if the pandemic had ended, had never happened. We drank mimosas on a sunny patio under a glassed-in enclosure that made the two of us feel as if we were dining in a terrarium.

I had remained grimly reticent. Agnes had never seen me this way. It had to do with her Uncle Roger. He was her father's brother. Hard to believe. Maybe he'd been adopted. I just felt sorry for the man.

Agnes had asked her mother about this, but Shirley had perfected the art of dodging such questions and never explained the Roger situation. It was as if Shirley couldn't be bothered because Roger wasn't from the O'Meara clan, her side of the family.

Agnes had seen that I enjoyed her company because my intelligence required little from her to make me laugh and feel whimsical. I liked feeling this way. She thought me handsome and told me so, which, finding it an embarrassment, I asked her to stop. Agnes had taken one photo of me in a blue shirt, the blue of the sky in April early in the morning after a rain has blown through the night. In the photo I'm wearing a slightly darker blue blazer and slacks. The kicker for Agnes was my shoes in that picture; they were mahogany-colored loafers and shined as if dipped into varnish.

She had never seen me in jeans. I didn't wear them. She'd asked me why one time and I'd said I'd worn my share of dusty denim as a boy in Texas. My slacks, never cuffed or pleated, spoke of me as a gentleman, a lover, a courtesan of sorts, though Agnes never heard me suggest the slightest interest in other women. Such an appealing scent infused her memory whenever she thought of me, one that blended licorice with a slight trace of almost lemony cologne. Unlike her parents, I didn't smoke. Always there, fond of her, I was a man who didn't need Christmas as an excuse to give her presents.

I bought her a camera, a used Leica M6 Classic, a model she'd once told me about, which had blown her away. "I thought you'd like it, but please don't insult me by asking me what it cost."

She agreed not to. There was a bit of father and daughter between us, but I didn't mind. Her father was gone, after all. There still existed a small vacancy that I could fill. She didn't even need to bring it up. It was as if she knew, had thought about it, and didn't find it strange or disturbing.

I was different in that, especially after Derek, I was on the genteel side and yet prone to a slight hedonism. I burned rapidly when I got too much sun. I had no sisters or brothers. No family at all. I could talk finance and investing, but I suspected that would bore her, which it did, so we talked music. I brought her flowers, mostly roses, and chocolates. I insisted she come to my apartment each Sunday for a meal, one that I'd cook for the two of us. I looked funny in an apron, less at home in one than my mother ever did. While cooking, I'd sing along to music I liked, music she often didn't know, one more harmless reminder of our age difference.

Agnes would watch me cook and think of ways to photograph me in that silly apron and I'd laugh and say, "Not on your life, no pictures of me like this."

Our Sundays together reminded her of how when her father would cook a barbecue on the back patio during the summer, also in an apron, and Shirley, tanned, drink in hand, would saunter in and out of the kitchen with supplies for him, from tongs to sauce ingredients to another drink. Shirley would wear her cinnamon hair pinned up, and she'd scuff along in sandals, a flowing batik-pattern dress, a necklace made from coral or Bakelite. She and her Daddy would toast each other, beaming, increasingly inebriated as the sun began to settle and it was finally time to eat.

She remembered how her father would touch her mother repeatedly in front of everyone, without shame, making all sorts of sexual innuendos as he talked. It had seemed natural to her. They were married and in love, after all.

Agnes was sure she never really knew if her father was faithful or up to no good, but she could admit she didn't mind. She grew up accepting that he was a friendly sort and understood it was wrong the one time he cornered her alone in the living room and said he knew he shouldn't touch her mother like that, not there of all places, in front of his own children. Creepy as it was, Agnes viewed this as her father's privilege. No sooner would he confess to being too egregiously sexual, he would touch Shirley there again, softly, his hand moving gently up and down over the front of her pelvis while Shirley, drunk, blushing, giggling, would then shove him away with a loud, "Stop it, you lecher. Not in front of the kids. How many times do I have to tell you?"

Agnes found that I enjoyed hearing such stories, my own childhood nothing like hers whatsoever. She'd go on about her father's hands wandering to press and squeeze against her mother's bottom, her stomach, her breasts, on the cheek, holding her throat which led him to kiss her on the lips while meat sizzled and smoked on the brazier and Shirley, just as drunk, just as openly carnal, folded and kissed her husband in return without squirming away.

Even though Agnes understood as she got older how lewdly and inappropriately her parents had behaved, especially since all three of their siblings were usually present, it still struck her as acceptable. She'd liked it. Keeping to a pact with her brothers, she'd never discussed this behavior with anyone. Until now. With me. I was flattered. I thought it a bit crass, but they were married, after all, and in the privacy of their own homes.

"At least they weren't doing that to you and your brothers, right?"

"Right. I guess."

Weren't all parents equally as promiscuous when they'd had too much drink in the summer sun? Reflecting back, seeing how sordid it was, she understood better why her mother had kept Daddy in view when possible. Why she was worried when she learned that Daddy often visited Agnes in Providence to go to the movies. Nothing untoward or remotely sexual ever happened, though. She just got to know her father better and outside of their home.

For better or worse, both her parents had been there for her and that's how she wanted to think about and share her experiences with them. They'd been there for her First Communion, and her Confirmation. They showered presents on her each Christmas and often provided the one special gift she asked for, if within reason. They did the same for her brothers.

They'd given her the first SLR camera, an Olympus, that she'd owned. Her father taught her about the ravishing Sophia Loren. Her mother taught her about actors she admired such as Sidney Poitier, Sean Connery and Richard Gere. "Aim high, aim for a gentleman," she liked to say. "He doesn't have to be rich, but he should be trustworthy and a barrel of laughs to be with."

This, said Agnes, is how she felt about me. She'd never felt the same way about Derek.

"I just outgrew him, I guess. It was bound to happen."

She said she understood this now. Any thrill she once felt thinking about the criminal realm Derek worked in by night had long ago passed. She wanted stability, affection and, she could admit it now and it wasn't painful, someone who would soothe her as a man she could rely on. She also needed a man who wouldn't disparage her for her sexual relations with women, though she wasn't going back to Holly ever again.

"That's over too, but I don't regret it."

Why should she? I didn't mind. I had a calloused and yet not unappealing attitude that had come, I believed, with age. "I just don't care about you and Holly," I told her. "It's none of my business. I know Holly. I've spoken to her many times. I think she'd agree with me that you and I are apt for each other, if that's the right word, because we already know we can't have children together. Not that I want any because I don't. So let's just see how it goes. Honestly, Agnes, I hate to sound morbid, but I don't want to die alone. And neither do you, I think."

I never made her feel ashamed of being the younger one, less experienced, her former boss, wanting to discover, to ask questions, to turn over new pages in a book of life that didn't end. I encouraged her to listen to more opera, as well. She did, tearing up the first time I played for her Mirella Freni's version of *O Mio Bambino Caro*. I watched her as she'd listened. Smiling wistfully when the aria had ended I'd remarked, "Learn, Agnes. Learn and learn some more, it's what this life is all about."

⁓✦⁓

If asked to, I couldn't explain it, but in the wake of my departure from the lost world I can say there were nights when I knew that my angel of death hovered nearby. I heard that angel breathing. It wasn't a man or a woman. It was both, as if a mythical creature, and would appear all of a sudden not from without but from within, hiding inside me and waiting for the appropriate moment to emerge and allow me a glimpse before hiding again in every shadow of every room I ever found myself in.

You see, I don't want this only to be my story. It's Holly's, Derek's, Ginger's. It's ours, too, I suppose, and I can share all sorts of details about Agnes and me, along with my fears and concerns about getting involved with a younger woman, but I think these details would bore you. As a man, I've always found the female mind, in all its incarnations, more challenging and intriguing than that of the male.

Agnes appealed to me in so many ways. She was a source of an infinite number of surprises. Sometimes, like my angel of death, she would be waiting in front of my apartment building, just standing there boldly with camera in hand, saying she knew when I went to the gym and wanted to greet me upon my return and spend the night with me. Other times, it was the way she'd sneer unimpressed by a comment I might pass that she'd deem sexist or stodgy. On some occasions, she'd talk me into sneaking with her to the rooftop of my building, knowing I had to pay the doorman a bribe to unlock the security door and let us do as we pleased up there.

Sometimes we'd kiss or sit on a blanket with a bottle of wine as if having a picnic. Most of the time, that rooftop was a playground for Agnes to shoot her photos. I'd just stare out at the Hudson River, fighting off the wind, my eyes following whatever boats might be passing along.

NINETEEN

AGNES HURRIED TO PUT ON LONG UNDERWEAR and heavy socks before she grabbed her camera bag for a night of capturing as much man-made light in Manhattan that she could find. This pursuit of night shots for her archives of Doomed Landmarks demanded she push herself. It felt right to do so, kept her alert and motivated to believe photography was going to save her from despair, and that she wasn't a failure.

When I asked her about Derek, she told me she didn't know where he'd gone. This worried us both. For all we knew, he could be dead. Agnes had phoned Holly, who'd said she didn't know either, but she wasn't worried at all. She'd said Derek had time-tested survival instincts and knew how to adapt. "He'll be just fine," Holly had told Agnes. "You're the one I'm concerned about."

It could have been that Holly was lying. Agnes didn't think so, but I did. I thought we'd both have to live with whatever Holly decided to share, assuring Agnes she might be disappointed if she put too much faith in her. I was pleased that she was enjoying her time with me. That she liked the advice I gave when she asked for it. I believed my role was to encourage her to be flexible and get on with her life in her own unique way.

After arriving from Queens by subway to Manhattan it felt right to Agnes, with the usual fumes of peril in the air, to be out alone after dark. She was accustomed to these fumes. She liked seeing that there were increasingly more people about, many of them younger, already vaccinated, she supposed, just as she was. As I was, too. Not that the vaccine made any of them less dangerous, especially at night.

Neither of us felt trapped any longer. The deep Covid abyss which seemed to me a bizarre fever dream the more I thought about it, began to shrink and move rapidly farther behind us, part of another less salutary life. Even the politics were changing. Judging by polls, a new mayor, a black man and a former cop would soon be elected. According to some web sites, Governor Cuomo was rumored to be in hot water over a litany of indiscretions.

Agnes was refreshingly indifferent to any of that. She remained obsessed with her pictures, using her trusty and fast lightweight Minolta SLR with a handful of easily changeable lenses. And her new Leica too. What she didn't always take with her was her Nikon F-1 with its bayonet lens. This camera, as I understood it, was still her preference for daytime shooting.

Lurking along, hunkered over, skittish and sly, Agnes sought to discover and select her shots and use the money wisely that she'd spent on film. Though she had money now, there was no reason to be frivolous with it. She knew she could borrow from me if she wanted to, but it wasn't necessary. She'd already paid back the sum she'd borrowed, and she'd entrusted me with $50,000 to decide how best to invest it. We worked on this together, and I taught her how it was done at the most rudimentary level. Though I'd be long gone in the floating world when it happened, my hunches at that time regarding pharma stocks would prove to be correct ones, garnering Agnes significant dividends when she sold them before they crashed.

It didn't surprise me to learn Derek had given her that sum in two large envelopes full of cash. It wasn't money from his mother's will or an insurance policy or part of his inheritance, some of which he intended to share with Agnes once the paperwork cleared. The $50,000, which was only a percentage of what he'd left her, had been drug-dealing profits. Agnes had known some of his hiding places, and she'd been raiding them indiscriminately and setting the money aside in a shoe box she'd kept hidden in one of her closets. So, this cash coupled with what Derek had given her, if managed with prudence, would set her up for life financially.

At first, Agnes hadn't known what to do with it. I advised her to store some of it, in cash, in a safe place. I advised some modest stock purchases, adding to her savings account, and making make small, bi-monthly deposits of about $2,000 dollars into a Vanguard account that I'd helped her open.

"It's all rather conventional, so the IRS won't get suspicious," I told her. "Play your cards right and you won't be poor, not ever again. Hate Derek all you want, but all that drug money is going to take care of you."

"I don't hate him," she said. "How can I?"

She said she couldn't even think about Derek or money, not now, not when she needed to think about images, to *focus*. Life for so many was about greed and she understood this, she did, money allowed an illusion of liberty. However, for her, it had never been a goal or a motivation to live. She said she was grateful to me for the investment advice because she believed, if careful, she'd always have enough money to shoot and process as many photos from negatives as she wanted. She could create a budget. She wouldn't always need to stop when she hit her 48th frame each outing. She could splurge, too, on some new darkroom equipment. Maybe even a new enlarger.

Maybe she would. Maybe she'd upgrade her wardrobe too, and dine out with me at some of the restaurants, only a few of which had not re-opened, that she'd always wanted to try. Maybe she'd travel, though travel still felt like a nuisance with all the ever-changing guidelines that varied country by country to accompany all the fear-mongering rumors of maybe even a fourth wave of the virus.

Conversely, playing it thrifty would contribute to the battle against global climate change. This was a cause dear to her heart. All that silver in the developing chemicals she used wasn't helping the environment one bit. However, if she stopped shooting film manually and went only digital, regardless of her reasons, she'd be like all the others. She didn't want that either.

Agnes had to admit she felt different, renewed, more optimistic. Was it really possible that the Covid era was ending? She said she felt giddy thinking that more than ever she could push herself and experiment. For years, she'd been aching to achieve this freedom from money worries. Her principal rule would remain unchanged. Every shot counted. She catalogued them in her pursuit of history and of one memorable image. Now, she could so without any guilt or concern over where her financing would come from. If Derek wasn't in Queens, then he most likely wasn't dealing any longer. She'd put his wicked drug money back into the world as a means of supporting art galleries and artists and social causes she believed in.

Yet doubts remained. Why now, she asked me, when she'd never been more comfortable? What was wrong with her, anyway? Why was she doing this to herself? She shouldn't have any doubts at all. This felt so weird to her, she said. Like it was a mind-set she was stuck in, and one that nobody else cared about. Nor should they. Why couldn't she admit that she'd rather suffer as a dilettante, her work ignored, shooting film, feeling alone in her battle against conformity? Her reasons for such a stance hadn't changed. Nothing political or professional. I told her that she liked any convenient rationale for complaining. She'd go to her grave with this as part of the pathological impulse that had led her to photography and the arts in the first place. She didn't like that I'd said this, but she'd heard and respected the painful kernel of truth in it.

When night shooting, Agnes sought out neon emanations which she altered through different filter combinations, making the words of a sign, for example, as abstract as possible. She'd gone through a phase of shooting car headlights as they passed, or producing images of long vibrant chaotic colored lines, but she'd tired of that conceit, thinking it gimmicky. What she was hunting for now were reflections within prisms within reflections. A neon or a traffic light against a metallic surface, a reflection that bounced and squiggled back captured in the chrome border around a car window, or any pane of glass for that matter. These reflections tended to find her. They whispered or else they leaped out. She never knew where to walk or to look, her eyes open, keening, the thrill of the hunt tingling inside of her.

Shooting had become fun again. She felt happily childish in her hunger, though the streets still felt like deflated arteries hollowed out by the pandemic. Doorways and buildings evacuated, the hum around her vibrating at a lower pitch. The air more pregnant with peril. Though she always shot at night alone, she began to feel more often that I was with her. She talked to me about choices she could make when it came to framing a certain emanation that might seize her. She found it a pleasure, as did I, to talk over drinks in the evening, or coffee on the mornings when she'd sleep over. Whenever possible, she'd steer her way toward a topic which I confessed I still didn't understand, namely the havoc of emotions known as love. Pardon the pretense in my saying this, but if I were a Shakespearian character, my tragic flaw would be an inadequate comprehension of what those four letters mean. Yet in how many movies do characters say "I love you?" All the time, am I right? Of course, I am.

An ache swelled in my heart whenever thinking about the implications of such a sentence, those three words sometimes blurted out in a swoon of ecstasy. Agnes appreciated my fears. She was patient with me. Did I love her? She'd asked me this. I told her outright that I didn't know. That in truth I was getting closer to figuring out this love question as perhaps the core purpose of my existence, but I didn't feel I knew Agnes or myself well enough yet to say it without wincing. She said I was over-thinking it. That I wanted love to be something perfect. That it wasn't. That love defined itself as one went along, and I shouldn't worry too much about it.

If only it were that simple. I feared she'd take umbrage at all this wishy-washy thinking from one older than herself, but she didn't. This relieved me to no end. She thought my fears rational and said that she'd be disappointed if a man my age didn't guide his words and deeds according to a measured amount of restraint, especially when it came to matters of the heart. She liked this about me. "There's hope yet for the two of us," she said, teasing me.

There was time, as well, though she griped that I talked sometimes as if I were so old. I wasn't. I admit it soothed my ego to hear it. She'd tell me repeatedly I should be at ease with my patience and reserve, that they were qualities she admired. So, I took her advice. I began to relax. We both did.

I found myself spending more time really enjoying the books I read, the strolls I took with her, the small meals I lingered over in her company or else alone poaching in solitude. Seated at night in my apartment, I'd venture down one of my Texas music rabbit holes, head-phones on and listening to Guy Clark, Townes Van Zandt, or to Redd Volkaert playing his Telecaster. I'd close my eyes and imagine Agnes out there in the dark, poised, balanced, her lens open for long expo-sures hoping to create fusillading strobes of green, pink and yellow. Taking succor from Jackson Pollock, much of what she shot at night was intended to represent the cosmological explosions of colliding energy forms that define our every waking moment.

Other nights I'd listen to Régine Crespin, or Kathleen Battle, nur-turing my passion for divas and arias. I'd linger in the ethers that their voices would send me to. I'd relive some of the long conversations I'd had with Agnes, how she'd sink into gloom over whether there was a market for her images, or whether she'd ever achieve notoriety. During such talks, I'd ask why she cared about markets. She had money to live on. An apartment in Queens. No danger that Derek was going to trouble her. Now was the time for her to be an artist. If she needed someone to help sell her work, I would perform the task, gladly so. In the meantime, she needed to reach down deeper, work longer hours in the darkroom, obsessively so, fulfilling herself, actualizing her vision.

If the bashful smile on her face was any indication, Agnes revered the way I nudged, soothed and motivated her in this way. She'd look at me as if shocked by what I'd said, as if hearing it expressed for the first time. Her eyes would widen. This look of bright eagerness would over-come her and, as if ten years younger, she'd lunge toward me and we'd hug and kiss and before long were making love to each other.

She confessed she didn't miss Derek. Was that wrong? No, I told her. Derek probably didn't miss her, either. She yearned to explore, discover, make statements and impressions. She always had, but in this new incarnation she'd begun doing it with more verve and effervescence. She started to trust herself, admitting it was okay that she didn't care how others accepted her shots. They were about her inner life, after all. Her struggle to find sanctity, to make the best of her diurnal rebirths and epiphanies. They weren't just about the pandemic or her miscarriage any longer. They were about moving on from these experiences and learning to see again.

I cheered her on. I listened. We spent many an evening at my place. First, a quiet dinner. Some wine. Some music. Some lovemaking. It was divine. Then she'd head out alone with her camera, returning usually around three in the morning. I'd be long fast asleep, but by noon we'd talk and she'd tell me she was finally getting somewhere. She'd had it with markets, compromises, needing approval and waiting with all the other sheep to be slaughtered. What was the point of residing in a free country if she didn't feel free to honor, use, exploit, value and pursue her freedom?

To hear her tell it, Agnes spent an inordinate amount of time crouched behind parked delivery vans because they allowed her to hide while using her handy 80-200 Vivitar zoom with its stacked polarizer and star filter and one of her last rolls of 1600 speed Fuji *Superia* film. Agnes said that it had been years, going back to 2016 since she'd been able to feel so unencumbered by a fear her work wouldn't please an imaginary audience. It was that same year, 2016, she'd started using this Fuji film, and it had been expensive at $15 dollars a roll, but when still available online she'd purchased bricks of it, spending about $1,000 dollars. This was a large sum for her at that time.

Her suspicions that this film would be discontinued had turned out to be right, but now she feared it might not give her the color saturation she wanted because the rolls were beyond their expiration dates. This was why she also shot with another all-manual Pentax SLR and a telephoto and only a UV filter, using Kodak *Portra* 800 film. Two hoped-for images, two cameras, two kinds of film. Only she knew the details of her experiments, and none of them would matter if she didn't get excellent shots.

She didn't like to use flash when shooting at night because it might call attention to herself. When she shot neon of any kind, she took her sweet time, ever deliberate. There could be nothing urgent or hurried in her process, particularly since most were taken as extreme close-ups and demanded a coordination between her breathing and her hands. To help her with this, she used a collapsible mono-pod to steady her telephoto lenses. She often set the monopod on parking meters or metal newspaper boxes or truck fenders.

The more I saw of Agnes, the more I took a fragile pride in the salubrious effect I appeared to be having on her. She was as thin as I'd ever seen her, a glint in her eye, and she'd get so excited, almost gushing, when she talked about her work. "It's all about the details," she'd say. "The film I use, the light or a lack of it, optimal color saturation, the night pricking at my conscience, bleeding through its neon, staining the cracks in the city's armor before dawn comes to expose them all again."

Agnes. How could I not be fond of her? Did I love her? Perhaps. No, of course I did. I was head-over-heels in love. Yet what was the rush? What was the need for definition? I believed that what we were both doing, if honest with ourselves, was self-serving, true, and destined. In her case specifically, she was serving not a hobby but a reason for being. She didn't need a profession. She needed an affirmation of her desire to make her mark. If she shot thirty-six frames, she'd be lucky to get one pair of worthwhile images. It would still cost her dearly to process the negatives, but that's where the money she now had could come in handy. No matter how many pictures she shot, one or two superb frames validated her daily expenses. They also validated my support.

As far as printing was concerned, she went to her friend Hannah at PrintSpace, who'd color-balance the images before cropping them according to agreed-on specs. Agnes paid a tad extra for these, depending on whether Hannah produced the image on satin, matted, pearl or glossy paper.

We continued to speak about love, just the two of us. Derek and Holly came up in conversation less and less often. She said no, a woman shouldn't *need* a man, shouldn't need anyone, but that didn't mean she shouldn't spend more time with me.

I asked her, "What happened? It's all different now, isn't it?"

"Nothing," she said. "Everything. That's the beauty of it. Just time and some decisions."

Nothing felt wrong. It was too good to be true, but I wasn't about to fight it.

⟞ↄʋↄ⟝

I never tired of enjoying her photos. They hung in each room of my apartment. Agnes was an artist in the sense pursuing art in the way Beethoven defined it, meaning she was perverse and selfish. Like Andre Malraux, she saw art as a revolt against fate. Like Ralph Waldo Emerson, her art was a jealous mistress. Like Nietzsche, she viewed art, ultimately, as the proper task of life. I strung this quartet of geniuses together in my imagination not only due to excessive reading, but to a recently finished crossword puzzle in which the four longest answers to the puzzle's main clue answered the question: What Is Art?

I harbored the conceit that I was creative, too, though I'd never admit that in public. If I could even brook such a statement it was only because what I found in Agnes was an energy, feckless and petulant, that I was growing comfortable with and had never known as an only child. This might also be why I had become a producer rather than a director. I'd learned from studying masters of cinematography such as Sven Nykvist, among others, how demanding Agnes's discipline could be. This hadn't made my interest in photography any less fervid. If anything, it had deepened my respect for it.

What had any of this to do with my abiding lack of certainty when it came to defining love? I couldn't say. Love's definition, I'd always thought, was central to our nature as humans. It was a motivator behind the desires that fueled our choices. Love made it necessary to change its defining parameters as we changed. I began to believe my definitions were not inaccurate. Agnes listened as I aired them out, and she supported them. Maybe love was just learning to trust one's intuition? Or maybe, better still, love was knowing that you didn't know.

A person fell in or out of love, just as Adam and Eve had fallen from grace in the garden. Such a fall couldn't be blamed on the serpent. Or could it? Nor should the apple be seen as guilty. All Eve's fault for taking that bite? Wait a minute, hadn't Eve come from Adam's Rib? So it was Adam's fault. As if love wasn't a paradisiacal experience? As if it were a sin? Nobody really knew, and such freedom I felt, such a liberation overcame me when I nurtured such a thought.

It was once so much easier for me to think about love. Now, feeling so joyously buoyant and lifted by my growing fondness for Agnes, it left me stung by its many thorns. But so what? Not a problem. I could with ease define the love for a long car trip from, say, Florida to Montana. I could define the love of rolling smoothly alongside the Hudson up the West Side Highway with Gene Ammons blowing sax on the radio at four o'clock in the morning. Love defined itself with ease when many years ago, back when I knew so much, when I got tired on a long road trip, which meant my companion would take over the wheel allowing me to nap.

I could love a woman, a man, a child, if I could love myself. Could I love a woman if I didn't understand her or myself? Did I understand anything? I had no ready answers. I mistrusted anyone who said they had. Perhaps, at last, the snakes of wisdom were creeping into my beard.

Life with Agnes offered such felicity. She didn't mind cooking now and then, and she'd cook for us while naked in her apron. I'd watch her rosy bottom, feasting my eyes but feeling no guilt since it was consensual and in my own home. She never complained about an occasional cockroach, or a fume of garbage from the alley outside my apartment window. That old apartment Derek had left her with was far worse and I knew it.

Nor did she mind telling me outright when neither one of us wanted to cook that we should dine out by candlelight on nouveau cuisine prepared by international chefs whose names neither of us could pronounce correctly. Waffles, wine or winging it, so to speak. The polarities in the life we'd begun to share were serving to define, for me, gradations between strata, distinguishing lust from affection from desire from other forms of love, love, love. My dearly beloved Agnes could be the royal queen of my utopian fantasies, or else a Lolita-like fire of yearning that crackled in my old-man blood, but love itself, as I'd suspected all along, was not sex, was not any one mood or object or state of existence.

Agnes, I believed, knew this too. She had learned well from her experiences with Derek and Holly. The sexual element between us was often a vigorous tussle and release, a dazzling eclipse to be repeated as the tides of promiscuity ebbed and then began their slow heated surging again.

Seated there in my kitchen, soaking in her energy, beaming at Agnes, I yearned to define love. It had to be and it was more than the percolating carnal heat, the emotional states that intrigued and sometimes drained me. I'd always been intimidated by and infatuated with women, gloriously and ridiculously vulnerable to their wiles, though I'd never gotten as intimate with any of them as I had with Agnes. All she had to do was glance at me a certain way in order to incite a trickle of curiosity, hunger and, at times, melancholy. Was this part of love, too?

Indeed, it was, but what of marriage? Such a leap of faith would mean accepting my as yet incomplete definition of love. Marriage was certainly on my mind. Did couples marry out of fear, or was it for security and money? This was a fair question. It rubbed against my notion that the marriage contract was sacred because it was grounded in sacred love. But love wasn't sacred. Love was everything. My, my, was I one confused bachelor.

I turned to friends I trusted. I asked Avi, who'd been married a long time. Did he still define love for his wife as anything near to how he'd defined it when they'd first met? Avi had been startled by my question, ascribing it to me spending too much time home alone during the pandemic. Then I told him I'd met someone. "I'm crazy about her, Avi. Just crazy."

This changed Avi's response. I swear I heard him smiling over the phone. For years, he'd wondered why I'd stayed a bachelor for so long.

Avi told me, in his opinion, that love's definition changed in terms of how the love was expressed, but the core feelings and impulses were still the same inimitable mystery. There was some part of an answer in this for him, but it wasn't enough. Not for him. Not for anybody. It wouldn't be enough for me either.

I should consider myself warned. Avi believed love was tied to desire and the sexual, especially that core element of it, yet how define love for a pet or a child or a project? This kind of love was about hoped-for results, the steps of nurturing, shaping and development. There was never any guarantee such love was requited, which made it similar to married love, but it wasn't the same because the goal was more concrete.

"Love," he said, sounding a dark ironic laugh. "Ennis, we should make a movie."

I thanked Avi. We were still close friends, after all. The pandemic hadn't created any wedge between us. Maybe we could return to producing movies, even though we both knew that given the economic situation with most investors that this wouldn't happen.

I might create a series, though, suitable for one of the streaming outlets. It would be a love story. No more gangsters. No more Fentanyl. After talking with Avi about love, I had enough to ponder before I wrote another word of any new screenplay. Plus, I had the script Agnes and I were still working on. It, too, was about love.

I looked at Agnes seated across from me in my tiny kitchen, sipping her coffee. I couldn't define what I felt in terms of love, but it was there. I felt something remarkable, like a warm glowing expansion in my chest. It was tied to and fed on my desire for Agnes's mind, her friendship, her smile, her personality, her silly jokes, and all the imperfections in her body. If I married her, I could love her in a way that no other man would be allowed to.

Or was it lust I felt for her youth, the cheerful bounce in that body of hers? Some lust was there, brewing within me, without question, but there was awe, a beatific contentment that simmered under my skin. I didn't want to reduce it to what I believed were the rigidities of lust. This transcended lust, and I felt lifted by it. I felt I was "seeing" Agnes, convinced at last I'd been given an opportunity that, for once, I had the nerve to seize on.

TWENTY

Keep it a secret, Holly. Ma? She's gone. Her apartment too. Yeah, I sold it. Agnes in the other apartment, living that old life in Queens, but for me, all of it, gone, gone, gone. Never became the man I thought I was. Had to get on with my life. It was the best way. Holly you can come with. We can both get tanned sipping Pina Coladas on the beach.

"So what you thinking?" Holly asked him.

They were in her apartment. It was roomy and sometimes, with the windows open, it smelled of the sea.

Belize, he thought, but he wouldn't say it. Not yet. Too soon. "I'm thinking, you in?" said Derek.

Holly said there was nothing much for her to do anymore. She was sick of everything, had hit a dry spell. It happened. All made worse by Covid. Her life had become dreary and she was sick of all the days she'd only seen sunshine when it had peeked through the big window in her apartment late in the afternoon, or else she went out to the balcony to watch before it dipped below the horizon. She was getting thinner too; she'd never been this skinny in her life. *But do you still find me attractive?*

"Sure I do," he said. "What you talking about? You got a figure that don't quit."

She leaned on him, running one hand down his chest. "But am I really?"

"Really what? Don't beg, Holly. It ain't becoming." Ma used to say that to him. "Why would I lie?"

"Because you're a gangster and a drug dealer." She ran her hand into his jeans and began to fondle his crotch. "Derek. I don't want to be alone."

"We'll find our way. Don't you worry."

He twisted, pulling her hand away. He then grabbed her both her arms and lifted her with ease off the sofa and carried her toward the bedroom. "See, if you were fat I couldn't do this."

It had never happened so fast, so spontaneously and with such wild abandon with Shooter. Happened explosively all the time with Holly, any way he wanted. From behind, with her on top, and he'd go down on her and lick and nibble, she was so clean with a smell he liked.

She'd let him slap and bite her now and then. She'd slap back and bite his ear and when they were done they were really done. Wiped out. Then he'd sleep like a king and forget all about Ma and the life he was leaving behind.

Though he could afford it, he didn't take her out to eat. Didn't work that way with Holly. She had other friends for that. She had her own money and liked to show it off. Sometimes, she'd show him off too, but not very often. Fine with him. She paid and went where she wanted to go. She got him vaccinated finally. Took him shopping, bought him clothes. A pair of leather pants. Tight around his legs. A black shirt too. All in black. She bought him a necklace made from real gold, or so she'd said.

How could he complain? She liked to spend.

They drove around in her fine car, a BMW. Wasn't like home, but he'd get used to it. Nothing would ever be like home. Ma's ghost was helping him understand this. He had to think of Queens as more than home now, it was the past, a fairy tale, and he'd never go back. Sure, he missed it, but he wanted to stay alive. Hassan, those who wanted to kill him, they'd never find him. They'd only know that he'd bolted. That he wasn't around. Without a word. And now somebody else was cashing in, pushing the poison. Fine, let sleeping dogs lie.

Providence was full of hicks and loudmouthed morons that thought they were so tough. Too many of its restaurants were still closed, but he didn't care. He was there for Holly. The sex. It was a pit stop, nothing else. He'd stay for as long as needed before Holly got bored. She might come with if he agreed to it, and she might not. He didn't want her to rush any decisions. That was the beauty of it. No hurries, no worries. Endless sex. New threads. Nice meals. More sex.

In the morning, which for Holly was never before noon, she'd make coffee for him. It had an aroma that perfumed the apartment and made him feel like somehow he'd ended up in this heavenly place and couldn't believe his good luck. She'd wear a pink nightie that barely covered her ass and he'd grab her big hairy pussy and make her wet whenever he could, since she didn't wear any panties. He'd kiss her all over and they'd start going at it again and maybe around two in the afternoon they'd shower and sit together over coffee and whatever he wanted, if he was hungry. Holly would say no problem and call for delivery. They'd eat and then maybe smoke a joint and then go for a cruise down to the sea in her car.

So many days like this Derek had lost count, but he didn't care about time. He wasn't thinking as much about Ma not like in the early days though she was still there, she'd always be. *Ma I miss you.* He'd never thought he could feel so friggin' happy. He stopped looking over his shoulder all the time. He breathed differently. Slept better, too, and sometimes would wake to a stillness that was so unusual it unnerved him. Wasn't used to it. He'd look at Holly sleeping there, an angel, a devil, all his for now.

Holly said she was feeling happier too, better than she'd felt in a long time. She was really into the sex, couldn't get enough. Holly knew, too, how to get out and find beaches that weren't all that crowded because they usually went on weekdays when most folk were working. They'd take long beach walks together but never get too romantic, which was fine with him. He'd spend time alone at those beaches. Holly would too. She was good like that. She gave him his space. He'd stare at the waves and he'd listen and he'd feel himself flooded with memories of Ma and Buzzy and Queens, who he'd been and what he'd said, so many close shaves, so many nights sweating it out, risking his life with addicts and other dealers and so many memories that he couldn't choose one, it was impossible, so he let them stream through him as the waves rolled in and rolled out, each one restoring and cleaning his soul.

There was one time when it, *the subject*, came up. They were on a beach in a place he'd never heard of, some kind of island they'd needed to cross a long bridge to get to, but it was nice. Holly said maybe they'd keep driving and if the did they'd need to cross another bridge so they could get to Newport and have dinner there. The whole state was one long bridge after another. What the hell, why not? This was living, especially after Covid.

They got fresh air, listened to the sea, walked the beach. What a life. Sex, beaches, restaurants or delivery. Could be a whole lot worse. Just so long as Holly didn't get any ideas about commitment now that Shooter and the triangle game was out of the picture.

Damn, but she was getting ideas. He could read her. "You know," said Holly. "We've been together two months."

"So? Who's counting?"

That had ended it. He turned mean, ice cold, glaring at her. He hadn't liked doing it that way, but it worked. There was still *the subject.* He brought it up. "I mean, I never pull out. How you control that?"

She usually had this peaceful look on her pretty face, like she was enjoying life because she was an angel and it was, for her, an endless frolic in heaven. But don't cross Holly Greene. Don't doubt her. She had smirks, daggers and all sorts of ways to stab an enemy in the back. Derek knew he hadn't seen the worst of them. He didn't want to. He went easy and he got along.

"I have everything under control," she said.

"It's a woman thing. I get it."

"No you don't, Derek. Don't kid yourself. Just do me a favor and don't ask me again."

He said he wouldn't. They'd live. Really live. Sure, it was a risk going in without protection, but why not take it? The innocent days with Ma were gone and this made him sad about being part of a family that was no more, he and Ma a kind of couple, something that used to be. Made him feel angry too. He'd done nothing to deserve this. Just like he'd felt with Shooter after her miscarriage.

—⌇—

They started planning his move to Belize. Best time to go was summer. Cheapest. Not the tourist season. Holly wasn't sure she'd go. She was still thinking about it. She was cooking more too. Always in the kitchen now and this was a new obsession with her. She said she was fed up with delivery and restaurants and wanted to eat more, eat better and to gain weight. In her opinion, she was way too skinny, it wasn't healthy.

"You sound like Shooter now," he said. "Never happy about how you look."

"You shut up about Agnes. She's my lover too. She's off limits. We have no right. Neither of us. She's out of our lives and I hope she's happy now. She deserves to be."

Fine, whatever, he could deal with Holly's loyalty. He wasn't about to argue. Maybe it was better this way, coping with a problem by not dealing with it, pretending it wasn't there. Not that Shooter was or had ever been a problem. He'd done the right thing by letting her go. He was sure of it now. Just as sure he was glad not to be dealing anymore. To think of all the scumbags he'd had to trust until he had cash in hand and could walk away. Or else run. Never trust a junkie or a user or a dealer. Never. So glad he was out of that life. Buzzy and even Ma's ghost had told him he'd done good.

What he had now was all he needed. Holly. Going down on her sweet pussy. Sex in the morning and sex at night. She drank cocktails with funny names, but she didn't smoke much weed and didn't like talking about hard drugs, though her medicine cabinet was full of prescription bottles that he stayed the hell away from. This proved she was high all the time. Downers, uppers, all of it legal and prescribed. None of it any of his business.

The meds explained her mood swings. Holly had what she liked to call, laughing at herself, her "first world problems," like which kind of olive oil to use and whether she should use liquid or powder forms of laundry detergent. She had her therapist, her meds, her yoga, her Pilates, her eccentric rich friends and all her books, but she seemed to spend most of her time alone sulking, brooding, using solitude to keep herself at ease and under control.

They never talked about this. She was a complicated woman. He didn't mind. He preferred it that way. Shooter had tried hard drugs, she'd gone to a shrink but she hadn't liked it and had avoided prescription meds. She'd also been a chatterbox, but with Holly it was all secret silent codes like he had to read her little tics and grimaces and smirks to figure out what she was thinking. Not much spoken language at all, and on her meds all the time, a glassy look to her eyes.

Finally, he sneaked a closer look at the pharmacy inside her medicine cabinet. It made his Fentanyl trade look kind of amateurish and lightweight. Holly and Elvis, he thought, peas in a pod. It was probably gonna end in a bad way.

Why should they talk more? He thought he wanted to, but not really. He didn't want to love anyone either. He just wanted to get his rocks off, enjoy his pleasures. Besides, he couldn't trust women, couldn't trust anybody. Not Shooter, nobody. People were too secretive, too afraid. It was like they put on their Covid masks over the masks they already wore all the time. Even with all the sex, he wasn't fucking Holly. He was fucking her body. Her mind was elsewhere. He'd felt the same way with Shooter. It was weird.

———⁓⁓⁓———

Nobody understood love. Why the fuck should he? Sure, Holly was cooking up a storm now and he felt grateful to her for the meals, the company and most of all going down on her, but any love as he saw it wasn't a reason for commitment. Not this time. Been there, done that. Holly should know better and she acted liked she did, but the truth was she didn't get it. Not at all. She was spoiled, doped up, an airhead living in a fantasy world and unwilling to accept that Derek Kotas, for one, didn't feel the emotions or the need for companionship that Holly Greene did.

Earth to Holly. Time to change the game. Belize was out. He

wouldn't go there. She'd try to visit him there, but she'd never find him because he'd be in South America. Ecuador, to be exact, and it would be fresh again and he'd meet a nice Latina woman who could cook.

This was no time to start talking or sharing plans. He wasn't interested. Nor did he know how to tell her anything. It seemed Holly felt it from him because she'd started talking more, a lot more, wouldn't turn off the gab and there'd be that glassy look in her eyes as if the meds were kicking in, and she'd breathe like she was hyperventilating and overheated, drinking wine in the kitchen, walking around with food in her hand all the time now, saying it was time to grow up and how she, neither one of them, could always choose running away as an option, that sometimes you had to stay and tough it out for the good of the relationship.

What kind of talk was that? Good of the relationship. Stop talking smack, Holly.

He'd gotten comfortable growing distant. He was almost frigid at times and there were harder lines in his many faces, the many masks he wore, all of them as if chiseled into his features. Set there. Hard as concrete.

She was getting softer around the chin, too. Pudgy in places. How did that happen? She'd always been so skinny. It was from sleeping all day, and the meds, and all the Italian food and the deliveries from Federal Hill, and the Italian bakeries eating calzones and cannoli and lasagna. Lots of red wine. Sleeping later and later. Eating too much pizza. More wine. No exercise. Slower sex. Sometimes sleeping all day, especially when it rained. Complaining she didn't feel well and off to the doctors again, or so she said, though she could have been going anywhere.

Who knew what her prescription meds were doing to her body. She'd lock herself into her bedroom and stay on the phone. She'd start crying out of the blue. There were nights on the phone with her mother she'd go on and on yakking while eating a whole box of chocolates and downing a bottle of wine.

Something was up. Any idiot could see it. He'd seen Shooter go through some phases but nothing like this roller coaster ride, this steady plunge Holly was taking. He didn't have the patience for it. He didn't really care either. Sex was fine, but when he looked at Holly now the first thing that came to mind was that the worst thing had happened. That he'd knocked her up.

He never brought up *the subject.* He didn't have to. He found her pregnancy test kit in the rubbish bin next to the toilet. Almost three months now they'd been together. It all made sense.

He didn't know what the hell to do. Holly probably wanted to keep it. Sure, sure he should have insisted on them using protection, but all that freewheeling, liberating sex, compensating for what went down with Shooter. Those restaurant dinners, cocktails, weed, drinks, her meds and more sex, it had slowed her down, tired her out. Everyone gets older, some faster than others. She got more emotional now, easily triggered, took a lot less. Yeah it all made sense, but she had to be sensible enough to know he wouldn't marry her, not in a million years. The last thing he wanted.

He started to avoid her. Didn't want to talk. She played it her way and started, in return, avoiding him, maybe thinking that he'd view it as punishment. She even made him sleep on the couch some nights. The whole thing had shifted. Maybe she wanted a kid. Could be. Hard to say. Probably. It would give her something to live for. He'd never trusted Holly; she was fun and a great lay, but not the kind of woman you married, so he couldn't say he'd *stopped* trusting her. Truth be told, he trusted nobody. Holly should have known this.

Not one second more of their time together would lead anywhere. His marriage to Shooter had shown him he'd never really wanted a mate for life. Never wanted much of anything except to chill out alone in his own way, at his own speed. It was the miscarriage and Ma's dying that had cemented this idea.

For him, the right answer to conventional life was one word: no. He had cash and he'd start fresh somewhere. He'd just keep Holly thinking Belize, figuring she was already scheming how she could get herself a place there so she could come after him with her kid under one arm. She'd want his money which, compared to hers, was chicken feed. Still, she'd want it all.

He started sneaking time on her laptop, doing research, clearing the browser afterwards so she wouldn't know the sites he'd been searching. He didn't have a phone any longer. He had nothing. Totally off the grid. Paid cash for everything.

Maybe Florida. The economy was good there and they'd gone easy on masks and lockdown protocols, basically giving the finger to the rest of the country. He could buy a cheap place there, not South Beach in Miami of course but in other areas that weren't as popular. Get himself a trailer on a slab. Change his name. Grow a beard. Live in sandals. Just disappear one night on a Greyhound bus and never look back.

After their last argument, with Holly suggesting he start working somewhere, he'd started drinking. He normally didn't drink, but he didn't want to be, as she'd put it, "part of a couple looking after each other."

He'd had enough of that nonsense. The drinking was a sign. It meant he understood that Holly wanted her hooks in him. The time had come. The best he could do for himself was to split with his few happy memories intact. He wouldn't go back to being the bad-ass dealer he'd been. He could, but he didn't want that. Re-invention was always possible, only this time in a new place. None of the stench of death and Queens around him, and all his memories of Ma.

Best part of all this was that he didn't feel connected to anything in the same way any longer. Drinking helped him muddy all the precise thoughts in his head. Razor blades of insight that gave him a headache. The whole thing was simple. Keep away from Holly. Don't let her get too close. Then, on the sly, ditch Providence. How much of an imbecile he'd been. He didn't want, he *needed* to move on. One cheap bus ticket and a gym bag full of all his cash. As Buzzy used to say, travel light and it's easy to blow Dodge at the drop of a dime.

———⁓———

Miami by bus for now. Maybe Ecuador in the future. Cuenca, to be exact. He'd have to see and make adjustments, but he'd fit in down in Miami, he was sure of that. Eventually, with the help of some friends active in the Miami trade community, he'd make his way and establish himself. He'd shave his head and grow a huge beard, change his look completely. Maybe use a different name. See about changing it legally. Bone up on Spanish. Maybe use a name that sounded more Cuban, more Latino. One friend, Miranda from Brooklyn, sold real estate in Dade County and she'd agreed to help. Miranda was single. There'd be sex.

Nobody to talk to. Fine with him, even though his back felt sore from so many hours on the bus. Somewhere south of Charlotte now. He'd planned a little bit of an itinerary, starting with a friend of Buzzy's, an old-timer named Del Rivera who owned a building with his son in Miami not far from where the old Orange Bowl football stadium used to be.

Derek would rent a room, no questions asked, no names exchanged. He'd pay a few months in advance. All cash transactions. There was two-hundred-grand in the gym bag on his lap. A ton of money if he managed it right. The rest was in an account back in Manhattan and he'd leave it there for as long as possible and then, one day, empty the account, sink it into an investment of some kind. That would happen later on, much later. The two-hundred G's would last him a long time. Couldn't plan too far in advance. Had to see how the landscape developed.

Just relax. Let the bus roll through the night. No other choice.

He believed he'd be safe in Miami. Miranda's suggestion of Cuenca and starting a new life there sounded pretty good. She'd been a few times and wouldn't mind going back. Maybe he and Miranda could become an item. He could whip himself into shape, and Miranda would teach him Spanish. A little bit each day. Pillow talk. It was the best way to learn. He'd picked up enough Spanish in school and on the streets growing up. Wouldn't be a problem.

Derek imagined himself walking a beach and listening to waves. He had to start fresh. Shooter, Holly, they had their money, their dreams, their new lives. Nothing he wanted.

Ma might not have approved, but Ma wasn't around anymore. Buzzy would approve. He'd understand completely. A man had to choose, and it was all different now, which meant he had to think differently about himself. It showed maturity.

He'd start by tanning himself all day long. Get his whole body shaved so that his skin would be smooth like a pomegranate. He'd wear a hat and sunglasses all the time. He'd live for the day, the moment, and avoid all the assholes that had moved down there from up north.

Only Miranda. She was all he'd need, but he couldn't rely on her too much. She'd be there for him, help him get started. She wasn't the type who talked a lot and that was always a plus. The Covid nightmare was finally going to end up in the shitter where it belonged.

He wore his loose dark T-shirt over sweatpants and he was bursting with feelings, from relief to a strange giddiness. Never felt easier to carry so much cash with him. He couldn't go back, of course. Not for a long time, if ever, but why would he want to? That life was over, but this new one could be great. He was proving to himself that knowing versus thinking he knew, and then versus experiencing, they were all different. Some guys never got to that lesson until it was too late.

He was lucky. He'd gotten this far. Maybe he was wiser, but he couldn't say he'd made it until he had a new mask on and was perched under a beach umbrella. He'd be holding a rum drink in one hand, shaking the keys to his new apartment in the other. Why not him? Other guys, some of them douchebags, had pulled it off. Yeah, why not him?

TWENTY-ONE

Holly, alarmed at the sight of herself in the mirror, had decided. She would continue to do yoga each day, as she had before her pregnancy began. She'd take each bout of morning sickness in the same way she'd learned to take people – one at a time.

She'd already broken the news to her mother, who at first wasn't dismayed. However, by turns, her mother had sounded disgusted and angry, unwilling to accept there would be no father involved in raising the child. Nonetheless, she'd promised, though begrudgingly, her full support. Anything Holly needed, at any time, just ask.

Where had they gone, those years from 15 to 25 to 35? They'd vanished. Agnes, too, was out of the picture now. She'd never learn Derek was the father of her child. Maybe if it was a girl she'd name it after Agnes. If a boy, she'd name him after her father. The best way to view this pregnancy was as an unorthodox but creative way for the three of them to extend their lives as a family. Sick, really, but it felt right as the twisted conclusion to the triangle game. Derek: out of the picture too. Good riddance. He'd played his role. Wherever he was, let him stay away and not come back. So typical of him, so much the act of a cowardice to go sneaking off into the night.

Neither Derek nor Agnes existed any longer. All her life she'd acted as if she needed them both, loved them, but what she'd loved was the idea of them as her extended family. Just an idea and not one she required any longer. What she'd failed to understand was the truth that she loved no one more than she loved herself. She was incapable of loving someone else completely. This was why she saw Derek's cowardice as a gift. Let him be off. She could never marry. Men spread their seed, but they were mostly an inconvenience. Her years in psychotherapy hadn't taught her that. She'd learned it early and on her own. There was her Daddy, of course, but he was an exception, and to think of him was to place herself back in childhood which was so far away now, as if another person's life.

What she could tell herself was that she wasn't a flop. She wasn't an ignoramus either. She knew she was selfish and preferred to view herself as a spoiled little princess. So be it. Her mother would continue to spoil her. So be it. Mother would always be there for her with Daddy's money, with her maternal warmth, gifts, encouragement and, of course, she would dote on her new grandchild. Nothing was going to change that and, thought Holly once more, saying the words out loud to herself, "So be it."

I'm going to live finally. She'd give herself and her baby all they needed and deserved. Really, such a naughty game she was playing, but life could be a dazzling soiree again. A new energy was streaming into her blood, filling her, she could feel it. *Why did I wait so long to get pregnant?* To be a mother, what a blessing, she thought. The very idea was painting her days in fresh vibrant colors. It felt perversely diabolical yet so wonderfully natural, artful and satisfying. It was her own destiny, no one else's. A statement against the pandemic and all the idiots determined to run the world into the ground.

Her baby was going to be raised as one who countered all the world's suffering by bringing love in all its needed dimensions. Her baby would bring to the world a renewed sense of purpose. Having the child would improve her, and eventually this child would work to improve the world. Her child would be cautious and creative and, of course, she'd be a girl. Holly would teach her to fight lies and cruelty wherever she found them.

She'd already met with her mother's attorney. She would attest officially that she didn't know the father's identity. Any comments about her depraved morality be damned. She had decided to keep the baby with a complete awareness of the challenges that lay ahead. She might be full of guile and selfishness, true enough, but of love too, brimming with it. She'd swear to this on any bible. Life again had drawn a circle, proving that to live was to create more life.

TWENTY-TWO

Once on the roof of my building, able to feel the weight on my shoulders dissolve, I walked lightly to edge and leaned over with care, arrested by the motion of a black trash bag pushed along by the wind. The bag was like a black archipelago unmoored and blowing under a gloomy sky the color and texture of hammered silver metal. That bag could have been me, crossing a sea of cinder-colored asphalt that shined in places where the street lights, when turned on during the twilight hours, would catch my erratic gleaming.

How I loved thinking about such effects. So did Agnes. She lived to imprison them.

Watching the empty bag drift, I thought with a sleepy twinge of eroticism about a shapely woman's body, the figure of a nude, the torso, *figura serpentinata* coiling up through gravity born as an image of woman out of the hands of a sculptor fingering mere clay. A female body. Eve. A womb. The serpent. The apple. Adam's rib. They were all one. To live was to writhe and twist out of darkness toward an eternity of darkness, to make one's passage over waves that rose and dipped like the sternum of a slumbering giant.

Me, I was a male ogre. Adam. The rigid torso. The shaft with its ribcage and suggestions of power and muscularity. I viewed life, the body, as one. I prescribed to a consciously metaphorically bleak reminder of the interplay between genders, human wastefulness and the futility of striving for achievements.

I studied the bag in motion. I saw how it started to morph into a large black crow spreading its wings. The light in the sky darkened momentarily to an ashier tone and softened the bag's ebony shine and glimmer so that it blended in and became difficult to see.

When it drifted near some pigeons, it scared them off. Pigeon wings flashed like quicksilver, sparking at once in a primitive unrehearsed choreography. This no one could photograph. Why would anyone want to? It was too private a transcendent treat.

For a moment the pigeons flew together so densely that they surrounded the trash bag to conceal it from view. They rose as one body, one figure, a stuttering of silver gashes and jabs against the sky that lasted briefly, leaving the trash bag to look stranded, deflated, like a puddle of oil.

The pigeons veered upward in consort with each other, crossing and dropping and looping between rooftops, aloft, ascending toward what I hoped was heaven. There had to be such a place. This earthbound conceit, all this science and alleged knowledge couldn't be the sum of our experience.

An occasional few veered away from the others as droplets of rain came on, at last, forcing me to consider finding cover under eaves above the access door. However, I didn't move. I let the rain, as it began to fall harder, pelt me on the head while I continued to watch the trash bag, the rain holding it in place, whisking its dimple scars into tiny pools and puddles that expanded, the rain steady now, slanting down, pushed by the wind, forcing all that I saw to blend into one large blurry mash of pewters and glossy shale. I should hurry in from the rain. I should do a lot of things.

The city, seen best as always from any rooftop heights, had treated me again to one of its small movies and I didn't feel disappointed. Was watching a trash bag the best I could do? Simply put, yes. I felt satisfied, relieved, much lighter and indifferent to the doubts and queries that had brought me to this roof in the first place.

I thought of the void, the colossal unknowing we live with, a collective angst and emptiness in the lives of people below and around me. I saw them teeming on the far horizons, each like a pale mark etched into shiny street macadam seamed with scribbled lines of tar. I saw a steel ladder, fixed accessory to an older brick building next door. Visible through the bleary gusts, its rungs were rusted yet bolted in place. After all my visits here, and there had been many, this was the first time I'd really seen this appurtenance. It would take Daredevil, one of my favorite comic book heroes (mostly because he was blind) a split second to use such a ladder. Daredevil could get anywhere from moment to moment in his comic-book universe.

I saw as Daredevil's creator must have seen, the roof slate and copper flashing. It shined wet, explosively, like the stretched black tarps that Fellini had used to create an ocean effect in one of his later movies – was it *Roma*? I couldn't remember.

Did I love Agnes, really? I did. Would she marry me? I just couldn't say. I hoped so. Undoubtedly, I would ask. I'd come, finally, to this conclusion. Me. Daredevil.

There were benefits to certain forms of commitment. They brought the promise of a new life, one shared in a way that Derek had been unable to share with Agnes. I sensed from Agnes she sometimes missed the insecurities of her old life. She had matured out of the state of curiosity that was once enough to drive her to create day by day, fearlessly so, as if creating was the only reason to stay alive.

Lies, lies, lies. She was creative, to be sure, but she was no different than anyone else. She was filthy with lies. So was I, for that matter. I wasn't Daredevil, and she wasn't Wonder Woman. Those heroes thrust themselves into pursuits of truth and justice while leaping over ventilation caps that gleamed like polished zinc saucers and inverted kitchen pans. They saved others because they didn't need to save themselves.

Heroes. The word rhymed with zeroes. In some ways, the unreal had become more real to me than "we the people." To be human; what did that mean? One had to be more than just a torso in tights, endowed with extra powers, trapped in a perpetual cyclone toward mighty feats of salvation.

How could there be good if there wasn't evil? Steam spread and swayed in a tango between two rising wisps away from a duct that curved like an inverted fish hook. How many thousands of miles of ductwork kept this city from suffocating itself? Nothing was more important than breathing. This was what the pandemic had taught me and, I'm sure, many others.

The next dystopian event would likely involve water. Either too much or too little. Air, fire, water. The body. The very ducts that carried the air we all breathed and shared had carried a toxin we'd learned to protect ourselves from. How demented was that? No one was killing me, Agnes, or anyone else. Each of us were killing ourselves.

I was nothing special at all. I did my so-called work by remaining unseen. I played along to the tunes of others with their inner fiddlers. No, I wouldn't jump off the roof. I wasn't that vibrant an echo of life in all its despair. I was like a song still unheard because it needed the proper coloratura soprano. Yet no such soprano existed.

There was no time like the present to die slowly. Time's inevitable drag offered its tugs and flights. I grew less modern by the minute, more cautious, masked without wearing a mask because my face was already the mask. I coped with memories of my initiations, feeling vacant, hearing the mother figure in me ask why I'd turned out this way.

You're all right, Agnes. And if not, you'll be all right.

Nobody really got away with pure love. Betrayal got mixed in.

The hunger for acceptance, this was the part of me, almost childish, that worried me the most. As Agnes had said, I was one of the "good guys" and we often got screwed by the likes of Derek. Perhaps. But I knew how to embrace and avoid the Dereks out there. I got things done.

I was in love. It was like wearing a new suit. I'd make a loyal husband. Maybe we'd buy a little house together. The thought coaxed me along, the cozy allure of it, a break from the old and a headfirst dive into a sparkling new unknown. Was I afraid I might be content? A part of me wanted to scream, to demand an answer, but instead I just stood in the rain, shivering, my shirt soaked and starting to cling to my flesh.

There was a time when I wanted each film I produced to bring a sustained moment of painful awareness. I wanted to make viewers endure and see the frustrations that they felt had led them to seek out and be fortunate enough to discover such a film. The pretense of that, my alleged artistic vision, astounded me. Sickened me, as well. I'd even gone so far to think that once my films were viewed by enough people, the world would change somehow. I had wanted to alter, to even erase viewer preconceptions, to cleanse their minds, to reconfigure them through shock and malice and, yes, even love. Not just for sport or vengeance, but out of compassion, as if life itself didn't already do that for them.

Agnes was like me in this regard. She believed her photos, each and every one, would represent all that was wrong, right, charming as well as puzzling to any viewer. A couple of pretentious hacks, that's what we were. We deserved each other. We could age gracefully, boring ourselves to tears with insipid conversations about art over dinner. To absorb a new hurt by creating a new vision was possible, but someone often had to be blamed for creating that hurt. Just as someone else inside of us had to find and shape that new vision.

※

My tiny apartment grew quiet and began to shrink. Agnes, deep in thought, had the floor if she wanted it. Hours might pass before she opened her mouth.

I'd wait. I was with her, but I still didn't believe it. Falling in love couldn't just happen. It had. Yet I had to prove it, so I moved to my one big window and stared at Tenth Avenue. A cab now and then headed uptown as if pumped there toward the next set of lights. A colossally empty metropolis compared to what I'd once known it as.

With my back to her, I heard Agnes asking, "Ennis, be honest with me, do you still want to do this?"

I said nothing. I waited. Then I turned and faced her. "Honestly, since you asked, I'm not sure. I'm not certain I ever did, you know, want anything."

"I can find someone else."

"To love you or to write a script with you?"

"The script."

"Oh that," I said. "I thought you meant something else."

"No, Ennis, I'm not talking about my feelings for you."

"I knew that. Sure, I did. I knew that all along."

It was a lie, of course.

As I absorbed the look on her face, I saw by the softening clouds in her eyes that she wasn't struggling to cut through the tangled brambles inside of me. I was easy for her. I only thought myself more complicated than I really was.

Let me be plain. I was the one still trying to find what I needed to see. The one who admired that one of us had found the courage to face the other directly and really share. Love had embraced me. Agnes had embraced love. There was a difference and she viewed it with clarity and comprehension.

I'd run out of energy. I felt myself sinking into melancholy. I started recalling salad days in Austin and how hard I'd worked. Brainy and anti-social I would not drive a truck as my father had. I'd live my own sweetly sculpted Texas-sized existence, naïvely so and by the dictates of tossed coins. One side of the coin, the head, meant performing good deeds and achieving heaven. The other, the tail, meant choosing sin and the fires of hell. It had been up to me. It still was, but that simplicity was gone now. Maybe it would come back. Maybe not. I knew, at least, this uncertainty. Just as I knew I would ask Agnes to marry. Not in my apartment, though. I would go to her, to Queens, and I'd kneel on that floor in her living room that reeked of photographic chemicals. With wine and flowers, I'd propose knowing that she would answer yes.

Maybe that old simplicity wasn't yet gone.

TWENTY-THREE

What had I said to her during our last time together? *I think I need to help keep you well, to be with you more often. All the time.* I didn't mean that, not really, did I? *Of course I mean it, Agnes. It's simple. I don't want to lose you.* Lose her? She was the one afraid of losing me. Didn't I see that? My words had forced her to see she'd been reading me incorrectly. I should have known that she had a difficult time expressing her feelings, many people did, especially towards those they loved.

Agnes groaned a little, shifting about on the couch. I would need to understand these allowances. Why did everything always have to be so difficult?

We locked eyes on each other. I think I appeared defeated, a man coming to realize this was likely his last opportunity to be with someone.

Agnes spoke candidly as if to clear the air. "Derek was a bastard and a prick."

I laughed and smiled. "But he was lucky to have you."

Agnes leaned forward, elbows digging into her thighs. She was unable to make eye contact. I said I wanted, in a physical sense, to be closer to her, but I hadn't been willing to show it. I looked away. I'd never liked direct eye contact. At times, I could be quite evasive. It must have been obvious to her I didn't know how much of myself I wanted to be vulnerable. Agnes understood this. She could empathize, but I doubted I liked doing so. What she needed to hear was an open admission of my commitment, not subtle though generous suggestions.

In a gentle way, like a bit of hushed nocturnal jazz, Agnes said. "It isn't easy, this, not for me either. You know this, Ennis. You know this."

I nodded once, then twice, saying I understood. Then I looked away again, returning to that window of mine where I spent hours it seemed savoring my view of Tenth Ave. I went there often as if it were an oracle. As if there was nothing more left inside of me, no useful or extravagant displays of pathos that I could mine from within and bring up to show her.

Hovering at the window, sighing, I let myself grow distant, allowing Agnes to realize again that none of the discomfort she felt had anything to do with her. It was about my own doubts, some anger I felt toward myself, some misgivings and confusion regarding my responses to the pandemic and to what appeared more and more to be the end of my career as a producer. So many regrets I had, buried under my skin, that I was unwilling to abandon.

Agnes had never been selfish or irresponsible. Nor had she tried to manipulate me. I saw that clearly, didn't I? Of course, I did. And of course it was painful to accept that neither of us had any idea what was in store for the future, but we'd both lived long enough to know it unwise to expect fairness or sudden fortune.

Poor Agnes didn't know what to say to me. She had no words left. She had her thoughts, mental pictures, and the silence. All she could muster was a lugubrious sigh. Feeling silly and melodramatic, she labored to remain placid as the silence bloomed around her, an unusually solemn one that I suspected wouldn't last for long. Not if I could help it.

I felt as if the two of us were sinking into soft loam. We'd been dropped into the room so that it could smother us. I felt again a cloudiness in my mind as I heard her breathing. *Who are you Ennis, will I ever find out? Who are you?*

"Agnes, I profess to you that I'm one of the kindest, most loyal, intelligent and resilient men that you'll ever met. I want to set up a visit on this coming Tuesday. A visit to your Queens apartment. I come to you. I insist on it."

I sounded eager and nervous. She asked me why Tuesday. I replied why not. It was going to be special. I'd bring a bottle of Syrah, a French label, wine I knew she liked.

"Agnes, I want to spend some leisurely time with you, but in your domain for a change. Where you feel most comfortable."

"I'm comfortable here," she said, sounding startled. "Haven't you noticed?"

"I said *most* comfortable. Your world completely. Not mine. We can order a pizza or Chinese. You know, keep it simple."

After some thought, she agreed to this. She said Tuesday seemed as good a day as any. It was if someone who knew her well was sending a message, a positive one. I thought to myself: we're a Tuesday couple, after all. I didn't really know what that meant. Unconventional, I suppose that's what it meant, what we were, but not as proudly so as we'd once been. We were having a mellowing effect on each other. A positive development, to be sure.

I paid close enough attention to hear her thoughts, but what I heard shook me. It was never exactly what I expected. It proved she'd always be a step ahead of me. I was the easy read. Not her.

After she left and I was alone, I felt my body begin to shudder. Then, miraculously, I began to think about my mother and I started weeping.

I couldn't control myself. I wept thinking she would have wanted to be there, to see me standing at the altar. I just kept weeping and weeping, half of me relieved and full of joy, the other half in agony. So much had changed, so very much, and would never be the same again.

———✺———

It was while walking, planning future moves in my head, that I spotted this old bearded homeless man who smelled quite foul and was holding up a creased cardboard sign that read: *$2 Tell Me Off*. Toothless, he was working his gums over some food a stranger had been kind enough to give him. He chewed with a forward and backward motion and occasionally noisy side-to side-slurps as he watched people in masks scurry by.

I stopped and observed from a distance how he studied the people. How he guarded his cardboard sign, and how he gummed to death his last morsel of food. Here was a soul to envy in a way, one so downtrodden that he existed outside of the clamor of self-pity, promotion culture and the pains of disappointment.

For him, there was no army of banned, cancelled, corrupted, sold-out, hacked, indoctrinated, damaged, triggered, lied-to, terrified, infuriated, condemned, authorized, censored, suppressed and infiltrated souls to make up the meme extravaganzas and revisionist freedom narratives that spoke for the times he was living in. *God love you, man, whoever you are.* I sauntered up to him and quietly handed over a twenty dollar bill, shocking him, but when he started to speak, I scooted away, my bottle of Syrah in its brown bag wrapped under one arm.

I didn't pause or turn to look back. I believe I heard him shout some words of thanks.

Later, after I bought a small bouquet of roses for Agnes, my hands now full, I saw an even more wretched looking panhandler. A vivid crimson flushed his dirty neck. An unshaven face so grimy it was difficult at first glance to know what his race was, as if that mattered. He held a paper cup and served up a pitch about helping a man in need.

Three young women, cute, with masks on and make-up and phones, one of them with a Hello Kitty keychain on her backpack, looked shocked by the sight of this half-man-half-cur who reeked of the sewer. His clothes were soiled, torn, his face riddled with pustules.

He passed his cup in front of them, shouting so crudely that one flinched, afraid, holding on to her friend's shoulder. The panhandler didn't stop, though. He sneered and shouted nonsense, growing louder as a way to scare them until they moved on.

Why didn't scenes like this ever appear in a movie? I knew the answer, but I didn't feel like examining or sharing it. What I knew, and all that mattered, was that my next move was not part of any dream of stardom or renown. My next move would be to accept that it was only by grace and pure luck that I hadn't ended up as rabidly desperate as that poor man.

My move after that would also be an admission. I would need to include Agnes in every thought I had. She who I deemed more important than myself.

I'd had an awakening. I was not moving on. I was standing still. Attaching myself to another form of stasis. If Agnes was a rock, then I'd be one of her barnacles. I'd find myself by giving away all of my best to her. I took a grand and glorious comfort in this thought.

I remember thinking, too: *I am going to die.* This thought, as well, just bubbled up and burst within me. I'll tell you the reason I think I had it. I was in love and had accepted love, and love, to quote a Victorian-era sentiment, is as much a form of death as a form of renewal.

Sweet, sweet death, and as I drifted back to 8th Avenue at 23rd where DoNuts used to be, one of Agnes's favorite vintage eateries, I stopped and let out a sigh. No weeping. No sorrow, either, as I realized that my running around in Gotham was over, finally. As an outsider bit of Texas cornpone fancying himself as tough as George Jones, or as sweet as Miranda Lambert, I was about to move on. Where? I didn't know. The future wasn't going to happen in any way I thought it would, or wanted it to. They were behind me, all those crudely fashioned pipedreams.

Everything, including my life, would soon be at an end. Death was not avoidable. The only way to respond was to saddle up, ride and forget about new horizons.

Lucky for me – no, not luck but impecunious management of money when I had it coming in – I wouldn't need to find a job. I had more than enough to cover the price of a car and our move. It wasn't that I only wanted to depart from the city and all its bleak renditions of soulless reality, it was that I had to. The time had come. I knew this deep in my bones. I was going to live according to love's illogical dictates, even while knowing love in all its forms would always wither on the vine.

I'd been viewing love and life and death in the wrong way. These were not end-points but rather shores that spoke of cyclical ways to define the human experience. Blessing us, demeaning us, instructing us, they weren't a curse. We had to learn, without fear, how to stop believing we needed to comprehend them. We simply just had to live. Passions themselves were a form of death. They were forms of change. They were tides.

As I walked, lifted by these thoughts, every city on the planet struck me as too big, too noisy, too expensive. My fortune had been to find Agnes before I'd gotten too old. I feared that she wouldn't say yes, but I knew it was a paltry fear, an absurd one. Agnes loved me body and soul. She knew how to love. Everything about us being together smacked of joyous inevitability.

I stood on 23rd Street slumped in the shade of a brick building that once housed a coffee shop. I remembered meeting someone there named Barney Power who'd been working behind the counter for decades. In his white apron and shirt, Barney's face was worn smooth and greasy by deadening air. I remember the dim light of that coffee shop, the wee hour nights when I'd stop in just to sit and listen to the murmurs and chinking of ceramic coffee cups and saucers. My memory of Barney loomed in spare washed-out tones, the slight rosiness of the urban landscape at twilight or early in the morning. All of that Manhattan, the one I'd adopted, embraced and thought I knew, had continued to disappear. Not much of it remained and it deserved to be set free. The longer I stood there alone, observing my past, wading through such a specific memory, the less I knew myself. The city no longer had any use for me, nor did I have uses for it. Avi and I had talked, of course, but talk was cheap. I would never again produce a film. I would never invest or gamble with my money. The time had come to wait, to listen, to stand like a tall reed at the edge of a marsh and let the wind nudge me gently back and forth.

The more I'd seen of the city's alterations – and they didn't take long, just a few months, ask any urbanite – the less I mourned the passing of another Barney Power, another coffee counter or deli, another steak house or Italian restaurant, Indian eatery, Thai palace, jewelry shop, hardware store, and, of course, I was old enough to remember blocks along Broadway in the low teens near Union Square when I walked briskly from one used bookshop or antique shop to another. In those days, the idea of being in Manhattan was a boast, part of a grand plan. I was bold and brassy enough, and stupid enough to be there simply to show all the doubters that a Texas kid of modest means could make himself into a suave self-deprecating tycoon who played major symphonies in mostly minor keys.

I should have been dancing on air. Instead I felt exhausted. A turgid sense of mourning infused my blood and it was reminiscent of what I'd felt during the first years following my mother's death. I felt like I'd been had, stolen from, dealt yet another bad poker hand. I'd played everything wrong. I thought about how long it had taken me to get over my mother's death. I'd never even addressed my father's death. I'd just avoided it and kept running. Had I really gotten over anything? Do any of us? Yet I would do it all again. The thought made me as bonkers as everyone else out there. You hear me Barney Powers? Bonkers, all of us.

I'd journeyed inside of myself to a place where I could re-think everything. There, the loneliness I felt, the fear, its melancholy, didn't gnaw at me as much as it had when younger. During daylight hours I was still able to take long walks alone and remember with fondness my mother's loving smile. It was at night with no one at my side that I felt imprisoned within regretful memories, unable to break free of them. This, too, is a form of love. I'd had enough of doleful elegiac serenades and the maudlin cello concertos in my head. I had my mask on and somewhere to be. I had roses and a bottle of red for Agnes.

My heart was, indeed, brimming full of joy. The smile on my face grew broader as I headed down into the subway to catch a ride to Queens.

❧

Ennis, I'm waiting, where are you? I heard Agnes so clearly. I told her I was there, I was with her, just as Ginger was there too. Both of us in that dusty Queens apartment with its drafty windows.

Ginger and I had found each other again. We'd commiserated with our angels. We each kept trying to reach Agnes, but she kept fighting us off. Perhaps that was why Agnes ached so much, sitting there depressed and alone on that sofa, slumped in front of the television as if she'd been speared in the ribs.

So, nobody move. A scene from our final movie, the one Agnes and I wrote together, plays out. On set, the time has come for another shot. Everyone is ready. The camera is about to roll. This has always been my favorite moment in the movie-making process, when the cry "hold the red" sounds from either the director or assistants and all becomes still.

Time doesn't pass. Every person on set, no matter how nervous, bored or restless, remains suspended in a slightly agonizing stasis teeming with expectation. What I hear as I look on is my breathing, little else. Then, as if snapped awake, time thrusts me forward and words from the actors start to fill my ears. Each of them moves, as rehearsed, hitting their marks as the next, the newest, perhaps the best scene in the film begins to unfold.

This sense of anticipation, of achieving possible excellence, this is what I will miss most now that I've ceased paying dues in the lost world. After all, I made a reputation as one who gauged self-worth in terms of what one accomplished, not what one hoped to achieve.

So, I stop. I turn backwards, away from time and rivers. I drift through the floating world, back and forth in time and space. The angel of death did not slay the wrong man, with all the shades of a Hitchcock mystery that such a statement implies. No, the angels hit their targets, and Ginger reminds me of this, and so do my mother and father. They are all there, all my loved ones.

In Ginger's case it was her body giving out, and in mine it was a display of spontaneous and lethal violence. A few drive-by bullets were sprayed into the air, one of which struck me. I can't blame Derek, even though the bullets were meant for him.

Now, it all would have been different if I hadn't been walking on that street, or if I'd chosen to take a cab from the subway to Agnes's apartment. I'd still be standing and breathing among you. But I didn't. You see, after arriving to Queens by subway, I decided to walk. I wanted some fresh evening air. I'd also decided, without thinking about it excessively, to try a different route, one I hoped would get me to my destination in less time.

I have learned the name of my angel. Hassan. He was raised under difficult circumstances without parents or a stable home. A feeble well-intentioned grandmother had been the only one who'd shown him right from wrong in one of those apartment buildings in a Hunt's Point neighborhood that one survives – *if* one survives – as a badge of honor.

Under brutal circumstances, Hassan had learned how to avoid trouble, but he wasn't what he appeared to be. He wasn't a cocky skilled assassin riding in the back of a black SUV with tinted windows, both hands on a Glock. No, he was a scared kid doing "a job" because of a vendetta and a belief he owed it to himself, and because it was a way to show others, all just as lost as he was, that he could play God.

Who knew *all* the details of his circumstances? Derek? Maybe. I certainly didn't. Hassan fired that Glock, stunned for a moment by how it kicked back and sent tingles into his shoulder. Nothing like the way thugs handled guns in movies. He sprayed those bullets, making sure he hit his target before the driver, who never stopped the SUV, gunned the engine so they could disappear into a screeching turn at the nearest intersection.

Another drive-by homicide in the lost world. With the pandemic winding down, and life cheaper than ever, they were on the rise throughout all five boroughs. As usual, police officers arrived to do their jobs. A young black man had been murdered. Wrong place, wrong time. This man had priors too. The perps had likely killed him as part of a gang shooting.

The perps had also killed a white man (me) and, tragically, a black girl, a teenager who lived in the neighborhood. Three senseless deaths. It would make the evening news, hardly causing much of a stir. Another brutal occurrence in a city of blurred and squiggling neon lines.

Cops asked questions. As they do, of course, knowing the first 48 hours are crucial to getting useful information. They went door to door up and down the street. Most of the residents said they'd seen nothing, just heard some gun shots. A couple of bullets had smashed apartment windows and scarred two parked cars.

Hassan maybe felt sick about killing that teenaged girl. He believed as an assassin that he needed to care about one thing – that he didn't miss his target. Now it was time for him to run and hide. It was possible his two murders by mistake would be the end of his own life. But that third murder, it was a mistake too. The victim was black. He wasn't Derek. Hassan was supposed to kill Derek.

Man, thought Hassan, it had all gone wrong. Hassan hoped the friends who were helping him disappear would make good on their promise to keep his location a secret. They knew he was just a minor player and maybe, eventually, he'd be found. Then again, maybe not.

The police would look for him while the incident was hot and they'd hope one of his so-called friends would play the Judas role to earn his own street cred. Such betrayals were common.

So, in short, the details of my story are that I died by chance along with two others, all of us taking stray bullets merely by being at the wrong place at the wrong time. I can't speak for the others, but in my case I was there in Queens because I was on my way to propose marriage to a woman I loved. Is there dark irony in that? You bet there is. Too bad I'm not around to make a movie about it.

⸺◦◦◦⸺

Nobody except me knew I was on my way to ask Agnes for her hand in marriage. My friend Clint from UT Austin days had long ago been granted power of attorney regarding my will. Because we weren't yet married there'd be nothing in it for Agnes. Not a penny. With Clint carrying out his duties, my chosen charities would fill their coffers.

Video footage went viral on the internet. There was phone camera footage recorded by a thirteen-year-old boy in the neighborhood who was happy to cooperate with the police. The SUV plate number was visible. As was Hassan, though in a hoodie, his head sticking out the rear window, both hands on the Glock as it fired, swaying slightly from side to side.

More information came in. Ennis Railsback, the dead white guy, was a film producer.

Some wondered why, as they heard the story, I was visiting such a neighborhood. Did I have family members there? Had I been involved in illicit forms of behavior?

One neighbor, a Latino barber interviewed by local reporters from the New York One channel, related mournfully as if fed up, that "It used to be nice around here, okay, but now it's done. All these gang-bangers, ain't even safe out on the street no more. That poor girl, terrible shame, she was a nice girl, deserved better."

Hassan watched that TV interview alone while hidden in a basement room provided to him by a member of his posse, crew, gang, extended family, call it what you will. None of them could be trusted. The sliver of hope he clung to was that his face couldn't be seen on the video because he'd covered it with his hoodie. Though he felt sick about killing that girl and that other dude, a brother, he didn't care about some middle-aged white guy that shouldn't have been there in the first place.

Derek hadn't been iced. Hassan was still angry, still at large, still seeking vengeance. The only thing he cared about now was his own life and his ride showing up on time to get him to the Newark bus station where he'd roll first to Cleveland and then Chicago. There, he'd meet a friend of a friend who'd put him up for a while until things cooled down.

※

In a daze, my Agnes – yes, all mine now – sleepy, tired, unable and unwilling to taste food, her lips gummy, sealed shut. Her body collapsing as if she were a raft carried off by the brutal currents of a river. This river pulled her and she bounced along, water in her nose, her body twisting as she dodged the low tree limbs that extended out from the embankment. She bobbed along, the river slashing time into snippets and chunks. She remembered pieces of conversations, of moments with me, advice I'd given, a peculiar look on my face, my habitual gestures, our lovemaking, our slow prolonged meals, our carefree walks in city parks, our sadness that museums were still closed. I was gone, never to return. Yet always there as if I'd never left. It took all the energy she had to drag her body out of that river and into bed each evening, and out of bed again in the morning. She couldn't eat. She might never eat again. She didn't go out. She stayed in her pajamas all day and cried while sipping either coffee or tea. She found refuge and energy in cleaning the apartment. This helped her stop crying for a while. She found it liberating to begin throwing items away. Anything at all that reminded her of the past, of Derek and of me went into plastic bags that were twisted up and tied at their tops and piled one atop another on the sidewalk.

She couldn't bear the thought of her photographs, or being in the dark room, or of holding a camera. As more time passed, she was able to shower and dress and at least go out for milk and coffee. She bought more cleaning supplies. More boxes. When she wasn't cleaning, she'd sleep on the couch in her clothes. There were no more long days of developing her photos, no more of the soft old Agnes. Sharper lines had begun to etch themselves across her forehead. Her jeans began to fit her better. She felt lighter. She brushed her teeth at least four times a day. She combed her hair for hours, ever so slowly, just gawking at herself in the mirror and wondering who she was.

What had happened to her life? What had she done to deserve such a fate? She defrosted the refrigerator, emptying the freezer and throwing away all the food there. She threw out all the alcohol in the apartment. She boxed up all her knick-knacks and vintage collectible items, deciding once she had the energy she'd bring them to a vintage shop and sell them for whatever money they might bring. She moved about robotically in a state of numbness, and when she listened to music it was at a low volume, brooding ambient spatial soundscapes, no lyrics at all, that coaxed her to the sofa where she'd lie and sleep at all times of the day.

She had stopped taking pictures or even thinking about photography and it didn't bother her at all. She didn't care. She preferred to do nothing, to be alone, to hear the sound of her own breathing. She liked not needing to speak. Weeks passed this way. Though the weather was warmer, she refused to venture outdoors. She ordered delivery now and then, but after only a couple of bites she abandoned the food until it attracted flies. She tossed out her bong and all her paraphernalia related to smoking pot. She scoured the bathroom, and her bedroom, shocked by how dirty the space she lived in had been.

Stunned and dismayed to realize that for years she'd been unable to pass a single day without indulging in self-medication in one form or another, she asked herself what kind of a sickening person had she been. She read constantly, mostly novels, putting the books into a carton once she was finished with them. Not a single word sank in or stayed with her. What stayed was the smell of the pages, the little naps she fell into while her mind tried to absorb the language and make sense of it. She piled book after book into that carton which, once filled, she left on the sidewalk. Let someone else read them and escape. Let someone sell them and make a little money. Very little. They were old dog-eared paperbacks and many of them reeked of photographic chemicals.

She binged, too, on so many episodes of so many programs from streaming platforms that she couldn't distinguish one from the next or even recall their storylines from day to day. She dreamed of the programs she watched and talked to the characters while in her sleep, awakening in the middle of the night, soaked in sweat and sometimes in tears. She'd hurry to her bathroom and shower and then change into fresh pajamas and turn on the television and start watching another program, any one of them, the content didn't matter so long as there was noise and light and motion until she fell asleep.

Holly never returned calls, her emails or texts, so she stopped trying to reach her. The message was clear. Holly was out of her life. Amen. The time had come. Another month and she'd have to renew her lease on this apartment. She wasn't going to renew. She'd had it with Queens, with Manhattan, with big dreams of big achievements in the big fine arts. She brought all her cameras and photographic equipment to B and H photo and sold every bit. They bought everything at rock-bottom prices, happy to own such a haul for such a small investment.

Good for them, she thought. *They'll profit by my generosity.* Other hopefuls would come along to devote years to unlearning how to see, perpetually ensconced in a delusion that their experiments in aesthetics made a difference.

Where would she go? It wasn't important. The destination would come to her. What helped was travelling light. Out went the clothes in trash bags. She left them on the street. The trash bags disappeared. She didn't bother phoning her mother. She would, she hoped, eventually find the nerve, but she wasn't yet ready for Shirley, ever the resilient social butterfly, who just wouldn't understand. Or maybe she would, but Agnes didn't want to be anyone's daughter. Nor did she want to be the girl from Barrington. She was just plain Agnes, stripped down, the one Derek used to call Shooter, though no one, if she could help it, would ever call her that again.

She had no desire to even think about Derek, let alone speak to him. She didn't care where he was, or even if he was alive. She cared about me, she missed me, but she told me she had to let go. She did this by burning her photos. She decided to keep her negatives, nothing else. They were catalogued in three-ring binders, each strip cut to fit into acid free sleeves. Page after page of negatives, each page labelled.

This is what she'd leave behind, not the photos, at least not those she still owned. If others were out there on walls or in albums, let them stay there.

The pleasure was hers, night after night, as she stepped out to the little courtyard area behind the kitchen. This tiny and damp sanctuary of mossy bricks and leaky gutters and drainpipes and neighborhood cats and the occasional rodent was where she liked to work. Here she kept her trash bins, clearing a space on the bricks, laying one photo down at a time, using a cigarette lighter to ignite them at all four corners and watch them curl and turn to ash, leaving their smell on the air.

Sometimes, she cried while watching the images turn to black. Other times, for no reason at all, she felt elated. The best times were when she felt the experience bodily, as if she were rising into the sky with the ashes. As days turned into weeks, she saw her body growing leaner, the look in her eyes colder, less willing to embrace anything warm or gentle. Doors kept slamming shut in her dreams so often and at various tempos and volumes and so rapidly that they sounded like either snare drums, timpani or kettle drums, and sometimes all three at once to deafen her. There were some that sounded like primitive tom-toms pounding out two beats and the word "Ennis…Ennis…Ennis…."

She missed me. She longed for me. Images burned and their ashes danced and swished back and forth in a way that soothed her, as if they were wind-tossed snowflakes, telling her she'd done it, she'd found the strength, that she wasn't dying, she was just getting on without any concern for what the future might bring.

For my man my Ennis the one I'd fallen for. Covid protocols. No funeral. A posting online, just another death, another body bag. The morgue, the cemeteries were full of them. I'd brought her to such soaring heights, and ultimately so much disappointment. A crude exit and one she believed I didn't deserve. Not for the man she loved, and who understood her better than any man she'd known, had been on his way to see her that Tuesday, as planned. Judging by evidence, he was bringing her flowers, wine and, she thought, her female intuition told her without question that he was going to propose marriage.

I would have said yes, I hope you know that.

Nothing I'd ever said to her directly could prove this, but Agnes believed, and correctly so, that I loved her and wanted to spend my life with her. She'd learned of my death not only from televised news coverage of the drive-by incident, but because she'd decided to break a precedent when she received a call from an unlabeled number she didn't recognize on her phone. Usually she ignored such calls. Most were from credit card companies or political campaigns. She decided to answer and heard a drawl from a man named Clint.

She knew a little about Clint, having recalled my mentioning him. She'd never met the man. An attorney based in Texas, he'd been my friend in Austin. We'd kept in touch over the decades. A man needs an honest lawyer, they're hard to find. This was Clint, who told Agnes that other than my own driver's license, his business card was the only other identifying document found in my wallet. The police had phoned Clint and asked about his relationship to me. Since there didn't appear to be surviving kin, would Clint come to the morgue to confirm identify of my body?

He agreed. All the way from Dallas. Now, that's a friend. I'd described Clint to Agnes as more of a typical Texan in that he was lanky and preferred to wear a tall hat and snakeskin boots, though Clint didn't sport such apparel while in Manhattan. He arrived buttoned-down and somber, having been vaccinated twice, and boosted and having taken an anti-body test, as well. This hadn't been required of him in Texas, but Clint wasn't one to spur caution. We had a fraternal relationship and spoke often on the phone. During the week I'd been shot he'd tried to call a few times about niggling legal questions, and after repeatedly getting no answer he'd decided something was wrong. This was why he wasn't surprised – as he might have been – when the phone call came from the police.

Agnes liked that Clint spoke so slowly and with a drawl. She liked his politeness, introducing himself, making sure he was speaking to Agnes Bailey Kotas and no one else, and then offering his sincere condolences. Speaking about me to Clint sent eruptions through Agnes, shaking her body, striking her with such force that she began bawling. She would call back at a later time. She apologized best she could. Clint said he understood. To call anytime. He'd be expecting her.

Clint, ever patient, waited three days until Agnes called back. Holding back sobs, Agnes regained enough composure to tell him she was grateful. That I'd spoken highly of him as a loyal friend. Clint explained he was in Manhattan, that he planned to meet with Avi and some lawyers there. He didn't have keys to my apartment, and he assumed Agnes had a set. He'd assumed correctly. It was a simple matter. The police had the keys that had been in my pocket, but they weren't willing to hand them over.

If Agnes cared to, and Clint hoped she would agree to, she could visit the apartment with him. This had to be done. Agnes said yes, she understood this, and the following day she met Clint at my apartment and apologized for her emotional outbursts, her unsteadiness, generally. Clint, a gentleman, said there was no need. He had all the time in the world to take care of business that, unfortunately, had to be done.

Agnes used the time to gather some of her own belongings. She'd left them behind at my apartment. Some of them she still needed. Most she wanted to sell. Clint explained that legally Agnes was free to take what she wanted. He thought I would prefer it this way, an assumption on his part which was correct. They emptied the apartment as quickly as possible, renting a van and purchasing boxes from a shipping store. They also phoned charity agencies that came and took away larger cleaner items with re-sale value.

Throughout her time in my apartment, Agnes experienced spasms of relief mingled with gratitude. One morning, seated alone sipping coffee by the window that looked out on Tenth Avenue, she felt my presence. I was there with her. I knew she heard my voice. I was suggesting she was doing the right thing, that I'd always be with her and felt closer to her in ways more profound than I'd felt while in the lost world. I assured her I was doing well in the floating world, that I didn't want her to suffer but to find her way. She shouldn't fear the grief, anger and loneliness that had been overwhelming her. She should accept it and know it wouldn't pass, but that its ferocity, in time, would diminish.

Agnes shared none of this with anyone. Having finished her coffee, she began one by one to fill boxes, forcing herself not to deliberate too long even while swamped in memories. There were small pieces of antique furniture, items from various films, and various appliances. She insisted Clint take back to Texas framed photographs she'd taken of me, and of the city, and the original artwork I'd purchased over the years, including an oil of Texas bluebonnet country by Porfino Salinas.

Clint, shrugging, went along. "If you insist."

"I don't insist," she told Clint. "I know. It's the best way."

Along with some designer brand clothing, watches and jewelry, Agnes helped herself to signed first editions, my music, my movie posters, my collection of autographed scripts and vintage Hollywood memorabilia, deciding to take it all and, once home, choosing to sell some of it on eBay, on Craigslist, and to find dealers locally who were willing to buy it from her. She didn't want to keep much of it. She just wanted more money, which was okay by me.

Clint helped, but he tended toward reticence. Agnes felt too drained and desolate to stir up conversation, yet they managed to be cordial and get to know each other a bit. They ordered their lunch each day from a neighborhood eatery whose menu I kept pinned under a magnet to my fridge. In the evenings, Agnes took him out to dinner. Together, getting acquainted, they worked all day, and strolled in the late spring air at night. Agnes mourned the fact they couldn't yet attend a Broadway show, and that the museums were still closed. Clint, divorced, without children and a bachelor, didn't mind. He worked at his laptop in his hotel room and in my apartment, changing it into an office as he filled out forms and spoke on the phone with the proper authorities to help set into motion the process of closing all my accounts. He scheduled meetings with banks and financial advisors, as well as cleaners who would come once the apartment was empty and he'd be flying back to Dallas. It would be as if I'd never even lived there. He didn't have to tell Agnes I preferred it that way.

———∽∽∽———

Agnes, sometimes many times a day, still broke down into tears. This was common when she was alone. She cried and cried until spent. Then she slept. She kept selling her and my own belongings until the Queens apartment was nearly empty. What remained was a mattress in her bedroom, a table and two chairs in the kitchen, an overstuffed easy chair and a TV in the living room.

Then one day it happened. She had an epiphany. She'd already told the landlord she'd be moving out. It was about mid-May and she'd awakened at two in the afternoon, the sun beating down on her mattress through the pair of windows in her bedroom. Her epiphany made it clear that she was all wrong, that she shouldn't stay imprisoned as a victim. The easiest first path would be the one of least resistance. She phoned her mother and begged to move back to Barrington to live for a while until she felt capable of living somewhere alone.

Though Shirley had been made aware of what had happened, her reaction still surprised Agnes. She said that she, too, felt depressed. She feared that Agnes might become suicidal. Derek had abandoned her. Holly had too. She'd fallen in love with me. Now I was dead. All by chance, so rudely, so thoroughly. How dreadful, all of it.

Shirley said, "Honey, I've had it with life as I know it. I want to start over. I've already joined AA. I'm going to try. It's possible. Please, Agnes, come. You could help me. I need you. You need me. We could help each other, just for a while anyway. I'm so glad you found the courage to call."

At first, Agnes, in shock, had been hesitant. She hadn't expected this. Did her mother really want her daughter back? Did she really want her mother? Well, she'd been the one to call Shirley and ask. There was no denying their lives as mother and daughter would always be intertwined, so why not accept it and help each other out. But shouldn't it take longer? Shouldn't it be more difficult? It seemed awfully quick, and almost easy. Then again, there was no timeline or rulebook for adapting to the death of a loved one. Relationships endured if they allowed room for amendments and healing, so after repeated calls and long conversations, Agnes softened and Shirley softened and they both agreed to an arrangement. One year. No more.

Agnes kept promising Shirley it wouldn't even last that long. It would be temporary; she'd start devising plans. She'd saved money. Lots of it. She didn't tell Shirley how much, or that it had come from Derek's dealing narcotics. Summer was coming. A new normal was emerging and they were adapting to it. She'd had time to sell nearly all her things, as well as mine, to various dealers in the city, and online. She'd soon get rid of her TV and mattress and easy chair and pack a suitcase and take a train to Rhode Island.

Shirley said she'd meet her at the Providence station. "Why don't we stop in and see Holly while we're there?"

"We're not talking," said Agnes. "It's over."

"But why? You and Holly were like sisters."

"Not anymore. It's a long story. Please don't ask. You don't pry and I don't pry."

Plans were set, though Agnes knew she couldn't count on Shirley not to snoop about. She was her mother, after all. She worried. Her curiosity was natural, a bit excessive but typical of any Mom, and if she learned anything it wouldn't include a word about the triangle game and Agnes's physical relationship with Holly. They were through. Agnes would stand her ground. Shirley would never learn the truth. It was best that way for all concerned.

What surprised Agnes next was that there were two phone calls, one from a woman at a bank who wanted to confirm that Agnes had known Mr. Ennis Railsback, that they had been lovers and I had been her former employer. Another from a man, rather abrupt and suspicious but just doing his job in law enforcement, or so Agnes had supposed. She answered his questions about where she'd been that Tuesday, listening as the man lamented that drive-by incidents were becoming so common that most people didn't pay them much attention. Agnes wasn't sure she agreed with this, though she concurred with the man when he said the tragedy was that upstanding citizens such as myself, the young man and teenaged girl, all with clean records, had become homicide victims.

Was there comfort to be taken in such a bleak attitude toward violent acts of serendipity? Agnes didn't think so. At last, at last, she got the hell out of Queens.

❧

Once in Barrington, and with Shirley's help, she found a used car to purchase. She'd stopped drinking and smoking pot completely and would stay on that track. Forging a pact with her mother, they both agreed to exercise and eat right. Not many gyms were open yet, but that wouldn't stop them. Her mother had a Stairmaster machine in the basement that Agnes was welcome to use. They planned to walk each day to Rumstick Point.

One day, her mother brought home a puppy, an adorable mongrel cross of mostly chow and spaniel that she'd gotten from a friend. Agnes named him Ennis. This increased their walks to three times a day, sometimes more. Agnes bought a bicycle too and began riding it as part of her daily routine, using a trail that ran not far from the house.

They spent more time together, driving to Colt State Park in Bristol, taking long walks there. They drove to Westerly to visit one of Shirley's friends, and to Jamestown and Newport, as well. They kept to a healthy diet and only occasionally allowed themselves to cut loose and enjoy dessert and "have a good cry" as Shirley put it, over a sad movie. They watched lots of movies together, chatting as if girlfriends getting reacquainted after a long absence. It seemed to Agnes as if for the first time they were finally getting to know each other. She'd underestimated

Shirley's wit, intelligence and generosity. It was a pleasure to be there for Shirley when she signed off Zoom from AA meetings, and to add a different slant to what was clearly a new and different narrative for them both. As Agnes viewed it, they were like a pair of slightly bruised and mature peaches, still lovely and sweet and to be handled with care.

Shirley encouraged Agnes to set up a dark room in the basement and start taking pictures again, but Agnes refused. She walked Ennis, and took him on drives. She trained him to obey different commands. She didn't miss big city living. Alone, she rode her bike to the tiny coves along the Narragansett Bay where she marveled at a sunrise or the sun dropping into the waves and spreading like an apricot brandy, the air rife with fumes of wild honeysuckle. Why had she ever left such a beautiful place? What had she been trying to prove?

Holly's absence and what Agnes viewed as her betrayal of their friendship became, with time, less of a source of anguish. Agnes held firm and never discussed any of this with Shirley. There was no need. Shirley had her own demons, having left some damage in her wake while drinking like a lush. Shirley took her solitary walks and had visits from different friends, though most evenings they prepared meals together. On weekends Agnes sometimes met with some of Shirley's AA friends, one of whom was married to man who owned a sailboat, so she and Shirley even went sailing a couple of times.

They were providing each other with what they needed: support, friendship, encouragement, sanctuary and time to heal. They started going to church together, though this was complicated by pandemic cautions still being observed, meaning that they watched the Mass online. She knew Shirley didn't like it, and why should she since the ceremony lacked any lsting spiritual resonance or social component. There were nights when Agnes imagined herself with me, longing for my body there in the bed with her. She missed the fight in me, the patience, my cautious ways of kissing her. I would never *be* again, though I'd remain alive in her memory. Maybe that was the meaning of heaven. It was the place the dead occupied in the forgiving minds of those still gadding about in the lost world. She had to admit, too, that in spite of death, she'd never felt so pleased to appreciate she was still alive.

Strange, she thought, it was as if I stood with her at her side. *I swear I can feel you, Ennis.* We were walking together through a scene in a movie rich with the pathos and the life-affirming spirit that I had always encouraged from the artists making the films that Avi and I produced. She'd been talking often by phone to her brother and more and more she felt drawn to taking her money and moving to Colorado to stay with him until she found her own place. She'd start fresh. She'd move eventually from Colorado to Wyoming or Montana or Nevada, one of those big Western states where she'd buy a pick-up truck and live modestly surrounded by miles of mountainous land. The natural world in all its glory would reveal itself to her as a subject to absorb and appreciate, but not to capture and photograph. Not at first. Maybe later. First, changes would need to happen and arouse within her a lasting sense of awe, a renewed passion and gratitude for any moment that held her in thrall, one tiny set of eyes under a vast implacable and slanting firmament.

It was the seeing, seldom the picture that counted. A new scene, a new moment was about to begin. Everyone was ready. So was she. Hold the red.

About the Author

John Michael Flynn has been Writer in Residence at Carl Sandburg's Connemara in North Carolina, and an English Language Fellow through the US State Department in Khabarovsk, Russia. He also writes as Basil Rosa. Previous short story collections are *Something Grand, Dreaming Rodin, Off To The Next Wherever,* and *Vintage Vinyl Playlist.* Poetry collections include *Restless Vanishings, Moments Between Cities,* and *Second Nature Third Eye Fifth Wheel.* His book of essays, *How The Quiet Breathes,* was published in 2021 by New Meridian Arts. Visit him at https://jmfbr1.blogspot.com/.

Fomite

Write a review...

Writing a review on social media sites for readers will help the progress of independent publishing. To submit a review, go to the book page on any of the sites and follow the links for reviews. Books from independent presses rely on reader-to-reader communications.

For more information or to order any of our books, visit fomitepress.com

More novels from Fomite...

Joshua Amses — During This, Our Nadir
Joshua Amses — Ghats
Joshua Amses — Raven or Crow
Joshua Amses — The Moment Before an Injury
Raymond Barfield — Dreams of a Spirit Seer
Charles Bell — The Married Land
Charles Bell — The Half Gods
Jaysinh Birjepatel — Nothing Beside Remains
Jaysinh Birjepatel — The Good Muslim of Jackson Heights
David Borofka — The End of Good Intnetions
David Brizer — Cacademonomania
David Brizer — The Secret Doctrine of V. H. Rand
David Brizer — Victor Rand
L. M Brown — Hinterland
Paula Closson Buck — Summer on the Cold War Planet
L.enny Cavallaro — Paganini Agitato
Dan Chodorkoff — Loisaida
Dan Chodorkoff — Sugaring Down
David Adams Cleveland -— Time's Betrayal
Paul Cody— Sphyxia
Jaimee Wriston Colbert — Vanishing Acts
Roger Coleman — Skywreck Afternoons
Stephen Downes — The Hands of Pianists
Marc Estrin — Et Resurrexit
Marc Estrin — Hyde
Marc Estrin — Kafka's Roach
Marc Estrin — Proceedings of the Hebrew Free Burial Society
Marc Estrin — Speckled Vanities
Marc Estrin — The Annotated Nose

Fomite

Marc Estrin — The Penseés of Alan Krieger
Zdravka Evtimova — Asylum for Men and Dogs
Zdravka Evtimova — In the Town of Joy and Peace
Zdravka Evtimova — Sinfonia Bulgarica
Zdravka Evtimova — You Can Smile on Wednesdays
Daniel Forbes — Derail This Train Wreck
Peter Fortunato — Carnevale
Greg Guma — Dons of Time
Ramsey Hanhan – Fugitive Dreams
Richard Hawley — The Three Lives of Jonathan Force
Lamar Herrin — Father Figure
Michael Horner — Damage Control
Ron Jacobs — All the Sinners Saints
Ron Jacobs — Short Order Frame Up
Ron Jacobs — The Co-conspirator's Tale
Scott Archer Jones — A Rising Tide of People Swept Away
Scott Archer Jones — And Throw Away the Skins
Julie Justicz — Conch Pearl
Julie Justicz — Degrees of Difficulty
Maggie Kast — A Free Unsullied Land
Darrell Kastin — Shadowboxing with Bukowski
Coleen Kearon — #triggerwarning
Coleen Kearon — Feminist on Fire
Jan English Leary — Thicker Than Blood
Jan English Leary — Town and Gown
Diane Lefer — Confessions of a Carnivore
Diane Lefer — Out of Place
Rob Lenihan — Born Speaking Lies
Cynthia Newberry Martin — The Art of Her Life
Colin McGinnis — Roadman
Douglas W. Milliken — Our Shadows' Voice
Ilan Mochari — Zinsky the Obscure
Peter Nash — In the Place Where We Thought We Stood
Peter Nash — Parsimony
Peter Nash — The Least of It
Peter Nash — The Perfection of Things
Michael Okulitch — Toward Him Still
George Ovitt — Stillpoint
George Ovitt — Tribunal
Gregory Papadoyiannis — The Baby Jazz
Pelham — The Walking Poor

Fomite

Christopher Peterson — Madman
Andy Potok — My Father's Keeper
Frederick Ramey — Comes A Time
Howard Rappaport — Arnold and Igor
Joseph Rathgeber — Mixedbloods
Kathryn Roberts — Companion Plants
Robert Rosenberg — Isles of the Blind
Fred Russell — Rafi's World
Ron Savage — Voyeur in Tangier
David Schein — The Adoption
Charles Simpson — Uncertain Harvest
Lynn Sloan — Midstream
Rana Shubair — And No Net Ensnares Me
Lynn Sloan — Principles of Navigation
L.E. Smith — The Consequence of Gesture
L.E. Smith — Travers' Inferno
L.E. Smith — Untimely RIPped
Robert Sommer — A Great Fullness
Caitlin Hamilton Summie — Geographies of the Heart
Tom Walker — A Day in the Life
Susan V. Weiss —My God, What Have We Done?
Peter M. Wheelwright — As It Is on Earth
Peter M. Wheelwright — The Door-Man
Suzie Wizowaty — The Return of Jason Green